MW01077333

1

Surviving the Dead Volume IV:
Fire In Winter

By

James N. Cook

COPYRIGHT

This book is a work of fiction. The characters, incidents, and dialogue are drawn from the author's imagination and are not to be construed as real. Any resemblance to actual persons, living or dead, is entirely coincidental.

SURVIVING THE DEAD BOOK FOUR: FIRE IN WINTER. Copyright © 2014 By James N. Cook. All rights reserved under International and Pan-American Copyright Conventions. No part of this text may be reproduced, transmitted, or stored in or introduced into any information storage and retrieval system, in any form or by any means, whether electronic or mechanical, now known or hereinafter invented, without the express written permission of the author and Amazon.com.

FIRST EDITION

Library of Congress Cataloguing-in-Publication Data has been applied for.

First Edition ©MARCH 2014

Also by James N. Cook

Surviving The Dead Series:

No Easy Hope

This Shattered Land

Warrior Within

The Passenger

The weight of lies will bring you down,
and follow you from town to town,
'cause nothing happens here, that doesn't happen there.
So if you run, make sure you run
to something and not away from,
because lies don't need no aeroplane,
to chase you down.

-The Weight of Lies.
The Avett Brothers

ONE

It's a hell of a thing, the threat of war.

It eats at you. It dwells in your mind. You find yourself constantly worrying over events you can't see or touch, much less control. Frustration builds because you have no choice but to trust distant strangers with the handling of things no one on this blighted Earth is possessed of sufficient wisdom to manage. But that was where I found myself, all day every day, sweating with anxiety over an enemy I couldn't see, couldn't root out, couldn't kill. And it wasn't just me, it was everyone. Every survivor in the country waited anxiously as the new President was sworn into office, insurgents and loyalists alike.

And now, wherever there was a spark of voltage equal to the task of powering a device, people bent their ears to HAM radios, or laptops, or cell phones, or plain old AM/FM, waiting to hear what the President was going to say. She had a huge responsibility, this new Commander in Chief, to ensure the continuity of the most powerful nation the world had ever seen. And, less glamorously, to destroy its enemies. Enemies that had taken root on what was once solid American soil.

The Midwest Alliance.

The Republic of California.

The flotilla.

Insurgents.

Marauders.

Slavers.

Famine.

Disease.

Nuclear winter.

Lions and tigers and bears. Literally.

And that was just here at home. The international situation was just as volatile, and just as likely to erupt into violence. Consequently, every eye in Hollow Rock was staring with rapt attention at either a bank of televisions set up in the VFW hall, or for a few beneficiaries of recent improvements to the electrical grid, in the comfort of their homes. Wherever they watched, they fidgeted, and worried, and listened.

But not me.

I was too busy running for my life.

"Where the hell did that horde come from?" Eric shouted as we sprinted along, two squads of troops running close behind.

"Good question. Why don't you go ask them?"

He made a hiss that could have been irritation or laughter or both. "Something tells me they're not big on conversation. This is a problem, Gabe. The weather is turning to shit, and we're a long way from home. What do you want to do?"

I looked over my shoulder, pumping my legs in the ankle-high snow. The burn in my thighs reminded me that in just a few short months I would be forty-one. My body seemed to think it was older.

"Running seems like a good idea. We should stick with that for now."

"Funny, Gabe. Real funny."

A voice called out from behind us. "Hey, you guys realize we're running *away* from the transport, right?"

I looked back to see Staff Sergeant Ethan Thompson hustling to catch up with us, his men fanned out in a loose skirmish line behind him, Sanchez and his squad bringing up the rear. Towering over them all was the dark, massive figure of Sergeant Isaac Cole, grinning broadly despite the army of ghouls converging on us.

"I know," Eric shouted. "There's an opening up ahead, over by the pawnshop. Let's head that way and see if we can get clear."

We pounded ahead, breath coming in short bursts from the sudden exertion. Snow fell around us in great smothering curtains, whipped along by a howling wind. It stung our eyes like needles, forcing us to blink against the bitter cold. My goggles bounced against my chest, but I didn't bother trying to putting them on. There was no time, and the distraction might result in a fall. Better just to keep moving.

It was mid-morning, but the sky above was a dull, barely visible brightness through iron gray clouds. The storm had moved in quickly, and if it kept getting worse, we would be facing whiteout conditions—proof positive winter hates us and wants to kill us all.

The pawnshop grew closer with painful sluggishness, step by agonizing step, like running in a nightmare against an invisible force bogging down my legs. The horde was a hundred yards behind, but the cacophony of moans made it feel like they were breathing down my neck. I shifted my rifle around to my back and opened up my stride, gaining speed and outpacing the men behind me. I may be getting older, but I have long legs, and I can run with the best of them when I need to. I reached the pawnshop first and nearly fell over as I slid around the corner.

Up ahead, a dark, shuffling mass surrounded the edge of the parking lot directly in my path. I skidded to a halt and stared, squinting against the wind, hoping against hope I wasn't seeing what I was seeing. For a moment, a shrill little part of me protested, railed against reality, told it to go away, desperately hoping it wasn't a wall of infected out there but something else. Something innocuous like a low fog, a tall snowdrift, a herd of buffalo, a pile of crashed vehicles, an abandoned police barricade, anything but an impenetrable swarm of the walking dead. That hope died quickly when a thunder of moans rolled through the air.

"Hold up!" I roared over my shoulder.

The other soldiers rounded the corner at a dead sprint, heads down, legs pumping, leaning on each other to keep from falling. I stood tall and held my arms out. "Goddammit people, STOP!"

They heard me and obeyed, feet scrambling for purchase on the icy ground. A few of them fell cursing in the snow.

"What's the problem?" Eric shouted.

I stepped aside and pointed.

"Ah, shit. Not good."

"Schmidt, get up here with the ladder!"

The young soldier dropped his pack, unzipped it, and quickly fished out the item in question. He undid the lashings on a three-foot telescoping plastic pole, then tossed his pack onto the roof.

Constructed of eight-inch aluminum struts and quarter-inch steel cables, the portable ladder could be coiled small enough to fit inside a half-empty assault pack. Its companion, the telescoping pole, had an S-shaped metal hook fastened to one end.

Although only three feet long when collapsed, the pole expanded to twelve feet. To use it, you simply looped one end of the steel cable around the hook, extended the stick to the rooftop, put your weight on the bottom rung, and everybody climbs up. The last man will have a tough time of it, being that there is no one left to hold the cables taut. But it's nothing a fit, well-trained soldier can't handle.

Schmidt—a tall blond kid whom Eric always called by his first name, Justin—quickly deployed the hook ladder, set it's sharply-pointed end firmly into the ice covering the roof, and planted his boot on the bottom rung. "All set," he said.

"Hicks, Riordan, on me." I ordered. "Everybody else, up the ladder."

The wind shifted direction to the north, driving the thick veil of snow away from my face and making it easier to aim. Hicks and Eric fanned out on either side of me, rifles leveled. The ACOG scope on my M-4 seemed to move of its own volition, the crosshairs coming level with the nearest walker's forehead. I squeezed the trigger and felt a small jolt as sixty-eight grains of 5.56mm lead alloy ventilated a dead skull.

Without thought, my hands moved a few inches, my shoulders shifted, half a breath expelled itself, another squeeze, another muted crack. Before the walker hit the ground, my eyes were already tracking toward the next target. While my body went to work, the rest of me drifted. I heard grunts of effort behind me as the troops climbed the ladder, urging each other to *go, go, go*. Eric's rifle cracked rhythmically on my right, while to my left, Hicks' M-4 pelted my shoulder with expended shell casings.

I racked up a score of seven before the walkers grew close enough to see clearly, veiled as they were by the snow. They emerged from everywhere, surrounding us on all sides, hundreds of them, no escape in any direction. The roof of the pawnshop was our only option.

My sights centered on a young ghoul, no older than fourteen or fifteen when she died, still somewhat recognizable as the person she had once been. Her clothes consisted of sturdy hunting attire, the kind of thing a long-time Outbreak survivor would wear. What was left of her hair was cut short, and her shoes had not yet fallen apart. She must have died recently, maybe a couple of months ago. From the missing gouges of flesh on her face and torso, it was obvious she hadn't died easy. I squeezed the trigger, the bullet did its work, and she collapsed.

"Eric, you're up!" Justin shouted.

"Okay, falling back."

Eric moved his rifle to his back and leapt for the ladder. I shifted to cover his lane, focusing intently and increasing my rate of fire to compensate. The weapon seemed to operate on its own, unthinking in its precision, guided by steady hands. Sometimes I wondered if it was me doing the fighting, or if all the years of combat had created a separate, symbiotic consciousness. An unconcerned, disconnected thing with all the necessary muscle memory and mechanics to get the job done, but none of the baggage.

Or maybe, after two decades of violence, killing had simply become as unremarkable as taking a piss.

Justin called out again, and I motioned to Hicks. Without a word, he lowered his weapon, executed a neat little heel-to-toe pivot, took three graceful running steps, and went silently up the ladder. He did everything silently, that guy. I could count on one hand the number of times I had heard him speak, and even then only in one or two word sentences.

Gunfire erupted over my head as the rest of the troops opened fire on the horde, driving them back and buying me time. "You're up, Gabe," Justin said. I slipped my weapon to my back and motioned him up the ladder. "You first, Schmidt. Go on."

He frowned, but didn't question me. While he climbed, I put my weight on the bottom rung to hold the ladder steady. He scrambled up quick as a monkey, propelled by strong young muscles nearly half my age. When his boots disappeared over the top, I began hauling myself upward. It wasn't easy; the wind pushed me like a giant hand and the ladder swung wildly. By the time I was halfway up, I was hanging nearly parallel to the ground, shoulder pressed against the cinder-block wall, arms struggling against gravity and friction.

With teeth gritted, grunting with effort, I kept climbing. My legs pushed. My hands moved purposefully from one rung to the next. Then, out of nowhere, my tactical sling drew tight around my chest and cut savagely into the skin of my neck. A brutal weight ripped at me, nearly peeling me from the ladder. I tilted backward like a seesaw until I could see my feet over my head. The hook above me bit deeper into the ice, knocking loose a tumble of white debris that barely missed my face. I held on desperately, growling through clenched teeth and craning my neck to see what had grabbed me. At the edge of my peripheral vision was a freakishly tall ghoul dangling from my rifle as if on a pull-up bar. It hauled itself up and tried to bite my back, but didn't quite make it. I heard its teeth clack together on empty air.

"Help!" I shouted. "I need help!"

For the first time in a long while, genuine fear gripped me. The ghoul dangling from my back couldn't reach me with its teeth, but its weight made it impossible to climb. The rest of the

16

horde pressed closer, gaining ground despite the hail of bullets ripping into them. I strained upward, but couldn't get the leverage I needed. The undead kept closing the distance, steady, unrelenting, mouths gaping wide. Their moans filled my ears, the stench of decay clung to the back of my throat. I let out an animal scream and hauled with everything I had, but made no progress. The rungs were slick with melted snow, making it difficult to get a grip. My arms began to tremble from the strain. The ghoul hanging onto me lunged up and down, jaws snapping mere inches from my back.

And then I was moving upward.

Two sets of gloved hands reached down and hauled on the ladder, but it was slow going. The ladder was small, only a couple of people at a time could reach it. The others crowded in but couldn't get close enough to help.

"Everybody get back!" Thompson shouted, exasperated. "Hicks, let go of the ladder and go kill some walkers. The rest of you too, goddammit. Cole, give me a hand here."

The hazy, bundled shapes of men shifted above me and the ladder fell back down. I almost lost my grip and shouted in terror, images of being ripped apart by ghouls drowning out all reason. The horde crowded close, pressing in on one another, bottlenecked against the wall of the pawnshop. If I fell, I would be right in the middle of them, on my back, defenseless.

I opened my mouth to scream but bit it back when the ladder lurched upward again. This time I could see the broad-shouldered outlines of Thompson and Cole pulling me up, hand over hand, slowly, gradually, cursing me for being so heavy. I set all my will and determination to hanging on, to not falling into that teeming, gnashing hell beneath me. My hands cramped, something burned angrily in my right bicep, a section of cable dug into my ankle hard enough to draw blood. But I held on anyway, squeezing tighter, ignoring the pain. An eternity passed, and then I could see over the edge of the roof. When I reached it, I shouted at Thompson and Cole to hold up.

"What's wrong?" Thompson asked, teeth gritted.

"There's a walker hanging from my back. If you pull me up, he'll be close enough to bite me."

Cole let out a frustrated hiss. "Well, we can't just fuckin' hold you all day, man. What do you want us to do?"

"I got this," Eric said calmly.

He walked over, drew his Ka-bar, sprawled on his stomach, and slipped the blade under my tactical sling. A few forceful sawing motions later, the strap split and the ghoul fell away, along with my rifle. The sudden release of weight sent Thompson and Cole over backwards, dragging me on top of them. We landed in a pile, cursing and pushing at one another. Eric's hands gripped my back and helped me to my feet.

"You okay, man? That was a close one."

"Yeah," I replied, voice shaky. "Too fucking close."

SPC Derrick Holland's voice drifted back to me, laughing. "You scream like a girl, Garrett."

He was still shooting at the walkers, back turned to me, yelling over his shoulder. I was trembling with spent adrenaline, hands cramped, breath coming in ragged gasps. That had been the closest I had ever come to being eaten by the undead, and it rattled me. My temper, constant danger that it is, sparked to life. I walked up behind Holland and leaned down close to his ear, pointing at the horde.

"How would you like it if I hung you by your ankles over those fucking things, you little smartass?"

He paled a bit, smile retreating.

"Got anything else to say?"

"Uh, no."

"That's what I thought. Keep your comments to yourself, Holland. You'll live longer."

When I turned around, Thompson and Cole stood with arms crossed over their chests, trying unsuccessfully to stifle laughter behind gloved fists. The other soldiers pretended to be occupied killing the infected, but I could see their smirks. Maybe they were as tired of Holland's mouth as I was.

After a couple of deep breaths, the frosty air cooled my temper. The tension in my shoulders eased, the burning in my face subsided, and I felt my fists unclench. Remembering my lost weapon, I stepped to the edge of the roof and looked down. The ghoul who seized it still clutched it in one desiccated hand, waving it mindlessly over its head.

"Fuck you, you rotten fuck," I said, and spit on its face. Schmidt was busy re-rolling the ladder. I stopped him and took it.

"What are you doing?" Eric asked, overhearing and walking over to stand next to me.

"Getting my rifle back."

"With the ladder?"

"Yep."

"How?"

"Watch."

I flipped the ladder over so the big hooked end dangled at my feet and slowly began lowering it, foot by foot, careful not to let it swing too much. The wind was strong, but constant, making it easy to compensate for. When it was level with my rifle, I maneuvered the hook toward the M-4's trigger guard trying to thread it through the small rectangle of metal. It took me a few tries, but I finally snagged it and pulled upward. The damn ghoul held on like a vise, refusing to let go.

"There's a cure for that," I muttered, drawing my pistol with my free hand. Taking careful aim, I fired a single shot. A .45 caliber hollow-point slug blasted a hole in the ghoul's forehead, splashing the corpse behind it with reddish-black gore, like hitting a melon with a baseball bat. The pressure on my rifle released immediately.

From my pack, I pulled out a small pouch of homemade disinfecting wipes and gave the weapon a good once-over. God only knew what kinds of diseases those filthy walkers had crawling on them. Schmidt took the ladder from me and stowed it his pack.

Behind me, Thompson and Sanchez ordered their men to cease fire. There were enough infected that trying to kill them all was a waste of ammo. The troops slung their weapons and gathered into a dejected huddle in the middle of the roof, muttering back and forth. The wind roared too loud to hear what they said, but their tone and body language spoke of worry. As I moved closer, Thompson saw me coming and waved me over.

"I think I have a plan to get us out of here," he said, stepping away from his men.

"I'm all ears."

He pointed up the highway, due east from the pawnshop. "It looks like the horde is thinnest over there in that field. If we can bottle up the rest of the horde at this chokepoint," he pointed at the narrow space between the pawnshop and an adjoining burned-out convenience store, "we can send one or two guys to get clear and circle back around to the transport."

I thought it over. The horde looked pretty thin where he indicated, but it was still damned risky. I said as much.

"All our guys have to do is move fast and hug the buildings along the highway," he replied. "You, Riordan, and Holland can provide overwatch until they're out of sight. By that point, they should be clear."

I didn't like it, but there was a blizzard moving in, and the horde wasn't likely to leave any time soon. I asked Cole to check the weather and temperature information from Central Command. His big fingers moved deftly over a ruggedized touch-screen device.

"Doesn't look good," he said, his deep voice rumbling in his chest. He pointed at the sky. "This storm is big as hell. 'Sposed to dump more than three feet of snow overnight. It's thirty-one degrees right now, but the low is only twenty-eight. You know what that means."

I breathed a sigh through my nose. "Yeah. It means we're fucked."

Twenty-eight degrees. Two degrees warmer than the twenty-six degree temperature required to immobilize the undead. How they managed to keep moving in sub-freezing temperatures, I had no idea. But move they did. The cold slowed them down, but unless it got below twenty-six Fahrenheit, it wouldn't stop them. And while thirty-two degrees may not have been a problem for the undead, it was more than enough to induce hypothermia in the living. We were dressed for the weather, but our tents and sleeping bags were back with the transport, not to mention our firewood. The only thing we had going for us was the couple of days' worth of food each man carried in his go-bag. We might freeze to death, but as least we wouldn't do it on an empty stomach.

Pulling my coat tighter around me, I trudged wordlessly to the side of the roof and faced the highway. U.S. Route 79, State Route 76, a two-lane stretch of blacktop cutting through the flat, desolate emptiness of Western Tennessee approximately sixteen miles from Hollow Rock. Snow had piled up six inches thick already, obscuring the faded paint on the crumbling asphalt, making the road a flat little stretch of white between drainage ditches. The footprints left by the infected were already filling back up.

I turned my head to the north and saw nothing but snow and walking corpses. To the south, the picture wasn't any better. The wind shifted again, directly into my face this time, forcing me to shut my eyes and look away. Behind me, approaching footsteps crunched softly over old layers of ice. By their heavy tread—and simple logic—I knew it was Thompson.

"Listen, Gabe, this is our best shot. You know it as well as I do. We don't have time to mess around. We need to ditch this horde and find shelter."

The fact that he was right didn't move me. In these situations, time permitting, I always like to take an extra moment, a few more seconds of analysis. Cover the options, puzzle out the permutations, try to find anything I may have overlooked, anything I forgot. A solution that minimizes risk to human life, but still accomplishes the mission.

In this case, nothing sprang to mind. I hated asking good men to do something that might get them killed, but given our current predicament, there wasn't much choice. There was a world of danger between our current location and our only hope of escape, and if no one braved it, we might all be dead before the next sunrise. In that light, the rationalization was easier.

Back before the Outbreak, I didn't watch much television, but I did watch a little. One of the very few shows I liked was *Dirty Jobs* with Mike Rowe. Rowe was a master of deadpan humor, and could rattle off one-liners better than Rodney Dangerfield. He had the unique ability to find the funny side of situations that would make most people retch. Poop splashing in his mouth in a San Francisco sewer tunnel, for instance.

Among his many memorable quips, the one I always thought cleverest was a bit called 'Safety Third'. Pre-Outbreak, anyone who ever worked anywhere encountered the legally required OSHA regulations conspicuously posted on corkboards—which in my experience were universally ignored—and had heard the ubiquitous phrase, repeated ad nauseam until it became so hackneyed and cliché it's utterance flowed swiftly into one ear and promptly out the other: Safety First.

Mike Rowe disagreed.

Safety First makes no sense. If you always put safety above everything else, you will never endeavor anything dangerous to begin with. Which is bad, because many a worthwhile task involves a tremendous amount of risk. Raiding supplies in an abandoned town rumored to be infested with the walking dead, for instance. Furthermore, if you always put safety first, you grow complacent in thinking someone else is always looking out for you. But in truth, the only person looking for you is *you*. Each person, each individual, owns responsibility for his or her life and safety.

The soldiers who had agreed to obey my orders in exchange for accompanying me on my supply raids knew the risks when they signed on. If they wanted safety, they could have just stayed home or, you know, *not* joined the freaking Army. Which meant, by definition, safety was not their paramount concern.

Their first concern was boredom. There wasn't much to do in Hollow Rock in the dead of winter except eat, drink, and fornicate. The first two they did with gusto, but a scarcity of willing partners made the third activity difficult to accomplish. Well, difficult for everyone except Cole, anyway.

Second, they were broke. The Army paid its soldiers in federal credits, which were only redeemable at military facilities. Out in the rest of the world—or 'the shit' as they called it—those credits were worthless.

Elizabeth Stone, the mayor of Hollow Rock and my current significant other, had agreed to provide shelter and food for the troops stationed with us for the winter, but anything else was on them. They couldn't trade their weapons or ammo because they needed them, and there wasn't much work to be had, at least until the spring planting season. Which left scavenging as their only way to obtain the items necessary to purchase sundries such as alcohol, coffee, sugar, bacon, and toilet paper, just to name a few.

Thompson was the one who first approached me, showing up during one of my private drinking binges at the newly opened Stall's Tavern, a cold glass of grain liquor in one hand, no doubt encouraged by our mutual friend Eric Riordan. The deal was simple: he would provide strong backs and extra rifles in exchange for a cut of everything we found. I told him there was only room for ten men at the most, being that Sanchez and his squad were my regular crew. He said that was fine since he only had eight men under his command anyway. Then I told him there were certain items the town needed which he couldn't skim from. He frowned, but nodded.

Thompson wasn't really in much of a position to bargain, which made me seriously consider pushing for more favorable terms. However, the frown on Eric's face notified me that doing so would incite his wrath. My skinny blond friend is a much more formidable man than he used to be, so in the end, I capitulated.

For the last six weeks, Delta Squad—one of four squads in First Platoon, Echo Company, 2nd Battalion of the 1st Reconnaissance Expeditionary Brigade out of Fort Bragg,

NC—had accompanied my crew on our regular supply raids. Although I was initially skeptical of their competence, they quickly proved themselves a valuable addition. My little salvage operation's profits had more than doubled since bringing them onboard.

Which brought me back to the problem at hand, and the risk our men would be taking fighting their way back to the transport. This wasn't the first tough situation we had been in, nor was it the first time we had had to fight for our lives. Hell, it wasn't the second, third, fourth, or fifth time. But these men kept coming back for more, the stubborn bastards. They kept showing up for work.

And that was the most important thing, their first priority: having work. They needed something to do, and anything beat sitting around the barracks waiting for another turn at guard duty. Having an occupation gave them a sense of worth, of dignity. And when you've got nothing else going for you, nothing to hang on to, dignity means a hell of a lot.

Their next priority was profit. You can't buy much with earnestness and smiles. If you want to purchase the little luxuries that make life enjoyable, you damn well better find something worth bartering for. I brought these men out here to make them rich, not babysit them. I gave them an opportunity, but made no promises and expected them to look after themselves. If they wanted to get home alive, it was up to them to make it happen.

Ergo, Safety Third.

"Ask for volunteers," I said, letting out a sigh.

Thompson nodded and walked away. The wind blew over the trees in the distance, and the clouds grew darker. I tied the severed ends of my tactical sling in a knot, loosening the strap a bit to compensate. My magazine was nearly empty, so I dropped it, stowed it, and slapped in a new one. Worked the charging handle. Checked the chamber. Made sure the safety was off. Kept my finger off the trigger.

Habits. Old habits. I wondered how long the good ones would keep me alive, and how long it would take the bad ones to get me killed.

TWO

Hicks volunteered first, like he always does.

A couple of other guys tried to go with him, but I vetoed them. Thompson looked at me like I was crazy.

"Gabe, we need you up here on overwatch. You're our only real sniper," he said.

"Eric is as good as shot as me, if not better, and Sanchez is coming along. Between those two and Holland, you'll have all the marksmen you need."

He stepped closer. "Look Gabe, I don't mean any disrespect, but these guys are half your age. They're smart, they're fast, and they're trained for this. Let them do their jobs."

"I'm well aware of my age, Thompson. I'm not the decrepit old goat you seem to think I am, and I have ten times as much training as any one of these guys. Don't worry, I can handle myself."

"That's not what I meant, Gabe."

"I know what you meant, Sergeant. Here's what you're not considering—I have more combat experience than any five of your men combined. Which means I know how valuable close fire support can be, especially in the form of a sniper. I can do more than just hide in the grass and bushwhack people, you know."

"I know, but-"

"Which one of us is in charge here, Sergeant?"

His stare turned cold. "You are."

"Exactly. Try not to forget it."

"I'm not questioning you, I just-"

"You have your own ideas about things, and that's fine. I'll listen to your input, but I'm the one who gets the final say. That was the deal, remember?"

He sighed, defeated. "Yeah, I remember."

"Good."

I turned around and shouted for the other soldiers to listen up. They gathered close, huddled together against the wind.

"Here's how it's going down. The first thing we have to do is cut off that end of the alley." I pointed toward the pawnshop entrance. "Sanchez, that's your job. Start dropping walkers in a straight line between the front wall here and the convenience store. Pile 'em up high. We have to make sure the horde can't get through on that side. Think you can handle that?"

He gave a thumbs-up. "*No problema, jefe.*"

"Good. Cole, I want you, Cormier, and Smith to wait until the pile is chest high and then clear the alley so me and Hicks can climb down without being overwhelmed. You'll have to work fast. Got it?"

Cole unslung his SAW and gave it a quick check. "Easy-peasy, baby."

Last, I turned to Delta Squad's grenadier. "Fuller, as soon as Cole and his guys clear enough space, I want you to put two HE rounds just past the back of the store. You see that car out there?"

He looked and nodded.

"I want those grenades between there and the back wall of the convenience store. That'll buy me and Hicks enough time to get clear. Got it?"

"You were a marine, right?"

I blinked. "Yes. Why?"

"The target area is barely forty meters away."

"About forty-five, actually, which is well outside an HE round's minimum arming range. Blast radius is only five meters. We'll be fine."

He looked skeptical. "Are you familiar with the term, 'danger close'?"

"More than you know. Listen, we're wasting time here. If you can't handle it, Private, just give me your piece and I'll do it myself."

His eyes narrowed a bit. He was a tall kid, with a bland face, dark hair, and inscrutable black eyes. But when roused to anger, his innocuous, affable veneer peeled away and the hardened soldier beneath glared out. "I can handle it, Gabe. Just keep everybody back, there might be shrapnel."

"Duly noted. All right everybody, keep your ears open and move when I tell you to. Any questions?"

No one spoke.

"Good. Take your positions. Sanchez, wait for my order."

"You got it."

In seconds, everyone was ready to go. Sanchez and four of his riflemen took position on the edge of the roof while Cole and his team trained their weapons in the narrow alley.

"Everybody ready?"

A round of affirmatives.

"Open fire!"

The pile didn't take long to form. The undead packed the short alley, making it a simple thing to stack them up. The ones still moving stumbled and crawled over their dead comrades in a vain attempt to get closer to the meal perched teasingly above their heads. Quick shots from Sanchez's men put them down, accelerating the process. When the heap reached halfway up the wall, I ordered Sanchez's men to cease fire and back off. As soon as they were clear, Cole's team went to work.

There is something incredibly nostalgic about the throaty *rat-tat-tat-tat* of an M-249. When you turn a corner and come face to face with several dozen insurgent troops armed with AK-47s and RPGs, there is nothing more comforting than the staccato rattle of a light machine gun. Except the panicked screams it elicits from your enemies, that is.

28

Cole fired his weapon from the shoulder, a difficult feat considering the SAW, with its hundred-round box of 5.56mm ammo attached, weighed well over twenty pounds. He maneuvered it easily, shuffling his feet and engaging targets with short, controlled bursts, blasting infected skulls apart like windblown confetti. The men helping him did the same with their smaller, lighter M-4s. I monitored their progress, and when it looked like most of the walkers were down, I tapped Cole on the shoulder.

"Nice work, gunner. Now fall back. The rest of you too, let's go."

Cole's team followed him back to the far side of the roof as Fuller stepped up and loaded his grenade launcher.

"Everybody clear?" he called over his shoulder.

"All clear." I said, and covered my ears.

"Fire in the hole!"

The launcher made its characteristic metallic *phump,* and a second later, a ball of fire exploded just beyond the infected Cole's team had put down. Arms, legs, torsos, and other bits of walking corpses flew spinning through the air, some landing next to us on the roof.

Fuller turned and knelt down, letting the pressure wave from the blast roll over him, already loading another round into the launcher. He shifted his aim a bit to the left and fired again. Another explosion rocked the pawnshop, shaking the roof under our feet and sending sheaves of ice crashing to the ground. It had been a long time since I was that close to a grenade going off, and I had forgotten how powerful they were. There was an odd hollow feeling in my chest, and my ears rang despite having covered them up. I shook it off and reached for Hicks' shoulder.

"Come on, time to move."

Drawing my knife, I ran to the edge of the roof, dropped to my stomach, and lowered my legs over the precipice until I began to slide down. My blade bit into the ice and slowed my descent until I had gone as far as I could without falling.

29

Raising the knife, I kicked away from the wall and dropped the remaining five feet to the ground. Even though I bent my knees to soften the landing, the impact jarred me all the way to my teeth. My knees let me know in no uncertain terms they didn't appreciate this kind of abuse. A second later, Hicks dropped to the ground beside me. Quietly, of course.

"Let's move," I said. Hicks nodded once and followed me.

The carpet of dead flesh beneath our feet was so thick we couldn't see the pavement, forcing us to step gingerly to keep from slipping and falling headlong into a mess of putrid meat and body fluids. Here and there, an arm or a leg moved weakly, still directed by infected brains not quite destroyed enough to shut down. We avoided them, not wanting to waste limited ammo putting them out of their misery.

It seemed to take forever to reach the end of the alley where we could put our feet back on solid ground. Beyond us, the dead had recovered from the blasts and were once again closing in. I turned and raised an arm, signaling Eric, Holland, and Sanchez to start laying down covering fire. They steadied their aim and went to work.

Now that his bullets were flying over my head, it occurred to me I may have dealt a bit too harshly with Holland a few minutes ago. All it would take was one slip of his aim, and I would be sporting a new orifice where it didn't belong. I resolved to apologize for my behavior, assuming I lived through the next few minutes.

The horde was thinner where we emerged, but still numerous enough to overwhelm us if we didn't move quickly. I set off at a dead run, Hicks following closely on my right. Without stopping, I raised my rifle and picked off a couple of ghouls who wandered into our path. Firing while running was a difficult skill I had mastered over a decade ago, and it had saved my life more times than I could count.

Hicks shifted his rifle to his back, drew a pistol from his tactical vest, and began firing one-handed. A walker hit the dirt with each squeeze of the trigger.

Impressive.

We kept at it for a few hundred meters, only firing when a walker got close enough to be a threat, and reloading on the run. The horde gradually grew thinner until we finally left the last cluster behind. When they were out of sight, I slowed to a steady jog, willing my heart rate and breathing to slow down. Hicks matched my pace, looking none the worse for wear.

"Let's stop for a minute. I need to get my bearings."

"Okay," Hicks said.

In the short time since we left the pawnshop, the storm had worsened dramatically. Visibility had dropped to less than ten meters, and gale force winds sent streamers of snow howling along like the world's biggest sandblaster. I put on my goggles and tied my scarf around my mouth. Hicks did the same.

"I think we're close to the transport," I said. "Let's get on a rooftop and see what we can see."

A restaurant nearby had a service ladder leading to the roof, but the bottom eight feet were covered by a security grate. Rather than waste time trying to break the lock, I put my back against the ladder and laced my fingers together. Hicks stepped into my hands, pushed up until he could plant one boot on my shoulder, then climbed the rest of the way to the roof. Once he was up, I backed off, took a couple of running steps, leapt for the lowest crossbar, and caught it on the first try. Brute strength got me up the next few rungs until I could get my feet high enough to climb properly. Above me, Hicks stayed low, eyes constantly moving.

Once I was up, I motioned to the false front facing the street. "Let's take a look."

Peering over the edge, I could barely see the other side of the highway. Everything was covered in a thick layer of white, but the shapes of the buildings were familiar.

"Okay, I know where we are," I said. "The cross street over there is Reedy Creek Road. We passed the transport a couple of blocks back."

Hicks squinted through his goggles, trying to read the road signs through the driving snow. "You sure about that? I can't make heads or tails of this place. Everything looks the same."

"Trust me, I'm positive. We need to head east on 79. The transport is only about a hundred yards from here, we just can't see it."

"You're the boss."

We climbed back down and followed the highway along one of the ditches flanking it. The wind blew directly in our faces, forcing us to lean forward and constantly scrape snow from our goggles. The drifts at our feet were already halfway to our knees and getting deeper. I began to worry how I was going to drive off the horde and get the others to safety. We were already in near-whiteout conditions, and things were only going to get worse as the day went on. Driving the transport away from town with little to no visibility was going to be damned tricky. But there was nothing for it. It was either that or freeze to death.

Ahead of us, the boxy outline of the transport began to resolve itself through the swirl of powdery white. Movement caught my eye near the driver's door, and I reached out a hand for Hicks' shoulder. A shift in the air brought a snippet of voice past my ear.

"...the fuck you start this..."

And then it was gone, replaced by the howling gale. Hicks heard it too, and we both hit the ground at the same time. I tapped his shoulder, forked my fingers at my eyes, and then pointed to the drainage ditch on our right. He nodded and began crawling toward it. Once over the edge, he worked his way forward to get a better angle on whoever it was checking out our wheels.

I backed off slowly, being careful to stay low and avoid sudden movements. Movement draws the eye, and the last thing I wanted was to be spotted out in the open with no cover. When I could no longer see the transport, I changed direction and belly-crawled to the other side of the highway before standing up and circling behind the closely packed buildings.

A block away, there was a narrow gap between Dixon and Lawry Insurance Agency LLC: Your Local State Farm Representatives, and Kelly's Konsignment Boutique. Both buildings were in surprisingly good shape, and probably contained a small fortune in salvage. The insurance agency undoubtedly had reams of paper packaged conveniently in nice big boxes, not to mention office supplies and computers. All of which were valuable, especially the paper. Then there were the clothes in the consignment boutique, most of which were probably women's fashions and children's wear, which would be in high demand come springtime. A busy little corner of my mind started tallying up how much bacon, wheat, chicken jerky, and whiskey I could trade all those items for, and what price they would fetch at one of the many trading posts along the Mississippi River.

The rest of my brain—the part actually engaged in living long enough to see my dreams of prosperity come to fruition— noticed the alley ahead was in the lee of the wind, making it much quieter than the highway beyond.

If I stayed low and moved slowly, the person by the transport would not be able to see or hear me, but I could see and hear him. Still, it was risky. I wished like hell I had brought my winter-pattern ghillie suit with me, but it was on the transport along with the rest of my gear where it wasn't doing me a damned bit of good.

Oh well. Safety third.

I slung my rifle back, drew my pistol, and dropped to my belly. The snow beneath me was deep, so I wiggled down until my chest hit the thick layer of ice at the bottom. Now I had a nice twelve inches of camouflage to hide in. I couldn't see anyone ahead of me, so I took a chance and tossed a few handfuls of snow over my head, coating my back. More snow joined it from the sky, slowly forming a concealing blanket.

The cold wasn't strong enough to muscle past my thick winter jacket, but it was only a matter of time. The longer I laid there, the more my body heat would melt the snow around me, and when that happened, the shivers would follow along in a hurry. Then there was Hicks to think about, hiding on the other side of the highway in much the same condition. I got moving.

Most people have no concept of how slow you have to move to avoid detection, how much patience you need to do it right. Growing up, my uncle—who raised me as his own after my father died—took me hunting every fall. He had the patience of a glacier, that man. He could move with geological slowness, his breathing under strict control, fully aware of every scrape of fabric and rustle of leaves beneath his feet. Sometimes, he would click the safety on his rifle, and I could swear my eardrums shattered.

By the time the good folks at Quantico got their hands on me, I was already an old hand at stalking, and I could out-shoot half the instructors. Naturally, I soon became the subject of much envy among my fellow sniper candidates. Even the instructors, who were supposed to be neutral third parties, had a bit of a love-hate relationship with me. It didn't help that on my last stalk I got within a hundred yards of the observation post before firing my two shots and reading the card. One of the instructors had a walker—the living kind, mind you, not one of the undead—running around in circles, insistently telling him 'sniper at your feet' and getting negatives until he was fuming, spitting mad. The poor guy almost fell off his stool when I stood up.

The snow piled on my back as I inched toward the mouth of the alley. Even without my ghillie suit, the man at the transport would have had to dig through the snow to see me. I kept my head down and timed my movements with the gusting of the wind. It took me about ten minutes to get where I wanted to be, and I was willing to bet the guys back at the pawnshop were getting worried. I hoped Thompson didn't do anything stupid, like send someone after me. If he tried, I hoped Sanchez could talk him out of it.

Slowly, gradually, I raised my head out of the snow, just enough so I could see over the drift in front of me. I had a good view of the transport and of the man looking it over. He squatted next to one of the fuel tanks, ear pressed to the metal, rapping on it with a knuckle. I shifted just a bit and looked up into the driver's compartment. Sure enough, there was another man, bundled up in rags, rifle standing next to him on the bench seat. He was hunched over, one hand moving around on the console from one switch to another, obviously trying to figure out which one started the big machine. The start button was purposefully not labeled because of situations like this. And even if the would-be thieves did find it, the engine wouldn't turn over without the key currently residing on a string around my neck.

The thieves' confusion was understandable, as the transport didn't look like a car, or a truck, or any other standard vehicle. It looked as if a farm tractor and a Yamaha Rhino had a baby, fed it steroids, injected it with growth hormones, and then hitched a trailer to its ass. The driver's compartment seated two, the passenger compartment behind it seated twelve with standing room for six more, and the trailer attached to the rear frame was big enough to haul two full-sized pickup trucks loaded single file. Its twin fuel tanks, currently three-quarters full of JP8 jet fuel, held fifty gallons each.

The Facilitator the Army dropped off with it had boasted its multi-fuel versatility was unmatched, and in a pinch, it could even run on a barrel of whiskey. I told him that was impossible, as no self-respecting Outbreak survivor would dare waste that much valuable whiskey on something as stupid as driving.

Pushing these thoughts aside, I shuffled back down into the snow and rested my head on the ground, eyes closed.

Decision time.

It would be easy to simply kill these guys and get back to the others, but that would leave unanswered questions. I don't like unanswered questions. I wanted to know who these men were, where they had come from, and what they were doing here. None of my men had found any signs of recent habitation during our initial sweep of the town, so we weren't dealing with locals. Meaning they either followed us, or arrived at the same time by coincidence.

It was possible they were just fleeing the horde, spotted the transport, and saw it as an easy escape. In their place, depending on how desperate I was, I might have done the same thing. Bearing that in mind, it would be wrong to simply kill them outright without giving them a chance to explain themselves.

Maybe they needed help. Maybe they were lost and starving. Maybe they knew where to find other survivors. Maybe their group was low on food or medical supplies and sent them foraging. Maybe they had families waiting on them, anticipating their return. In this age of desolation, stealing doesn't necessarily make a person evil. It just means they're in trouble and want to live. Maybe that was the case here. Maybe I could help them.

Maybe, maybe, maybe. I hate maybes. Time to get some answers.

Peering over the snow again, I waited until the one closest to me finished checking the fuel tank and walked back around to the driver's side. A few seconds passed. The man in the cab leaned down to talk to his partner.

Move now!

I popped up and walked quickly toward the transport, staying low, pistol aimed at the man in the cab. He didn't turn around. I circled to the back of the trailer and knelt, making sure to stay back so they wouldn't see me in the mirrors on the door. Their voices were clear now.

"…there's no start button like a semi, and I don't see a keyhole anywhere."

"Well, it's got an ignition system, that's for sure. Let's pop the hood and see if we can bypass it."

"You think you can do that?"

"Maybe. It's worth a shot. Watch my back, those soldiers might come back any minute."

"You got it."

Footsteps crunched in the snow, moving around the transport's front end. I heard the creak and rattle of the ladder. Door slamming. More crunching. More rattling as they loosed the retaining lugs on the hood. I waited until I heard the squealing of large hinges before moving.

The man from the cab had his back to me, facing the direction of the horde. I moved up quickly, gun trained on his back. When I was ten feet from him, I stopped.

"Don't move!"

He jumped and turned around, fumbling under his long, heavy coat.

"I said don't move!"

The one tinkering with the engine leapt down, but before he could run, Hicks burst up through the snow and fired two rounds just behind his feet.

"Shit!" he shouted, raising his hands. The man facing me was still trying to get under his coat. I put a round in the dirt in front of him, spraying his legs with stinging ice and asphalt. "Do you want to die?" I shouted.

He bolted for the other side of the street. I tracked him, finger tightening on the trigger. He finally got his hands on what he was rooting around for, spun quickly, and brought it up.

AK-47.

Game over, buddy. I double tapped him in the chest. He stumbled and fell backward with a howl, then, to my surprise, gripped his rifle, sat up, and tried to level it at me again. I aimed my next shot at his forehead, but it struck low, smashing through his teeth and blowing his brain stem out the back of his neck. The rifle clattered to the ground.

Swinging to my right, I trained my gun on engine-guy. "You want to join him?"

"N-no sir."

"Then keep your hands where I can see them. Hicks, cuff this asshole."

Hicks switched to his pistol and moved in. "You try anything, and it'll be the last thing you ever do. Y'hear?"

The man nodded. "Yes sir."

Hicks searched him, took his weapons and gear, applied the riot cuffs, and ordered the man to go flat on his stomach while he secured a set of zip ties around his ankles. Satisfied our prisoner wasn't going anywhere, I approached the dead man and picked up his rifle, looking for the manufacturers stamp. It was on the bottom, slightly forward of the trigger guard, spidery writing etched cleanly.

Chinese. Just like the Free Legion.

"Son of a bitch."

I searched the dead man's pockets, pulled off his boots, cut open the lining of his jacket. No hidden items, papers, or maps. Nothing to tell me where he came from, what group he was with, or what he was doing here. Aside from his clothes, all he had was a tactical vest. MOLLE, just like mine. Attached were six spare mags for the AK, a small first aid kit, flashlight, a couple of glow sticks, small roll of paracord, and a fire steel. Two pouches for water bladders were mounted to the back. One held water, and the other had a pair of black plastic handles protruding from the top. It yielded a pair of bolt cutters, a scavenger's best friend.

Underneath his shirt, I saw the distinctive U-shaped outline of body armor. I cut it off and looked it over. Two mushroomed .45 slugs less than an inch apart in the chest directly over the ceramic trauma plate. A testament to both my marksmanship and the quality of the armor.

Well armed, and well equipped, but no food. Just weapons, water, and a few essentials. Looking the body over, it didn't look starved. He had been strong, well fed, in good physical condition.

Observe. Remember. Don't jump to conclusions.

I left the body on the ground, but gathered up his weapons and kit. A Kalashnikov and seven full magazines could buy a horse, or feed a family for a month. No sense in letting them go to waste. After stowing them in one of the storage compartments under a passenger bench, I grabbed a roll of duct tape and walked back around the transport. The prisoner was still lying on his stomach with Hicks' rifle pointed at the back of his head. I grabbed him and rolled him over, looking into eyes wide with fear. He tried to speak, but I stopped him with an upraised index finger.

"Don't worry, friend. Very soon, you and I are going to have a nice long chat. But for now, you're going to do exactly as I say. I'm going to put this tape over your mouth, and then I'm going to stuff you in the back of that vehicle you just tried to steal. My friend here is going to keep an eye on you. If you try anything, he'll throw you to the infected and watch them eat you alive. Any questions?"

He shook his head vigorously.

"Good." I ripped off some tape and sealed it over his mouth. Hicks helped me load him in the back and took a seat nearby, rifle trained on his head.

"You good to go?" I asked. He gave a thumbs-up.

I opened the bench containing the dead man's gear and took out the paracord and the water bladder. After snipping a short section of cord, I stuffed the rest in my coat pocket and then cut off the top of the bladder. On my way out, I noticed Hicks staring at me.

"Fishing tackle," I said. "The bait's outside."

"Gotcha."

Unhitching the trailer was the easy part. I wasn't worried about leaving it behind; it would only slow us down, and we could come back for it after we dealt with the horde. Getting what I needed from the thief's dead body, however, was markedly more difficult.

The next couple of minutes were gruesome, but necessary.

THREE

The others were right where I left them.

Thompson and Sanchez were arguing, probably about whether or not to send someone to search for me, but stopped when they heard the transport approaching. A few infected in the back turned and stared at me hesitantly, as though unsure which meal to pursue before deciding canned food wasn't their thing.

As they turned back to grope uselessly at the pawnshop's roof, I spun the transport around in a wide circle, backed up close to them, and jumped out. The next part was going to be tricky, and I would need to work fast.

Trigger Happy, as I had designated the dead thief, was chained to transport's rear brush cage like a prize marlin. I unhitched him and dragged his body closer to the horde, about thirty feet away. The paracord tether on his ankles drew taut as I stretched it as far as it would go. Several dozen ghouls in the back caught the scent of fresh meat and began shambling my way.

"That's right, fuckers. Come and get it."

From underneath my coat I took out the dead man's water sack. I had it filled with his blood and tied off the open end with a piece of cord. It was messy work hanging him upside down and opening a vein, but critical to my plan. I hadn't drained him completely, just enough to fill the bag. The cold was already making the blood lumpy and viscous.

I turned the bag upside down, punctured it with my knife, and aimed it over the ghouls' heads. A strong push on the back sent a thin stream of blood arcing through the air. I waved it back and forth like a fire hose, dousing as many as I could.

The effect was immediate.

To the infected, fresh blood is akin to a bonfire on a moonless night. They can't track scents over long distances like animals, but at close range, the smell whips them into a feeding frenzy. Every ghoul in the horde caught the scent and snapped their faces toward the crimson fluid raining from the sky. I heard a thousand ear-splitting cracks as they began chomping their teeth together, ravenous eyes bulging, noses turned up to triangulate the scent. They turned and shuffled in a tidal shift, inevitable and strong, bent on a single purpose.

When the bag was halfway empty, I set it down, grabbed Trigger Happy by his hair, lifted his head, and slashed his throat. With no heartbeat to pump out his blood, I had to lift him up by his belt and swing him back and forth in a wide arc. Maroon liquid splashed the snow, still warm enough to melt the ice beneath. When the gout slowed to a trickle, I dropped the body and splashed it thoroughly with the remaining blood from the bag. The ghouls grew closer, advancing within twenty feet.

Sprinting back to the cab, I dropped the water sack and fired two shots in the air to make sure I had everyone's attention. Clearing the ladder in two steps, I slammed the door and gunned the engine. The cab didn't have a rearview mirror, obstructed as it was by the passenger carriage, but the mirrors on the door showed me what I needed to see. The horde had forgotten about the men behind them, slowly converging on the dead body in the street. I eased into first gear, intending to roll forward with the speedometer's needle bouncing just above the zero peg, but the transmission ground angrily as I backed off the clutch. The transport hitched and convulsed, caught a gear, and lurched forward a few feet before blowing a puff of oily smoke from the exhaust stack and stalling out.

"Shit. That's not gonna work."

I cranked it again, shifted gears with authority, and revved forward at ten miles an hour for about fifty meters before stopping. The engine idled in neutral while I stared at the side view mirror waiting for the horde to reappear. There was nothing but snow.

Heartbeats hammered in my ears, barely audible above the ceaseless wind. I mumbled impatiently, cursing and tapping my fingers, but the mirror remained white and empty. I counted to sixty, then seventy. Eighty. Ninety. At a hundred, I decided to run back and try to get the horde's attention again. But just as I opened the door, I saw the first swaying figure appear followed by many others. It occurred to me then the temperature had dropped, and the ghouls weren't moving as fast as they usually did. A toddler could have outrun them.

Impatience, Gabriel. It's as good as stupidity. Slow down. Think.

The dance went on for the better part of an hour, me driving a short distance ahead, the horde catching up, and the whole thing repeating. When the odometer told me I'd gone a mile, I stopped, jumped out, and cut the cord binding Trigger Happy to the transport. With the severed end in hand, I stared for a moment at the dead man's body.

Where it wasn't covered in frozen brown blood, his skin had gone nearly as white as the falling snow. Even though he had tried to kill me, it felt wrong, somehow, just leaving him there without at least a word or two to mark his passing. I walked over and paused. The man's blank eyes stared lifelessly at an indifferent sky. Not accusing, or pleading, or anything else. Just empty.

Less than two hours ago, he had been a living man with a head full of memories, and hopes, and wants, and a life story. Once, some woman had held him close and cooed over him as new mothers do. Maybe his father had done the same, or maybe he didn't. He might have relatives, or a wife, or children. I would never know. Now, he was just a sack of meat about to be devoured by a pack of ravening monsters. Probably not how he thought he would end the day. I went back to the transport, retrieved his shredded jacket, and laid it over him.

"Sorry, fella. Should have thought twice before you reached for your gun. I gave you a chance to live, but you didn't take it. Made it a case of you or me, and it damn sure wasn't going to be me. For what it's worth, you helped me rescue my men. That's something, I guess."

Snowflakes fell on his dead eyes, sticking to the dry surface. Left there long enough, he would freeze until some scavenger came along to feast on him. I doubted the infected would wait that long.

Back in the cab, I leaned my head close to the small window to the passenger compartment. "Hang on in there, Hicks. It's about to get bumpy."

"I'm set. Go for it," he shouted back.

I gunned the engine and swung the transport in a broad circle, plowing through the field next to the highway. As I went over the ditch, I heard the prisoner bounce off the floor a few times and let loose a muffled shout. The frozen earth beneath the snow provided good traction for the transport's oversized wheels, and I managed to push the engine close to its top speed of thirty miles an hour on my way back to the pawnshop. The horde drifted by on my right, their forms ghostly gray in the pale distance. Once around them, I bounced over the ditch again, straightened the wheels, and put the accelerator to the floor.

"You alright back there?" I shouted.

"I'm fine."

"What about the prisoner?"

"Still breathing."

Good enough. As I neared the east side of town, I heard the unmistakable crack of gunfire echoing ahead. M-4's, not the deeper, malicious clatter of AK's. I gave the horn two long blasts to let them know I was coming. The gunfire ceased immediately.

When the pawnshop came in view, the troops had already climbed down and were busy dispatching the remaining infected. Most of them were cripples and crawlers, too damaged to move as quickly as their more able-bodied brethren. Once the main force had passed beyond sight, the noise of the living in close proximity had kept these few stragglers from leaving. I parked the transport, left the engine running, hopped out, and drew my falcata.

"You want some help out there?" Hicks shouted, face near a window grate.

"Nope. Got it under control. Just hang tight."

The first infected I came to was a male, big, clothes long since disintegrated. Most of its left arm, shoulder, and the left side of its face were gone. Big chunks bitten out of the legs, right calf muscle just a thin strip of gristle. Much of his skin had sloughed away revealing grayish black muscle tissue beneath. He had been dead a long time. Maybe since the beginning. He stepped strongly on one leg, stumbled along with a little hop on the other, nearly lost his balance, righted himself, and started again. The one hand he could still raise reached for me, fingers curled into claws. His teeth clacked together again and again, the sign of a ghoul who hadn't eaten in a long time. I let him get within a few feet before I hacked his arm off just above the elbow. He didn't seem to notice. My next swing came straight over the top, splitting his head down the middle. A quick boot to the gut freed my blade and sent the ghoul tumbling backward in a limp heap.

Another came on behind him, oblivious to its cohort's death. I set my feet and cut its head off with a single backhanded swipe. Its body stiffened, shuddered, and dropped. There were a few dozen others, but I only got nine of them. The two squads of soldiers cut down the rest of the ghouls with brutal efficiency, always working in pairs, alternating between attacking and defending.

Except for Eric.

He always fought alone, a short Y-shaped length of wood in one hand, his thin rapier-like sword in the other, darting in and out, each lunge piercing an eye socket and sending a walker to its final rest. He was well practiced and could put down infected twice as fast as any man in the crew. Most of them laughed at his choice of weapons until they saw him in action and witnessed the swift, deadly expertise with which he worked. Now, they stayed out of his way.

When it looked clear enough, I called the crew over to the transport and gave them a brief rundown of my encounter with the two thieves.

"You know," Eric said, "it did seem a bit odd to me, you swinging a dead body around. I wondered where you found him."

"Now you know. All right, gentlemen, we need to go pick up the trailer and load as much stuff as we can before the horde gets back. Try not to kill my prisoner until I've had a chance to question him. Got it?"

I got a round of acknowledgments as the men broke away and filed into the transport.

It took less than ten minutes to retrieve the trailer, re-hitch it, and begin loading it up with salvage. Eric and I stayed busy moving among the men, pointing out which items to bring and which to leave, triaging what was most valuable and in demand. We cleaned out all of the computers, paper, and office supplies in the insurance agency, most of the children's clothes and winter wear in the boutique, and then moved on to a nearby hardware store. Unlike many such businesses, this one didn't look to have been looted too badly. As we cleaned it out, I felt the mental gears begin to hum along, singing a tune I wouldn't have listened to under other circumstances.

"What do you say we hit up the gun shop on the other side of town?" I asked Eric. "Just for shits and giggles."

He thought about it for a second. "You might be onto something. This place hasn't been looted very much, except by the Free Legion. They just took the food and medical supplies. The Midwest Alliance kept them flush with weapons and ammo, so they might not have bothered with the gun shop. Or maybe they just booby trapped it and left it for later. That seems more their MO."

"MO?"

"Yeah. You know, *modus operandi*."

"You a cop now, Riordan?"

He glared, but it only lasted a few seconds before he grinned sheepishly. "I guess I've been hanging out with Sarah too much lately."

I laughed and clapped him on the shoulder. "Sarah's good people. Keep at it, you might learn something. Now let's round up the crew and see what loot we can find."

Finished with the office and the consignment shop, the crew piled into the transport and we set out for the small gun shop I spotted on a side road leading into town. It was in the same direction as I had led the horde, so we wouldn't have much time. I let Eric drive while I knelt on the bench and held a quick conference with Sanchez and Thompson through the small window.

"As soon as this thing stops, have four men set up a perimeter. Me, Riordan, and Fuller will breach the door and do a safety walkthrough. Once I give the all-clear, have your men start loading everything they can carry, starting with ammunition. Then guns, knives, clothes, holsters, anything that looks useful. I want this place cleaned out. Understood?"

They both nodded.

"Now don't forget, this used to be Legion held territory. There could be traps anywhere. Any of your men see something that doesn't look right, make sure they know to step away and call me over. Got it?"

"Yes sir." Thompson said.

Sanchez nodded. "You got it, chief."

"All right. We're almost there. Brief your men and stand by." I sat back down and turned to Riordan. "You're familiar with Legion traps right?"

"Yep. Disarmed a few, once upon a time."

"You mind sweeping the entrance? Make sure there's no surprises?"

"Not at all. But if I end up as a grease spot, scoop me up and put me in a bag, will you? Make sure Allison has something to bury."

"Just watch yourself and remember what I taught you, and you'll be fine."

When we arrived at the shop, I rapped my knuckles on the window grate and shouted the order to get ready. Sanchez and Thompson called out affirmatives and began barking instructions at their men. Brakes squealed as the transport bounced over the curb to the parking lot and Eric slowed the big vehicle to a halt. I already had my door open before we stopped, one foot on the ladder, weapon at the ready.

When the big tires finally rolled to a halt, I hit the ground and swept the parking lot with my rifle, scanning for movement. I didn't see anything, but with the storm worsening, visibility was extremely poor. There could be infected anywhere, or more raiders. We needed to make this quick.

"Clear," I called out. Eric repeated the same from his side.

Moving in tandem, we began converging on the shop's entrance. Behind us, Page, Hicks, Cole, and Holland formed a perimeter around the back of the transport. Fuller followed us to the entrance and stacked up behind me against the storefront. Eric took up position on the other side and began checking the door for traps. Near the bottom, he spotted something connected to one of the hinges and gently brushed the snow away from the wall, revealing dead brown grass beneath.

"Sneaky motherfuckers..." He squatted down to get a closer look. I tapped Fuller on the shoulder and motioned him back.

"What have you got, Eric?" I asked.

"Same setup I've seen a couple of other places. Pipe bomb full of Pyrodex and ball bearings with a shotgun shell trigger. AKA, a fucking homemade claymore. It's been out here forever, probably doesn't even work now."

"Don't take any chances," I said. "You need help disarming it?"

"Nope. I got it, just give me a minute."

He worked slowly, moving with meticulous care. His back blocked me from seeing his hands, but I was fairly certain he was disconnecting the tripwire and removing the trigger mechanism. It's what I would have done, anyway. After less than a minute, Eric let out a breath and upended the pipe into the snow, spilling out the ball bearings.

"Okay. The door looks clear, but we'll need to open it slowly. There might be another bomb on the other side."

"Hey Gabe?" Fuller said from behind me.

"What?"

"Why are we wasting time disarming traps on a door?"

I frowned at him over my shoulder. "You got a better idea?"

He removed two concussion grenades from his vest and held them up. "Actually, I do."

I looked at the grenades and felt a flush creep up my neck. He was right, and I should have thought of it myself. Over two and a half years of conserving ordnance for life-or-death emergencies had made me stingy, and it hadn't even occurred to me to just blow the door, along with any traps connected to it. I swallowed my pride and nodded.

"You're right. Good thinking, Fuller. Eric, fall back. We'll breach with explosives."

He frowned at me and moved back. "That information would have been very useful two minutes ago. Y'know, before I risked my life disarming a bomb."

I ignored him and took cover, calling out to Fuller. "Whenever you're ready, Private."

A second later, I heard the grenades clatter against the plexiglass doorway. Three seconds after, the detonations hit me with a one-two punch right in the chest. Peering around the corner of the transport, I saw the door lying flat on the ground a few feet into the darkness beyond the entrance. Some of the brickwork around the opening had crumbled, but otherwise it looked structurally sound.

"Let's move."

We didn't bother stacking up beside the entrance before going in. If there was anyone inside, they definitely knew we were coming. Eric took point and led the way through the smoke and dust, calling out a reminder to turn on our tactical lights. I had already done so, as had Fuller. Once through, Eric peeled off to the right, rifle up, barrel swiveling wherever his eyes tracked. White LEDs lanced through the darkness. I broke left with Fuller close behind.

At a glance, I could tell the shelves were still well stocked, nothing knocked over or in any kind of disarray, except for a few display stands just inside the entrance. The door had knocked them down on the way by, scattering orange hats and camouflage beer cozies across the dusty floor. The blast also shattered the front windows, but the ones on the sides of the building were still intact. The dust on the floor looked undisturbed for the most part, no telltale footprints betraying the presence of others. Fuller and I made a quick circuit of our side, carefully working our way toward the checkout counter. As we approached it, I heard Eric call out all clear.

At the counter, I stopped and lowered my rifle. The place looked like someone had simply closed up shop and never returned. The guns were still on the racks, ammo still on the shelves. Nothing had been disturbed.

"This is really weird," Fuller said. "I haven't seen a gun shop like this since before the Outbreak. You know, not trashed and looted and shit."

I nodded, feeling my eyebrows come together. It didn't make sense. During the Outbreak, frightened, desperate people had descended on places like this in droves and taken everything they could carry.

"Maybe the town was evacuated before things got bad here," Eric said, stepping around a tall shelf. "I remember one of the Legion raiders saying something about that."

"Then where did all those walkers come from?" Fuller replied.

I turned and looked out the shattered doorway to the transport. An idea began to form, and I didn't like where it led.

"I'm not sure, but I know someone who might be able to tell us."

FOUR

His name was Patrick Folsom.

I might have said it was a fake name if not for his Illinois driver's license. He carried it in a worn leather wallet along with credit cards, some family pictures, old business cards, and a few rumpled dollar bills. The address was 1310 Joliet Drive, Aurora, IL. The pictures showed a plump, beardless Folsom with a pretty young woman and two pre-teen boys. The edges were worn from frequent handling, the images faded.

"I'm assuming this is your family?" I asked.

He was propped up on one of the benches, hunched forward, arms and legs still bound. We were alone in the passenger carriage except for Hicks, who looked on silently with his rifle aimed at Folsom's head.

"They were," the prisoner replied.

"Outbreak?"

"Yeah."

"I'm sorry to hear that."

He looked up, laughing incredulously. "Really? Well that just makes my fucking day. How about you untie me and we can hug it out?"

I put the pictures back in the wallet and held it up where he could see. "You know, you're the first person I've met since the Outbreak who still carries one of these things. Most people threw them away a long time ago. Any particular reason you still have it?"

He gave an incremental shrug cut short by his bindings. "Sentimental I guess. Just wanted something to remind me of better times, back when I had a life."

"In my experience, most people try not to think about those days. Makes it harder to deal with their present reality."

"Good for them. Now are you gonna tell me what you want to know, or what?"

I had been monitoring his body language, and had not noticed any classic signs of anxiety or deceitfulness. He seemed, if anything, merely annoyed and physically uncomfortable from being hunched over. That in itself was an opening, but I would have to approach it carefully. Start out the easy way. If I didn't like what he told me, I could always beat the truth out of him later. I wanted to avoid that, if possible. There was no rush, and torture doesn't always yield the best information. People will say anything to make the pain stop.

"What did you do before the Outbreak?" I asked.

Again, the smile. Shake of the head. "I worked for a bank. Loan officer. I golfed on the weekends, went to my kids' baseball games, ate fattening food, drank too much, fucked my wife every chance I got, and told my sons I loved them every day. Then the world went to hell. When the Outbreak crossed the Mississippi, we packed our shit and ran along with about twenty million other people. We had an SUV full of water, clothes, food, camping gear. The one thing we didn't have was a gun. My wife always hated the things, said she didn't want one in her home."

He laughed then, but there was no humor in it. His eyes grew raw, gazing back across the barren distance of post-Outbreak years. For a brief time, he forgot his continued existence hinged on the next few sentences out of his mouth. I rapped a hand on the bench beneath me, bringing his attention back to the present. When he glanced at me, I made a twirling motion with my index finger.

"Most people stopped at the refugee camps in Topeka and Wichita," he continued, "but we kept going. Our third day on the road, we blew a tire somewhere on I-70. Middle-of-nowhere. A couple of guys in a truck stopped and offered to help us, but as soon as they saw what was in the back, one of them drew a gun and pointed it at my oldest son. Told us to back off or he'd shoot him. So we backed off. They took everything, all of it. My wife begged them to leave us some food and water, but they just laughed. They drove away and left us with nothing. So we did the only thing we could do; we started walking. Found an abandoned farm. The house was burned down but the barn was still standing. We holed up there for a few months, melting snow for water, eating whatever we could scavenge. My wife found a gun in a trailer park and, lo and behold, decided it was a good idea to keep it. In December, she came down with a cold that got worse and worse until it turned into pneumonia. She died in her sleep. My kids got sick a couple months later from some bad water we drank. They died hurting, and there wasn't a goddamn thing I could do about it. I held their little bodies while they burned up with fever, and I cried like a baby. When it was over, I dragged them down from the loft and tried to bury them, but the ground was frozen and I was too weak to dig a grave. Then, as if losing my whole goddamn family wasn't bad enough, a pack of wild dogs showed up. Three pit bulls and a couple of half-dead looking mutts. I tried to scare 'em off, but it didn't work. Bastards damn near killed me. I had to hide in the loft and listen to them tear my kids apart. I almost killed myself then; I had the gun in my hand, barrel against my temple, round in the chamber. I couldn't protect my wife, couldn't protect my kids, could barely protect myself. But I didn't do it. I waited until the dogs were gone, and then I left. Now, here I am."

He kept his head down while he talked, staring at the ground. I leaned back against the wall and watched him for a long, silent moment. His story was bad, but it was far from the worst I had heard, horrifying as that is.

"That's a lot of information, Mister Folsom."

"I figured it would save time," he replied. "Now, how about we get to the part where you ask me what you really want to know?"

"You in a hurry?"

"I'm tired. Tired of being cold. Tired of being hungry. Tired of being scared. I'm sick of the fighting and stealing and running and never getting a goddamn decent night's sleep. Ever since my kids died, not a day goes by I don't ask myself what the fuck I think I'm doing. You ever think about that? What the point of all this shit is? There's nothing left to live for. Nothing but hunger, and fighting, and pain until eventually I get sick, or bit, or somebody kills me for my shoes, or some fucking animal gets ahold of me, or I grow old and can't do for myself anymore. Then where will I be? No. Fuck it. You're just going to kill me anyway, so ask your questions. I'll tell you whatever you want to know. All I ask in return is you make it quick. I've suffered enough."

He was looking at me now. No challenge or defiance, just resignation, eyes hollow and empty, staring out from that desolate place we go when things get bad. That place of recognition when you look down and see that yes, indeed, that is a bullet hole in my torso. Yes, that RPG really did just disembowel me. Yes, those really are my intestines dangling around my ankles like deflated balloons. Yes, the nice policeman really did just say my father was killed in a mine collapse. No, I'm sorry son, your mother's cancer is inoperable. Yes, those really are the walking dead, those mindless, fearsome, unrelenting things I fought in so many third-world hellholes and yes, this is a worst-case scenario. Then the phone rings and it's 'Hey Gabe, there's some serious shit going down in Atlanta. Red Plague. Yes, I'm sure. Grimes got bit, man, I just wasted him. I'm bugging out. See if you can't get in touch with the old team, okay? Later.'

And then there is the sitting in the chair, and the disbelief, and the urge to scream, but you don't. You look at the gun, and you think about the future, and you make a decision.

For some, the survival instinct is always there and it will not be denied. It is insistent, strident, an irresistible force. It says NO, you will not give up after all this. Not after what you've survived. Suck it up, pick up the phone, and do what you have to do. You still have one friend left in the world. Tell him what he needs to know. Then you take your hand away from the gun and you get your ass moving. Survival instinct is a tough lady, hard as nails and sharp as a lover's bite, but she keeps you hanging on.

Then again, some people shuffle that voice aside. Beat it, simmer it, send it down the road until it's just a shrill little noise whining in the distance, too faint to listen to or care what it's saying. That's when people go for a high dive with no pool. When they play William Tell with their cerebellum. When they knot a rope, and stand on a chair, and carve something into a wall before they jump.

But not me, not yet. Gabriel Garrett's iron is not bound by faulty welds. This tall, muscled, calloused, scarred, scruffy, loose-limbed, hard-fighting scrapper doesn't go down that easy. But he knows every man has his limits, and he's never had any children. Never had anything with a woman that lasted more than a year. And he has certainly never watched his family die or listened to his children's corpses being torn apart by ravening dogs. He can't imagine living with that kind of crippling dysphoria. He can, however, see how it might take the fear of death and reduce it to an annoyance no worse than the prospect of indigestion after too many hard drinks.

Not for the first time, I wondered what it would take to drive me to that point.

"I won't say I'm not going to kill you," I said, "because you never know how these things will work out. But it's not my immediate intention. I want information, and if you give it to me, I might let you go. Or I might take you into custody and turn you over to the local sheriff."

"Sheriff? You fucking kidding me? There's still cops around here?"

"Of a sort."

He laughed. "Well don't that just beat all. Where the hell are you from, anyway? Where'd you get this…thing we're sitting in? You with the Army or something?"

"I'll ask the questions."

"Right. Well, go ahead and ask them already."

I drew my knife and stood up. Folsom's eyes grew angry. "What kind of sick fuck are you, man? I told you I'll answer your questions. You don't need the knife."

"Relax." I bent down and cut the ties binding his ankles. He was able to separate his feet and sit up a little straighter.

"Thanks."

"You're welcome."

I sat back down and cleared my face of all emotion. It was a trick I had practiced extensively during my days with the CIA. Smooth out all the planes and lines, relax the brow, tilt the head down slightly so my cheeks and jaw appeared shadowed, set the mouth in a firm, straight line. Because of my pale gray eyes— think Siberian husky or timber wolf—it produces quite the dramatic effect. As if to say, no matter what you have been through, no matter how bad you think you have suffered, things can always get worse. Much worse. And I am the harbinger of your misery. The effect was not lost on Folsom.

"Who was the man I shot?" I asked.

He shifted uncomfortably. "His name was Jimmy. Don't know the last name, everybody just called him Jimmy."

"You don't sound too broken up about his death."

"I'm not. Guy was a belligerent asshole, always running his mouth and doing stupid shit. Nobody liked him, but he was good in a fight, so we kept him around. Said he was a marine back in the day, served in Iraq. We always sent him places to get stuff. Food, medicine, booze. He liked doing that kind of shit, liked the rush. We took turns going with him. You know, to keep it fair."

"Who is this 'we' you keep mentioning?"

"The crew we were travelling with. There's seven of us now, seeing as you killed Jimmy."

"Where are the others?"

"Not far from here. I could show you on a map."

I reached back and rapped a hard-knuckled tactical glove against the wall. Cole asked me what I needed.

"Can you bring up an area map on your tablet and bring it in here, please?"

"No problem."

I turned back to Folsom. "Are you part of a larger group?"

"Yeah. The Midwest Alliance. You probably heard of them."

"I have. What are you doing this far south?"

"Scavenging. Scouting. Trying to stay alive."

I nodded slowly and leaned forward in the cramped space until my face was only about a foot from Folsom's. He looked up as I drew close and I could see the striations of dark brown iris around his wide pupils. The next question was important, and I wanted to be close enough to catch him in a lie.

"Where were you leading that horde?"

Folsom went still, just for a moment. Tiny flick of muscle above the cheekbone, slight dilation of the pupils, barely perceptible intake of breath. But it was there.

"Look man, we were just trying to get away. Those fucking things came out of nowhere. We saw your vehicle and thought, you know, what the hell. Figured you and you men were dead anyway. I know it's a shit thing to say. But that's how the world is, you know?"

I kept my gaze steady as I sat back, expression blank. Fabricated a slight narrowing of the eyes and a nod, as if confirming some inner debate. Despite the cold, Folsom began to sweat.

"What else?"

"That's it man, swear to God. Like I said, I'll tell you where to find the others."

"Of that I have no doubt." I was still holding the knife in my fist, knuckles perched on the edge of my knee. The black-coated blade lay parallel to the ground, a clear line of delineation between what Folsom was hoping for and what I had the power to give him, quick or slow. I let the knife and the silence sit there for a while, its own dire suggestion.

"I'm pretty good at spotting lies, Folsom. I believe you about your family. I believe you about Jimmy, and the people you're with, and the Midwest Alliance. What I don't believe is you didn't have anything to do with that horde."

"Look, man-" he started, but I held up a hand, the one with the knife in it. His eyes locked to it, a bead of sweat dangling from one worried eyebrow.

"Here's what I think," I said. "I think if I was going to send people to round up a horde and lead it somewhere, I would send a team of no less than six, but no more than a dozen. Eight sounds about right. It's hard, dangerous work with a strong possibility of casualties. A man would have to be highly motivated to attempt something like that. Desperation, greed, anger, extortion, and old-fashioned bat-shit lunacy are the usual culprits. You don't look desperate to me; you're too well fed. Greed is a possibility, but it doesn't feel right and I trust my instincts. Extortion doesn't make sense because you don't have any family left. And I'm going to go ahead and say you're not crazy, which only leaves one culprit. How am I doing so far?"

He remained silent, eyes locked on the knife. The door opened at the back of the transport and Cole appeared in the doorway. "Got what you need, boss," he said, holding the tablet out to Hicks, who took it and brought it over to me. On the screen was an interactive map of McKenzie and the surrounding area. I turned it around so Folsom could see it.

"Here's what's going to happen, Mr. Folsom," I continued. "You're going to show me where the other people in your crew are. You're going to tell us everything we need to know to take them prisoner, peacefully. Then my men and I are going to move out and apprehend them while you and a couple of my best guys stay behind. If your intel turns out to be wrong, or you lead us into a trap, or I don't radio back with a pre-arranged password at a pre-arranged time, those men are going to go to work on you. You will beg for death before they're done, and when they are, they will feed you alive and screaming to the infected. If you want to live, or at least get that quick death you were talking about, you had better damn well deal on the level. Do I make myself clear?"

Folsom paled visibly. "Yeah. I understand."

"Good," I said, offering my least friendly smile. "Let's get started."

FIVE

They were spread out over three locations.

Each one was a waypoint where a two-person team waited to take over leading the horde. While they did so, the rest of the team would set a hard pace and move ahead to establish new waypoints further down the line. There, they would snatch a brief rest until it was time to take point again. It was a surprisingly well-coordinated operation, considering they had no radios and no long-range communications. They operated solely by experience, and by being able to predict what the other members of their team would do in any given situation. The kind of thing that takes practice.

Lots of practice.

I drove the transport to within a mile of the nearest waypoint, which put us four miles from McKenzie. My plan was simple: Riordan, Cole, and Fuller would come with me to take down the first group of Alliance goons. Sanchez and three of his men would move to the next waypoint and apprehend the insurgents there. Same story for Thompson, Holland, Vincenzo, and Page. Hicks and the rest of the troops would hang back with the transport to keep Folsom under guard and respond with reinforcements where necessary. If all went according to plan, they would be in for a very dull wait.

To avoid any chance the bad guys might somehow warn each other, I decided all three strike teams should attack in tandem. Hicks got the job of coordinator, which he was not happy about, but didn't argue. Rather, he simply glared at me, shook his head, and muttered what may or may not have been a grumbled curse. Personally, I didn't know what he was bitching about. He got to hang out in the warm, heated confines of the transport's cab and orchestrate a very simple snatch-and-grab operation while the rest of us froze our asses off. By the time my team reached our destination, I was starting to regret not taking the job myself.

When we reached it, I decided the waypoint was a good choice of location: a strip club. I might have thought it was something else if not for the sign featuring a silhouette of a buxom woman sporting what appeared to be booby tassels with the words LIVE NUDE GIRLS plastered beneath. Sounded better than DEAD NUDE GIRLS, I suppose. Although, as screwed up as I've learned people can be, there might be a market for that somewhere.

The club had no windows and only two entrances, one in front and one in back. Both doors were heavily reinforced steel, not the clear glass typical of more reputable establishments. It was a squat single-story structure with the beginnings of a deep snowdrift forming around the back entrance. The snow on that side had been hastily shoveled away, and I could see two distinct sets of footprints leading in both directions near the door.

If Folsom had kept going on his way and not encountered my crew, it would not have taken him long to make it this far. Driving the transport to within a mile had taken just over half an hour, and then another twenty minutes to hike in on foot. While we waited, the transport covered the five miles to the second waypoint, and then another five miles to the third. The insurgents at all three locations were most likely settling in for a nice long break, grabbing a bite to eat, maybe a nip from a bottle of hard stuff, looking forward to a good night's sleep. All of which worked to our advantage.

Normally, I would have waited for nightfall and attacked then, but we only had a few sets of NVGs and it was only going to get colder. I wanted to take these people into custody as quickly as possible, and then haul ass back to Hollow Rock. Central Command needed to know what was going on out here.

The hard part, as always, was the wait. After roughly two centuries of shivering silence—which my lying bastard watch told me was no more than an hour—Hicks finally conducted a round of terse radio checks to ensure all strike teams were in position and standing by. All affirmatives.

"Roger that," he said in his West Texas drawl. "All teams proceed on mission. Happy huntin'."

Eric and I went out ahead and set up overwatch on the north and south sides of the entrance. The others stayed out of sight behind the treeline. The two of us were less than fifty yards from the door, but we were well hidden by the thick snowfall. I had switched to my trusty SCAR 17, even though I was running low on ammo for it, and swapped out my ACOG for a 1-6x VCOG scope. Eric had done the same with his M-4, and since he had volunteered to take point, had further armed himself with a handful of M-84 stun grenades.

Much like the breaching charge currently resting against the small of my back, and many other items in my private inventory, the flashbangs were a gift courtesy of the U.S. Army. And by gift, I mean Thompson, along with the other squad leaders in First Platoon, embellished their combat reports to not altogether truthfully emphasize the hostile and dangerous nature of marauder disposition in the immediate vicinity of Hollow Rock. Thus, Central Command approved their request for additional armor, weapons, ammo, and various explosive ordnance, a portion of which Thompson then appropriated from a recent supply drop and promptly wrote off as having been used to root out and eliminate pockets of insurgents harassing innocent traders on the highway.

Along with a promise to use my ill-gotten gains for the purpose of protecting Hollow Rock and her citizenry, the items I requested had cost me a case of whiskey, thirty pounds of chicken eggs, and four jars of instant coffee. All to be shared with Thompson's men, of course. Specifically his platoon sergeant and commanding officer.

Let's hear it for capitalism.

While I freely acknowledge the criminal nature of purchasing black market hardware from impressionable young staff sergeants, even those who operate under the watchful approval of their direct chain of command, I also have to acknowledge—both for my own well-being and that of my men—that hunting salvage in the wastelands is a dangerous way to make a living. But such danger can be mitigated by the judicious employment of strategy, tactics, requisitioning of the proper equipment, and occasionally blowing shit up.

Ergo, my current situation.

I turned and motioned to my team. They had fanned out behind me at ten-yard intervals, eyes watching all approaches. The plan was simple: Eric and I would breach the door and execute a dynamic entry with Fuller backing us up. Cole would move around front and cover the other entrance with his SAW. If anyone tried to escape, it was his job to make sure they didn't get far. The rest of us would deploy the flashbangs, move in, and cuff-and-stuff the bad guys. Folsom had told us there would only be two of them, but we weren't taking any chances. If it came down to a question of us or them, my orders were to shoot to kill. Apprehending the insurgents was the main goal, but it was not more important than getting home alive.

Each strike team only had one man with a radio—me, in my team's case. I had only requisitioned five long-range handhelds from the Militia's armory and was now sorely regretting not grabbing a few more. The worsening weather was making hand signals difficult as the heavy snowfall had reduced visibility to just shy of ten yards. Folsom, Riordan and I would be fine, but Cole would be too far away to see us once the action started.

At my signal, the big man slowly worked his way down the hill to speak with me. When he was close enough, I motioned him near.

"When you hear the breaching charge, that's your cue," I said. "Riordan and Fuller know not to come out the front door if they can help it, but you never know what might happen in these situations. We may not have a choice. You follow?"

He smiled, white teeth standing out against dark brown skin. "Don't worry 'bout a thang, I got this. Ain't gonna be no friendly fire today. Just do what you gotta do, bossman."

I clapped him on the shoulder and sent him off to his firing position. It was something close to a hundred meters away, so figuring his pace at a meter every four seconds, I waited until seven minutes had passed before signaling the others to advance.

We proceeded carefully, stopping often to wait and scan for movement. Nothing. Just the wind in the trees, and the sand-like rattling of snow over ice. No tripwires. No jury-rigged alarm system. No booby traps. No sign whatsoever of a properly established perimeter. Just obvious footprints in the snow.

Either this was an exceptionally clever trap, or the insurgents inside the strip club were not expecting company.

Or maybe it's something else. Maybe they have good reason not to set up a perimeter or hide their tracks. Or maybe they're just tired, and didn't feel like making the effort. You've seen people do dumber things. But never assume, Gabriel. Never assume.

The only course of action was to proceed with the breach, so onward we went. The three of us stacked up on the entry side of the door. Eric gripped the handle and turned it slowly, only applying pressure to the latch in case there was a pressure-triggered bomb on the other side, or a weapon rigged to shoot.

"Locked," he said.

We switched positions and I reached back for the breaching charge, peeled the cover off the adhesive strips, pressed it over the bolt, and activated it. Riordan and Fuller had already fallen back and covered their ears. I followed them, and two seconds later, the charge detonated.

The explosion was brief, sharp, and powerful. It traveled through the wall and thumped me in the back. The door rattled open with a shudder, bashing loudly against the cinder-block wall on the other side. Eric was already moving into the opening, two flashbangs in hand. He stopped just shy of the corner, pulled the pins, and let them fly.

"Flashbangs out!"

Almost immediately, we heard the twin *CRACK-CRACK* of the grenades bursting, impossibly loud in the small space, and then two brilliant flashes of light. If there was anyone within twenty feet of the entrance, they weren't happy. I didn't hear any screams. Eric used his tactical light to quickly scan the door for wires, then signaled he was moving in.

I broke left while Riordan and Fuller broke right, weapons up, eyes scanning for movement, searching for traps and anything resembling the outline of a human body. The interior of the strip club was pitch black where it wasn't illuminated by our tac-lights. I smelled dust and wood rot. The ground felt gritty and slick under my feet. Gray-coated tables and chairs occupied the floor in scattered disarray in front of an equally dusty stage adorned with several tarnished stripper poles. A chest-high bar dominated the entire wall furthest from the back entrance. There was an open space near the front door that extended between the two main bodies of tables and ran parallel to the stage. I kept my rifle trained on the bar, moving back and forth. Eric and Fuller split up to search the tables.

"Clear," Eric shouted.

"Clear," Fuller answered.

"Eyes on the bar!" I ordered. "Eric, hit it now!"

That was when things went sideways.

As Eric's hand went to his vest to grab another flashbang, the barrel of a Kalashnikov appeared over the bar. The hand holding it, and the person attached to it, remained behind cover. As the rifle opened up, firing randomly around on semi-auto, Eric and I dropped to the ground.

Fuller wasn't quite as fast.

The rifle was pointed almost straight at him when it appeared. The first two shots went wide right, but the next two staggered the young soldier back a step. He shouted in pain, took a knee, and squeezed off a burst from his M-4 at the wood paneling directly below the rifle. His rounds stitched a line all the way to the floor. A shout of pain rewarded his efforts

As Fuller demonstrated, there is a big difference between concealment and cover. Concealment simply hides you from your enemies, but doesn't necessarily offer any protection if you are discovered. Cover is something that can actually stop a bullet. The latter is, in many cases, much more difficult to find than the former.

The three of us had neither.

If the bad guys were standing up, I would have seen them. Which meant they were either crouching or lying down. My guess was lying down. We probably caught them while they were asleep, woke them up with the breaching charge, and then scared the shit out of them with the flashbangs. Any other time, I might have ordered them to surrender. But I had nowhere to hide if they opened fire through the bar's flimsy wood, and they had just shot one of my guys.

Although equipped with a suppressor, the SCAR was loud in the confines of the building. I fired on semi-auto, rapidly placing powerful 7.62mm NATO rounds at two-foot intervals through the bar. Fuller kept firing at the spot below the Kalashnikov where the scream had emanated from, while Eric began stitching rounds through the bar in my direction, obviously intent on meeting me in the middle. I emptied an entire twenty round magazine, reloaded, and emptied another one. Eric did the same. The chamber of Fuller's rifle latched open after expending the last round in his P-mag. Rather than reloading, he slumped over on his side with an agonized groan. My first instinct was to render aid, but it would be useless to do so until I knew the building was secure. Getting myself killed wouldn't do Fuller a damn bit of good. There was a chance Cole had heard the commotion and was on his way, but I couldn't count on that. I just hoped Fuller could hold on a little while longer.

There was just enough light for Eric to see me without having to swivel his rifle. I called out to him and signaled to flank right. He nodded, and we rose to our feet at the same time, moving at the same speed toward the bar. Words were no longer necessary. We had fought side by side so many times each of us knew instinctively what the other would do.

When both of us were in position, Eric drew a flashbang, pulled the pin, and tossed it over the bar. I turned my back to it and closed my eyes, hands over my ears. Eric did the same. The bar absorbed most of the blast, but it still made my ears ring and put spots in my vision.

As soon as the shock dissipated, we went over the bar and hit the ground simultaneously, rifles up, alert for danger. Ten feet in front of me, a bullet riddled body lay on its side. It was male, medium build, short, dressed in heavy clothes, big nasty exit wounds on the neck and upper back. Bullet holes and bits of flesh speckled the wall behind him. Blood had spread in a rectangular pool, confined by the narrow space. Arterial spray on the shelves and cabinets, and a few smears on the floor around his shoulders. He had squirmed a bit before expiring, and he was definitely, undeniably dead. There is a certain stillness that settles in when the lights go out for good. No slight tremor of heartbeat or respiration, no tension in the muscles and nerves, no blood pumping from open wounds. Just a slow, sluggish spill.

The air was thick with the stench of evacuated bowels. I raised my rifle and put a round through his head, just to be extra sure. When you have trained as hard as I have, old habits die hard. Eric watched dispassionately.

"I thought there were supposed to be two?" he said.

"That's what Folsom told me. The other one might not be in the building. I'll get Fuller patched up. You and Cole go conduct a perimeter sweep."

"Good thinking."

As we were turning to hop back over the bar, a squawk of metal on metal screeched behind Eric, the sound of rusty hinges protesting sudden motion after prolonged disuse. In the small window framed by Eric's knees, I saw the lid of a hatch spring upward from the floor. I hadn't noticed it there with Eric in the way, and he had walked right over it without realizing what it was.

"Look out!" I shouted.

Another person might have turned around. If they had, it would have been their last mistake. Eric wasn't that stupid. Without hesitation, he bunched his legs and launched himself over the bar, arms and legs tucked to reduce his target profile, leading with his shoulders so he could roll when he hit the ground. As he went over, I caught a brief glimpse of the insurgent behind him—a swarthy, bearded man, surging up through the opening with pistol in his hand, aimed at Eric. I leveled my rifle and drew a bead on his forehead. He beat me to the punch and got off two shots rapid fire. Eric screamed. I stayed focused and squeezed the trigger. There was a low WAP of the bullet passing through flesh, bone, and wood paneling. Faster than my eyes could follow, the top of the insurgent's skull disintegrated in a crimson burst. There one second, gone the next, most of it splashed against the underside of the hatch behind his shoulders. He slid silently back down into the darkness. The lid fell and clattered shut.

On the other side of the bar, Eric lay on his back clutching at his lower right leg. Even in the dim light, I could see inky dark blood pouring out between his fingers. Both he and Fuller had been reduced to writhing, moaning agony.

"Riordan, how bad is it?" I said, rifle trained on the hidden trapdoor.

"Got my calf muscle. Hurts like a bitch. I need help, man."

"Any bones broken?"

He prodded gingerly at his tibia, then gently squeezed the muscle tissue above his fibula. A hiss of pain escaped him, but no scream. "I don't think so. It would hurt a lot worse if one of them was broken, right?"

"Yes. If you can squeeze your leg like that without screaming, the bones are fine."

A pounding of boots on frozen ground echoed from the back entrance. The door was still thrown wide on warped hinges, allowing grey winter light and swirls of snow to gust through the opening. I snapped my rifle in that direction, finger on the trigger. Then I remembered Cole was still out there, and took it off. The footsteps stopped. Cole's powerful bass thundered into the room.

"Mockingbird!" A pre-arranged verbal identifier.

"Blackhawk," I responded. It was the all clear signal, although technically I wasn't entirely sure if we were clear. The other pre-arranged response, red bird, would have meant I was under duress, and would have elicited a much different reaction from the big gunner. As it was, he stepped through the doorway, took in the situation with a quick visual sweep, and immediately went to Fuller's side.

"You gonna be all right, man. Tell me where you hit at."

Fuller moved his hands and gestured at the left side of his chest. "Took two rounds right here. I'm not sure if they got through my body armor. Goddamn this hurts."

Cole put his first-aid kit on the ground next to him and went to work. I peeled mine from my vest and tossed it next to Eric. "See if you can get the bleeding stopped. I'm going to make sure we don't have any more company, and then I'll be right back to help you. Think you can hold out until then?"

Eric reached for the kit and began unzipping it, speaking through clenched teeth. "I'll be all right. Just don't be all day about it."

"Right."

I approached the trapdoor and realized why neither of us had seen it. Latticed rubber matting lay over top of it, the kind with lots of holes and channels to keep bartenders from slipping on spilled drinks. After kicking the mats out of the way, I saw the hatch lay flush with the ground, no handle visible, caked with a thick layer of dust. My knife barely fit into the crease between the panel and the surrounding floor, but once in, the lid lifted easily.

Shining my tac-light into the hole, I spotted the swarthy man who shot Eric. He had landed on his buttocks, sitting upright, ruined head listing over to one side, limp hands lying palms up on the floor. I put another round straight down into his chest. The body shook a little with the impact, but made no other reaction.

The space was too tight to lead with my rifle, so I unslung it and laid it on the floor with the handle toward me. If I needed to, I could hop up, grab it, and bring it to bear. But I hoped I wouldn't need to.

With one hand, I drew my pistol. With the other, I unhooked a couple of chem-lights from my vest, popped them, crouched over the hatch, and tossed them into the yawning darkness beyond the ladder. Sliding forward, I hung upside down through the hole and swept the room below me with my pistol. No movement. I had expected to see a storage room piled with cases of liquor and boxes of bar napkins, or maybe an underground utility shed. But the basement was neither of those things. In the eerie green luminescence of the chem-lights, the room was wide and open, with wood-paneled walls, tastefully arranged oil paintings, darkly stained tables and chairs, and a wet bar at the far end. The bar was flanked by a desk supporting a money counting machine, and another desk with an array of envelopes, lockboxes, and duffel bags. Whatever this place had once been, I was guessing at least some of its operations had been less than legal. I was tempted to climb down and have a look around, but more pressing matters required my attention.

I sat up and keyed my radio. "Sierra Lead, Sierra One. How copy? Over."

"Loud and clear, Sierra One. Over."

"Give me a sitrep. Over."

"Sierra Two and Sierra Three both report targets engaged and apprehended. One enemy casualty. Headshot, courtesy of Sanchez. The other three are alive and well. Request to commence extraction. Over."

I sighed. I had been worried how the other, less experienced teams would perform, and here I was with two wounded men. Some leadership.

"Proceed with extraction, Sierra Lead, but make it fast. I have two wounded. Repeat, two wounded. As soon as everyone is on board, proceed to my twenty for medevac. Over."

"Acknowledged, Sierra One. Will commence extraction and proceed to your twenty for medevac. ETA thirty mikes. Will advise Hotel Romeo to prepare for casualties. Can you advise as to the extent of the injuries? Over."

I hopped up on the bar, swung my legs to the other side, and made my way over to Eric. "Assessing now. Stand by."

"Copy. Standing by."

Eric still lay on his back, leg in the air, hands pressing gauze pads to his wounds. Beads of sweat ran down his forehead emitting ghostly steam in the frigid air. His lips were pressed into a hard blue line, face pale with agony, breathing rapid and shallow. Blood soaked the gauze, but the bleeding had slowed from a pour to a drip.

"Okay, buddy. I need you to move your hands for a minute. Gotta let me see what I'm up against."

Slowly, he released his leg and lay his arms down at his sides. I peeled the bandages away and shined my flashlight on the damage. It looked as though the bullet had entered just outside the center muscle of his calf about eight inches below the knee, traveled through the muscle at an angle, and exited less than half an inch from his fibula. Smaller caliber, maybe a .380. The exit wound wasn't much bigger than the entry wound, indicating the bullet had not deformed significantly before exiting. Must have been a copper jacketed round, passed through him too quickly to tumble. A lucky break. He had lost some blood, and the tissue damage would keep him sidelined for at least eight weeks, but with time, and a little physical therapy, I figured he would make a full recovery. I told him as much.

"Great. Sounds wonderful. Now can you put a bandage on it and get me some goddamn painkillers, please?"

As I started dressing his wound, I called over to Cole. "How are you looking over there?"

The big man had sat Fuller up as straight as he could go and was busy wrapping a pressure bandage around his ribcage. "First round hit the trauma plate. Busted it, but didn't get through. The second looks like it hit the thin part of the Kevlar and deflected a little, but it still tore a hole through-and-through a few inches below the armpit. Looks like he might have a couple of broken ribs."

"*Might* have broken ribs?" Fuller wheezed. "I feel like there's a knife in my side every time I breath."

"Anything life-threatening?" I asked.

Cole shook his head. "Not if we can get him to a doctor in the next few hours."

"Good enough. Hicks is en route with the transport. We just have to keep it together until they get here."

I reached a hand toward my radio and advised Hicks of Riordan and Fuller's injuries. He informed me he would pass the information on to Hotel Romeo—phonetic initials for Hollow Rock—where Doc Laroux would be waiting when we got back. She was going to be pissed at me for letting Eric get hurt. Something told me the Safety Third argument wasn't going to help in this case.

Finished dressing Eric's wound, I started back toward the bar to search the dead bodies. The wind outside howled louder than ever, whipping through the open door and sending up choking plumes of thick dust.

"Cole, when you get done with Fuller see if you can get that damn door shut."

"No problem," he replied.

My back was turned, but I heard him stand up, and the rustle of his gear as he walked to the door. Then there was a strange *crunch-scrape, crunch-scrape*.

My heart leapt in my chest.

"Shit!" Cole yelled.

I tried to raise my pistol, but the big man was in the way. His leg came back and then shot forward with tremendous force. There was a clack of teeth slamming together, and I saw the body of a small child flip end over end out the door, the back of the head cracking loudly against the top of the doorjamb as it spun through.

"Walkers!" Cole shouted, reaching a hand over his shoulder for his bar mace.

I heard several moans coming from the doorway, maybe four or five of them. Cole strode forward, lifted his mace high over his head, and swung it downward. Skull bones crunched and brain tissue splattered outward against the walls. Cole raised his leg and booted the body out of the doorway before following up with another overhead strike. And another, and another, each one punctuated by a booming front kick—standard technique for keeping a doorway clear when attacked by the infected. At the edges of his bulk, I saw limbs flailing and pale, ragged bodies thrashing against one another. My hands itched to draw my short sword and join the fray, but there wasn't enough room. Then, as quickly as it started, it was over. Cole pulled a rag from his pocket and began cleaning his mace. He turned and motioned me over.

"How many out there?" I asked.

He moved to one side. "Come look."

I walked over and peered through the door. "Shit," I said, succinctly.

A horde was gathering outside.

A big one.

SIX

"They must have been nearby when we got here," Cole said. "Maybe scattered around, blinded by the storm. Came when they heard the commotion."

"You're probably right," I replied. "No way we can fight off that many. Let's see if we can get this door shut."

Eric asked, "Hey, what do you want us to do?"

I looked over my shoulder. He had struggled to a sitting position and was reloading his rifle.

"Try not to bleed too much," I said. "If Cole and I get killed, shoot as many infected as you can, but make sure you save one bullet for yourself. In the meantime, look around and see if you can find a bottle of something strong. I could use a drink."

"You're fucking hilarious. Really."

He and Fuller dragged themselves further inside, groaning and making plaintive little hissing sounds until their backs were against the bar. Then they laid their weapons over their laps and waited, eyes closed, drawing deep breaths, clearing their minds against the pain. Possibly praying, in Eric's case. He did that sometimes when things looked bleak. A foxhole Catholic if I ever saw one.

I stopped praying a long time ago. Figured out no one was listening.

Cole and I stepped outside and tried to lever the door shut. The heavy-duty hinges were warped, steel collars twisted against bent pins. Looking it over, I figured we could get it shut, but only by pushing from the outside and booting it into place. Once closed, it would take two men with crowbars to get it back open. Or a few breaching charges. The infected had neither.

"Okay, here's the plan," I said. "You go back inside, keep an eye on Riordan and Fuller. I'll jam the door in place, wait for the transport from a good safe distance, and try to lure away some of these walkers. I'll hang on the radio. When I spot the transport, I'll give them my position. If I can't get to the transport, I'll catch up with you down the line."

Cole looked at me like a third eye had suddenly sprouted on my forehead. "Have you lost your ever-lovin' mind? To hell with this door, man. This place has a basement, right? Let's get down there and wait for backup."

"No. We don't know the full extent of Fuller's injuries. Broken ribs can do all kinds of nasty things to internal organs, and if we try to get him down that narrow ladder, we're only going to hurt him worse. We can't risk moving him until the transport gets here with a stretcher and proper medical equipment. Besides, if you hide in the basement, the smell of all that blood is going to draw the infected like flies. They'll pack in there tight as sardines, and the moans of the ones inside will draw the ones outside to the door. They'll gather so thick against the entrance it'll take a bulldozer to move them out of the way. How is Hicks supposed to rescue you through that? Shoot them all? We can't waste that kind of ammo, and there's the risk of somebody else getting hurt. I can't have that, Cole."

"Look, Gabe, what you're saying makes sense, but-"

I cut him off with an upraised palm. "This is not a negotiation. This is what we're doing. End of discussion."

He frowned at me, eyes intense. He was an inch shorter than me, but outweighed me by thirty pounds of solid muscle. And he was quick. Damned quick. If he decided to make an issue of things, I doubted I would be able to stop him without causing both of us serious harm. From the look on his face, I could tell he was thinking about it. I raised an arm and pointed at the walkers. There were nearly a dozen within thirty meters of us.

"Cole, we don't have time for this. When you signed on to my crew, you agreed to follow my orders. Did you not?"

The intensity wavered. "Yeah. But come on, man, this is crazy as hell. You gonna getcha self killed."

"No, I won't. I've done this kind of thing before, Cole. Trust me, I know what I'm doing."

He took half a step back, tension draining, shaking his head. "Famous last words, man. Famous last words."

He stepped inside and walked over to his SAW. Picked it up. Looked it over. Placed it on a table and sat down in one of the many chairs. "Good luck," he said. "You gonna need it."

"Just hang tight. We'll be out of here in no time." I grabbed the door, planted a boot against the wall, and heaved with everything I had. The hinges cried a despairing screech. I shoved with my shoulder and cursed the door in three languages until it was just a few inches from the jamb. Then I backed off, took three running steps, leapt into the air, and applied all my weight into a two-footed dropkick. The heavy steel slammed home with a bright clang and the pop of several hinge collars breaking. My satisfaction lasted as long as it took me to rebound from the door and land flat on my back. The snow offered some padding, but it still hurt.

Getting back to my feet, I looked around at the converging infected, trying to estimate their number. The wind had shifted, making visibility a little better than it had been earlier and allowing me to see thirty or forty meters through the stinging snow. Even in that small expanse of real estate, there were at least fifty undead.

I had deliberately left my SCAR in the strip club, as I was down to my last three full mags for it, and I didn't want to waste them on infected. I still had my Sig .45, but only thirty-six rounds of spare ammo in that caliber. Forty-five ammo was even harder to find than .308, so I didn't want to use it either. I dropped my assault pack and unzipped a compartment on the side. Within was a Sig Sauer Mosquito—a small .22 caliber pistol—and a screw-on silencer.

Because it is small and light, .22 ammo is perfect for use against large numbers of undead, assuming they are within twenty-five yards. I had a brick of 750 rounds, which would probably be enough to deal with the horde confronting me and then some, but then there was the problem of reloading. I had five full magazines including the one in the pistol, but that only accounted for fifty rounds. The only solution was to make every shot count and reload on the run. I fished out the 750 round brick, poured a portion of its contents in an empty pouch on my vest, re-stowed the ammo, zipped the pack, slung it over my shoulders, and drew my falcata.

My best bet was to get back to the highway, follow it south where the transport was coming from, and try to find some high ground to defend. The pistol in my right hand and the sword in my left were a comfort, especially the blade. Swords might not have much range, but they never run out of bullets. That said, when there are infected nearby, a gun is never a bad idea. I knew as long as I had those two weapons, I could hold out for a very long time.

I took a few moments to read the horde and determine a route through them. Threading one's way through a crowd of the hungry dead is much akin to mountain climbing. One does not just go at it without a plan and a clear sense of direction. If you do, the end result will most likely be a painful, screaming death.

The easiest way to plot a course through a horde is to observe the terrain. Walkers follow the path of least resistance, which is why they are so often found on highways and game trails and the clefts between hills. They generally stick to flat, level ground, they tend to circle large land formations unless there is prey at the top—in which case they will climb relentlessly to reach it—and they seem to abhor large bodies of water. Not that they won't wade into them, they will, but it takes a lot to get them to do it. Whatever it is that keeps the ghouls ambulatory, it does not like being submerged.

Western Tennessee is very flat. There are hills and even the occasional deep ravine, but for the most part, manmade structures or trees are the only ways to take the high ground. The snow was coming down way too thick to see any tall buildings, and since I had not been down this particular stretch of road before, I couldn't call the location of one from memory. So I did the only thing I could do.

Start moving, and kill anything that gets in the way.

The snow was deep on the road, making it hard to tell where the asphalt began and where it ended. A biting wind pushed hard against me, sending clattering snowflakes dancing across my goggles. My breath formed an icy fringe on my scarf, creating a scraping circle of cold on the lower half of my face. The drifts had piled up well over my ankles, making for tough going even on flat ground. I was already a little fatigued from the strain of the day's events, and I knew I only had a few miles, five or six at the most, before my strength began to flag. I needed to find a place to hole up, and I needed to find it fast.

My path brought me straight into a cluster of six infected, all of them torn, naked, and barely recognizable as human. Probably dead since the Outbreak. As they came closer, a voice came unbidden to my mind from a time long in the past. A voice with a name I had not thought of in years: Lundegaard. No first name, no mister, just Lundegaard. No accent either. National, regional or otherwise. The most bland, boring voice you can imagine from a bland, boring man. A man who wanted his lessons to stick, but be otherwise completely forgettable.

"You will find that no matter how much extra ammunition you carry on your person, it will never be enough," he said, all those years ago. *"There will almost always be more infected in areas with significant outbreaks than there will be bullets to deal with them. Therefore, it is important to manage ammunition expenditure carefully. One of the most effective ways to do this is to alternate between firearms and non-ballistic weapons. Each of you will have your own preference for non-ballistic weapons, but at the very least, it should be something you can use at close range, something you have a fair amount of proficiency with, and something that can withstand damage from frequent violent collisions with very dense human skulls. Research and Development is working on designs for new weapons that may be issued in the future, but for the time being, we leave this choice of equipment at each operator's discretion.*

Now, let us discuss the philosophy of use as it pertains to the aforementioned alternation between what I will henceforth refer to as simply 'guns' and 'bludgeons'. Please note that bludgeon is a generalized term that includes both edged and non-edged weapons.

Whenever a tactical situation permits it—always bearing in mind that personal safety is of paramount importance and you must defend yourself in the manner you deem most expedient— you are wholeheartedly encouraged to utilize bludgeons to dispatch revenants whenever possible. Doing so reduces ammunition expenditure, which, in addition to reducing costs to the company, increases your long-term chances of survival should you become stranded during a mission and extraction is not immediately practicable.

A simple tactic, one that each of you should be able to master with very little difficulty, is to assess how many revenants you can dispatch with your bludgeon and never attempt to exceed that amount in close combat. In other words, shoot them down until their number is sufficiently reduced before you proceed to splitting skulls."

Six infected was usually no problem for blade work, but in this case, it would be dangerous because they were packed closely together. The dynamics of fighting a horde change depending on the distances between walkers. If there is a lot of space, say twenty feet or so, it is not necessary to engage at all. Just serpentine through the ranks and make sure to stay away from grasping hands. At ten feet, assuming you have the right weapon, you can kill a straight line through a horde at a brisk walk and, as long as there aren't too many of them, emerge unscathed. At five feet, your best bet is to try to find a way around. Your chances of winning through are slim, but improve if you have a team of well-trained, well-armed fighters helping you. At less than five feet, you are walking into certain death no matter how many friends you have. If a horde that tightly packed surrounds you…well, like I always say. Save the last bullet for yourself.

I raised the pistol and sighted in. The walkers were less than twenty feet away, but the strong wind forced me to aim a little to the right. The one in the lead was nearly as tall as me and skinny as a willow branch. Its skin, where it hadn't been stripped away by the elements, was a mottled gray, stained black with old crusted blood. A flaccid remnant of shredded genitalia dangling between its emaciated legs was the only recognizable indication of gender. It had been a man, once, but now it was just another monster. I squeezed the trigger, and it walked no more.

I tried hard not to notice any details about the next three I shot. With a memory like mine, you don't want to focus too closely on things like that. Those kinds of memories stay with you and rear their ugly heads at the strangest times. By distracting myself with the mechanics of aiming and firing, I could almost ignore the pitiful, shambling figures blurring beyond my pistol's front sight.

With two left, I lowered the gun. No sense wasting ammo on so few. A quick glance around showed there were more walkers nearby, but none within striking distance. At least none that I could see. Ahead of me, beyond the whirling barrier of wind-driven ice, I wasn't so certain. I adjusted my grip on my sword, assumed a relaxed stance, and waited.

My falcata is an unusual weapon. The version I carry is a twenty-first century blacksmith's interpretation of a sword that dates back to the Celts of the early Iron Age. Iberian mercenaries used it to devastating effect back in the Second Punic War and the conquest of Hispania. Roman soldiers reported encountering howling warriors swinging leaf-shaped blades so sharp they could cleave a man's helmet and shield in a single blow. They legions familiar with it were so impressed they eventually adopted it into their own infantry, the ancient world equivalent of a sidearm.

Mine is much larger than the swords used by those fierce little guys, and heavier as well; just over three pounds out of the sheath. It has a sharp, forward-curved blade that narrows in the middle and widens out at the top—kind of like a Kukri—giving it the impact force of an axe while maintaining the cutting edge of a sword. The tip is sharp enough to stab with, but a falcata is designed primarily for cutting and chopping. At these tasks, it excels.

Against the infected, it is ideal.

The last two came into range at the same time. You have to be careful fighting them this close; the infected are slow, but can lunge quickly across very short distances. And if they get their hands on you, your chances of survival drop dramatically. Fortunately, there is a simple solution to this problem.

Cut their filthy arms off.

My first attack was two looping slashes in a figure-eight pattern that sent the arms of the closest walker thumping wetly to the ground. I backed off a step and repeated the procedure for the second one. Neither seemed to notice.

For the next part, I did much the same thing Cole had done back in the strip club. A quick downward slash at a forty-five degree angle to the crown of the head, wrench the sword free, watch the reddish-black brain matter spill out of the gaping hole, and then apply the boot. As the first one toppled backward ass-over-head, the last ghoul lunged for me, mouth gaping, a guttural hiss in its throat, stumps wobbling in comical impotence. I shoved it back with a firm hand to the chest and let the sword whistle through the air. Again the gore. Then the boot.

I flicked the blade to the side and passed it through the snow a couple of times to clean off the accumulated brain tissue. There was no sense in sheathing it, however. No telling when I would need it again.

I stepped over the fallen corpses and moved on.

*****

One mile, eighteen dead ghouls, and fifteen minutes later, I found what I was looking for.

There was a steep incline leading away from the road that seemed a little too symmetrical to be a natural formation. At a distance, its upper half was indistinguishable from the gauze of snowfall and gunmetal clouds overhead. On closer inspection, it turned out to be a berm built up the side of a highway overpass.

The snow covering its slope was nearly to my thighs, but I managed to struggle my way to the top.

The bridge was still intact under almost three feet of white stuff. Visibility was much better at that elevation, allowing me to see a few hundred meters in all directions. I expected to spot at least a few infected nearby, but there were none. The wind must have covered the sound of my passing enough so they couldn't track me. Looking away from the highway, a broad blanket of field stretched off toward a cluster of abandoned houses. On the eastern side of them, bordering the highway that ran across the bridge, the field sloped downward toward a flat, asymmetrical depression with a thinner layer of snow cover than the surrounding terrain. By the flatness and the shape, there was only one thing it could be. I smiled, drew the Mosquito, and fired a shot in the air.

Ten minutes passed with no sign of the horde. I raised the gun and fired again. More waiting. By my watch, another ten minutes went by. My hands were going numb, and I had to stomp my feet on the hard-packed ice to maintain feeling in my legs. I kept reminding myself to be patient and remember the cold slowed the ghouls to a crawl, and there was nothing to be gained by acting in haste. I paced the length of the bridge in the middle where the snow was thinnest, kicking my feet in front of me to clear a path. After two passes, I had worn a knee-high furrow through the saddle-shaped drift. After ten passes, I began to warm up a little and increased my pace to a slow jog. At fifty passes, I slowed down to avoid breaking a sweat—the absolute last thing you want to do in sub-freezing conditions.

And then I saw them.

They were packed tightly together, converged into a single mass snaking along the highway and the surrounding fields. Where there were patches of trees, they stumbled through them, bouncing from trunk to trunk. Milky white eyes peered hungrily through the wind, noses in the air, desperately trying to catch the faintest trace of prey. In the low pewter-colored light, their unblinking eyes seemed to shine with preternatural luminescence. I fired again and watched their heads swivel in my direction. The ghouls along the leading edge saw me first, sent up a keening wail, and began stumbling toward the bridge.

The screeching sounds of undead multiplied, amplified, and followed me down the hill. I stumbled through the freezing powder and wished like hell I had brought along a pair of snowshoes. Not a mistake I intended to repeat.

I took my time working my way toward the depression in the field. The ghouls couldn't see any better than I could, as visibility was still extremely poor. Every fifty yards or so I turned, shouted a few obscenities at my adoring audience, and then proceeded ahead, making sure not to gain too much of a lead.

Finally, I reached my destination and looked around, gauging the distances involved. The easiest course of action would be to circle around the periphery of the depression and wait at the other side, but the proximity of the ghouls was not going to allow that. They would catch up to me and divert their course, which would defeat the purpose of coming down here to begin with. The only way for my trap to succeed was to go straight across, and quickly.

I stepped forward and put a tentative foot onto the ice. It creaked a little, but held firm. Just to be on the safe side, I laid flat and shimmied across on my stomach, arms and legs wide to distribute my weight as much as possible. As I crawled, numbing cold filtered through my heavy winter clothes enough to make me shiver. Creaks, cracks and groans announced my passing, giving me nightmare visions of plunging through jagged ice into freezing water. I shook my head to clear it, controlled my breathing, and kept moving. When I reached the other side and stood up, a buzzing tension released from my shoulders and jaw muscles.

Now for the fun part.

I had timed my crossing perfectly. The ghouls arrived at the other side of the level expanse within moments. The first of them stepped heedlessly out onto the ice, oblivious to the danger beneath their feet. I edged back a few steps, hands on my weapons, ready to flee in an instant if my plan failed.

The undead drew closer, more and more of them stepping away from the frozen shore. Their moans increased in intensity. Grasping hands rose into the air, as if they could reach me from where they stood. The snap of teeth clacking on empty air built to a maddening crescendo.

"Come on, come on," I whispered. "Just a little further."

On they came, more and more of them, the ice popping and wheezing in protest. I backed a little further up the low rise toward the highway to get a better view. About twenty yards up, I spotted something jutting skyward like a raised bump on the smooth skin of snow cover. I ran over and brushed off the top layer to reveal a square green utility box. A sticker next to the handle warned me high-voltage equipment lurked within ready to electrocute any hapless soul stupid enough to pry it open. I brushed off more snow, cracked off the ice with the hilt of my sword, and climbed up.

At best estimate, there were over two hundred ghouls headed my way. They had all begun crossing the ice except for a dozen or so stragglers bringing up the rear. The icy seal over the frozen pond continued its creaking and groaning, but did not break. The lead ghouls were nearly three quarters of the way across and growing more agitated with every step. As they approached, eyes locked unwaveringly at the tall, meaty meal across from them, the ghouls on the outer edges began to swing inward, converging on their intended prey. The horde slowly assumed a teardrop shape, the point stabbing inexorably in my direction. They packed in tighter and tighter until they were shoulder to shoulder, bouncing and jostling against one another. The ice screamed louder and louder until, much to my relief, a huge section in the middle gave way with an agonizing CRACK. In an instant, nearly a hundred ghouls disappeared beneath the surface, swallowed by cold black water.

If I had been listening from a distance instead of watching, I would have thought I was hearing a gun battle. The cracking of ice increased in frequency until it became an ear-splitting, staccato cacophony. Ghouls vanished left and right, their expressions remaining unchanged even as they plunged beneath the merciless ice.

Finally, the cracking stopped. Only a few ghouls remained, most of them crowded around the opposite shore of the large pond, wasted faces registering primitive confusion. A moment ago, the ground in front of them had been solid. Now, they stood knee deep, thigh deep, and in some cases, chest deep in freezing water. I walked calmly around the shore until I was within twenty yards, raised my pistol, and went to work. I burned through the remaining rounds in my current magazine before switching to my falcata.

As I swung, making sure to keep my breathing steady and my balance firm, I regretted not bringing a hatchet with me. I could have destroyed the ghouls much faster and saved wear and tear on my sword. After the last corpse went down, its head flying one way and its torso the other, I cleaned the blade with a few handfuls of snow and examined the edge. There were a few small nicks in the finely-crafted steel. I ran my thumb over them with a grimace, and a promise to work the blade over a whetstone at my earliest opportunity. For now, it would have to wait.

After cleaning my sword and drying it carefully, I turned my attention northward. With any luck, the road back to the strip club would be clear of undead. Time to find out what was holding up the cavalry.

"Sierra Lead, Sierra One. How about a sitrep? Over."

"En route, Sierra One," Hicks replied. "Sorry it's taking so long, visibility is shit. I'm taking it easy, don't wanna run this pig off the road. I know we got wounded, but we won't be gettin' nobody home if I get stuck in a ditch. Over."

"Acknowledged. I'm activating GPS. Get a fix and tell me how long until you reach my position. Over."

I made my way back to the bridge, activated my radio's GPS, switched antennas, and waited. A glance at my watch told me it would be dark soon. I wondered how Fuller and Riordan were holding up.

"Sierra One, we have your twenty. Looks like we're about a half-mile south, heading straight for you. You must be close to the highway. Over."

"Standing on an overpass, actually. You should see me here in the next few minutes."

It was three minutes, in fact, before I heard the throaty rumble of the transport drawing near.

SEVEN

There wasn't enough room in the passenger compartment.

Three men from each squad rode on the transport's roof, feet dangling over the side, rifles in hand. I was less than ten feet over them when the big vehicle slowed to a halt beneath the overpass.

"Let me guess," I called down to them. "Too many prisoners for everyone to fit."

Holland looked up and waved a hand. "Come on, jump down. We ain't got all day."

I stepped over the rail, climbed down until I was dangling from the bridge by my fingertips, and dropped the last couple of feet to the roof.

"I'm on board," I said over the radio. "Let's get moving."

Taking a seat just behind the cab, I settled in and tried not to shiver too badly as the transport bounced, squeaked, and clanked its way to the strip club. A few infected dotted the road here and there. Hicks ran down the ones that got in the way and ignored the rest. Five minutes from the bridge, the booby-tasseled vixen on the strip club's sign came into view.

"This is it," I said, keying the mike. "Titty bar on your left. That's where they're holed up."

"Roger that. Looks like there's a few infected wanderin' around the entrance. Let the other guys on the roof up there know, will ya?"

"Ten four."

I called out the appropriate warning, drew my .22, and eased toward the ladder on the passenger side. As the transport's tires crunched to a halt, the two doors aft of the passenger carriage opened and spilled out eight gun-toting soldiers and militiamen. The six men on the roof and I climbed down while two others stayed behind to watch the prisoners. Hicks and Page stayed in the cab, as required by protocol. My protocol. I made it a point to always leave at least two men in reserve in the transport, foot on the gas pedal, in the event we had to beat a hasty retreat. It had saved our lives three times already.

Once on the ground, I shouted for Holland and Sanchez to form up on either side of me, then directed Thompson to grab three bodies, get inside, and get to work on Fuller and Riordan. Cole heard the commotion and opened the front door, SAW in hand.

"Over here," he shouted.

I had the other troops form teams to clear out the undead, melee weapons only. The last thing I needed was the crack of rifles drawing more walking corpses down on our heads.

Moans drifted hollow and warbled through the shifting wind. Rather than risk losing people in the near-whiteout because they couldn't see or hear each other, I had the men divide the small parking lot into sections, like cutting a pie. The club was at our backs, and each team was responsible for protecting their section. Zone defense, so to speak. Two troops with suppressor-equipped rifles took up position on our six to repel any undead approaching from the other side. I ordered them not to fire unless they had no choice—ammunition was growing scarce. Once in position, we set our feet, clutched our weapons, and waited.

There were less than a hundred walkers, but they still outnumbered us by a wide margin. With our weapons and training, it was manageable, but I'm not stupid enough to think any fight is too small to be my last. I shouted to the other teams to make sure everyone was within earshot. They were.

"Remember, fight as a unit. No cowboy heroics. If you get too many to handle, back off and use your rifles. Maintain muzzle discipline at all times. Anyone hits a friendly, I'll fucking kill you myself. If you need help, ask for it. Everybody clear?"

I got a round of acknowledgments. These men knew their business enough that my admonishment was redundant, but it made me feel better to say it. It also served the useful purpose of reminding them who was in charge. In the absence of strong leadership, discipline is the first thing to break down. When that happens, good men die. I wasn't having that. Not after the way I had let Fuller and Riordan down.

The infected slowly closed to within fighting distance. I ordered the men to stay calm and hold back, one open palm in the air. I waited until I could count their bloody black teeth, and then dropped my hand.

"Attack!"

With a roar, the soldiers went to work. I added my voice to theirs as my falcata carved a bloody path, sending smashed brain tissue and decapitated heads crashing to the ground. On my left, Sanchez viciously pounded away with what he called his war hammer. It consisted of a three-pound sledgehammer head, which he had ground down at the ends so it resembled a small metal football, and then attached a twenty-four inch hickory handle. He swung it in a diagonal, looping percussion, like hammering railroad spikes. Except the spikes were undead skulls, and he was driving them into their own necks.

On the other side, Holland was doing his usual frenetic kicking and cutting routine with a pair of tomahawks. His first victim caught a 'hawk to the forehead, went stiff as a board, and slowly began tipping over sideways. Holland helped it along with a spinning hook kick, pried his weapon loose, backed off a few steps, and waited for the next few infected to trip over the body. When they did, he severed their brain stems with precise, well-practiced chops from the spiked end of his tomahawks.

At some point during the fighting, when the infected had bunched up in front of us and I was about to give the order to fall back, I heard a thundering bellow and saw Cole ripping into the ghouls' left flank with his bar mace. I called out for the men on that side to fall back and reinforce the opposite flank so Cole would have room to swing. The other troops, though winded and muscle weary from fighting, redoubled their efforts, their confidence buoyed by the human engine of destruction bashing a swath through the infected.

Through the press of bodies, a massive walker shoved two smaller ones out of the way and reached for me, bellowing like an angry bull. The bastard was nearly seven feet tall, with a great swaying lump of belly and flopping loops of pale intestine dangling where the skin had been eaten away. One of its arms flopped uselessly at its side, but the other made it past my blade and clamped onto my shoulder, fingers gouging painfully into the thickness of my deltoid. The pressure was immense, the concentrated power of human muscle unconstrained by pain or buildup of lactic acid. No involuntary signal from the brain to release when capillaries burst, or fingernails ripped out, or when bone crushed the flesh attached to it. Even in life, his grip would have had the strength of a steel vice. In death, it threatened to rip my arm open despite the protection afforded by the tough fabric of my clothes.

I roared in pain and brought my sword up in an underhanded slash. The razor-sharp blade split flesh and bone as easily as paper. The pressure released immediately. The creature lunged forward at the waist, mouth open, teeth bared, rotten breath threatening to make me gag. I leaned back to avoid it and watched its teeth clack together less than three inches in front of my face. Dropping my weight, I hopped back a step, corrected my stance, and brought my falcata down in an angled overhand chop. The spring steel sank into the ghoul's cranium, cut downward across the eye socket and cheekbone, and exited clean through on the opposite side. An oblong section of skull, brain matter, and half of one eyeball slid free and fell to the ground. The ghoul swayed on its feet for a second, then hit its knees and fell forward on what was left of its face.

I kept swinging, moving from one target to the next, right shoulder sore from exertion, left shoulder burning from the big ghoul's grip until, as often happens in combat, I found myself standing with blade in hand, breath ragged, goggles spotted black with blood, eyes casting about for danger, heart pounding in my ears, desperately searching for the next threat through the swirling blizzard wind. But there was no enemy in front of me. I looked around at the other troops who stood clustered together in similar states of exhausted confusion, weapons clutched, but nothing to swing them at.

In hand-to-hand combat with the undead, one falls into a sort of myopia, concerned only with dispatching the nearest foe in sufficient time to bludgeon the next one. When mired in that red-tinged miasma, the sudden absence of creatures trying to kill you comes as a shock. Then there is the dawning clarity of victory, the shouting, the whooping, the brotherly slapping of hands upon tired backs.

My troops were not immune to this endorphin rush of relief, the chemically enhanced knowledge they had fought, won, and would live to fight another day. Sanchez and Holland stepped closer to me, and although their scarves concealed their mouths, I could see the grins in their eyes.

"Nice work, gentlemen." I said, and held out my sword as though reaching for a fist bump. Holland tapped it with one of his tomahawks, followed by a clank from Sanchez's hammer.

"*Pinche muertos* didn't know who they were fucking with," Sanchez said.

I smiled back at him, then raised my voice and turned to the other men. "All right fellas, playtime is over. Sanchez, Cole, rally your men and set up a perimeter. It's getting late; we need to get back to Hollow Rock before nightfall. You all know what to do. Let's get it done."

Cole and Sanchez acknowledged and started barking out orders. In a matter of minutes they would check their troops for injuries, have them clean and sanitize their weapons, and prepare to move out. While they worked, I went to check on Fuller and Riordan.

Inside the club, Thompson worked beside a propane lantern and had just put the finishing touches on a fresh bandage over Fuller's injuries. His hands moved with the swift, deft assurance of someone who knows what he is doing. Thompson had been an EMT before the Outbreak, and while he didn't have access to all the medical technology of his previous life, he had plenty of experience patching up wounded soldiers using whatever materials he had on hand. From the drooping of Fuller's eyes, I guessed Thompson had administered a vial of rare, precious morphine. Riordan was still clear-eyed, but obviously in pain.

"How are they doing?" I asked.

"Riordan's injuries aren't severe. Tissue damage mostly, ripped up the muscle pretty bad. He'll need stitches, antibiotics, and a couple months of rehab, but he'll be all right. Sorry, buddy, but you're sidelined until that leg heals up." Thompson patted Eric on the shoulder, who twisted his mouth ruefully.

"Yeah, I gathered that."

"Fuller, on the other hand, has at least two broken ribs. He'll also need stitches and antibiotics, and he'll probably be laid up in bed on pain meds for at least a few weeks. Doc Laroux might have a different opinion, but that's my prognosis."

I nodded, suspicions confirmed. "Think it's safe to move them?"

"Considering today's shenanigans, I don't think it's safe *not* to move them."

"Agreed. I'll go get you a stretcher, an IV, and some fluids. As for you, Eric, on your foot."

"Har, har. Help me up you overgrown bastard."

I grabbed his hand and hauled him up from the floor. He hopped on one leg, me supporting his good side, all the way to the transport. I helped him into the passenger seat in the cab, gave him a couple of bootlegged oxycontin I kept in my pack for emergencies, and told him to stay put.

"Shouldn't be a problem," he said, downing the pills.

Moving Fuller was a more delicate operation. Thompson and Cole secured him to a backboard, and the three of us, along with Sanchez, laid him down on the floor of the passenger car. Due to limited space, the number of soldiers riding on the roof went from six to ten. I pulled rank and informed them I would be driving, and to fight out the seating arrangements amongst themselves, but do it quickly. Fuller's condition wasn't getting any better.

With all the soldiers loaded in, I drove north along Reedy Creek Road until I reached the location where Hicks had left the trailer. After re-hitching it, I threaded a path through a few back roads to Highway 22 and turned south. From there it was a straight shot to the 77/364 bypass around Huntingdon—a town we had cleaned out a few weeks ago—and then Old State Highway 1 all the way to Hollow Rock.

It was slow going. The storm was in full swing and visibility was down to just over twenty yards, forcing me to creep along at ten miles an hour. I had to stop several times to scout ahead and make sure the road was clear. Lucky for me, even raiders and hijackers stay inside when the weather turns bad. Finally, with an hour left before nightfall, the western wall of Hollow Rock came into view. I breathed a sigh of relief and turned onto a dirt trail—well traveled even in the dead of winter—that swung around to the north gate. On the way, I keyed the radio.

"Watch commander, this is G&R Transport and Salvage, requesting entry. How copy? Over."

Sarah Glover's rich contralto crackled from the speaker, stirring old feelings best left unspoken. "Copy, Gabe. That blue-eyed Texas boy on your crew called in a little while ago, said you had a couple of guys wounded. Can you confirm that? Over."

"Affirmative. Did Specialist Hicks inform you of their injuries? Over."

"Sure did. Doc Laroux is prepping the O.R. right now. What about you, Gabe? Are you okay?"

There was a gentleness in her tone that tugged at something deep in my chest. Old feelings, faded, but still carrying warmth, the buried embers of an abandoned fire. She was a married woman when I fell for her, and smart enough to see what was happening to me. Sarah had kept her distance until I was cured of my infatuation, and when my eyes cleared, the flames died down, and my brain started firing on all cylinders again, she had been kind enough to offer forgiveness and friendship I didn't deserve.

My track record with the fairer sex is spotty at best, consisting primarily of a litany of one night stands, brief romances of three months' duration or shorter, and one marriage that lasted all of a year before my ex-wife decided enough was enough. The years since had been lonely ones, and in that isolation, I had grown unaccustomed to having women in my life, even as friends.

All that changed after arriving in Hollow Rock, especially as pertained to a certain tall, curvy, doe-eyed, smooth-skinned, lithe-muscled, passionate, intelligent, strong-willed brunette by the name of Elizabeth Stone. She of the soft lips, the sparkling laughter, and the urgent passions, who just happened to be the mayor of the fine township beyond the gates at which I awaited entry.

Then there was Allison, Eric's woman and the town's only doctor, who had decided I was worthy of allowing into her life, her home, and her confidence. Three good women, all anxious to curb my destructive appetites and nudge me along on the straight and narrow. It was a welcome change, if bittersweet.

"I'll be all right once my men are looked after," I replied. "You got somebody opening the gate? Over."

"Nolan and Harper are working on it right now. Stand by."

I stopped the transport in front of two massive concrete-and-steel doors and let the engine idle in neutral. Flurries of snow beat feebly at the windshield while the wipers fought to keep the streaks at bay. The exhaust stack sent up a thick plume of smoke that seemed vulgar next to the white landscape. Eric shifted in the seat beside me, head nodding lazily as he strained to stay awake. The painkillers had done a number on him.

"Wha's taking s'long?" he slurred.

"Waiting for the guards to unbar the gate. Be just another minute."

"'Kay." This time, when he nodded, his head did not come back up. He slumped over against the door, arms limp, head tilted at an uncomfortable angle. A quick check of his pulse found it slow, but strong. I pushed him back against the seat, shifted his head so it rested against the window, and let him be.

There was a clang from the other side of the gate, a low grinding of pulleys turning, and then the doors swung slowly inward. I waited until they had parted wide enough to permit entry, and then put the transport in gear and rumbled through. As soon as the back edge of the trailer had an inch's clearance, the guards began wheeling a pair of hand cranks in the opposite direction, pulling the heavy gate shut as quickly as they could. They had learned long ago not to take chances when it came to ghouls or marauders piggybacking through.

I couldn't see them through the snowfall, but I knew there were two sentries on duty in opposing towers, both armed with high-powered rifles and LAW rockets, ready to rain down fire if things went pear-shaped. I had no intention of provoking them.

One of the ground-level sentries was Quentin Reid, the newest addition to the Hollow Rock Sheriff's Department. He was an earnest and dedicated young man, but a bit green in the horns. He stepped up the ladder and shined his flashlight around the interior of the cab.

"Sheriff radioed down and said you got prisoners," he said.

"Yep. Six of them, trussed up in the back under armed guard. You want to take custody?"

"Not right now. Ain't enough deputies on hand to watch 'em. Think some of your boys might help us out?"

"My men have been through the ringer, deputy. They're exhausted."

"It'd be just for a little while, maybe an hour or two until I can get some more bodies down here. I'll talk to Lieutenant Cohen and see if he can spare a few people from the Ninth to keep watch overnight."

"I'll ask for volunteers, Quentin, but if they say no, I can't make them. Their job is done as far as I'm concerned. Now can you speed this up? I have wounded."

"Right. Just make sure you and your boys stop back by when you're done. We still have to search y'all for bites. Rules are rules."

"You have my word."

He stepped down, did a quick inspection of the men in the back, and then waved us on.

First stop, the clinic. Allison and a rough-looking squad of nurses took Fuller and Riordan off my hands, the latter carried bodily by Thompson and Cole. I remained ensconced in the cab, wrapped in the warm comfort of my own cowardice, but still caught a hostile flash of amber-colored eyes as Allison glanced my way.

I was going to get an earful from her in the not too distant future, and so was Eric. At least the Blond Wonder would be unconscious or stoned silly for the worst of it. I had no such reprieve.

With the others back on board, I drove a couple of blocks down to the sheriff's office. Sarah was waiting in the parking lot when I pulled in, bundled up in a thick sheepskin coat, knit cap pulled down to her ears, rosy cheeked, arms crossed over her stomach, shivering in the cold. I stepped down from the cab and walked into a tight hug. Her arms were thin and strong, not quite making it all the way around my torso.

"It's good to see you back safe, Gabe."

"Fuller and Riordan weren't so lucky."

She pulled back from me and looked up, concern written in her pale blue eyes. "How bad are they hurt?"

"Thompson thinks they'll be okay, but they'll be laid up for a while. Going to need lots of pain meds and antibiotics."

Sarah grimaced. "Doc says we're running low on that stuff."

"We're always low on medical supplies. Worst case, I'll put in a call to General Jacobs."

"He'll want a favor if you do. He always does."

"If it saves lives, it's worth it."

She stepped close to me again and placed a gentle hand on my arm. "Just make sure you don't get roped into something you can't get out of, Gabe. You know nothing would please Jacobs more than to slip a leash around your neck."

"Believe me, I'm familiar with his stripe."

The back of the transport opened and the soldiers began helping the six prisoners to the ground. They had cut the zip ties constraining their legs but left their hands bound behind their backs. Two soldiers escorted each of them, rifles jammed into their kidneys, narrowed eyes begging for an excuse to pull the trigger. The men of First Platoon had all seen combat against marauders and insurgents, and had no patience for their kind.

Sarah turned her head to look at them, the fine threads of muscle in her neck taut against her skin. A single lock of bright auburn hair dangled from her knit cap, just begging to be tucked behind the charming curve of earlobe. It was an effort of will to keep my hands in my pockets.

"I better get these guys booked," she said. "What's the charge?"

"Hell, pick one. Sedition, armed robbery, attempted theft of government property, conspiracy, you name it. We caught 'em leading a horde this way. Damn near a thousand strong. There a law against that yet?"

"There is actually. President signed it a month ago."

"No shit?"

"No shit. It's called necro-crime. Covers a whole laundry list of charges. Sabotage, terrorism, destruction of property. Or in this case, conspiracy to commit murder. All capital felonies in Union territory, punishable by summary execution. Uncle Sam has no further interest in fucking around."

"Jesus, I didn't know that. Looks like these boys are in deep shit."

"We all are, Gabe. And it gets deeper every day. Can you come by in the morning and fill out a statement?"

"Of course."

"If the government doesn't want them, they'll be tried here in Hollow Rock. You'll be called upon to testify."

"That's not a problem."

She walked toward the entrance and held the door open while the soldiers and prisoners filed in. When they were through, she cast a final wave in my direction and followed, letting the door swing shut on its own.

I waited in the transport, engine idling, hands in front of the heater vent. Outside, the snow fell steadily, blown sideways by the wind. I watched it pour down and felt an old familiar anger begin to well up, directed at the person responsible for the mayhem that seemed to follow my every step.

If he would just settle down and stop trying to solve everyone else's problems, he might actually have a chance to build a life. But every time he turns a new page, he finds a new and improved way to splash blood all over it.

"What the fuck were you thinking, Gabe?"

Silence.

"What kind of Rambo bullshit was that? You damn near got two people killed, one of them your best friend."

More silence.

"It's not your job to fight the government's battles anymore. Last I checked, you had an honorable discharge. Did you re-enlist when nobody was looking?"

The cab stayed willfully quiet but an answer came anyway, unbidden. Words spoken in anger years ago, the last thing my ex-wife ever said to me just before she slammed the door in my face.

You are what you are, Gabriel. And you always will be.

EIGHT

The blizzard was gone by morning.

A two-and-a-half foot thick blanket of snow covered Hollow Rock, piled nearly head-high along roads and sidewalks where a small army of volunteers, guards, militiamen, and soldiers had shoveled it aside. The sky was mostly clear except for broad bands of cirrostratus clouds clinging to the eastern horizon. A red, gold, and orange sunrise burned through the low stretches, while the streaks at higher altitude stood out stark and crisp against a cobalt sky. I paused on the porch to stare at them for a minute or two, struck by the simple, crystalline beauty of a cold winter morning. My good mood lasted as long as it took me to walk through the door of town hall.

Elizabeth stood in front of the floor-to-ceiling windows in her office, arms crossed under the swell of her breasts, back turned to me, morning sun suffusing the edges of her frame. I called it the Worried Pose, one of her many mannerisms I had picked up on in the last few months. A few errant strands of hair not constrained by her ponytail stood out bright copper in the golden light.

"This is bad, Gabe," she said. "The Alliance has never openly attacked Union territory. The Free Legion were puppets, a proxy act. This is direct action."

"It was an attempt at direct action. And it wasn't exactly an open gambit."

She turned to me, her usual subtle smile absent, lines creasing the sides of her mouth, eyes puffy from too little sleep. "How do you figure?"

"Plausible deniability."

"Speak plainly, Gabe. I'm too tired for riddles."

I let out a breath and pinched the bridge of my nose between my fingers. "The Alliance is going to disavow everything. Even if we can get a confession from all the prisoners, which we won't, the Alliance will say it's a lie. A ruse by the Union government to start a war. Without solid evidence, the President will face tremendous pushback if she tries to launch an attack. Not the kind of thing you want less than forty-eight hours into your presidency."

Liz uncrossed her arms, hands going to her hips, lips pressed in pensive line. "I hadn't thought of it that way. So maybe it's not as bad as we think?"

"Oh, it is. Every bit as bad, and worse, probably. The Alliance sent a team of experienced ghoul wranglers against us knowing full well that if they failed, they could simply deny involvement with little chance of repercussion."

Liz shifted from one foot to the other, one hand idly scratching her graceful neck. "You really think Central Command would let them get away with it? After what happened with the Legion?"

"What choice would they have? Whoever is running the Alliance's PR campaign is doing a masterful job. They have more than half the loyalists and almost all of the independent city-states believing they want to create a separate, peaceful nation and establish commerce with the Union. With all the other problems people are facing, it's an attractive sales pitch. After all, who wants a civil war? People have enough to deal with right now. Just let the Alliance create their own stupid country. What's the harm?"

"That's bullshit. The Alliance hates the Union. For Christ's sake, where do people think all the marauders out there are getting their weapons?"

"The truth has nothing to do with it, Liz. It's what people want to believe, so they believe it. And the Alliance does nothing to discourage them."

"So that begs the question, what will it take to convince them?"

I shrugged. "Most Americans never took Al Qaeda seriously until the nine-eleven attacks."

She frowned and put her hands on her hips. "Do you think it will come that?"

"I sincerely hope not."

Elizabeth nodded slowly, moving to sit down next to me. "And if the Alliance had succeeded with the horde, their people would have just left it at our doorstep and high-tailed it back to their own territory with no one the wiser."

"Exactly. A smart play. But I don't think they were going to settle for simply leaving the horde at the gate. It would have created an inconvenience, but not a devastating one."

"I don't know, Gabe. It would have been a hell of a problem."

"Yes, but nothing we couldn't handle. I think they planned to take it further."

"What makes you say that?"

I pretended to study my fingernails. "Intuition. Deductive reasoning. Experience. And the small matter of several Semtex charges found among their equipment."

She sat up straight, eyes wide, face going pale. "What?"

"Walt hasn't given you his report yet?"

"No, he's still busy questioning the prisoners."

I let out a breath and slid down further in my seat. "They were going to try to blow a section of the wall, I think. Probably on the south side, where it's all made of telephone poles."

"Oh my God."

I laid my hand on her thigh and squeezed gently. "Hey, we stopped them. We know they're after us now. We can take precautions, beef up security on the wall, double up the patrols, give First Platoon something to do other than dig latrines and shovel snow. We've been here before, Liz."

"I know that, Gabe. But what if you hadn't stopped them? How many people would have been killed?"

"Don't waste your time on what-ifs, sweetheart. You'll drive yourself crazy."

She smiled then, unexpectedly, and it was like the sun breaking through the clouds. Some of the deeply etched lines smoothed from her face, making her look ten years younger. Her eyes grew warm, the color of dark chocolate.

"I like it when you call me that," she said.

"What?"

"Sweetheart. It sounds a little odd coming from you, so surly and gruff. It's enough to make a girl think you're not as unassailable as you look."

I smiled back, pulled her close, and kissed her gently. "Then I'll have to do it more often."

I kissed her again, meaning for it to be just a quick thing, but Liz's fingers slipped around the back of my neck and held me, lips growing soft and urgent. Her tongue touched mine, sending a jolt of electricity go all the way to my heels. She kept me there long enough that I began to seriously consider brushing the papers off her desk. But then, to my disappointment, she pulled away, one hand lingering on my face, thumb tracing a scar under my right eye. Her smile faded, replaced by the look of concern that had rarely left her in the last few months.

"We were supposed to have some peace and quiet with the Legion gone," she said. "Things were supposed to settle down."

"Nature abhors a vacuum, Liz. The Legion controlled a big chunk of territory smack in the middle of three major trade routes. Now that they're gone, all the little fish want a piece of the action."

She let out a weary sigh and sank deeper into her chair, hand rubbing at her eyes. "And now this thing with the Alliance. When does it end, Gabe?"

I didn't have an answer to that, so I held her hand and stayed quiet.

*****

Sheriff Walter Elliott took my statement over breakfast at the VFW hall, then asked me to walk with him to his office. Never being one to pass up a chance to gather intel, I agreed.

At the station, he sat down behind his desk and removed his hat. It was new; his old one had suffered a tragic death in the mud outside Stall's Tavern while he and I were breaking up a bar fight. I happened to have a few Stetsons in storage at the time and traded him one—to which he affixed a brown band with a miniature sheriff's star—in exchange for his last twenty rounds of .45 ACP.

He put the hat on his desk the proper way, brim up, the crown perched atop a stack of papers. I sat across from him in an uncomfortable metal chair, a far cry from the lushly upholstered leather in Elizabeth's office. The steady noise of a multi-fuel generator, one of several donated by the Phoenix Initiative, sent a gentle hum through the walls of the police station.

"They're denying everything, of course," he said.

"What about Folsom? He's the one who told me how to find the others."

Elliott shook his head. "Says he had nothing to do with that horde. Says the only reason he talked is because you threatened to torture him."

"Lying bastard."

"Did you?"

"Did I what?"

"Threaten to torture him."

My eyes narrowed, jaw growing tight. "I didn't exactly have time for a detailed interrogation, Walt. Not with over a thousand infected breathing down my neck."

"I can't say I approve of your methods, Mr. Garrett."

I counted to ten before answering, willing the heat creeping up my neck to slow down. Then I spoke slowly, measuring each word.

"I don't remember asking for your approval, Sheriff. And before you go passing judgment, you remember one of those sons of bitches tried to kill me, and you think about those Semtex charges they were carrying."

Elliott stared for another moment, then leaned forward and rested his elbows on his desk. I heard a rasp of stubble as he passed a hand across his face.

"Would you have done it?" he asked.

"If I thought it would save lives, or if I thought I could gain information to make this town safer, yes, I would have. But only if I was sure."

Elliott nodded, not making eye contact. "I radioed a report to Central Command and e-mailed copies of their statements, photographs, fingerprints, all of it. Not sure how much good it's going to do. Depends on how much of the old federal databases are still intact."

"Shouldn't be a problem. Ishimura says those databases are in the Archive."

"Mr. Ishimura says lots of things."

"He's delivered so far, hasn't he?"

Elliott's chair squeaked as he leaned back, arms crossed over his chest. "Yeah, but I don't trust him. Nine out of ten questions I ask him, he can't answer. Just says 'sorry Sheriff, that's classified', then expects me to find any damn thing he asks for. It's startin' to get on my nerves."

"He's trying to restore the power grid, Walt. That's not an easy thing to do. And lots of people in this town wouldn't have heat in their homes right now if not for him."

The sheriff's sour expression softened a bit. "I know that. But all the secrecy makes me nervous. This is a small town, Gabriel. Everybody knows everything about everybody. I'm not used to having strangers around."

"Wasn't that long ago I was a stranger."

A faint smile creased the deep lines around his eyes. "True. But you're one of the folks, now."

He reached across his desk, took my report, stapled it, and put it in a folder. Wrote something along the tab I didn't catch. As he was putting the stapler back in the desk, he hesitated.

"I don't suppose you found any office supplies yesterday, did you? We're running low around here."

"Actually, I did, and I'm willing to let some of it go. For the right price, of course."

"Of course." Elliott frowned. "All I can trade you is food from the municipal supply. If I had anything else, I sure as hell wouldn't be coming to you for staples."

"How about information?"

"Excuse me?"

"I ask questions, you answer them, and I decide what the answers are worth."

"Sounds like a bad deal."

I offered my most affable smile and held out my hands. "Maybe I'm feeling generous, Walt."

"Contributing to the public good, is it?"

"Something like that."

Watery blue eyes glared at me, did the math, and decided it was worth it. "Strictly off the record, you understand," he said. "Anybody asks, I'll call you damn liar."

"My lips are sealed."

He made a whirling gesture with one hand. "All right then, go on. Ask away."

"What's the next step in your investigation?"

"Right now, nothing. The prisoners aren't marauders, they're insurgents. They admitted their affiliation with the Midwest Alliance on the record, which puts the whole mess under federal jurisdiction. The only thing I can do is keep them on ice and wait for instructions."

"What do you think the feds will do with them?"

He shrugged. "One of three things, probably. They'll fly 'em off to Kansas and we'll never see 'em again, or they'll pass the buck and make me hold a trial on whatever charges they dream up, or they'll give 'em back."

"Give them back?"

"Send them back to the Alliance."

I went still. That possibility had not occurred to me. "Why in the hell would they do that?"

"They probably won't. We have a case here, especially with your testimony. But it happened a few times with the previous administration."

"How?"

Elliott scratched at the back of his neck. "Let's say you're a citizen of the Alliance. You get caught on Union soil doing things Union citizens don't appreciate, so they truss you up and haul you to the local constabulary. Let's say the constabulary, like us, is under treaty. They conduct an investigation and present their evidence to federal authorities. Now let's say no real harm was done, and the case for the prosecution isn't that strong. The administration doesn't want to touch off a civil war, so, in an act of good faith, they return said offenders with a stern warning that although the patience of the federal government is considerable, it is not without its limits. The Alliance apologizes for the incident, proclaims their innocence, condemns the act, and offers assurances the offending party will be dealt with harshly upon his or her release into Alliance custody."

My initial reaction was anger, but then I scratched at the stubble on my chin and thought it over a while. "That's actually smart maneuvering on the administration's part," I said.

Elliott looked owlish. "How do you figure?"

"The last thing the federal government needs right now is a war on two fronts. If things escalate with the Alliance, you can bet the beer money the Republic of California will throw their hat in the mix. Even if we beat them, which isn't a sure thing, it would be crippling to all parties involved. Let's face it, if ROC forces and the Alliance thought they could take us, we would have been trading leather months ago."

"I thought we already were."

"Not yet, we aren't. Not in earnest, anyway."

"Really? 'Cause I seem to remember a bit of trouble with some yokels calling themselves the Free Legion."

"That was kid's stuff. You remember the Iraq War, right?"

Elliott blinked a few times. "Of course. What does that have to do with anything?"

"The insurgency. Some of the troops were locals, but most were recruited from elsewhere. Syrians, Jordanians, Palestinians, Saudis. Hell, we even ran into a few Serbians. Most of them were young Muslim men, not soldiers or anything, just regular guys. Worked day jobs during the week, fought the jihad on the weekend, then went back to work on Monday. The problem they ran into, initially, was scrounging up enough weapons to fight us with. At least until the Iranians got involved. That was when things went from bad to worse. They supplied the insurgents with military hardware, and in exchange, the Ayatollahs got the satisfaction of believing they were contributing to the downfall of the Great Satan. This situation with the Alliance isn't all that different. They source their gear from the ROC, who probably brought it over from North Korea or China or wherever the hell they came from, and then the Alliance trades those weapons with anyone looking to make trouble for the Union. Take the Free Legion, for instance. Strong leadership, halfway-organized military structure, a clear objective that lines up with the Alliance's agenda. And if it all goes tits up, it's an easy out for the Alliance. What evidence do we have of their involvement? How can we prove they were supporting the Legion?"

Elliott ruminated, fingers drumming on his desktop. "None, and we can't. Not enough to please the populace, anyway. The Legion's leadership died in the fighting, and they were the only ones who knew where the weapons came from. Who the suppliers were. That explains why the previous President didn't raise more of a fuss over what happened last year."

"Exactly. I'll bet you there's a whole network of arms dealers out there, and we haven't the faintest clue where to look for them."

"But Gabe, I still don't see how giving the enemy their troops back is a smart move on the Union's part. Especially if they were actively working against us."

"That's just it, Walt. Think about it. If we execute every asshole we catch trying to play saboteur, pretty soon we're going to have a lot of blood on our hands. That's going to incite the Alliance citizenry and give their government, such as it is, all the excuse they need to retaliate. By only prosecuting the slam-dunk cases, the administration saves face among loyalists. Meanwhile, the Alliance has to eat a big slice of humble pie and apologize to the Union in order to quell the fears of their own people."

Elliott held up a finger. "I think I found a hole in your logic there."

"What's that?"

"The glue holding the Alliance together is their mutual hatred of the Union. The Alliance government doesn't have to play ball with us. Their people *want* a war."

"That's where your wrong, Walt."

"How so?"

"Have you ever heard the term groupthink?"

More blinking. "Can't say as I have. Is that a real word?"

"It is. It's a psychological phenomenon common in governments, business organizations, and political parties; a culture of conformity that discourages independent thinking and disagreement. Anyone who challenges the consensus of the greater body, regardless of how valid that challenge might be, is considered disloyal. This produces deviant outcomes. People thinking they are always right, everyone else is wrong, and their logic is unassailable, no matter how divorced from reality it might be."

One of the sheriff's bushy eyebrows came up half an inch. "Okay. I'll pretend I followed all that."

"In other words, it's a bunch of people sitting around telling each other what they want to hear, and shouting down anyone who says different."

"That makes a lot more sense. Hell, I've been in the room when that happened. But what does it have to do with anything we've been talking about?"

"I think there is a huge disconnect between the Alliance's government and its people. The ruling body wants a fight. They see the Union as an existential threat, and they want us out of the way. I think the people want peace and independence, and I think that is what stayed the previous President's hand where another might have launched air strikes. Your average Alliance citizen has no love for the federal government, but they're in no hurry to take on what's left of the military. Even diminished as they are, our armed forces are still the most powerful on the planet. If it comes to a brawl, the Alliance loses no matter what. Why do you think they issue a public apology every time one of their people gets caught?"

Understanding dawned in the sheriff's eyes. "I see where you're going with this. Even if they win, the Alliance will lose too many people and burn up too many resources to recover. And that's their best case scenario. Worst case, we beat them, wipe their fortifications off the map, and the survivors have nothing left to go home to. They'll be fodder for every bandit and slaver in the wastelands. Their people know that, and they're putting pressure on their leaders to avoid war with the Union at all costs."

"Exactly. And while it's unlikely, there's also the nuclear threat. The last President stated publicly it wasn't off the table.

The people of the Alliance don't want any part of that, and wisely so."

"So what was the point, then? Why go after Hollow Rock? What did the Alliance think they were going to gain?"

"Gain? Nothing. The Legion was cannon fodder. It wasn't about what the Alliance stood to gain, it was about what the Union stood to lose. We lost troops, we lost Special Forces operators, we lost ammo, and explosives, and an AC-130 gunship. They're not making any more of those things, you know. With every bullet we fire, every soldier we lose, every aircraft that crashes, our capabilities are diminished. It's not a quick, fiery death the Alliance has planned for us. It's the death of a thousand cuts."

The sheriff went quiet for a while, leaning back in his chair, one hand over his mouth, gaze vacant and brooding. I listened to the generator buzzing through the wall and thought of how strange it was to hear manmade noise after nearly three years of silence.

"How long do you think this is going to drag on?" he asked, finally.

"Probably until the Alliance government decides it's not worth it anymore. Maybe the ROC will launch an offensive and force everyone's hand. I don't know. All we can do is keep our ears to the ground and wait."

"That's the part I hate. The waiting." He leaned forward and made a show of opening his stapler and turning it so I could see the finger's width of tiny metal brackets within.

"So what's this conversation worth to you, Gabe?"

NINE

It was never my intention to go into the salvage business.

I blame Eric.

One night, not long after the destruction of the Free Legion, when First Platoon had settled in, and the other troops sent to aid us had departed, my oldest and best friend showed up at my doorstep with a broad smile and a bottle of Buffalo Trace. I was surprised to see him; he had left town two days prior to scavenge for supplies and wasn't expected back for at least two more.

I pointed at the hooch. "Where, might I ask, did you find that?"

He held the bottle up and turned it, letting the candlelight catch fire through the amber liquid. "Long story," he said. "How about a drink?"

I waved him in and took a seat in the kitchen while he poured us both a tall one. The whiskey was just as smooth and crisp as I remembered, and I felt a sudden mournful longing for my home state of Kentucky. Many years had passed since I gazed across the rolling green pastures or walked among the limestone hills, and I missed it terribly. Strange, considering how during my teenage years I yearned so badly to get the hell out of there. Didn't know how good I had it, I guess.

Eric spun a chair around and sat across from me, arms draped over the back, cocky grin creasing his month-old beard. "Gabe, my man, you and I are about to be very, very rich."

Leave it to the Blonde Wonder to start on a dramatic note.

"All right," I said. "I'm listening."

"You remember how the Legion had all those supply depots scattered around their territory, right?"

"You mean the ones the Army just spent the last six weeks cleaning out?"

"The same."

"What about them?"

He leaned closer and lowered his voice. "They missed a few."

My hand stopped halfway to my face. There was no sound in the room for several long seconds.

I said, "Is that a fact?"

"It is."

"How many?"

"Four that I know of. Maybe more."

From one of his cargo pockets, he produced a hand-drawn map and smoothed it out on the table. "I got this from Grayson Morrow before I infiltrated the Legion. It shows the location of eight supply depots, four of which I know for sure the Army didn't find. I'm guessing Lucian didn't know about them, forgot they existed, or neglected to mention them during his interrogation. Considering what Steve was doing to him at the time, the oversight is understandable."

I remembered the departed, yellow-eyed Green Beret, and the coldness I had seen him demonstrate on occasion. I remembered the things Eric had told me about him, such as his penchant for severing the Achilles tendons of captured enemy combatants. I thought about finding myself on the wrong end of one of his interrogations, and shuddered.

"And this map can tell us where they are?"

"It can."

I took another sip of bourbon. "How much are we talking about?"

"Can't say for sure, I've only seen one of them. But let me tell you, Gabe, it was a fucking gold mine. Crates of AKs with 20 rifles each, whole shelves of ammunition, boxes of home-canned vegetables, dried meat, medical supplies, toilet paper, sugar, coffee, even a few crossbows. Shit like that is worth a fortune."

When I put my whiskey on the table, my hand did not shake, but it was a near thing. I said, "That's a lot of weight to haul around, Eric. How do you propose we bring it here?"

"Funny you should ask. Before I came over, I stopped by the VFW hall and had a word with my friend Ethan Thompson. I asked him what it would cost for a private audience with his commanding officer, and he got me in for the paltry sum of a fifth of Captain Morgan."

"I heard the lieutenant was a cheap date. What did you talk about?"

"You know Central Command is sending us one of those Facilitator guys, right?"

I nodded. "General Jacobs mentioned something to that effect."

"Well, as it turns out, they're sending a shitload of equipment along with him. It's en route by train, scheduled to arrive the day after tomorrow. According to Lieutenant Jonas, the shipment will include a pair of multi-fuel troop transports. He says they're supposed to be like ATVs, only bigger, and can cross just about any type of terrain."

"Interesting. What else did he say?"

"First Platoon will be responsible for most of the equipment, but they're only taking one of the transports. The other will belong to Hollow Rock, care of Mayor Elizabeth Stone."

I felt my face stretch into a grin. "Municipal use only?"

"That would be my guess."

I turned my glass on the table a few times and tried not to look too smug. "I'm a fair hand at most things mechanical. Somebody's going to need to put that thing through its paces when it gets here. I'll wager I can talk Liz into letting me take it for a spin."

Eric finished his drink and reached for the bottle. "I bet you can."

Nine days later, we were two of the wealthiest men in Tennessee.

*****

The business occupies two buildings.

One is a rather sizable freestanding auto-repair facility, long since disused, which I bought for next to nothing. After clearing out anything not worth trading, Eric and I hired our good friend Tom Glover to help us mount bars over the windows, wall up the bay doors, and install a circle of iron pilings to keep out anyone with access to a vehicle. A short time later, we improved it further by adding battlements to the roof that could stop a heavy machine gun, and set up an overlapping perimeter of concrete highway dividers in the parking lot. The warehouse is where I store the majority of my inventory, less a few hidden caches scattered throughout the surrounding area, of course.

Contrary to popular belief, I am not paranoid.

I am aware.

There is a difference.

The other building is the Hollow Rock General Store, also purchased on the cheap from its world-weary octogenarian proprietor. It is the public-facing part of my operation, and is managed quite competently by Miranda Grove, a former slave of the Free Legion.

Long story short, Eric freed Miranda from horrifying sexual abuse at the hands of the Legion, and she is now fiercely loyal to him. Additionally, she has a good head for business, is as pretty as she is personable, and keeps the con men, thieves, and hucksters at bay. All in all, a great person to have running your business for you.

I was on my way to said business, having just left the police station and dreading the contentious task of divvying up yesterday's salvage, when I heard the unmistakable sounds of a struggle echoing near Benny's Barbershop.

Moving quickly, I eased along the wall to where it turned into an alley, stopped, peeked out briefly, and stepped back. The alley was empty, so I turned the corner and advanced silently, rolling my weight on the sides of my boots until I reached the back of the building. Out of instinct, my hand crept toward the butt of my pistol.

The rear of the barbershop stood parallel to the back of another set of buildings one street over, most of them standing empty. In the snow-covered space between, two young boys were engaged in a vigorous fistfight. I recognized both of them.

The bigger one was tall, sandy haired, pimple faced, and strong in a wiry, adolescent sort of way. He was fourteen years old, his name was Uriah Cranston, and, despite his size, he looked to be getting the worst of the exchange.

Uriah, much like his father, Roy Cranston, was a vicious, loudmouthed bully who took great pleasure in causing misery among his peers. He had never been caught doing anything serious enough to garner the attention of Sheriff Elliott, but he wasn't entirely off the radar either. Everyone knew his reputation, and made sure their kids steered clear of him. But in a town surrounded by a twelve-foot wall with only one school, there was only so far the other kids could go. Uriah knew this, and used it to his advantage.

The thing about bullies like Uriah Cranston is they operate in a mental vacuum. They do not understand the concept of relativity. They inflate their egos by preying on those they perceive as being weak, and thus delude themselves into thinking they are strong people. This belief persists until they run up against the real thing, and when that happens, all their narcissistic, ego-supported walls come crashing down, leaving them struggling with the cold reality that they are not nearly as indomitable as they thought they were. Judging by Uriah's opposition, I had a feeling I was about to witness the end of his ill-perceived invincibility.

As I watched, he threw a wide haymaker that sailed over the smaller boy's head and cost him a one-two combo to the floating ribs. The punches staggered him back a step, arms clutching his sides, breath whistling through a bloody nose. He

114

gritted his teeth and moved in again, trying to rush the smaller boy with a flurry. Two punches deflected from elbows and forearms before the smaller kid deliberately ducked his head, allowing a straight left to land on the crown of his skull. The bone on that part of the human head is dense and strong, and Cranston howled as his knuckles ran afoul of the laws of physics. I winced in sympathy, hoping he hadn't just broken his hand.

"Had enough yet, Cranston?" the smaller boy asked calmly.

"Fuck you, you little shit!"

A chuckle. Shake of the head. "You're insulting yourself, idiot. Maybe you didn't notice, but this *little shit* just kicked your ass. But hey, if you want to keep on being stupid, go right ahead. I got all day."

Cranston answered by throwing a handful of snow at the other boy's eyes and following it up with another kick aimed at his groin. The smaller boy avoided both by simply turning and hopping back. The momentum of the kick caused Cranston to slip on the ice and topple over backward. The smaller boy's eyes hardened as he rewarded Uriah's efforts with a boot to the same ribs he had punched only seconds before. As Cranston curled up into an agonized little ball, the smaller boy threw another, less vicious kick at his temple. There was a dull thud, and Cranston's eyes went blank.

For nearly a minute, he lay in the snow, face slack, breath coming in involuntary spasms like a fish out of water. When he again had his wits about him, he groaned and tottered to his feet, wobbling on unsteady legs.

"This ain't over, faggot," he said, speech slurring.

"I hope not. Busting you up is the most fun I've had in months."

Cranston stumbled away, hunched over, crimson drops staining the snow in his wake. The smaller boy watched him go, stance loose, hands curled at his sides, breathing steady, just as he had been taught. Only when his enemy had rounded the corner did he permit himself to relax.

"That was nicely done," I said.

The boy jumped about a foot in the air and turned to face me, feet braced, hand reaching for the Buck Nighthawk in a sheath at the small of his back. I held up my hands and laughed.

"Easy now, son. Don't go all Ginsu on me."

Brian Glover lowered his hands and broke a relieved smile. "Sorry Gabe. Didn't realize it was you."

"That's all right. No harm done."

"Listen, don't tell my mom and dad about-"

"Don't worry, kid. I've been there. There's nothing wrong with standing up for yourself. Especially not to a little bastard like Uriah Cranston."

"Thanks. You know how my parents are."

"No worries." I hooked my thumbs in my belt and tilted my head toward the street. "Hey, I'm headed over to the store. Why don't you come with me? I found some shoes I think might fit you while I was out yesterday."

He smiled and trotted over, the too-old sternness of an Outbreak survivor fading slightly. I like kids, generally speaking, but it pains me to talk to them anymore. Young faces shouldn't look so harsh and…well, grown up. I turned and headed back down the street, Brian falling into step beside me.

"Hey Gabe?" he said.

"Yeah?"

"What does Ginsu mean?"

I sighed deeply, causing a blast of white vapor to paint the air in front of me. "Brian, I love you to death, kid. But sometimes you make me feel old."

*****

The crew was already standing around the front porch, huddled in their coats and shuffling impatiently.

Tied to a rail around the side of the store was a surly-looking draft horse, muzzle in the snow, snuffling around for scraps of grass while Hicks carefully brushed its thick fur. He had unhitched the massive animal from a nearby wagon, which the troops would use to haul the crew's payment back to their respective barracks.

Knowing how anxious they would be, and unable to resist an opportunity to mess with them, I whispered to Brian hang back. He gave me a conspiratorial wink and slowed his steps. I approached the store at a leisurely pace, whistling a little tune and gazing around at the brilliant dusting of sparkles reflecting from the snow. Seventeen anxious faces watched me, their body language growing agitated. There should have been nineteen of them, but Riordan and Fuller were not going to be up and moving any time soon. They deserved a visit and a plate of hot breakfast from Mijo Diego, but that would have to wait until I paid my crew.

"Nice of you to show up, chief," Holland said. "We were starting to think you forgot about us."

I shrugged indifferently and stopped to break a few icicles from the awning. "You know, it always strikes me as remarkable how you jackasses show up at the crack of dawn on payday, but when it's time to hit the road, I have to send runners to hunt you down. Why is that, do you suppose?"

"Hey, I'm always on time," Hicks said, glowering.

I turned to him. "You know what, you're right. You *are* always on time. In fact, you're the only one who is." I turned to Brian and gestured at the lanky Texan. "What do you think, compadre? Should I give him head-of-the-line privileges?"

Brian put a hand to his chin and made a show of giving Hicks a stern appraisal. "You know, my dad always tells me it's important to be punctual. Says it shows respect."

"Indeed it does. Step on up, Specialist. You earned it."

The soldiers raised a chorus of insults and curses, a few of them hurling snowballs. Hicks flashed a rare grin, crossed his hands in front of his hips, and made a crude pelvic-thrusting gesture.

"Suck it, bitches. That's what you get for bein' lazy."

I unlocked the front door and stepped inside, followed closely by Hicks. Brian stayed outside to join an impromptu snowball fight rapidly escalating between Delta Squad and Sanchez's militiamen. Being that the Army contingent was outnumbered, the boy elected to reinforce Cole's diminished fire team. I allowed myself a quiet smile, listening to the good sounds of laughter and camaraderie. It reminded me of some of my better days in the Marines, the ones not stained with memories of violence. Those were hard years to be sure, but even the darkest times have their bright moments.

Miranda was already there, like always, moving among the crowded shelves, muttering, and updating inventory logs. Her long blond hair was coiled in a severe bun and stabbed through with a couple of pencils, forming an X on the back of her head. Though bundled in shapeless, rough-spun clothes and completely without makeup, she was a stunner. She straightened when I came in and blasted me with a full-lipped, blue-eyed, dimple-cheeked smile. A ray of sunlight splashed across her face, turning her eyes into gleaming jewels and making my heart skip a beat. I kept walking, but behind me, I heard Hicks's footsteps scrape to a halt.

"Morning Gabe," she said brightly, bustling over and flipping through pages on her clipboard. "I'm just about finished adding up yesterday's haul."

"How's it looking?"

She paused long enough to stand on her tiptoes and give me a light peck on the check. I tried to ignore the tingling on that side of my neck as she held up her paperwork. "This is the log from the day before yesterday. We haven't moved any of the new stuff over yet, so the info for the warehouse hasn't changed. Sheriff Elliott signed out the transport this morning and sent Deputy Reid to pick up a shipment of firewood down near I-40. I reserved it for the rest of the day when he gets back."

"What about the stuff we're not selling? Did you hire some guys to help us move it yet?"

She tilted her head at the roughhousing numbskulls beyond the front door. "The boys already volunteered to do the heavy lifting."

"Well done. How did you talk them into it?"

"They're helpless against my feminine wiles."

"Figures. So what's the tax situation?"

She flipped to another page and pointed. "We have six of the eight items on the request sheet. Four of them are under quota, two barely meet it, and the other two are way over, so I'll get them on the shelves ASAP. The clothes are going to move quickly, but I don't think we should sell them all. Reverend Griffin stopped by yesterday and told me a lot of families are struggling right now. The cold weather has been especially hard on the children."

She stepped closer to me and hit me full force with her baby blues, voice pitched at that perfect balance between beseeching and admonishment. "There's a donation drive this weekend, Gabe. We have plenty to spare."

A woman with a good heart and pretty eyes is a fearsome thing. They can get damn near anything they want out of a man, and all too often, they know it. I crossed my arms, tapped my foot, and pretended to think about it, but only briefly.

It is a known fact around Hollow Rock that while my prices are very reasonable, I run a business and not a charity. However, I am occasionally afflicted by bouts of conscience that bring out my inner philanthropist and diminish large portions of my hard-earned inventory. Furthermore, I have a hard time obsessing over profit margins when I see kids running around with wool blankets for shoes and coats sewn from bed sheets stuffed with straw. Miranda knew this better than anyone.

119

"Not a bad idea," I said finally. "I'll leave it up to you what we sell and what we give away."

She rewarded me with another peck on the cheek, bringing a flush up my neck. "That's very kind of you, Gabe."

From the corner of my eye, I caught Hicks smirking. I cleared my throat and gestured to the clipboard. "What about the stuff from the hardware store and the gun shop?"

Miranda flipped another page. "You really hit the jackpot there. It's going to take me another hour or so to finish counting the ammo. About a third of the forty caliber and nine-millimeter is going to the sheriff's department, as well as a thousand rounds of .22 long rifle for the town guard. Other than that, we're in the clear. I suggest we sell the hunting cartridges— buckshot, 30.06, the usual—and about a quarter of the pistol caliber stuff. Also, the shovels, tools, chains, and para-cord. Those are always in demand. The rest we should put in storage. Folks are going to need it come next spring."

I glanced out a window at a frost-encrusted tree. "Isn't spring supposed to start in three weeks?"

She sighed and put her clipboard on the front counter. "Yes, but something tells me it's going to be late this year. Again."

Thinking about the cold made me notice the conspicuous absence of a fire in the woodstove. I squatted in front of it and began shoveling out the old ashes. "What about this guy?" I tilted my head at Hicks. "We got anything left over for him?"

Miranda slapped a palm against her forehead and blushed furiously. "Right! Of course. I'm so sorry, Caleb. You're so darn quiet, I forgot you were there."

I stood up and swiveled a stare between the two of them. "Caleb?"

Hicks looked at me like I was stupid. "I do have a first name, you know. Middle one too."

"Right. I guess I just never heard it."

"Probably 'cause you never asked."

"What's your middle name?"

"Theophilus."

I blinked twice. "Seriously?"

"Yep. Named after my great-granddaddy."

"Huh. Caleb Theophilus Hicks. I'm not sure if that makes you less of a redneck, or more."

For the first time I could remember, Hicks laughed. "You're one to talk, Kentucky. You ever hear yourself when you get to drinkin'? Sound like Hank Williams with a throat full of glass. Sing like it too."

Miranda's musical laughter filled the room, and I found myself smiling right along. "To hell with both o' y'all. Go on and get your loot, Caleb Theophilus Hicks. And make sure the rest of those hooligans out there know to come in one at a time."

The soldier's smile stretched the scars on his face. "Will do."

Once I had a fire going, I stepped outside and called Brian in. The instant he looked at me, Sanchez nailed him in the ear with a fist-sized snowball.

"Hey, come on, man," the boy shouted, laughing. "I wasn't ready."

Sanchez reached down to reload. "Mercy is for the weak, kid. This is war."

Brian made it through the door a fraction of a second ahead of the next volley. White powder burst against the window as he slammed the door shut, still giggling and pawing snow out of his ear. I shook my head and motioned him in.

"Come on, son. Take off those ratty old boots and let's see what we got for you."

Brain did as I asked, then walked ahead of me in his stocking feet toward the storeroom. I noticed he had begun walking with the same silent, even tread as Eric, but kept his eyes moving and his shoulders loose the way I had taught him. It brought a smile to my face, right up until he stopped, went stock still, and flushed all the way to his ears. I crept over and peeked around the corner where he stared.

On the other side of the store Hicks stood with his back against the wall, Miranda pressed flat against him, her hands around the back of his neck, locked in a grasping, passionate kiss.

TEN

I swore Brian to silence, hustled him over to a display stand, and pretended to explain to him the finer points of fishing lures until Hicks left with his percentage of the salvage. Afterward, Brian helped me stock the shelves and tidy up the store, occasionally glancing over to share a guilty grin.

One by one, the rest of the soldiers and militiamen came in to collect their pay. There was a great deal of bitching, moaning, and attempts to negotiate for better goods, but Miranda handled them with deft firmness until they at last loaded their boxes into the wagon and trundled off. Brian followed soon after, thanking me profusely for his new boots.

I stood on the front stoop and watched him walk away, a tight, aching knot in my chest. When I was a younger man, I had always expected I would start a family someday. Wife, kids, grandkids, all of it. But now, my forty-first birthday was looming, and still no wife, no kids, and certainly no grandchildren. None that I knew of, at least.

There was also the small matter of the end of the world, and roughly seven billion flesh-eating monstrosities polluting the planet. Things like that tend to have a disruptive effect on family planning.

When Brian turned the corner out of sight, I went back inside. The stove had warmed the store enough to peel off my jacket and wool sweater, so I hung them by the front door and took a seat on a low stool in the storeroom. I was quiet for a while, watching Miranda work. I might not have noticed it on any other day, but there seemed to be a bit more spring in her step. A certain jauntiness over and above her usual sunny nature. Her cheeks were flushed, and a small, delicate smile curled her lips. A secretive smile.

"So how long has it been going on?"

She looked up from where she knelt beside a shelf. "How long has what been going on?"

"You know what I mean."

Her hands, previously occupied writing labels on cardboard boxes, hesitated for the barest instant. She recovered quickly, continuing her work with casual ease.

"Is this one of your jokes, Gabe?" she said, affecting an irritated tone. "Because I'll tell you, I don't have time for it this morning. I have a lot to do before the store opens, and it would be nice if you would get off your butt and help me. I know you're the boss and all, but I can't do everything around here by myself."

Duly chastised, I grabbed a sharpie, picked up an inventory log, and went to work at another shelf. "I'm not mad you didn't tell me, Miranda. If anything, I'm happy for you. But you have to admit, it is a bit soon. I'm just concerned, is all."

The scratching sound of her marker ceased. No rustle of clothes or shuffle of boots on concrete. The rasp of her breathing grew more rapid. Sharp footfalls marched to the end of her row, turned the corner, and stopped in front of me.

"What's that supposed to mean?"

I faced her, unabashed. "Miranda, this is me you're talking to."

She glared a few moments longer, chest heaving, muscles twitching in her jaw. I stood my ground and looked her in the eye. The ice between us persisted for a solid minute before it finally began to thaw.

"It's not too soon."

"Are you sure?"

"Yes."

I put my sharpie down, walked her over to my tiny office, and gently pushed her into my chair. Sitting on my desk, I took one of her small hands in my massive paws and held it. She withstood the full effect of the patient, fatherly stare for approximately thirty seconds before her bottom lip began to tremble.

"I'm ready, Gabe. Really, I am. I can't spend the rest of my life hiding in this store."

"I know."

"Caleb is such a sweet guy. So polite and quiet and gentle. He's not like the other guys around town."

My eyes narrowed. "What other guys?"

"You know what I mean, Gabe. The looks, the leers, the whispers, the subtle and not-so-subtle flirtations. I've lived in my own skin long enough to know what men see when they look at me. Sometimes I feel like I'm not a human being; I'm just a piece of pretty meat. That's how the Legion treated me, like a goddamn sex doll. I thought things would be different here, but now, I'm not so sure. Men are pigs no matter where you go."

"Present company excluded, I hope."

She turned her face up to me, smiling tearfully, and my heart just about crumbled. "Of course. You're one of the good ones, just like Caleb."

She sighed and took her hand back, arms crossed, twisting side to side in her chair. "I feel different when I'm with him, you know? He treats me like a person. He makes me feel...I don't know, special. He sees me for who I am and likes me anyway."

I reached down and brushed a stray lock of hair from her face. My hand looked like an old catcher's mitt next to her porcelain skin.

"Who you are, Miranda, is the strongest person I've ever met. Most people wouldn't survive what you went through, much less have the courage to start over and greet each day with a smile. Sometimes it's genuine, and sometimes it's through tears, but you smile anyway. I'm a sorry excuse of a man, darlin', but you give me hope I can do better with my life."

She picked up one of my hands and kissed an oversized knuckle. "Gabe, the only thing you're a sorry excuse for is a singer."

I laughed from somewhere deep inside, picked her up like a child, and pulled her into a bear hug, careful not to hurt her. She wrapped her arms around my neck and squeezed. She was warm, and her hair smelled like homemade soap, and I wondered what a father must feel like giving his daughter away on her wedding day. When I put Miranda down, a few stray tears flowed down her cheek. I brushed them away.

"So what's he like anyway?" I asked. "The boy hardly talks. I barely know him."

She wiped her face, smoothed her hair, and sat back down. I resumed leaning on the desk.

"I guess he's what you might call the strong, silent type," she said. "He thinks his scars make him ugly, but they don't. They add something. When I first met him, he was all mysterious and handsome, and kind of dangerous looking. Very attractive. I started flirting with him a little. I thought he would be shy, but he's not. Underneath that silence, he's very confident and smart. Some people around town see how quiet he is and think he's slow witted, but they're wrong. He's one of the smartest people I've ever met."

"Really? I mean, I never thought he was stupid or anything. I've seen him in action, so I know he's clever in a fight. But you don't have to be Albert Einstein to pull a trigger."

"You should try talking to him sometime, Gabe. He'll amaze you. He likes to read, did you know that?"

"No. What kinds of books does he like?"

"All kinds, really, but he especially loves the classics. Dickens, Faulkner, Dante, Shakespeare. And he loves poetry too. You would never guess just looking at him."

"No. I wouldn't."

"He writes his own. Keeps them in a journal."

I raised an eyebrow. "Poems?"

"Yep. Sometimes he leaves little ones on my pillow. Like this. It's my favorite."

She reached in a pocket and handed me a small square of paper. I ignored the implications of its former residence upon her pillow, unfolded it, and read:

Sapphire gaze,

in morning aglow.

Iron lives there,

and courage that grows.

No valley can hide you,

you are brighter than day.

I was drifting, and lost,

and you showed me the way

Defy you the darkness

with laughter and light,

for a heart is a burden

in the empty night.

Your smile sustains me,

you lend me your might.

From the depths you bring me,

you make everything right.

"What do you think?" she asked, smiling shyly.

"Question is, what do you think?"

"I think it's beautiful."

I handed her back the little slip of paper. "Remember what I said about seeing the strength in you?"

She nodded.

"I think he sees it too."

*****

Carmella Delgado runs two businesses: a laundry, and a restaurant. It's hard to tell which one is more successful.

She runs the laundry out of her house, and the restaurant stands a couple of blocks down the street. Constructed post-Outbreak, it is little more than a sturdy box built around a ring of fire pits with underground storage. In the summer, the cooking fires make the place unbearably hot, and the seating is all outdoors. In the winter, however, the heat is a blessing and everyone tries to squeeze inside.

Because I like to think ahead, I had placed my order with Carmella's son, Diego, the night before. Diego runs the place, supervised closely by a crew of old women armed with spatulas and tongs, who abide their days conquering tortillas and peppers for hungry townsfolk.

Mijo Diego had a limited menu that changed daily. They posted the day's options on a chalkboard by the front door, and you either ate it or you didn't. In winter, the food was mostly preserved vegetables, reconstituted dried meat, beans, and whatever ingredients they could source from the local farms. Sometimes they even managed to get their hands on fresh venison or pork. When they did, if you wanted some, you either got in line early or you missed out.

The smell of hot food hit me two blocks away and made my stomach gurgle. Upon arriving, I squeezed through the crowd and made my way to the folding table that passed for a counter.

"*Hola* Mr. Garrett," Diego said, smiling. "We have your food ready. Be careful though, it is still very hot."

He handed me a box filled with Tupperware containers still warm to the touch. I pulled it across the table and lowered my head, breathing deeply of hot peppers, roasted chicken, vegetables sautéed in bacon fat, and scrambled eggs. A stack of tortillas lay wrapped in a clean, square cloth next to the meat and vegetables.

"As always, please make sure you return the box and containers," Diego said politely. "They are not making any more of them, you know."

I assured him I would as he pulled my file from a box and marked down what I owed. He showed it to me, and I approved with a nod.

Diego didn't make local customers pay up front, although the rules were different for travelers. Considering what most of his regulars used for trade, it just wasn't practical. Like most businesses in town, in order to eat at his restaurant, you had to open an account. The accounts were kept in a row of filing cabinets behind the front table, each one in its own folder. It took a crew of six people to fetch, sort, and maintain the records. Since paper was in short supply, Diego maintained his records on thin slats of wood and wrote on them in charcoal. When someone paid their bill, he quite literally wiped their record clean. Each customer was required to settle their account before the end of the week, as well as return all containers and utensils to be washed, sterilized, and reused.

Delinquent accounts were a rare thing; Hollow Rock is a small town, after all. But it happened from time to time, and when it did, Diego didn't waste time or energy sending out debt collectors, or involving the sheriff's department. His punishment for failure to pay was far, far worse.

He simply refused to serve you again until you paid your tab.

I had heard stories about people who got behind on their bills at Mijo Diego, and the lengths some of them went to in order to settle their account. At first, I had dismissed these stories as small town gossip.

Then I tried the food.

I am no longer skeptical. If anything, those people didn't go far enough.

The steaming bounty went into the basket on the back of my bicycle, held securely in place with a pair of bungee cords. Five minutes of pedaling brought me to the doors of the Hollow Rock Medical Clinic, where I paused to center myself and gather my courage.

Beyond those doors was one Allison Laroux, M.D., a woman who cared deeply for me, but was madly in love with Eric Riordan. The same Eric Riordan who had taken a bullet in the leg less than eighteen hours ago while helping me detain a group of insurgents. Going after said insurgents had been my call to make, and I had known good and well the Blonde Wonder would rather die than let me face danger alone. So his injuries were, by definition, my fault.

"Come on, Gabe. Fear is the mind killer. Just get it over with."

I decided to treat it like a mission. If I moved quickly, stayed quiet, and didn't bring attention to myself, perhaps I could escape unmolested. I ducked my head, shrugged into my hood, grabbed the food, and moved. The lobby was empty save for the guard at the front desk. I recognized him; he was one of the regulars on the night shift. That worked in my favor. He was probably tired, bored, and ready for his watch to be over. I needed him to get in—the door accessing the recovery rooms was locked and only the guards had keys. As tired as he was, I could probably get past him with a minimum of noise.

He looked up as I pushed the doors open with my back, hands occupied with the food. I raised my face enough for him to see it through my hood.

I said, "Mornin' John. Slow night?"

He nodded wearily. "Just the way I like 'em. Here to see your boys?"

I nodded. He stood up, jingled a set of keys until he found the right one, and let me in. As I stepped through the door, he put a hand on my arm, stopping me.

"Whatcha got in the box there?" he said. "Smells delicious." He leaned over my shoulder trying to get a better look. I would have screamed at him, but it would have drawn too much attention. I faked a smile instead.

"Hands off, friend. It's for my men. I call it the gunshot special. It's given to all recipients of the Purple Heart, otherwise known as the Insurgent Marksmanship Award."

The guard chuckled heartily and released my arm. "All right then. Send them my best."

"I'll be sure to do that."

The hall was empty. There were four intersections between me and the recovery room. I set off at a steady clip, making sure to pie out corners before crossing. If Allison was standing in any of the passageways, I didn't want her to see me. There were a few alcoves and closets I could duck into if I heard her coming, but it would only work if no one saw me. This early in the morning, the staff would be a skeleton crew. My odds were good.

I got past two junctions with no problems. A nurse had her back to me at the third one, but I managed to inch quietly by and make it to the fourth undetected. I looked around the corner. It was empty. One last obstacle. I shifted the box to one hand, hurried to the recovery room door, turned the latch slowly, and slipped through.

So far so good. Now I just had to drop off the food, say a few words of encouragement, and make my escape. Disarming the emergency exit and slipping out through the supply room was an attractive option, but that would damage the clinic's security system. I am merely a *common* coward, not a heartless one.

No. The only way out was through the front door.

"Gabe, is that you?"

I jumped. I had been peering through the narrow, wire-grated window on the door looking for nurses or petite, dark-haired doctors with fiery tempers, and had almost forgotten about Fuller and Riordan.

"Hey, fellas," I said, turning around and holding up the food. "I brought you breakfast."

Eric was propped up in his bed, wounded leg lying atop a pile of pillows. His eyes were glassy, but steady.

"Thanks, man. Smells great. Mijo Diego?"

"You know it." I moved a tray next to Eric's bed and began laying out containers and utensils. Fuller lay flat on his back next to me, eyes closed, breathing steadily, arm connected to an IV. "Is he okay?" I asked.

Eric peeled the lid off his eggs and sniffed at them. "Yeah, he'll be all right. His wounds are worse than mine, so they gave him a stronger dose of painkillers. Don't bother trying to wake him up, he's out like a light. I'll make sure the nurses give him his food when he wakes up."

Excellent. That cuts my time in half. "So how are you feeling?"

He grinned. "Like I've been shot."

I gave the obligatory laugh, wondering how much opiate the nurses had given him to bring about such a bland, predictable joke. Eric was usually more colorful than that. He tested a forkful of eggs and groaned. "Oh, man. Even pickled, these peppers and onions are awesome. Everything is so bland these days, you know? Gotta have some flavor once in a while."

I cast a nervous glance at the door and pulled up a chair. Eric began piling potatoes and chicken on a tortilla. "So what did I miss?"

"Not much. Pretty much business as usual."

He shot me a look. "I mean with the insurgents. Did you talk to the asshole yet?"

By 'the asshole', he meant Sheriff Elliott. The two had never gotten along, due mostly to the old lawman's inexplicable antagonism toward Eric. I thought Walter would warm up to Eric after all he did to bring down the Free Legion, but so far, nothing had changed.

"Yeah, I talked to him. He's going to keep questioning them, see what he can find out. I have a feeling it's not going to be much. They admitted they were working for the Alliance, which makes it a federal matter. The sheriff's hands are pretty much tied. All he can do is wait for word from the feds."

Eric grunted and shoveled more potatoes into his mouth. "Whur uhut irinda?" he asked.

"I can't understand you. Don't talk with your mouth full."

He swallowed and took a sip of water. "Sorry. What about Miranda? She look over the haul yet?"

"Yep. Counted it up, scheduled the transport, and took care of payroll. Even convinced the crew to help her move the surplus to the warehouse."

"Damn. That was quick."

"She's an efficient girl."

"She seem like she's doing okay? You know, with me being shot and all?"

"I talked to her last night and explained your wounds aren't that bad. She took it in stride. Said she would pay you a visit this afternoon after she closes the store."

"That's good, man, I appreciate you doing that. Miranda's good people. Anything else going on? Any gossip?"

I thought about Miranda's budding relationship with Hicks, but decided to keep it to myself. That conversation would only delay my departure, and the longer I stayed, the worse my chances of escaping undetected.

"Nope," I lied. "Hollow Rock is a quiet place."

"It is now, anyway. Let's hope is stays that way."

He ate a few more bites, drained his cup of water, wiped his mouth, and lay back on the bed. "Sorry, but I can't eat all this. I think the meds are messing with my appetite. You mind boxing it up for me and giving it to one of the nurses? If there's no room in the fridge, they can just wrap it in a towel and set it outside. It shouldn't freeze before lunch."

"You going to eat it cold?"

"No way, man. Microwave. I'm dating the only doctor in town, remember? I get special privileges."

"Right. I forgot all about those things. Funny how you get used to doing without after a while."

"I know what you mean. That Ishimura guy is a miracle worker."

"That he is."

With a full belly, in a warm room, doped up on God knows what, lying under a blanket, Eric began to get droopy eyed. I sensed my opportunity.

"You look tired, amigo."

He nodded drowsily. "Yeah, it's the meds. I'm all loopy and shit."

I stood up and patted him gently on the shoulder. "Tell you what, I'm going to head out and let you get some rest. Let Fuller know I stopped by, okay?"

He made a vague gesture with one hand. "Sure, man. No problem."

I made quick work of gathering his food, took out my trusty sharpie, tore the bottom off an empty box of rubber gloves lying in the trashcan, and wrote a brief note of instruction for the nurses regarding Eric's leftovers and Fuller's uneaten breakfast. That done, I hurried to the door and peered outside. All clear.

Sensing victory, I opened the door and stepped out into the hallway. I got about two steps before a pretty, petite woman in a white coat rounded a corner, stopped in her tracks, and glared venomously.

"There you are," she said.

My stomach hit my shoes. My shoulders slumped. My chin fell to my chest.

Shit.

Busted.

ELEVEN

It is amazing how much space a small woman can occupy when she is infuriated.

I had been in Allison's office before, several times, and it had always seemed spacious, never cramped or confining. There was enough room between walls and desk and chairs to put patients at ease, so they would not feel boxed in. A doctor quite often gives people bad news, and whoever built the clinic knew the recipients would need room to breathe.

With Allison standing less than three feet away, barely eye-to-eye with me despite the fact I was sitting down, I felt as if I were locked in a cage with a large, angry animal brandishing claws and rows of pointy teeth.

"What the fuck were you thinking, you idiot?" she said, hands on hips, face red, chin jutting forward. Allison rarely cursed, so I knew I was in trouble.

"I was thinking someone needed to stop those insurgents. They were leading about a thousand ghouls toward Hollow Rock."

"But why did it have to be you, Gabe? Why did it have to be Eric? You're not in the military anymore. This town has a militia and a whole platoon of soldiers. Why didn't you just come back and tell the sheriff, or the mayor, or Lieutenant Cohen? They would have sent troops after the insurgents. They could have stopped the horde. That's their job. It's why they're here. It's why the mayor gives them food and puts a roof over their heads, so people like you and Eric don't have to fight anymore."

"There was a blizzard last night, Allison. They might not have made it in time. They might have been overwhelmed by the horde, or the insurgents might have escaped. Any number of things could have gone wrong."

"Yes, but that's the risk soldiers take when they decide to become soldiers. You say things could have gone wrong for the Army, but what happened when you decided to handle things yourself? What about Eric and Private Fuller? Didn't go so well for them, did it?"

I had been looking at the wall, and the ceiling, and the floor, and anywhere but at Allison. But when she said that, when she took that cheap shot at me, I looked up. Somewhere deep in my chest, the old fire began to burn.

"You know, Allison, last year you told me you were tired of working hard and getting shit on for it. Well you know what? Now I know how you feel. Every time I save this town from disaster, all I get is grief. Maybe you forgot, but this whole fucking place would be overrun with marauders if not for me. All these patients you're treating wouldn't be healing, they would be dead. This clinic wouldn't have electricity, it would be a pile of rubble. You wouldn't be standing here bitching at me for saving lives, you would be chained to a floor somewhere wondering who was going to rape you next. So don't you point your finger at me and call me the bad guy. I stood up for you, and everyone else in this town, when no one else would. The least you can do is show some goddamn respect."

Allison went still, the color draining from her face. Without realizing it, I had stood up and now loomed over her, hands balled into fists, teeth clenched. My voice had steadily grown in volume until it thundered off the stark white walls. Behind me, I heard shuffling feet edging closer to the door and people whispering. Closing my eyes, I counted backward from ten until my breathing slowed and my pulse returned to normal. I sat back down. My hands uncurled and went slack, dangling between my knees.

"Listen, I'm sorry Eric got hurt, okay? And you're right, it's not my job to fight this town's battles anymore. But Allison, you have to understand, Eric and Fuller knew what they were getting themselves into. They could have said no. They could have walked away. They knew the risks, they knew the danger the horde and the insurgents posed, and they chose to fight anyway. I might not be in the Marines anymore, but I care about this town, and I will not stand idly by and let the Alliance, or marauders, or slavers, or anyone else threaten my home. I *will not*. So don't stand there and tell me I shouldn't have gone after the insurgents. It's not just the responsibility of the Army or the Militia to protect this place, it's everyone's responsibility. Every man, woman, and child who lives here. And if they are not willing to take on that responsibility, if they are not willing to meet that challenge, then everything we're doing here is a waste of time. Because this place will *not* survive."

There were any number of reactions I might have expected from Allison at that moment. It would not have surprised me if she yelled at me again for letting Eric get shot. I would have quietly accepted a lecture that saving a town doesn't give me a license to behave recklessly. She could have admonished me not to lecture her about sacrifice, considering everything she had done for Hollow Rock. If she had slapped me in the face and said never to talk to her like that again, I would have meekly sat there and taken it.

But that's not what happened. What happened was the worst, most disarming thing she could possibly have done.

She put her hands over her face and started crying.

Great shuddering sobs racked her. A heartbreaking, hiccup-like noise broke loose from her chest. Tears spilled out from between her fingers. Her legs gave out and she went to her knees.

I sat there with my mouth open, too stunned to move.

Allison handled things on a daily basis that would make most people run screaming for the hills. She had brought children into the world, and sometimes, watched them die. She had personally delivered crushing news to patients and families. She had pulled bullets out of soldiers and militiamen, amputated infected limbs, and performed surgeries to repair horrific injuries. And through it all, she always maintained a clear-eyed, professional calm. Nothing ever seemed to rattle her. So seeing her huddled on the ground crying like a toddler with a skinned knee was, to put it mildly, fucking disturbing.

137

"Hey, hey, calm down now," I said, kneeling beside her. "Look, I'm sorry I yelled at you, okay? I didn't mean any of that stuff. That was just anger talking."

She took her hands away from her face and glared at me. "I'm not crying because you yelled at me, you idiot!"

I tried to talk a few times, but nothing came out. Her face went back to her hands, sobs unabated. Lacking any other ideas, I reached out and put a gentle hand on her shoulder. She responded by sliding down onto one hip and leaning into me, faced buried in the hollow of my chest. I sat down and wrapped my arms around her, rocking back and forth, whispering little comforting things. We stayed that way for a while, her crying, me trying to calm her down. A crowd gathered outside the door, peeking in through the window.

I shot them a look.

They left.

Finally, she calmed enough to let me help her into a chair. "Allison, what's going on? This isn't like you. You don't break down like this. You're the freaking iron lady of Hollow Rock."

She wouldn't meet my eyes, just sat there looking small and miserable. I kneeled next to her and took her chin in my hand. When I turned her face to mine, her amber eyes were full of tears.

"Hey, it's me, Allison. You're friend, Gabriel. Remember me? Look, I'm sorry I got mad, but I'm over it now. Just tell me what's going on, okay? You've got me worried."

She reached up and took my hand in hers, holding it in her lap. "If I tell you, you can't tell Eric. Promise me."

"That depends on what it is."

She looked at me again, firmly this time. "Promise me."

What was I supposed to do? She was crying. "Okay. I promise."

"I'm pregnant."

I froze. There was a ringing in my ears that grew louder and louder. I felt as if a gigantic hand was pressing me into the floor. Allison narrowed her eyes and gently slapped me on the cheek.

"Are you okay?" she asked. "You just went really pale."

The ringing stopped. I stood up on shaky legs, walked around the desk, and sank into a chair.

"Well, that explains a lot."

*****

Later, as I stumbled numbly down the street, I found myself in front of Stall's Tavern. It was not uncommon to find myself there—in fact, it had become something of a second home. But I had not gone there by force of conscious will. I had been walking with no clear sense of direction, vaguely aware of people passing me on the street, wondering just how in the hell I was going to look my best friend in the eye and *not* tell him the woman he loved was carrying his child. A commotion near the front door distracted me as a man pushed through a crowd of people and stomped angrily toward the lobby. I recognized him.

Roy Cranston.

My heart sank.

It was almost noon, and the lunch crowd had swarmed the place, all of them regulars who showed up nearly every day. Among them was my good friend and one of the most skilled tradesmen in town, Tom Glover, father of Brian Glover, the kid who had just beaten Uriah Cranston bloody a few hours earlier.

The trouble started by the time I pushed my way inside.

"Where's your son, Glover? I want to see him right now."

Tom calmly wiped his mouth, set his napkin on the table, stood up, and squared off with Cranston. He spaced his feet shoulder width apart, forty-five degrees from his opponent,

139

arms relaxed, head slightly forward, weight shifted back so he could swing his torso one way or the other. I watched his eyes become unfocused and center on Cranston's shoulders, just the way I had taught him. If a punch came, he would be ready for it.

When I first met Tom, he was gaunt from lack of nutrition. But eight months of good food and hard labor had restored his health and added twenty pounds to his frame. Knots of hard muscle lined his arms and wide shoulders, and though he was only about two-thirds Roy's size, I put their strength about even. Furthermore, Eric and I had spent as much time training him as his son, and although he didn't have Brian's raw talent for combat, Tom could handle himself just fine.

"Before I explain to you how you're not going anywhere near my son, how about you tell me what the problem is?" he said.

"My son came home beat up and bloody, and said it was your boy that did it." Cranston took a step closer, clearly not understanding the danger he was putting himself in. He was a big man, nearly as tall as me, but lean and rangy. He was fond of stepping into people's personal space and looming over them, not realizing how stupid of a thing it was to do.

I took a moment to assess the situation. The dining room was spacious, lined wall to wall with tables. At this time of day, customers occupied every available seat including the bar. Tom would not have much room to maneuver, which would work in Cranston's favor. What would not work in Cranston's favor was the tool-belt draped over the back of Tom's chair, and the twenty-three ounce, long-handled framing hammer less than an inch from Tom's fingers. Tom's forearms were nearly as big as most men's biceps, and I knew he could swing that hammer as if it weighed no more than a twig.

"First off, Roy, your son is a bullying shit, just like you. If he got his ass beat, he probably deserved it. Second, if Brian did it, I'll be the one to punish him and not you. Third, you had best take a step back and get your stinking liquor breath out of my face before something bad happens. You might scare these other folks around here, but I been around the block, son. You don't impress me."

140

Cranston's face went red. He lifted a hand, finger outstretched, intent on poking it into Tom's chest. Tom caught his hand halfway there, calloused fingers squeezing. Roy winced and tried to pull away, but Tom's iron grip held him in place. Even though I was standing eight feet away, I could hear Cranston's knuckles pop.

"That's the last time you try to lay a hand on me, Cranston. Now do the smart thing and walk away."

Of course, he did not do the smart thing. He lifted a fist and swung it at Tom's face. I stepped forward to intervene, but it was a waste of effort. Tom released Roy's hand, ducked the punch, and fired an uppercut into Roy's groin. The big man gasped and hunched over, mouth open, face drained of color, eyes bulging. Tom moved again, pushed Roy's head to one side, and slammed a hammerfist into his brachial nerve. Roy's legs went limp.

I reached Cranston's prone body at the same time as the owner of Stall's tavern, my good friend Mike Stall. The lanky old cowboy pushed his hat back, hooked his thumbs in his broad leather belt, and stared down with a disgusted look on his face.

"I tell you, Cranston, you ain't got the brains God gave a turnip," Mike said. "You're about as useless as bird shit on a saddle. Gabe, help me throw this idiot out of here, will ya?"

I helped Mike haul the half-conscious man to the door, feet dragging the ground behind us. Once outside, we took him around the back of the building and propped him against a wall. Mike placed a hand on his chest to keep him from toppling over.

Just to be on the safe side, I bent one of his arms into the crook of my elbow and applied a wristlock. If he struggled, all it would take was a little squeeze, and Roy would be standing on tiptoe begging for mercy. When Roy's eyes cleared enough to understand what was happening, Mike slapped him. Hard.

"Hey, you listening?" he said.

"Let go of me." Roy started trying to push away from me, so I applied a little pressure to his wrist, drawing a hiss of pain. He stopped struggling.

"Now listen here, Cranston," Mike said. "You can't just go storming into my place and startin' trouble with folks. Stall's Tavern is a family establishment, and I will not have people brawling on the dining room floor. You got that?"

Cranston glared angrily. "That bastard's son beat up my boy. You expect me to let that go?"

"First of all, Tom Glover is a good man and a friend of mine, and I don't ever want to hear you speak ill of him again. As for your unending litany of grievances with damn near everybody in town, I don't give a rat's ass what you do, Roy. But if you got a problem with somebody, you ain't gonna handle it in my tavern. If somebody hurt your boy, you go take it up with the sheriff. Don't bring that foolishness around here. Understood?"

Cranston looked down and nodded.

"This will not happen again, Roy. If it does, I will ban you for life. Are we clear?"

"Yeah. We're clear."

"Good. Now get on out of here, and don't come back for a week."

I released Cranston and watched him stalk away on unsteady feet until was out of sight. Mike turned and looked at me.

"I hate to say it, but he got what he deserved."

"Things like that have been happening a lot lately," I replied.

"Yes they have. I tell you, Gabe, everybody is gettin' a little too damned comfortable around here. All the unity has about gone out of this place. Folks ain't pulling together like they used to."

"What do you mean?"

"You weren't here during the Outbreak. You didn't see how it was, then. Folks were scared to death. The end of the world was a big-ol' shitstorm, and it was headed straight for us.

142

People started panicking. Fights broke out. Folks started stealing from each other. It was bad. Real bad. Then the mayor called a town hall meeting and laid out her plan, and everything changed."

My curiosity was piqued. Elizabeth had never talked about what happened in Hollow Rock during the Outbreak, and I had never asked. I got the feeling it was a touchy subject.

"What plan was that?"

He held his arms out as though giving a speech. "Build a wall. Defend your homes. Stand and fight. Hold the line. That was what it boiled down to, those four slogans. She even put up signs and posters all over town, like war propaganda. I'll be damned if it didn't work. Got everybody all riled up about stopping the infected. That's what holds people together in times like that, you know? Distract them, get them moving, give them something to do other than worry. It was brutal hard work building that wall, but she was out there with us every day, sweating in the sun and working herself half to death. Surprised a lot of folks when she did that. She was a big woman back then. Bet you didn't know that, did you?"

"No, I didn't. She's always seemed so fit."

"Hasn't always been that way. She was what my granddaddy would have called a 'big healthy girl'. But like I said, building that wall was damned hard work. She must have lost forty pounds in two months. Folks started worrying about her, thought she was pushing herself too hard. Didn't stop her, though. Ain't no quit in that woman. It's why everybody likes her so much."

"Wow. I didn't know that."

"She never told you?"

"I get the impression it's not her favorite subject."

Mike chuckled. "I suppose not. Those were hard times. We lost a lot of folks that first winter."

His smile faded, eyes growing distant. "But we're doing better now. Got you and Eric to thank for that. I don't believe

I've ever said it, but you boys did a hell of a thing for this town last year."

I waved off the compliment. "Ah hell, it was as much self-preservation as anything else. But if really want to show your gratitude, you can clear my bar tab."

The old cowboy grinned and started walking toward the front of the building. "I'm grateful, Mr. Garrett, but I ain't *that* grateful."

*****

Back in the tavern, Tom had resumed his seat and was finishing his lunch. I stopped at his table and nodded to him. One of his employees, a brick mason named Gilroy, tossed his napkin on his plate, stood up, and motioned to his chair.

"Go ahead and take my seat, Gabe. I got to head on back to work anyway." I thanked him and sat down.

"Let the guys know I'll be along in a little while, Gil," Tom said. "Gotta stop by the sheriff's office and give my side of the story."

"Take your time," Gilroy said, grinning. "Nice work by the way. You just did what everybody around here has wanted to do for years."

Tom waved him away and focused on his meal. A waitress stopped by to take Gilroy's plate and ask if I wanted anything. I told her I would like a cup of Mike's famous herbal tea, and no, I would not be ordering lunch. She smiled and headed for the kitchen.

"Gilroy's right, you know," I said. "You handled that asshole pretty well."

Tom shrugged. "Cranston's an idiot. I don't care for fighting, but I don't abide bullies either."

Although he was trying to hide it, I could see the tremor in his hands. Not from fear, just the adrenaline dump that comes after a fight. "You okay?" I asked.

"I'm fine," he said. "I've handled worse things than Roy Cranston."

A memory flashed by of a stretch of highway not far from Hollow Rock, and twenty-three armed men ambushing us, disabling our vehicle, and forcing us to retreat into the woods. I remembered Tom's face as he huddled behind a fallen log, rifle in hand, fighting for his life shoulder to shoulder with his son. By comparison, Cranston didn't seem like too big of a deal.

"I suppose you have."

He pushed a few potatoes around on his plate, mouth turning down at the corners. "I just hate it had to happen here, you know? Word will be all over town before I finish my lunch."

"You're probably right. I should go with you to the sheriff's office and give a witness statement. Make sure Roy doesn't try to say you attacked him or something like that."

"I'd appreciate it."

I drank my tea while he finished his lunch, then we stopped by the bar on our way out. Mike was polishing glasses while keeping a close watch over the crowd. He knew very well how excited people get in the wake of physical violence, and sometimes that excitement can result in additional altercations. I felt sorry for the offenders if they decided to get stupid. There was a leather sap just inches from Mike's able hands, and he had no qualms about using it.

Tom slid his heavy tool belt across the bar. "Hey Mike, you mind holding onto this for me? I gotta go by the sheriff's office. I'll pick it up on my way back to work."

"Not a problem, my friend." He made a small gesture, and Tom leaned closer. "I hate to ask you this, but you think you could steer clear for a few days? It might help keep the peace if you let things settle down a bit. Do you mind?"

Tom looked sad, but shook his head. "Of course not, Mike. And I'm real sorry about all this."

Mike took the tool belt and stashed it under the bar. "It ain't your fault, Tom. I appreciate you being understanding."

"Is it okay if I send my guys over for carry out?"

"That'd be fine."

"Thanks. I'll see you later, Mike."

Word had already spread to the sheriff's office by the time we got there. I can't say I was surprised; gossip is a favorite pastime in Hollow Rock. Sarah waited for us in the foyer, her face hard with anger.

"Are you all right, sweetie?" she said, wrapping her arms around her husband.

"I'm fine. You should see the other guy."

"Oh, believe me, I'll be seeing him very soon. I've just about had it with that son of a bitch. He'll be spending the next few days in lockup on half rations."

"Come on now, honey, there ain't no need for all that. I beat him down in front of about a hundred people. I'd say he's been punished enough."

Sarah didn't looked convinced. "He's a damn nuisance, Tom. He doesn't appreciate how good he has it here. There are a few people around town who think the rules don't apply to them, and Cranston is one of them. They're about to learn the hard way what happens when you ignore the law in Hollow Rock."

Tom smiled and kissed his wife on the cheek. "I feel sorry for those people. I really do. You hear this woman, Gabe? This is why I stay on the straight and narrow."

Sarah's eyes softened, and she punched him on the arm. "Go give the sheriff your statement, butthead. I have a citation to issue."

"Yes Officer Glover."

She broke a smile. "That's *Deputy* Glover. Get it right."

"My apologies."

The sheriff took both our statements and assured Tom he'd be having a very personal, very one-sided conversation with both Roy Cranston and his son in the not too distant future.

"What about Brian?" Sheriff Elliott asked. "Did he really get into it with Uriah?"

Tom held up his hands. "Honestly, I don't know. I'll find out though, you can count on that."

I grimaced and held up a hand like a schoolboy. The cat was out of the bag, so there wasn't much point in staying silent. "Actually, it's true."

Both men looked at me.

"I saw them out behind Benny's Barbershop. Brian worked him over pretty good."

Tom glared. I didn't meet his eyes. "When exactly did you plan on telling me about that?"

"I'm sorry, Tom. I told him I wouldn't say anything."

"Gabe, I know you don't have kids, but come on. You know better than to keep something like that from me. I'm his father for Christ's sake."

"I may not have kids, but I remember *being* a kid. I remember if you dragged grownups into a dispute, you'd never hear the end of it. Brian stood up for himself against a notorious bully. He's a tough, brave kid, and I'm not trying to make things any harder for him than they need to be. Besides, you know how he is. He'd be eaten up with guilt for a few days over not telling you, then he would confess. Tell me I'm wrong."

Tom stared for another moment, then looked away. "I guess you're right. Still, though, you can't keep things like that from me, Gabe. I'm his father, and I have a right to know what's going on with my son."

"All right, it won't happen again. I give you my word."

He nodded once. "Fair enough."

We stopped to say goodbye to Sarah and parted ways. I sensed Tom was still unhappy with me, but didn't try to explain myself any further. Tom isn't one to hold a grudge for long, so I figured I would give him a few days before trying to patch things up.

As I walked home, I thought about Allison, and Brian, and the Cranstons, and the thousand other little dramas playing out between the citizens of Hollow Rock. I thought about life in the city before the Outbreak, and how isolated it had been. When a man could live within a square mile of a hundred-thousand people, and feel completely alone.

Most people kept to themselves, content with their computers, iPads, cellphones and the filtered, touch-free cybersphere that had replaced the simple arts of introduction and conversation. No one wanted to talk to you, and you were expected to not want to talk to them. At least not outside the social constructs set aside for such purposes.

Even then, in bars and organized social gatherings, there was an established protocol. For example, one did not simply go to a bar alone. To do so was to incite pity, and mark oneself as socially destitute. If you wanted to attract members of the opposite sex, you had to have a minimum of one other person in your party, preferably two or more. Four seemed to be the optimum number for both men and women. If you had three wingmen, and spotted an alpha female with three pack members in tow, your chances of catching their attention were exponentially greater than attempting such a feat with any other number.

But try to meet people outside of a bar, or a dinner party, or church, or a dating website, and people branded you with contemptible adjectives such as 'weird' and 'creepy'. As though attempting to connect with another human being was a crime punishable by social excommunication. I can't remember how many times I would walk into a coffee shop, or a restaurant, or a café, and see people, couples, even families, sitting together at tables, all of them staring at some sort of a screen, faces blank, complete silence hanging between them. I would fight the urge to stand on a table and scream, 'For crying out loud, why don't you just TALK to each other?'

I always wondered what could be so interesting on those little devices it distracted people from their tragically short lives, from the thousand touches and shared moments it takes to build a marriage, or that their kids were growing up and they were missing it.

The world was different, now. No cell phones, and very limited computer and internet access. No signs in windows emphatically declaring FREE WI-FI. People had to interact verbally, in person. When they got together at Stall's Tavern, or the VFW hall, or a town meeting, they actually carried on conversations. People who had been neighbors for years, but had never spoken, suddenly started learning about each other. Sometimes it was wonderful and exciting, and other times it bred conflict. But it always created a new relationship, for good or ill.

The problem was, you never knew which way things were going to go.

TWELVE

I had the shop to myself the next morning.

It was Miranda's day off, and Eric was off his feet for the foreseeable future, leaving me as the only person to mind the store. Which meant instead of working out, or training with the militia, or teaching a martial arts class at the VFW hall, I got to spend the day haggling and arguing with the general public.

I really needed to hire more help.

As always, the store was neat and tidy when I arrived, the shelves stocked with the day's merchandise, and the inventory logs updated. There was nothing for me to do but unlock the door, flip the sign, and wait. I had enough time to plant my butt on the stool behind the counter before the chime over the door rang, announcing the first customer of the day. Not surprisingly, it was Federal Facilitator extraordinaire, Jutaro Ishimura.

Ishimura bounced into the store with his usual bright-eyed, smiling enthusiasm. He was quite possibly the most energetic individual I had ever met. Not in a bad way, not annoying or anything, he just always seemed to be in motion.

"Morning, Gabe. I heard you brought in some new inventory," he said.

"That I did, my friend. Got some desktop computers you might want to look at. Not sure if they're functional."

"That's okay. At the very least, there's copper wire in the fan motors. Let's take a look."

I stood up and walked toward the storeroom. Ishimura was one of a very few customers I allowed back there. We proceeded to the appropriate shelf, stacked nearly to the ceiling with PC towers.

"Holy crap," Ishimura said. "That's a lot of computers. Where did you find them?"

"Come on now, Jutaro. You know I don't divulge that kind of information. Got to protect my business interests."

He looked at me, smiling his toothy grin. "I'm not looking to cut into your business. I just need wire, and lots of it. Electricity doesn't conduct itself."

"Actually, it kind of does. You just have to create a difference of potential."

He raised an eyebrow. "So, you understand electronic theory?"

"I'm not a complete dunce on the subject."

"That's great. I could really use some help with-"

I cut him off with an upraised hand. "I already have a job, thanks."

He looked genuinely disappointed. His gaze shifted back to the computer equipment, a slight frown forming at the edges of his chin. It was the first time I had seen him look anything but enthusiastic. "Sorry. It's just...I have a big job to do, you know? I'm already behind schedule and it's such a pain in the ass to find materials. You should let me come with you on your next salvage run. I bet there's tons of stuff I could use out there."

"I don't know, Jutaro. It's pretty dangerous."

"I can handle myself."

"Really? You have combat training?"

"Actually I...nice one, Gabe. You almost got me."

"What do you mean, almost? You just told me you have combat training."

"No I didn't."

"Sure you did. I could tell by your reaction."

He shook his head. "You're crazy."

"Really?"

On a hunch, I threw a punch straight at his face. Not full strength, or full speed—and I fully intended to pull it a fraction of an inch before impact—but Jutaro didn't know that.

His arm shot up, the calloused edge of one palm catching me just under the wrist and deflecting the blow. I let my arm go limp, reversed the direction of my elbow, and caught his wrist. He struggled to pull away, surprisingly strong. He is not a big man, maybe five-foot nine, a hundred fifty pounds, but the muscles in his forearm were stringy and tough, much like Eric's. I might have expected that from an athlete, or a soldier, or a lifelong martial artist, but not from a scientist.

I let him go and stepped back, hands upraised. "All right, man, settle down. I was just testing you."

He looked angry. "Don't do that again."

"That was a good block. And that callous on your palm, it looks like you've spent a lot of time in the dojo. You any good with a firearm?"

"For Christ's sake," he said, disgustedly. "Why is everyone always asking me questions? I can't talk about it, okay? I can't tell you where I'm from, or-"

"San Francisco."

He froze. "How did you know that?"

"Your accent."

"I don't have an accent."

I shrugged. "Suit yourself."

He ran a hand over his close-cropped hair and let out an irritated sigh. "How much for all of it?"

"Depends on what you're trading."

"What do you need?"

"I'm running short of .45 ACP."

He rubbed his chin. "I don't have any of that."

"Can't you requisition it from Central Command?"

"No. I'm over budget as it is. Is there anything else you need? Tools? Fuel?"

"Got more tools than I can sell, and no use for fuel."

"But you have a generator in your neighborhood, right?"

"Had one. We donated it to the school so they can heat the classrooms."

Ishimura walked over to a stool, took a seat, and pressed his hands together, casting an avaricious glance at the computers. "I'm sorry, Gabe, but that's all I have."

"Actually, it isn't."

He looked up.

"You have information."

I watched a range of emotions play over his face. First was obstinance, the instinctive urge to stonewall me. Secrecy, evidently, was an integral part of being a Facilitator. Then came frustration, the knowledge that he had been given a difficult mission and insufficient resources to get it done. And if he failed, he would be held accountable. Next was a pensive look, the inner bargaining, the questions. How much can I get away with telling him? Can I trust him? What could go wrong? Finally, there was resignation. The knowledge he had no other cards to play.

If Jutaro had been a bad person, I would have smirked. But he wasn't. I pitied the guy.

"What do you want to know?" he asked.

I took a seat on a stool across from him, fingers steepled, debating where to start. "What are the Facilitators? Where do you come from?"

"I can't tell you that."

I stood up and headed for the front of the store. "It was nice seeing you again, Jutaro. Good luck out there."

"Wait."

I stopped, not turning around.

Jutaro let out a sigh. "I only know my part of it. It's highly compartmentalized. No one knows the whole operation."

I walked back to the storeroom and sat down. "Go on."

"They approached me when I was an engineering student at UC Davis."

"Who did?"

"Recruiters. Two of them. Typical government types. Dark glasses, suits, the whole thing. Homeland Security. Said they wanted to offer me a job."

"Doing what?"

"Training. They wanted me to participate in a training program for what they called 'disaster specialists'. Said it was a new project developed in the wake of Katrina. They wanted to train teams of engineers and scientists to go into disaster areas and restore infrastructure, render medical aid, repair critical facilities, that kind of thing."

"Didn't they already have people for that?"

"Yeah, but it was complicated. Involved a lot of civilian contractors and red tape. Very bureaucratic and inflexible. The recruiters said they were trying to create something leaner, more agile."

"Interesting. What did they offer you?"

"Money. What else? They said if I completed the program, the government would pay off my student loans and pay for the rest of my education."

"I can see how that might entice a broke college student."

"You have no idea. I was eating ramen three meals a day, bumming rides to school because I couldn't afford bus fare, even donated plasma. Anything I could do to scrape money..."

He stopped and looked at me, realizing what he was doing. His smile returned. "You're good, Gabe. Interrogation is a subtle art. What exactly did you do before the Outbreak?"

"This isn't quid pro quo. You want those computers or not?"

"Point taken."

"Good. Next question. What kind of training did they give you?"

He scrutinized me a moment longer before answering. "Highly specialized. They separated us into teams, each team focusing on something different. For me, it was electrical grids. How they work, how to repair them, what they're made of, ways to generate electricity, that kind of thing. It was intense, man. The program was no joke. A lot of guys didn't finish. Smart guys. I thought it was the hardest thing I would ever do."

He gave a short, bitter laugh, and peered down at the cuts and callouses on his hands. "Little did I know."

"So when did you go from being a disaster specialist to a Facilitator? What was the transition? How does it all tie in with the Phoenix Initiative?"

"Listen, I can talk about me, but I can't talk about the Initiative." His tone brooked no argument.

"All right then, tell me about your part of it."

"After the program, we all just kind of went back to our lives. I finished school, got a job, met a girl. Went back for follow-on training once a year."

"Back where?"

"It doesn't matter."

"That's not an answer."

He shrugged, but said nothing more.

"Fine. I'm going to assume something changed during the Outbreak."

"It did. Now, let me ask you a question."

"What's that?"

"How much have I earned so far? And just so you know, if it's not enough, I can always submit a request to commandeer those computers. This town has an Army presence. They could just come and take it."

I thought about First Platoon, how much they owed me, and how the Army still required soldiers to pay their private debts, and chuckled. "Good luck with that."

He wisely decided not to press the issue. "So how much is it?"

I pointed at the computers. "The bottom three racks. All yours."

"Very kind of you. How do I get the next two?"

"Answer a couple more questions."

"I've about reached the limit of what I can tell you."

"Then how about I sweeten the deal?"

"How so?"

"You said you want to ride along on a salvage run. Were you serious?"

A desperate hope sprang to life in his eyes. He swallowed a couple of times before answering. "As a heart attack."

"What happened to you during the Outbreak?"

He let out a breath and rested his elbows on his knees. "They came for me. It was during the early days, just after Atlanta. A couple of cops showed up at my apartment, said I wasn't under arrest, but the FBI wanted to see me. A matter of national security. Naturally, I was shocked. They gave me a few minutes to say goodbye to...anyway. The next thing I know, I'm at the San Francisco FBI office, then a Suburban with blacked out windows, then I'm on a military transport plane with a bunch of other people just as confused as me. We stopped twice, probably for fuel, and about sixteen hours later, I'm on an airstrip somewhere hot and tropical and I'm being hustled into an underground vault. That's when things got weird."

"Define weird."

"The first thing was the elevator. No buttons, just a card reader. The ride down took forever. Then they took me to my quarters, which looked like your average hotel room, and told me to wait. I heard it when they locked the door from the outside. Made a little click. Such a small thing, really, but I'll remember that sound for the rest of my life."

He stopped talking for a while and moved to one of the windows, eyes distant, staring out at the snow-covered town square. I had a feeling I knew what he was going through.

It always strikes me as strange how even the most devastating memories are so often shuffled back, clustered, lumped in among other things. For years at a time, they can lay dormant, unremembered, boxed-up mementos in an abandoned mental attic. But then something triggers them, and suddenly they are back with stunning force, dredging up smells and sounds and textures, sharp as the day they happened. They are powerful things, those unbidden recollections. They can stop a man in his tracks.

I went out front to give Jutaro some time alone.

A customer came and bought the last roll of paracord. He paid with a dozen eggs, a gallon of homemade chicken broth, and a pre-Outbreak candle. I would have given him the cord for any one of those things, but he offered all three.

Business. Not a charity.

The next customer came in less than a minute later. He saw the candle, broth, and eggs on the counter, and offered to buy all of them along with a ream of paper. I said the paper and the candle were for sale, but the eggs and broth were not. He asked if I was sure about that. I said unless he had some .45 ACP ammo to trade, then yes, I was sure. He told me he would be back in five minutes. He was back in three minutes and thirty-seven seconds with fifty rounds, still in the box, unopened, asking if it was enough.

In the interest of retaining his business in the future, lest he find out how much he had given away, I informed him I would have given him the paper, eggs, broth, candle, and half the inventory in the store for that much. I also informed him he should not show those cartridges to anyone, or tell anyone about them, and he should lock them up someplace safe when he got home.

"Are they really that valuable?"

"Yes, they are."

"You're an honest man, Mr. Garrett."

A disarming smile. Shrug of a shoulder. "Sometimes."

I would have settled for ten, but he insisted on paying fifteen. An idealist, that one. Concerned about rewarding honesty. So I relented and told him I would give him five rounds' credit toward his next purchase. I also told him to hang on to that ammo, and if he needed anything else, to come see me first. He said he would be sure to do that. I checked out the window so see if anyone else was coming my way. There was no one, so I went back to the storeroom and resumed my seat on the stool.

Jutaro continued his story without preamble. "Somebody brought me food a little while later. I tried to ask them what was going on, but they wouldn't tell me anything. Finally, after about four hours, a guy shows up and tells me to follow him. He leads me to an auditorium, a big one, the size of a small stadium. It had a big screen like a jumbotron hanging from the ceiling. I took a seat and waited. The place filled up in about half an hour, everybody asking each other if they knew where we were, why we were there, what was going on, did it have anything to do with the riots in Atlanta. Nobody knew anything, so we waited. Then they dim the lights and this face shows up on the jumbotron. I recognized him; it was the Secretary of Homeland Security."

Jutaro paused, going silent again. Impatiently, I asked, "What did he say?"

"He told us what was happening. The infected, the Outbreak, all of it. He told us the world was in deep shit."

"He actually said that?"

"I'm paraphrasing."

"Oh."

"Anyway, he says DHS agents would be meeting with us individually to help bring our families in. Warned us they could only take a few family members per person, no pets, so we should decide who our top priorities were. That fucked me up, man. Who should I save? Not a question you ever want to have to ask yourself. I told them about my parents, my wife, my daughter, my brothers. They said they could bring my wife and daughter, but that was it. I screamed at them, demanded they bring the rest of my family. One of them opened his jacket so I could see his taser and told me I should calm down. Said I could expect to see my wife and daughter in the next forty-eight hours. Until then, I was to remain in my quarters. They hooked a phone up to a wall outlet and told me if I needed anything, to pick it up and wait for someone to come on the line. Then they left."

"What happened next?"

Jutaro pointed at the computers. "I think I've earned that fourth shelf. What about the fifth?"

I sensed I was losing him, but I had been wrong before. "What about it?"

"I just don't see why any of this should be important to you. Nothing I'm telling you is worth what you're paying for it."

"You want that fifth shelf or not?"

"Fine. Ask away."

I thought for a moment, one hand idly scratching at my cheek. Jutaro was shutting down. I needed to loosen him up, rattle his cage a bit. I had hoped to shake out more information before reaching this point, but he was sharper than I expected. Time to show my trump card.

"It's hard to know what I should ask for next," I said. "Some of the things you've told me are the truth, and some are outright lies."

Jutaro sat up straight, eyes narrowing, posture aggressive. "Hey, fuck you, man. I've told you way more than I'm supposed to. You think I'm lying, I'll just take my shit right now and go."

"I don't *think* you're lying to me, Jutaro. I *know* you are. So stop with the theatrics. It's a good performance, but this ain't my first rodeo."

He glared for another moment, then burst out laughing. "Oh, man. You're good, Mr. Garrett. Really good. You almost had me going. Nice try. Seriously, though, ask your last question. I need those computers, and the day isn't getting any younger."

I went on as if he hadn't said anything. "When those agents put you on a plane, they didn't take you anywhere tropical. But the Outbreak started in April, so I'm guessing the part about it being warm was true. Nevada is pretty hot that time of year."

He froze, smile growing brittle, then vanishing. His mouth worked a few times, fractions of questions dropping to the floor. I stood up, moved within his personal space, and looked him in the eye. "And the training facility. Dahlgren Virginia. Right outside the Navy base. That's a long flight from San Francisco. Must have cost Uncle Sam a pretty penny."

"How did you…are you with the Initiative?"

"No. I'm just very good at what I do, Jutaro."

He began to recover a little. "And what is it you do, Gabe? I get the idea you're not just a simple shopkeeper."

"It's your wife and daughter, isn't it?"

No response. His mouth closed, eyes growing increasingly hostile.

"They're still there, aren't they? In the vault with the others. That's what they're holding over your head. If you don't finish this mission on time, what's going to happen to them?"

"What does it matter to you? Why do you care?"

"I have my reasons. Now, if you want those computers, and if you want to go with my crew on our next salvage run, you'll answer the question."

He threw his hands in the air, an exasperated hiss escaping his throat. "Yes! Yes, dammit, you're right. Okay? They have my wife and daughter. And if I don't finish this project on time, they'll be relocated to Colorado Springs."

"You say that like it's a bad thing."

"It's not, really, but they've gotten used to the vault. They like it there, it's safe. And if a war starts with the ROC, or the Alliance, they'll be protected. I can't let them get kicked out. I can't put them at risk like that."

"Folks here in Hollow Rock don't have that kind of protection. They get along just fine."

"Yes, but ask yourself this, Gabe. What about the people you care for the most? If you could move them somewhere safe, somewhere protected, where they could be happy, away from the undead, and marauders, and slavers, and war, and everything else in this fucked-up world, would you do it?"

I put my hands in my pockets and took a step back, gaze lowering. Jutaro closed the distance, reached out, and grabbed the front of my jacket. "Don't back down now, Gabe. Answer me. Would you do it?"

I looked up. "Yes. I would."

"Then you understand. You know why I'm working so hard. Why I'm sharing classified information with a man I barely know so I can get a few copper wires and have a shot at finding power lines and insulators. Because I will do anything, *anything,* to protect my family. They're all I have left and *will not* let anything happen to them. I will protect them, or I will die trying. That's why I'm here. That's what I'm working for. Are you happy now, Gabe? Is your curiosity satisfied? Can I have my computers now so I can go fix your goddamn power grid?"

I nodded wordlessly, feeling like the world's most thoroughly accomplished bastard. In my office, I opened a little safe and took out a notepad, a rubber mallet, a pen, and a unique hand-carved seal fashioned from a cylindrical piece of granite. I wrote a bill of sale on the pad, signed it, placed the stamp over the lower right hand corner, struck it with the mallet, removed the note, returned everything to the safe, and locked it. Back in the storeroom, I handed the slip to Jutaro. He snatched it from my hand and looked it over.

"I hope you don't expect me to thank you," he said.

"No, I don't."

He left without another word. I sat behind the counter for a few more hours, helped a few more customers, made a few more sales. At a quarter to four, after not seeing anyone for nearly half an hour, I closed the store and left.

On the way home, I watched the snow crunch under my boots and thought back to the last days of the Free Legion. I thought about General Phillip Jacobs, head of Army Special Operations Command, and my last meeting with him. I thought about the dossier he had shown me, the one marked as top secret. Not typical behavior for a high-ranking military officer, but I had done a great deal to earn his trust. Also, the dossier was twenty-six pages long, written in boring, mechanical military terminology. He had only let me look at it for a few minutes, five at the most. Probably thought I would scan the documents within, get a general idea of what I was looking at, and be duly impressed. After all, there was no way I could memorize a document so long and detailed in so short an amount of time, could I?

The thought put a smile on my face.

I often wondered how General Jacobs would react if he knew he had shown that dossier to a man with an eidetic memory. If he had, I doubt his attitude would have been quite so cavalier.

Truth be told, much of the information I pumped out of Ishimura was just to confirm things I already knew. Perhaps it is paranoia on my part, but it had occurred to me that maybe, just maybe, Jacobs was aware of my memory trick. Maybe he fed me bogus information to fool me into thinking I had won him over. Maybe the detailed information about the Phoenix Initiative contained in the dossier had been a smokescreen. He made it clear he wanted to recruit me back into the military, after all, and it was possible the dossier was just a ruse to win my trust. Dangle a little highly-classified information in front of me, pique my interest.

That particular doubt had been nagging me a lot lately, and the knowledge I could find out for sure one way or the other was what led me to turn the screws on Ishimura. It might have cost me a small fortune in computer equipment, but now I knew for sure Jacobs had been telling the truth. And in light of my conversation with Jutaro, I decided I had given the general too much credit.

He was not so clever as all that.

*****

Elizabeth was waiting for me when I got home. She smiled and stood up on the porch, arms outstretched.

"Come here."

I went. The arms were as warm and strong as ever, and so was the woman attached to them. Her fingers went to the back of my neck, toying with my close-cropped hair because she knew I liked it.

"I'm sorry I haven't been around," she said. "It's been busy at the office. This big junkman with pretty eyes brought a bunch of insurgents to town. Said they were leading a big horde of walkers. Had explosives and everything. Scared folks half to death."

"Sorry about that."

"Don't be. I'd rather they be scared than dead. Thank you."

"Least I could do."

She kissed me then, taking her time about it, hands in motion, hips pressing close against mine. It had been over a week since we had spent the night together, and we were both feeling pent up. I started walking her toward the front door, one hand fumbling for the keys in my pocket. She stepped backward, following my lead, urgent little noises breaking loose from her chest. I had just gotten the key in the door when, to my dismay, I heard the sound of tires crunching over gravel. Elizabeth heard it too, and stopped what she was doing to look over my shoulder. I turned around to see the sheriff's department's only working patrol vehicle—a blue Nissan Leaf with hand-painted decals—pulling into my driveway.

I could have chewed nails and spit out horseshoes.

It rolled to a stop a few feet from the porch, the electric engine nearly silent. Deputy Reid stepped out looking equal parts tense and sheepish. "Sorry to bother you, Mr. Garrett, but the sheriff sent me to find you."

The woman in my arms pushed gently away from me and stepped down from the porch. In the space of half a second, she transformed from Elizabeth, the warm, funny, passionate woman I was falling for, into Mayor Stone, the stalwart, confident, steely-eyed captain of the ship called Hollow Rock.

"What's the problem, Quentin?"

"You might want to come too, Mayor. We found a body."

"A body? As in a dead body?"

"Yes ma'am."

She shot me a questioning glance. I shrugged and held up my hands.

"Do we know who it is?" she asked.

"Sean Montford. He runs a pig farm outside the east wall, about two miles away."

Elizabeth's face drew tight, the worry and tension lines returning. "Dear God."

"You know him?" I asked.

She nodded. "He volunteers for the fall festival every year. He has a family, Gabe. Kids." Her attention shifted back to Deputy Reid. "What happened to him?"

Reid tried to speak, but nothing came out. He cleared his throat and tried again.

"It's bad, Mayor. Real bad."

*****

Deputy Reid was right.

164

It was bad.

The man who had once been Sean Montford, a mid-fifties pig farmer who had braved marauders, thieves, the Free Legion, and swarms of undead, who had protected his family and somehow kept his farm going despite incredible hardship, had been stripped naked and suspended from the stout branch of an oak tree, dangling by his ankles.

There was no question he had been tortured. Cuts, bruises, and horrific burns marred nearly every inch of his skin. His genitals were missing, as well as several of his fingers and toes. The deputies at the crime scene had done their best to locate them, without success. But as awful as it was, that wasn't the worst part.

The worst part was, despite being dead, Sean Montford was still moving.

"I'm sorry Sheriff. We can't find anything." Reid said, emerging from the treeline.

Walter nodded wearily, his tired eyes not moving from the still struggling Montford.

"Whoever did this must have taken them. Or maybe they killed him somewhere else and moved his body."

"Actually, I don't think it was either of those things," I said.

Walter tore his eyes away from the body and looked at me. "What do you mean?"

"Look at his mouth."

The sheriff stepped closer, eyes narrowing. He dropped to one knee, being careful to stay out of reach of Montford's flailing arms. I moved behind him and pointed. "His mouth is bloody. All his wounds were inflicted antemortem, meaning he had to have been restrained. I don't think he attacked anyone."

"Then where did the blood come from?"

"Look closer."

The sheriff reached into his jacket pocket and pulled out a pair of reading glasses. Tilting his head up to peer through them, he leaned in a bit farther. First came a sharp intake of breath, then the blood drained from his face, then he stood up, turned away, and ripped his glasses off, breathing heavily, hands trembling on his knees.

Sarah hurried over and clutched one of the old lawman's arms. "Sheriff, are you all right? What happened?"

"I'm fine, I'm fine. I just need a minute to breathe is all."

She turned to face me. "What is it Gabe? What did you see?"

I had to swallow a couple of times before I could say it. "There's a fingernail lodged in his teeth. I think it's his."

Reid took a few steps closer, brow knitted in confusion. "I don't understand. How would his fingernail get…" Realization dawned on his face. He ran to the edge of the clearing, hunched over, and was violently sick.

Sarah didn't look much better. "You mean they…they fed it to him? His…"

"Yes," I said. "I'm thinking they tortured him first, infected him somehow, and waited for him to turn. Then they fed him the parts they cut off."

Sarah made it a few steps farther than Reid before she lost it. Elizabeth was pale but composed. She turned away and walked to the gravel road, arms crossed tightly over her chest.

"Sheriff, I'm as sickened by this as you are," I said. "But I have to ask. Why am I here? I'm not a cop. Never was one. What do you need me for?"

He gathered himself with a few more deep breaths, stood up straight, reached into a pocket, and produced two pairs of rubber gloves. "Here, put these on and help me."

I didn't move. "Answer my question first."

"That's what I'm doing."

Confused, I did as he asked. We approached Montford's corpse together, the sheriff circling behind. "Do something about his arms for me, Gabe."

One side at a time, I caught his arms, applied a straight armbar, and broke them at the elbows. They dangled limply, the upper arms still flailing from the shoulders. It was hard to look at, but at least his hands were no longer a threat. Walter grabbed the legs and spun the body around. I understood immediately why they had sent for me.

On the dead farmer's back, carved deeply into the flesh, were four words:

GARRETT

DRAGONFLY

TWO GRAVES

I kept my expression neutral, allowing none of my reaction to show on my face. A cold feeling started in my stomach and spread outward into my arms, creeping up my chest. My pulse quickened, heart struggling under an onslaught of adrenalin, a classic fight-or-flight response. I did not move. I breathed slowly and evenly, willing my legs not to shake. My hands became tight fists in the pockets of my jacket.

I could not let them see. I could not give myself away, not here, not now. *Concentrate on your face,* I thought. *Control yourself. You know what to do.* Slowly, gradually, I knitted the eyebrows, pursed the lips, turned down the corners of my mouth. My pulse began to slow, leaving me feeling weak. But it allowed the tension in my shoulders to drain.

"Any idea what this means?" Walter asked.

I shook my head. My voice came out much steadier than I felt. "None whatsoever."

"You sure about that? Last I checked, your last name is Garrett. Looks to me like somebody's trying to send you a message."

I shrugged, hands concealed, still shaking my head. "I'm sorry, Walt. I don't know what this means."

"Is there anyone you can think of might have a grudge against you? Maybe someone from the Legion? A few of them escaped the fighting last year. Maybe they found out who you are and want revenge."

"That's a lot of maybes, Walt."

His eyes hardened. He stepped around Montford and squared off with me, voice growing in volume. "That's your name on his back," he said, pointing. "And a bunch of other nonsense that might not be nonsense. This man was murdered, Gabriel. He was tortured to death. He died scared and hurting, and whoever killed him desecrated his body. When I'm done here, I have to go tell his family what happened to him, and then I have to find out who's responsible. If you know anything, *anything* about who did this or why, you damn well better tell me right now."

I kept my voice calm and level. "Walt, I want you to listen to me, okay? I. Don't. Know. If I did, I would tell you. Did it occur to you that everyone in Hollow Rock knows who I am? Instead of looking at me, you should be looking at Montford. Find out if he had any enemies, anybody who owed him, or if he had any unpaid debts. Maybe whoever did this is trying to throw you off their trail. I think it's a little early in your investigation to be jumping to conclusions. Don't you?"

He stared hard, unconvinced. "You better not be lying to me, Gabe. Because if I find out you are, or if anyone else shows up dead with your name carved into their back, you and I are going to have a very long talk. And I *will* get the truth."

I stared back for a moment, then turned and walked away, shaking my head. The very picture of wounded indignation. "Deputy Reid, you mind giving the Mayor and me a ride back to town?"

He wiped his mouth and spit into the snow. "Be right there."

I stepped behind Elizabeth and wrapped my arms around her. She went rigid and gently pushed me away. "Not now, Gabe. Please."

"Sorry."

"It's not you, I just…"

"I understand. Come on, let's go home."

As Elizabeth climbed into the car, I cast a glance back over my shoulder at the sheriff. Sarah stood poised with her pocketknife in one hand, ready to cut the rope binding Montford's feet. Before she did, Walter drew his .357 and took aim. I saw his eyes close and his lips move in a brief prayer.

Forgive me, Lord, for what I'm about to do. I ask you to bless this poor man, and his family, and comfort them in their time of need. I ask you to forgive Sean Montford's soul for all his sins, and grant him peace and rest for all eternity. I ask you to help me find whoever did this, and bring them to justice, for the sake of all mercy and goodness left in this world. I ask you to lend me your strength that I might persevere, Lord, and I ask for your guidance on the path before me. Amen.

And then he pulled the trigger.

THIRTEEN

One the drive back to town, Elizabeth laid her head on my shoulder and clutched my hand.

I focused on staying calm, keeping my breathing steady, not letting my muscles tense. Waves of anger, guilt, sadness, and regret washed through me, burning me up inside. My teeth wanted to grind. My fists wanted to clench. A scream wanted to rip itself from my chest. And that old beast, that battle-urge, that red-stained, howling monstrosity, begged for release.

I wanted to let it go. To give in. But I couldn't. Not while Elizabeth was with me.

It wasn't easy, but I stayed relaxed. A warmth spread on my shoulder, soaked through my jacket, my shirt, into my skin. I closed my eyes and bent all my will to feeling that warmth, those tears of despair, of anguish. I put my arm around Elizabeth and drew her close, holding her tight. She sobbed gently, quietly, curled fists clutching me, clinging like a woman lost at sea, tossed in a storm. I held her, and stroked her hair, and did everything I could to fight the panic mounting within me.

As we passed through the gate, I had a sudden urge to confess. To tell her who had killed Sean Montford, and why. But the time for confessions had passed. Soon would be the time for action. Soon would be the time for retribution, and consequences.

The sheriff was right. Someone was sending me a message. They wanted to draw me out, flush me out of hiding. And they had chosen the perfect means to do so. I stared out the window at the passing countryside, feeling dread grow stronger by the second. The truth was obvious.

I had no choice.

I knew who hunted me, and he would not be denied.

*****

Eight years ago,

New York City

My control arranged the meeting in the bar at the Mercer Hotel.

He was fond of those kinds of clichés. Sometimes I wondered if they were his sole reason for joining the CIA, to live out some boyhood fantasy of being a character in a spy novel. It would not have surprised me in the least.

I took a seat next to him and ordered a drink. A ridiculously expensive drink poured by a stingy, condescending bartender. It never ceased to amaze me how much good money people spent on bad service. Not that I planned to pay for it out of pocket, mind you. Tolliver could put it on his government credit card.

"Nice work you did in Munich," Tolliver said, not bothering to look at me. "Eight sanctions, was it?"

"Nine. Our guy was dirty, just as you suspected. He's not a problem anymore."

"You're nothing if not reliable, my friend. Even if you are a jarhead."

"Spoken like a true squid, Lieutenant Commander. Now tell me, is there any special reason you made me come all the way to Manhattan? You know I hate this place. I'm assuming you have an office in DC. We couldn't just meet somewhere in Georgetown?"

"I have another job for you."

I put my drink down and looked at him. "That was quick."

"It's a dangerous world we live in, Mr. Garrett. Teeming with enemies foreign and domestic. Are you up to the challenge?"

"I'm here aren't I?"

"That's what I like about you. You have an excellent work ethic. Come on, let's retire to my office."

His office was a loft studio two floors up overlooking Prince Street, replete with the Mercer's famous high ceilings, spacious interior, and understated Christian Liaigre design, starting at a mere $975.00 a night. America's hard earned tax dollars at work.

I crossed the room to the large windows looking beyond the building's Romanesque façade to the bustling, brightly lit summer night beyond. On the street below, hordes of cabs jostled for supremacy among the waifish, high-heeled, Valentino and Louis Vuitton clutching socialites waving them down. Then there were the hipsters, the SoHo crowd, the not-so-fashionably-dressed artsy types with their insolent faces, and wise-to-the-world eyes, and their tremendous efforts to look as if they didn't give a damn about anything or anyone. A stark contrast to the carnivorous packs of Wall Street executives with their five-thousand dollar suits, impeccable grooming, and Ivy League class rings, out for a piece of moderately tipsy, elegantly fashioned tail. And surrounding these disparate factions, so much a part of the landscape they were barely noticed, were the homeless, the destitute, the people who lived in alleys and doorways and hidden places no one ever looked. The ones who couldn't make it in the big city but lacked the imagination or sanity to pack it up and try again someplace else.

On any corner you looked, mashed and melted together, stood these living embodiments of the pretense, extravagance, desperation, and pressure-cooker ferocity that comprised the beast called Manhattan. A land of tall buildings, taller egos, high art, high corruption, and some of the toughest, most hardnosed people you will ever meet. For a big heap of a country boy like myself, it was quite possibly the most unappealing of the great American cities. Then again, most New Yorkers probably thought Kentucky was pretty damned unappealing.

"I'm assuming the room is clean?" I asked.

Tolliver waved his hand toward a duffel bag on the bed. "It is, but I know you're going to check it again anyway. Knock yourself out."

I opened the kit and took out the necessary equipment. Starting with the camera detector, I swept every square inch of the room, taking my time and being careful about it. Nothing showed up in the viewfinder. Next, I switched on the bug detector and made another thorough sweep. It chirped near Tolliver's cell phone, but that was to be expected. The man was right. The room was clean.

"You're getting faster," Tolliver said. "That only took an hour."

"In our line of work, there is no such thing as too careful."

"Indeed. I've noticed you are a very careful man, Mr. Garrett. Now, if it's not too much trouble, could you sit down so we can cover the briefing?"

"Just a minute." I opened the minibar, took out two mini-bottles of 10 Cane rum and Coca-Cola, concocted a *Cuba Libré*, and took a seat at the table.

"Okay. Now I'm ready."

Behind his square-cut Armani glasses, Tolliver's eyes narrowed in irritation.

His hands went to his briefcase and began turning the combination dials. The briefcase looked ordinary, just a rectangular box encased in lustrous Italian leather, but that was where the normalcy ended. Rather than wood, the frame and casing were made of titanium, complete with a locking system impervious to nearly any breaching method short of a hydraulic press. And even if someone did somehow manage to pry it open, a small thermite bomb rigged in the housing would ignite, destroying the briefcase and the documents within, and causing grievous bodily injury to anyone standing within three feet. Just being near the thing was making me nervous.

Tolliver completed the unlocking process without incident, took out a manila file, and slid it across the table. I picked it up and read the stamp across the front.

"Operation Dragonfly. Very elegant. Who comes up with these code names, anyway?"

Tolliver took his glasses off and rubbed the bridge of his nose. "As usual, you're coming in at the tail end of a long investigation. Just read the file, please."

I opened the packet to the first page. Miguel Santiago Villalobos, age 48, currently residing in Guadalajara, Jalisco, Mexico, stared at me from a glossy photograph, the same photo I would find on his passport. There were other photos of him sitting, standing, walking, even a couple of shots from behind. Villalobos was short, maybe five-five, five-six at the most, bald, thick white mustache, slight paunch, the kind of middle-aged man you would walk right by on the street without noticing. But there was something in his eyes I didn't like. Something hidden. Something dark. Something that spoke of a casual indifference beyond the level of merely jaded, strongly into the territory of dispassionate. There was none of the usual light in his eyes, not like you see with normal people. His gaze was dead and blank and utterly without warmth. Like a shark's eyes.

I flipped through the rest of his file, memorizing the details. My memory trick is not automatic, it requires concentration, but I had honed the ability to a fine edge and could absorb written data much faster than most people can read. The key is to block out other input, let my eyes flow over the pages, and let the words etch themselves into my mind. Once registered, I could recall them at any time with precise clarity. A very useful skill to have in my line of work.

While most of the details of the investigation had been redacted, I gathered he was quite wealthy, born in a wealthy family, educated in California—Berkeley, specifically—and was the owner of Rezteca Holdings, a private equity firm headquartered in Guadalajara. He had inherited the business from his father, as he was the oldest of three sons.

I said, "I'm guessing Mr. Villalobos has been a bad boy."

Tolliver nodded. "You're not holding his file because he forgot to return a library book. He owns, among other things, several chains of hotels and car rentals. Quite a number of them, actually. All over Mexico. Charges exorbitant rates."

"Let me guess. Despite his exorbitant rates, his cars are always rented out, and all his hotels are constantly booked."

"Exactly. Typical money laundering scheme."

I put the file on the table and sipped my drink. "So which cartel is does he work for? And why don't they just buy him out? I'm guessing he gets a cut for his trouble. Why not eliminate the middle man?"

"That's a very good question. A question our analysts and investigators have been trying to answer for quite a while now. You see, the cartel pays him in cash for all the hotel rooms they never visit and the cars they never pick up, which is normal. Then he deposits the money in his accounts, puts it on the balance sheets as revenue, and tells the auditors, 'Hey, I don't discriminate. If someone wants to rent a room, I rent it to them. It's not my fault if they never show up.' Also normal. It's all done through his very modern and very thorough accounting systems, and unfortunately, it's all perfectly legal."

"So how does he funnel the money back to the cartel? And which one does he work for? You never said."

"*Las Sombras*. The shadows."

"I know what *las sombras* means."

"That's right. You speak Spanish, don't you?"

"Can we stay on topic?"

"Right. *Las Sombras* has been around a long time, mostly operating in the disputed territories southeast of Juarez. But now we suspect they've managed to muscle in on the Gulf Cartel's operations from Ciudad Acuña all the way to Nuevo Laredo. It seems they took a page out of the Gulf Cartel's own playbook and started hiring soldiers from elite military units. But in this case, it's not just Mexican special forces. They're hiring from all over the world. Their head of security is former SAS."

I whistled, shaking my head. "Sounds like the fucking Zetas all over again."

"Worse. They already own the police departments in their territory, and half the people living there either work for them, or know someone who does. They have eyes everywhere. Nobody gets in or out of their dominion without their knowledge. And they have zero patience for the other cartels operating nearby. There have already been more than a dozen beheadings. The videos were posted to Youtube."

"They sound lovely. How does Villalobos tie in to all this?"

"The money from the hotel and rental car operations goes to bank accounts in the name of Rezteca holdings, then it gets filtered through a dizzying array of subsidiaries to offshore accounts in the Cayman Islands. When we started digging through those accounts and the various businesses to which they were registered, we made a few enlightening discoveries."

I grinned and shook my finger at him. "Our guys hacked his account information, didn't they? Impressive. Those Cayman banks don't mess around when it comes to network security. Must have recruited some new talent down there at Langley."

Tolliver winked. "Need to know, Gabriel. Need to know."

"Right. You were saying?"

"The accounts in the Caymans are not solely held by Rezteca and its subsidiaries. There is another company listed on them. The Smith Group."

"And they are?"

"Ghosts. Ink and paper, nothing more. The Smith Group is a shell company owned by a vast array of other shell companies, all of them with Swiss bank accounts. It took years for our forensic accountants to track them all down, but when they did, they noticed a startling fact. Miguel Villalobos' name, or one of his many aliases, is on all of the paperwork. He's a control person on all the corporate charters, a principle in all the partnerships, a majority shareholder for all the publicly traded companies. He has his fingers in everything."

I sat back in my chair and let the weight of what Tolliver was saying sink in. "So he doesn't just *work* for Las Sombras, does he?"

Tolliver smiled, his teeth like fangs in the dim light. "No, he doesn't. Miguel Villalobos *is* Las Sombras. And he's coming here."

"To New York?"

"To the Waldorf Astoria, specifically. A three-day investor conference, hosted by Citadel out of Chicago. Heard of them?"

"Big hedge fund, right? Celebrity manager, always on CNBC?"

"That's the one. They're looking for new clients. Doesn't happen very often. The conference is invitation only."

"I'm assuming I'm invited?"

"Citadel has been most cooperative."

"How much do they know?"

"Only that a piece of favorable legislation is getting ready to expire, and if they allow a certain influential US senator's nephew and two of his associates to attend the conference, they can expect his vote, and those of his party, when the bill comes up for renewal."

"Sounds like a good cover. Except for the part about the two associates."

Tolliver sighed and rubbed his forehead, his tone hardening. "You will be working with a team on this one, Gabriel. It is not optional, nor is it open to discussion."

"Tolliver..."

"I know you prefer to work alone but this is a big one. We need this guy alive. He's not coming here without protection. He's not that stupid. A man like him has more enemies than he can count. He'll have his own security detail, and with his kind of money, you'll be facing a small army. A well-armed and highly-motivated army, comprised of at least a few special operations types. You're going to need help with this one."

I tossed back the rest of my drink, glared at Tolliver, and set it down hard. "Fine. But they better not be rookies, or I'm walking."

"Both are experienced and highly trained, just like you. In fact, you already know one of them."

"Who?"

"Anthony Rocco, formerly of the United States Marine Corps. I believe you two worked together in Fallujah, did you not?"

"We did. He's the one who got me this job."

"Excellent. Then I should expect this operation to go smoothly, right?"

I got up and started mixing another drink. "Don't ever say that, Tolliver. It's bad luck."

FOURTEEN

Deputy Reid kept his eyes straight ahead on the drive back to town.

There was no doubt he knew the mayor of Hollow Rock was weeping in the seat behind him. But to his credit, he didn't say a word. Not a backward glance, or even a look up into the rearview mirror. He stayed quiet and drove, once having to swerve around a walker that wandered out into the road. The young deputy may have been green, but he was not stupid.

Elizabeth got it together before we reached the gate, though her eyes were still puffy and red around the edges. After the usual inspections, Reid drove us to my house and pulled into the driveway.

"Do you mind if I stay a while?" Elizabeth said, reaching for my hand.

I said I didn't, but it was a lie. Montford's killer was still out there, and it was only a matter of time before another body showed up, or worse. The sooner I picked up his trail, the better. But to do that, I needed to outfit myself with the proper weapons and equipment, and then I needed to get back to the crime scene. It would be dark soon, and I sincerely doubted the sheriff would risk having his deputies out after nightfall. Or so I hoped, anyway.

I unlocked the door and held it open for Elizabeth. She walked inside, took off her boots, and lay down on the couch. The house was cold, with that brittle, hollow quality a room acquires when it has been empty for too long. The walls a little too close, echoes a little too loud.

There was a quilt in the coat closet, so I took it out and draped it over Elizabeth, careful to tuck it in around her feet. When I was finished, I leaned down and kissed her on the cheek, brushing her hair out of her face. A pair of dark, sad eyes opened as she reached up to me, fingers trailing across my jaw, thumb tracing over my lips. I knelt beside the couch and held her gaze, smiling, feeling a warm tightness in my chest.

There were narrow little crow's feet at the corners of her eyes, hairline fractures in the skin surrounding her mouth, thin creases along the borderland between her graceful jaw and strong, slender neck. It struck me as strange how, as a younger man, I found those small, superficial wrinkles unattractive. But now that I was older, I could not imagine being with a woman without them. They made a statement. They told me this woman had lived a while, and she knew things. That she had laughed, loved, made mistakes, succeeded, failed, and mourned. That she had known pleasure, and pain, and sacrifice, and indulgence, and all the thousand other things that add richness and texture to a life. Those little lines were perfect in their imperfection, beautiful in their unloveliness. They were the marks of a life lived with courage and grace through loss and hardship. They said this woman was no sheltered youngling with shallow concerns and an empty heart. This woman had depth, and sensibility, and strength of character, and if she cared about me, if I was lucky enough to have her in my life, then I was very fortunate indeed.

"You take such good care of me," she said.

I kissed her again, on the lips this time. "You earn it, lady. Every day."

I left her lying there and went into the kitchen to check the stove. A few embers still remained, glowing deep orange against the dark soot-stained metal. The addition of a few twigs and a little encouragement from the bellows sprang a new fire to life. I kept adding wood until it was a proper conflagration, then stacked larger logs around it. It wouldn't warm the house very much, but it was better than nothing.

The woodpile was low, so I replenished it from the shed out back, and then returned to the living room. Elizabeth's breathing had slowed, and she had wedged a throw pillow under her head. I touched her shoulder, eliciting a startled jerk.

"Sorry. Were you asleep?"

"Almost. I'm exhausted, Gabe. I have a hell of a day ahead of me tomorrow. Do you mind if I just rest for a while?"

"Not at all. You should move to the bed, though. You know how your back gets when you sleep on the couch."

She let out a weary sigh. "Yeah. You're right."

I followed her to the bedroom, tucked the blanket around her, gave her another kiss, and told her I might be gone a while. She mumbled a sleepy acknowledgment and rolled over, pulling the comforter tight around her shoulders.

I stood and watched her for a long moment, a little voice in my head telling me what a bastard I was. That instead of blood, I had the distilled essence of son-of-a-bitch running through my veins. That I was a miserable liar, and I didn't deserve a good woman like Elizabeth at my side.

I told that voice if there was one thing I was good at, it was keeping secrets. If things went smoothly, I would be back before morning. Maybe even before she woke up. If she questioned me, I would come up with some kind of excuse. Tell her I couldn't sleep and had spent the night double-checking the inventory logs at the warehouse. Something like that. As busy as she would be tomorrow, I doubted she would make much of a fuss. She would never be the wiser.

Assuming I didn't get hurt, of course. Or killed.

There was a moment of doubt. The nagging little voice grew louder, more insistent, raging at me to wake her up and confess, confess, confess. But I didn't. Because a man has a right to his secrets, and his shame. Because I was going to end this quickly and quietly, and there was no reason for Elizabeth to know what I was about to do. It was my problem and no one else's.

Such was my justification. Such was my stupidity.

I should have known better.

*****

When I bought the warehouse, back when it was still an auto repair facility, it boasted two offices.

One of them was fairly small. Just a desk, chair, a few shelves, and space for customers to sit down. I left it as it was. The other, much larger one—where all the paperwork, money, and an assortment of used auto parts were kept—I modified.

First, I cleaned it out and built the appropriate shelving and racks. Then I scavenged a heavy steel security door from the back of an abandoned restaurant and installed it in place of its flimsy aluminum predecessor. Next came the thick steel bar, held in place by metal brackets mounted to the concrete wall and secured with a massive padlock. I also set a couple of traps in the room that only Eric and I knew about. Entry into the room required two keys, which only Eric and I possessed, and knowledge of how to bypass the traps.

The first trap was simple. A string stretched from the door, to a pulley, to the trigger of a double-barreled shotgun. The shotgun was loaded with double-ought buckshot and mounted on a low table. Open the door too fast, and the shotgun goes off at about kneecap level. The perpetrator screams, cries, and bleeds until someone happens along and hears them. Then, assuming they survive their injuries, it's off to jail. Unless, of course, no one ever hears them. In that case, they bleed to death.

The other trap was a bit more complex, but no less diabolical. It involved sharpened railroad spikes, two-by-fours, leaf springs from a tractor-trailer, and a pressure plate hidden in the floor. Step on the plate without disarming the trap, and two concealed, spike-laden, spring-tensioned boards swing down from the roof to perforate the offending trespasser. To disarm it, one simply lifts the doormat and turns a lever to the proper position. When leaving, reverse the process, and the trap is re-armed. Simple, but deadly effective.

I should mention here that Hollow Rock has very strict rules about theft. To put it mildly, Sheriff Elliott has no patience for thieves and does not abide their presence in this town. As far as the law is concerned, if a thief is injured or killed in the commission of a crime, it is the thief's fault for creating the situation in the first place. Citizens have a right to protect their property by any reasonable means, up to and including the use of deadly force. Provided they post the necessary no trespassing signs, of course.

It does not pay to steal in Hollow Rock.

I unlocked the two locks, opened the door slowly, removed the shotgun string, set the lever to the safe position, and locked the door behind me. Taking out my flashlight, I shined it around the pitch-black room until I located an emergency lantern. Two minutes of winding the handle charged it, illuminating racks of weapons and equipment along the walls.

Since the defeat of Free Legion and subsequent re-opening of nearby trade routes, travelling caravans now stopped regularly in Hollow Rock. I traded with them extensively, usually for items to sell in the general store such as clothes, ammunition, soap, candles, vinegar, booze, that sort of thing. But I also let it be known that I was a collector of firearms, and would pay good prices for quality weaponry. Consequently, through the course of trade and by merit of my own explorations, I had amassed a rather impressive private arsenal.

The first thing I needed was NVGs and a good scope. The sun was down, and night would be falling quickly. Without night vision equipment, I would never pick up the killer's trail. There were several to choose from, but for this task, only the very best would do. The model I chose had been loaned to me by the Army the previous year for use on a rescue mission. After the mission, the officer who issued them to me, Captain Steven McCray, had died in the fighting. I held on to them, figuring someone would ask me to return them sooner or later. But no one ever did. And considering the NVGs and accompanying scope were the most advanced models ever built, capable of both night vision and thermal imaging with adjustability between the two, I wasn't about bring it up.

Next was weapons. I chose a suppressor-equipped LWRCI M-6 chambered in hard-hitting 6.8 SPC as my primary weapon, along with six full magazines. 6.8 SPC is extremely difficult ammo to find, and I only use it in dire emergencies. My current predicament qualified.

For a secondary firearm, I chose a venerable Beretta M-9, also suppressor equipped, and four spare magazines. I would have preferred my Sig, but .45 ACP ammo was in short supply. Nine-millimeter didn't have the same stopping power, but it was good enough to get the job done.

Next was my backup piece. Snub-nosed .357 Ruger revolver. Laser sight built into the grip. Paddle holster. No spare ammo. I figured if I had to use it, it meant I had burned through all the mags for the M-6 and the Beretta, and I was probably fucked anyway.

Last was blades and body armor. Primary blade: Iberian falcata. Secondary blade: Ka-bar combat dagger. Also a little Spyderco folding knife, just in case.

And for the grand finale, body armor. Dragon Skin. The best there is. Bought from a starving mercenary for the low, low price of a week's worth of food and five-hundred rounds of 5.56mm ammunition. Deal of the century.

I cleaned the weapons, checked them for functionality, outfitted a MOLLE vest with mag carriers and pouches, and donned the body armor. Last, I smeared Army issue face paint on all exposed skin, grabbed a rappelling harness, ghillie suit, and a length of nylon rope, and tied on a black headscarf. After a quick glance in the mirror, I reset the traps, locked the door, and headed out.

*****

The streets were empty when I left the warehouse. Night had fallen, and the icy wind had driven the townsfolk to their shuttered homes and the fireplaces within. Orange candlelight shone through windows, myriad beacons of hope and safety in the frigid darkness. The welcoming scent of wood smoke hung thick in the air, putting me in mind of hot food, comfort, good company, and a pretty brown-eyed woman with a heart-stopping smile, soft skin under a thick blanket, and the warmth of her body next to mine on a cold night.

The urge to go home and explain why I lied grew strong again, hammering at the inside of my skull, demanding to be acknowledged. It didn't have to be this way. I could apologize to the sheriff. I could ask for help.

But then would come the questions. The judgment. The hostile eyes. The whispers. It had happened before, after I left the Marines. There had been a neighborhood barbeque, and my ex-wife, and too many beers, and a drunken conversation with another veteran. I could only talk about the war when I was drunk, and only to someone who had been there. It felt good to talk about it then, to commiserate with someone who understood what it was like. The sand, the firefights, the fear, the heat, the constant worry that the person on a cell phone across the street was calling your location in to insurgents. Because all too often, that was exactly what they were doing.

We were loud. At first, the stories we told were the good-natured, funny kind. Stupid things people did in boot camp, drunken nights in dive bars, bare-knuckle brawls with squids on the waterfront. The usual bullshitting. But as we drank more and more, the stories grew darker and more violent. The times when we almost bought it, when we entered buildings on our feet and came out on a stretcher, when IEDs damn near blew us to kingdom come.

A man came over and suggested we shouldn't talk about those sorts of things in polite company. There were children around, after all. I threw a beer can at his head and told him to go fuck himself. He was just another useless civilian anyway. What the hell did he know about sacrifice? About pain? About watching your brothers get shot up and blown to pieces? Why don't you go hide under your momma's skirt, you fucking little cunt. You're not even a man, you're just a piece of shit. You need to keep your goddamn mouth shut when grownups are talking. I'll snap you over my knee like a fucking twig. Who the hell do you think you're talking to?

And then my wife's hand on my chest, her angry words in my ear, the wide-eyed looks of shock from my neighbors. People who lived beside me, who had to share a neighborhood with a murderer. A monster.

The smiles were always forced after that. The handshakes trembling and reluctant, even after I made the rounds and apologized. The man I insulted said it was no big deal, that he was sorry for provoking me. He was sweating profusely when he said it.

It was sixty degrees that day.

They teach you how to turn it on. To reach deep down and find the anger, the hatred, the fear. They teach you how to shape it, to use it, to turn it into something else. You learn your lessons well, they make sure of that. What they don't teach you is how to turn it off. How to make the nightmares stop. How to live when you are dead inside and only ashes remain where your heart used to be, burned up by all that anger and fear. And by the time you realize what has happened to you, it's too late. There is nothing left.

I heard that sad, angry voice again. Saw the disappointment in Karen's eyes. Felt the hangover pounding in my head on that hot summer day. The despair. The hopelessness.

You are what you are, Gabriel. And you always will be.

The door shutting, punctuating my failure as a husband. Then the drive back to my hotel, and the stop at the liquor store along the way. The whore across the street who marked me in an instant. The knock on the door after she had given me enough time to get good and roaring drunk. The money I gave her, and the shame the next morning when I realized what I had done. And that was just the tip of the iceberg. Then came the months of-

STOP IT.

Enough.

The less Elizabeth knew about my past, the better. This was my chance to start over, to build a new life for myself. And I was not about to let long-ago sins tear it apart. Not here, not now, not this time.

I closed my eyes, took a few deep breaths, and pushed against that shrill voice. I drove it far, far down, where its shouting was just a dim, unintelligible faintness in the distance. There was no turning back.

I had a job to do.

Time to get it done.

*****

My first obstacle was getting over the wall undetected.

Armed and armored as I was, I couldn't simply leave town through the main gate. My goal was to find Montford's killer, deal with him, and get back without attracting any unwanted attention. A dozen guards watching me leave town after nightfall while sporting full battle regalia was not the way to accomplish that.

There was an angled junction near the corner of Highway 70 and Dodd St. where the distance between guard towers was greater than anywhere else along the wall. Once the guards patrolling there crossed paths, they would turn around and walk back to their respective towers. The brief period when they would have their backs to each other would be my window.

The guards converged, exchanged an all-clear signal, and began walking the other way. When they had gone far enough, I emerged from cover and sprinted to the wall.

The inside edge of the perimeter boasts a six-foot trench, ostensibly to trap walkers if they somehow make it over. It provided perfect cover while I waited for the guards to make another pass. Beyond the wall, drifting over the spiked tree trunks and telephone poles that separate Hollow Rock from the rest of the world, I heard the distinctive moaning of infected.

A lot of them.

Not good.

Minutes ticked slowly by. Eventually, the guards' footsteps drew close again, louder and louder until they were directly overhead.

"Cold one tonight," one of them said.

"Damn right. Wish I'd have worn an extra pair of socks. My feet are like ice. How's things lookin' on your end?"

"Lots of walkers out there. Must be from that horde over in McKenzie. You hear about what happened there?"

"Yeah, a little bit. Somebody at Stall's place said Garrett's crew ran into some insurgents."

"Yep, that's what I heard too. Somebody told me they killed a few of them and took the rest prisoner. Not sure if that's true or not."

"Wouldn't surprise me none. Not after what happened with those Free Legion assholes."

Shuffling feet. Deep, weary breaths. The conversation had lulled, and both men were probably looking out over the field, not making eye contact, waiting for one of them to end the awkward silence.

"Well, I better get back to it. Shift's over in an hour, thank God."

"Lucky you. I still got three to go."

"All right then. Keep your eyes peeled."

"Will do. You do the same."

Footsteps again, growing fainter and fainter.

As they walked away, I tied a large monkey's-fist knot into the end of the rope and swung it a few times to test its weight. The idea was to wedge the knot between two of the wooden support struts above me and hope it didn't slip while I was climbing. A grappling hook would have been better, but it would have made too much noise. I needed to do this quietly.

Coiling the rope in one hand, I swung the knotted end upward, aiming for the bracing joists. I missed the gap on the first try, but got it on the second, tugging hard to make sure the knot was stuck fast. Satisfied it was, I went up arm over arm, quick and quiet, relying solely on brute strength. At the top, I transitioned from the rope to a support beam, hooked my legs over it, and let go, hanging upside down. With my hands freed, I pulled the knot loose and rewound the rope.

Waiting for the guards to make another pass was no fun at all. The boards dug painfully into my legs, pressure built in my head from the blood pooling in it, and although I had cinched my gear down tightly in anticipation of this moment, I kept expecting to see something come loose and fall noisily to the ground. Thankfully, it didn't happen.

The distant footsteps once again grew closer until they were right over me. The two guards exchanged another round of bored pleasantries before turning and walking away. I waited until the clomping of work boots on wooden planks faded, probably a few seconds beyond what was necessary, and then moved.

Hanging sit-ups have long been a part of my exercise routine, and all the endless, sweating repetitions served me well as I leaned up, gripped the board I dangled from, and swung my legs to the support post. Gripping it tightly, I moved my hands to a support strut, then another, and then to the edge of the catwalk. Pulling myself up, I checked both ways to make sure no one was looking. Both guards were still walking away, backs turned. I swung a leg onto the walkway, levered up, and rolled onto my back.

Standing up, I unslung the rope and looped one end around the post beneath the handrail. The boards were tough and sturdy, hand-cut from local hardwoods. Even as heavy as I am, I knew they weren't going anywhere. Next, I threaded the unknotted end of the rope through a figure-8 loop on the front of my rapelling harness and tied a quick slipknot, which I clipped to a carabiner on the back. The other end, I tossed over the wall. I didn't bother to check if anyone was looking. It was too late to turn back at that point, so I stayed focused on what I was doing.

Keeping the rope taut in my hands, I stepped up onto the angled space between sharpened logs and leaned forward, letting the line pay out slowly. When my weight was balanced slightly below my feet, I started running face-first toward the ground. It took four steps to reach the bottom. Once there, I disconnected the rope from the carabiner, pulled it hand over hand until the other end fell to the ground, quickly rewound it, and looped it over my shoulder.

Now I needed to get away from the wall, and quickly. The night was dark and cloudy, but the guards had powerful LED flashlights. If they heard me, the game was up.

After donning my NVGs and putting them on their thermal imaging setting, I set off across the spike-strewn trench surrounding the wall. On the other side, through the washed-out black and gray of the FLIR imager, I saw dozens of walkers that had wandered too close to the trench, fallen in, and impaled themselves on thick stakes. Some of them were face-down, some backwards, others lying on their sides, wicked spear points protruding through their ribcages. One had somehow managed to land ass-first, the stake running upward through its torso and jutting grotesquely from its mouth. It reached for me with a withered hand as I passed it by.

It was times like these I hated my perfect memory.

Others had missed the stakes altogether and shambled aimlessly in the bottom of the trench. They would be easy pickings for the extermination crew in the morning, but right now, they were in my way. Problem was, I couldn't kill them. If the morning crew found the dead bodies, it would send up red flags. For now, I had to go hand-to-hand. Never a pleasant prospect where the undead are concerned.

That's why God gave us boots and hard-knuckled Kevlar gloves. You're strong. You're in good shape. You can handle it. Now get moving.

I stretched my neck and shoulders, took a deep breath, and started running.

FIFTEEN

Only three walkers got close enough to be a threat.

The first was a little guy, so I leapt into a flying kick that sent him tumbling ten feet away. When you put two-hundred and fifty pounds of Marine behind a kick, it generates a lot of force. Especially if said force is concentrated in a striking surface the size of a boot.

The second one was big, almost as big as I am. The last thing I could afford was to let it get its hands on me. With the kind of strength it possessed, I would never be able to pry it loose without killing it. I ran to within four feet of it, checked my sprint, rolled to the side, and popped up behind it. A quick stomp to the side of its knee buckled its leg ninety degrees the wrong way. I dodged its flailing arms and kept moving.

The last ghoul was another small one, still recognizable as female, about Allison's size. Oddly, it was dressed in a military flight suit. A reverse heel kick spun it around and dropped it on its face. While it was down, I grabbed it by the neck and waist, lifted it up, and tossed it onto a nearby stake. It landed face up with the stake piercing its abdomen and slid down, streaking the stake with gore until it lay flat on the ground, struggling like a bug on an entomologist's pin board. The urge to put it out of its misery was strong, but I resisted. I had more important things to do.

After climbing the berm at the edge of the trench, I paused a moment, crouching low, assessing my route. There were roughly a hundred yards of flat, empty field between me and the forest. Scattered across it were the cold outlines of hundreds of infected, some of them in clusters, some of them spaced far apart. My best bet was to dodge the knots of mini-hordes, move quickly, and kick down the ones I could not avoid.

I had been concerned about leaving footprints in the snow, but it looked like I need not have worried. They would be indistinguishable amongst the innumerable tracks of the undead. Probably the first time in history a walker actually served a useful purpose. However, the problem with having lots of ghouls around to cover my tracks was that there were lots of ghouls around to cover my tracks. Worse, they had all heard me and were closing in.

One of the strangest things about ghouls is how differently they act at night. They are more active, more relentless, and make almost no sound until they are right on top of you. Many of them have their throats ripped out, making them especially deadly in the dark. Despite my extensive experience fighting them, and everything I learned as an operative at Aegis, I have no idea what causes this. What I do know is that unless you have a death wish, it is never a good idea to travel at night. But that was exactly what I had to do.

You won't win by counting all the ways you can lose. You've been here before. You know what to do. Now do it.

Looking behind me, I saw the guards had left their towers and were on their way back to the rendezvous point. Soon, they would be close enough to hear me. I could not let that happen. Time to move.

Thirty yards went by without incident. I skirted around a cluster of ten or fifteen undead, increasing my pace to maintain distance. Once around them, I passed one I had not seen, a very little one, just a toddler before it turned. It was close enough to lunge for me, its baby face twisted with mindless hunger, fingers curled into obscene little claws. Without breaking stride, I booted it the chest and sent it flipping through the air.

After dodging two more clusters, I sidestepped a pair of reaching hands and made it another forty yards before I had to fight again. There was a line of ghouls walking side by side as if in a skirmish line, separated from each other by less than ten feet. Going around them would cost me time I couldn't afford and force me to fight more infected. Not an appealing prospect. Better just to go right through them.

Aiming for the widest gap, I leapt into the air and hit the ghoul in front of me with my best flying punch. The hard plastic shell over my knuckles absorbed the brunt of the blow, saving me from a broken hand. The ghoul's sinus cavity collapsed with a sickening crunch as it fell backward. I tried to run over it, but my right foot caught its armpit and I went sprawling in the snow. Recovering quickly, I pushed myself up, kicked the ghoul's hands away, and kept running.

Finally, I reached the treeline. But there was no solace there, just more ghouls. My breath was coming in short, hitching gasps. My legs were weak from spent adrenalin. I had no time to rest, not with so many of them nearby. The ghouls had heard me, and they were coming.

Slow down, you big dummy. It's cold. They're sluggish. No need to wear yourself out. Use your head for something other than growing hair. You see all those trees? You see all those branches? You see how awkward and clumsy the infected are? You have a sword, right? Do the math.

Right. Branches.

I found a good one, a sapling. A quick swipe from my falcata felled it, and a few more chops trimmed it down until it was a seven-foot pole with Y-shaped branches at the end. Perfect for knocking down half-frozen walkers.

Referencing the map in my head, I turned northeast toward the highway. At a hard pace, I could reach it in less than half an hour. Once there, I simply had to outrun the infected and follow the road to the scene of Montford's murder. Then the real work would begin.

I made it exactly two steps before I heard a branch snap to my right. Turning, I saw a ghoul less than five feet away. Medium build, long dead, skin shredded, huge gouges of flesh missing from its chest and abdomen, throat torn out. No wonder it was so quiet. I braced my feet, aimed the sapling at its throat, and took two running steps. The branch hit it just below the jaw and shoved it backward, arms reaching for me as it fell. When it was down, I stomped on its ankle and heard a satisfying crunch. *That'll slow you down.*

Looking around, the next closest ghoul was ten feet away and closing. The plunging temperature had slowed its shuffling gait to a halting shamble, barely a mile an hour. I could outrun it crawling on my knees.

"Okay. Easy part's done. Now for the hard part."

I headed for the highway.

*****

As the pavement became visible ahead, it occurred to me that if Montford's murderer wanted to set a trap for me, the road to the crime scene was a good place to do it. I stopped and debated what to do next.

Sun Tzu once wrote that if you know your enemy and know yourself, you need not fear the result of a hundred battles. I knew my enemy, and I certainly knew myself. Problem was, my enemy had the same advantage. There was no doubt what lay ahead of me.

I was walking into a trap.

But I had no other way to track him down, and he knew it. He knew I would have to actually go to the scene and look around. That I would search for his trail in the darkness, and when I found it, I would follow it. Doing so would make me vulnerable, open to attack. He knew what kind of a marksman I am, and he would be taking no chances.

Sun Tzu also wrote that the mark of a great soldier is that he fights on his own terms, or he fights not at all. So how could I put this fight on my terms and not his?

You're a sniper. A sniper is a hunter of men. Don't let yourself be the hunted. Be the hunter.

Closing my eyes, I called up everything I could remember about the crime scene. Before leaving it earlier in the day, I had given the scene and the surrounding landscape a thorough scan, committing it all to memory. I knew I would be coming back, and I wanted to know the terrain when I did.

I played the events back, searching for something that could help me. There was the tree, and Montford's reanimated corpse hanging from it. No help there. Then there was the surrounding forest, bare branches stretching like skeletal fingers against the darkening sky. Not a good place to hide. Too easy to spot me there. I turned, gazing over the horizon, taking in the details.

There.

On a low hill, maybe half a mile away, the top of a grain silo cresting over the blanket of trees. Too far away for my rifle to be of any use, but not too far for my scope. I couldn't reach out and touch him, but I could sure as hell look for him.

It was a place to start.

*****

The pole broke halfway to the grain silo. As far from town as I was, I didn't see any harm in switching to my falcata.

The walkers were everywhere, hundreds of them. It looked as though the McKenzie horde had followed their noses to Hollow Rock, but dispersed over a wide area along the way. My blade was slick with gore by the time I reached the farm.

From a distance, the silos were the only distinguishable feature in the landscape. But as I got closer, I saw there were several large mounds of snow swelling upward from the surrounding flatness. I walked to the nearest mound and kicked the snow aside, revealing a rusted-out 1978 Ford pickup truck, tires flat, windows shattered, halfway collapsed to the ground. By next year, the only thing left standing would be the engine block. Eventually, even that would sink into the spongy earth.

The other mounds turned out to be a few pieces of farming machinery and the burned out remains of a house and barn. There was something familiar about the place, like I had been there before. Referencing the map in my head, I followed the highway lines and realized I was standing on the old Leary place. It brought to mind a story I heard not long after arriving in Hollow Rock about the people who had lived here, and what happened to them.

Seamus Leary had been a farmer. Old Irish stock, hard worker, God fearing, polite and respectful, avoided the devil's drink, generally well liked by everyone who knew him. Then the loosely-knit band of raiders that would eventually form the Free Legion came and murdered him, burned down his farm, destroyed his crops, killed his livestock, and kidnapped his wife and daughter. All because he refused to let them hide stolen loot in his barn.

The daughter survived the ordeal. She was one of the sex slaves Eric and I helped rescue last year. But her mother wasn't so lucky. They raped her so badly she started hemorrhaging internally and got an infection. When it was clear there was no saving her, the raiders shot her and left her body for the infected. They made the daughter and the other slaves watch, a lesson to them should they ever entertain delusions of trying to escape.

The Free Legion. May they burn in hell.

I shook the dark thoughts out of my head and proceeded to the grain silo. The ladder was rusty, but sturdy. I gave it a few shakes just to be sure and got a faceful of snow for my efforts. At least the ladder was stable.

After taking a few moments to clean the blood and ichor from my sword, I climbed the ladder to the top. The silo was about a hundred-thirty feet tall, offering a good view of the countryside. I looked for a place to set up, but the roof slanted toward the center at a steep angle with no flat spots to lie down. Not wanting to risk sliding off, I sat on the narrow catwalk and propped my rifle on the handrail.

The FLIR imager on the M-6's upper rail worked in conjunction with an adjustable Nightforce scope mounted behind it. I switched on the imager and peered through the scope's illuminated digital reticle. It was set at 10x magnification, but could go as high as 25x. If I were intent on doing murder, I would leave it at the 10x setting. But with the crime scene being over eight-hundred yards away, and my rifle's max effective range at about three-hundred fifty yards, I wasn't killing anything. Not yet, at least. This part was strictly recon.

My first problem was locating the crime scene in pitch darkness from half a mile away. That was where the FLIR device came in. After taking a quick compass reading, I peered through the magnified white, black, and gray image and scanned the forest below until I located the highway. At this distance, it was just a thin ribbon of smudgy white cutting through the undulating carpet of woodland. Increasing the magnification from 10x to 20x, I followed the sliver of road until I spotted the large, unmistakable outline of the massive oak tree Montford's body had been suspended from. Around it, suspended above the snow and just barely visible, was a square of thin white lines.

The fuck is that?

I cranked the magnification up to its maximum setting and looked again. The lines of the square stood out as clear, brilliant filaments about fifty yards on each side around the big oak tree. I had an idea what it might be and followed one of the lines to its source.

Low to the ground, just a few inches above the snow, was a bundle of exposed scrub and vegetation. Most people wouldn't look at it twice, but I wasn't most people. I knew that bundle of crud didn't belong there. If it had grown there naturally, it would be just as covered with snow as everything else. No, someone had placed it there deliberately.

I followed the rest of the lines and found three more such bundles, carefully arranged to avoid detection. I examined the lines again, and realized they weren't filaments, or string, or tripwires. They were far too straight, far too precise. There is only one thing that fires a straight line with that kind of precision.

Infrared sensors.

So that was how he planned to catch me, the sneaky bastard. This spoke to a level of planning and resources I had not anticipated. But for all his guile, he had not factored in the possibility I might have access to FLIR technology. That I might see the trap and be able to bypass it.

Quite often, when two evenly matched opponents engage in combat, victory and defeat hinges upon who makes the first mistake. And Montford's killer had screwed up right out of the gate by committing the unforgivable sin of assumption. Of underestimating his opponent's capabilities. Of saying to himself, *there's no way he'll have thermals. They're too rare, too expensive. The Army only gives those things to special ops guys. Garrett is a civilian. The best he can probably do is night vision. But even that would be a long shot.*

Wrong answer, buddy. I'm nothing if not resourceful. You should have known better.

Now that I had the initiative, the question became how best to use it to my advantage. In order to do any damage at all, I still had to figure out where my attacker was hiding. How far away was he? How did he plan to kill me?

Did he plan to kill me?

Maybe he wanted me alive. Maybe he planned to give me some of the same treatment he had given Sean Montford. If all he wanted to do was kill me, he need not have gone through all this trouble. He could have done it any time. Unless, maybe, he didn't have the right equipment?

I doubted that very much. Hunting rifles are quite common, even three years after the Outbreak. Ammo is tough to find in some places, but not impossible. He could have acquired a .308 or something bigger, equipped it with a decent scope, conducted surveillance, and waited for an opportunity. One shot, one kill, no more Gabriel Garrett.

But he hadn't. Why?

There was a strong possibility my theory was correct, and he wanted me alive. Considering our history, it wouldn't surprise me a bit. But there was also the possibility he didn't know for sure if I was in Hollow Rock. The more I thought about that one, the more it made sense.

Logic test number one: put yourself in your opponent's place.

There is someone I want to kill. I have information that leads me to believe he is in Hollow Rock. He thinks I died years ago. I want to use this information to lure him out of hiding so I can kill him at my leisure. How best to do that?

Answer: Sean Montford.

Implications: he knows a thing or two about Hollow Rock. He knows about the patrols, and the sheriff's department. He knows where to leave a body so the patrols find it. He knows that if I really am in town, the sheriff will find me and he will want to know what the words carved into Montford's back mean. He will want to know if I know who committed the crime.

The next part was a leap of logic. How did he know I would respond the way I did? That I would come out here alone? That I would not want anyone to know what happened all those years ago?

When in doubt, the simplest answer to a question is quite often the correct one. The simplest answer in this case?

He didn't.

He was guessing, playing a hunch.

Time was on his side, after all. He didn't need to get me tonight. If his plan didn't work, all he had to do was slip away and wait until things settled down. The sheriff would eventually call off the investigation, and everything would go back to normal. He could come up with a new plan and try again, meaning this wasn't necessarily intended to be an end game. He was fishing. Shaking the tree. Throwing shit at a wall to see what would stick.

Unfortunately for him, his plan worked.

Now I just had to find him.

SIXTEEN

From atop the grain silo, with my scope at its highest magnification, a thorough grid-pattern search of the area surrounding the crime scene yielded no results. If Montford's murderer was there, he had hidden himself well enough to fool a FLIR imager. My only option was to go down there and look for him. After descending the ladder, I donned my ghillie suit, drew my falcata, and got moving.

On the way to the road, between bouts of cutting down walkers, I thought about those infrared sensors. I thought about how difficult they were to set up in a well-lit building, much less outdoors. The killer must have set them up in the dark, after the cops left. Otherwise, the deputies would have found them. Which meant he was an expert at surveillance, something which further cemented his identity.

Another factor was the sensor's location. They were close to the tree, which meant the killer expected me to start my search there. If I were a little dumber, that's exactly what I would have done. Lucky for me, I'm not that stupid. The killer also knew that with the snow and the darkness, it would be tough for me to search for his trail and stay alert at the same time. It was probably how he planned to get the drop on me. Wait until I had my head down, then make his move.

Speaking of, how did he plan to take me down? Assuming he wanted me alive, how did he expect to pull it off? He had seen me in action and knew what I was capable of. Furthermore, he knew I would never allow myself to be captured without a fight. Did he really think he could do it working alone?

Simplest answer?

No. He didn't.

He was not that stupid. Someone was helping him. But who, and how many?

Again, I thought of Sun Tzu. *When an enemy is relaxed, make them toil. When full, starve them. When settled, make them move.*

The fundamental essence of an ambush is that you lie in wait. You settle in. You stay alert. But if they were hiding within ambush distance of the crime scene, why bother with the sensors? It was dark, but it wasn't *that* dark. If my enemy was who I thought he was, he was definitely resourceful enough to score some NVGs. Why not just watch and wait? Why go through the extra trouble?

Another simple answer: he wasn't close to the crime scene.

If he was clever enough to set up infrared sensors, he was clever enough to wire them to a radio transmitter. It wouldn't take much, Iraqi insurgents could do it with a cell phone. When I broke the beam, he would know I was nearby. Then again, there were also walkers and animals nearby. How would he know if it was a false alarm?

I knew how I would do it.

Video surveillance.

But why do it that way? Why bother with infrared sensors and video cameras and the heinous murder of an innocent man? The whole thing smacked of laziness. There was no discipline in this, no precision. It begged other questions.

If they weren't near the tree, where were they? If they didn't have eyes on the crime scene, where were they monitoring it from? And most importantly, how did they plan to take me down?

Maybe I was looking at this all wrong. Maybe the killer was not who I thought he was.

No, that didn't make any sense. There were only four people who knew about Operation Dragonfly.

Or were there?

I had always thought Tolliver worked independently of the Langley bureaucracy. That he kept the names of his operatives confidential to maintain separation between the boots on the ground and the people calling the shots. Nobody wanted to be the one sitting in front of a congressional committee if an op went sideways. They made sure there were enough degrees of separation to be hands clean if things went badly. The suits in D.C. only cared about results. They didn't give a shit who made things happen so long as they happened.

No. It had to be him.

But that still left the question of who was working with him. He knew better than to try to take me on alone. Mercenaries? The remnants of the Free Legion? Either one was a strong possibility.

Either one was also an assumption.

Just a few minutes ago, I had been gloating over how my opponent had made too many assumptions, and how it was going to cost him. And here I was doing the same thing.

Assumptions are bad. Assumptions get you killed. Knowing is better. What did I know so far?

I knew about the infrared sensors. I knew my enemy was not within two hundred yards of the crime scene, or if they were, they were extremely well hidden. I knew if they didn't have eyes on the scene, they had some other way of watching. I knew there was a very strong possibility they wanted me alive.

I knew they expected me to fall for their trap.

When you know an enemy is expecting you to do one thing, the proper strategy is to do the opposite. If they're expecting you to be in one place, attack from somewhere else. The killer expected me to start my search at the crime scene and expand outward from there. If his eyes were fixed in one direction only, then the element of surprise was mine.

I changed direction and headed north.

*****

There were more infected on the other side of the highway, but I didn't bother fighting them. The day's high temperature had only been thirty-four degrees, and it had dropped at least ten degrees since sunset. Immobilized, most of them now lay face down in the snow. Corpsecicles, as Eric called them.

I pictured the crime scene and drew a quarter-mile circle around it. Then I cut that circle in half, favoring of the northeastern side of the highway because the ground sloped gently upward in that direction. Not a hill, really, but higher ground than what lay to the south, the most sensible place to set up an ambush. I stayed to the outer edge of that circle until I reached its northernmost point, directly north of the crime scene. Beyond that point, the terrain sloped back downward leading to an expanse of flat, treeless fields. Not much cover out there. If the enemy was nearby, there was a good chance I was behind them.

Now for the hard part.

I adjusted both my FLIR imagers to their highest settings and started searching. For the first hour, all I found were frozen infected, an owl, and a small herd of startled deer. It was too bad I was hunting men, and not animals. I could have had some fresh venison.

Halfway through the second hour of searching, I picked up a heat signature. There was a thick stand of red cedars in the way, preventing me from seeing it clearly. I started to work my way around them, but then I remembered they provided good concealment. Going down on my belly, I crawled under fragrant evergreen boughs until I was close enough to see the source of the signature.

It was a house. A small one, more of a cabin, really. Maybe a thousand square feet of interior space, if that much. To my right, an overgrown gravel driveway wound its way through hundreds of yards of forest to the highway beyond. Referencing the map in my head, I figured I was about three hundred yards from the crime scene. Ahead of me was the crest of a long, low hill I hadn't noticed earlier.

It was a good location for a hideout. The sheriff and his deputies could have walked a two-hundred yard perimeter around where they found Montford's body, and they would not have seen this place. I only spotted it because I had approached from the opposite direction.

Clever bastards. They had planned this out long in advance.

Moving slowly, I removed my goggles and peered through the FLIR imager on my rifle. The walls were thin, but they were enough to obscure most of what was inside. Looking away from the scope, I saw there was no light coming through the windows. The heat signature was on the lower part of the wall closest to me, probably in a bedroom, a circle of brilliant white on the otherwise gray exterior. If I had to hazard a guess, I would say it was some sort of portable gas heater.

As Eric is fond of saying, only one way to find out.

I put my goggles back on and went around to the other side, moving in a low crouch. Ten feet from the house, I spotted a tripwire. Kneeling down, I could see it surrounded the house on all sides, rigged to little boxes tied to trees. On closer examination, the boxes were made of scrap metal with wires poking from the seams. Improvised explosives, and fairly sophisticated ones at that. Most IEDs I had seen since the Outbreak were triggered with bullets or shotgun shells. They were easy to make, and didn't require any special tools. These bombs looked electronic. Which would require advanced know-how, testing equipment, and a 3M soldering kit.

With a sudden sense of alarm, I realized that if they had rigged IEDs around the house, they could also have rigged cameras. Just as I thought this, I heard the faint sound of a door opening.

Time slowed down. My thoughts raced. I ran through everything I knew about video surveillance.

Unless a camera is mounted to a motorized turret, they only look at one area. If you are outside of the camera's field of view, you are invisible to anyone monitoring its video feed. To get comprehensive coverage of a place with as many approaches as this one, you would need dozens of cameras. The question was, how many did these guys have? It could not have been very many. Batteries and other sources of electricity were rare and precious. A person would have to expend a great deal of trouble and expense to mount more than four or five. If it were me, and I were worried about someone sneaking up on my hideout, I would not point the cameras out into the forest where they could be easily eluded. I would point them at a potential intruder's intended target.

I would point them at the house.

I backed off quickly, careful with every step, making almost no sound as I melted into the forest. When I felt I had gone far enough, I found a suitable spot and dropped to the ground, head down, eyes just above the snow, the trailing edges of my ghillie suit dangling in my vision. A man rounded the corner, walked a few feet to a hand-dug latrine, unzipped his pants, and proceeded to relieve himself. His outline stood out brilliant white through the infrared goggles. He started humming to himself. I eased my finger off the trigger.

Maybe I was wrong. Maybe this wasn't a hideout. Maybe the guy at the latrine really lived here. The presence of the IEDs didn't necessarily mean anything. Just that someone here knew how to make bombs out of scrap metal and old electronics. That kind of knowledge was rare, but not unheard of. It was a dangerous world, and it was not uncommon for people who lived in isolation to place booby traps around their homes. Hell, I had done the same thing at my old cabin in North Carolina.

On its own, the idea seemed plausible enough. But then there was the house's proximity to where Montford's body was found, and the infrared sensors. It just seemed a little too convenient. I examined the house, looking for signs of habitation. Normally at a place like this, there would be an outhouse, a woodpile, maybe a shed for storing perishable food. The remnants of outdoor cooking fires, a fence to keep the infected out. Looking around, I didn't see any of those things. No one had bothered shoveling the snow from the roof, the latrine looked recently dug, and the house was in a state of extreme disrepair. Another winter like this one, and the roof would probably collapse. It looked abandoned. *Felt* abandoned.

No. Something was wrong here. Slowly, I stood up.

I probably wouldn't be able to reach the man at the latrine before he finished his business, but I could make it to the side of the house and blend in with the ground. The man would have to pass within feet of me to get back inside. That would be my opportunity.

Seven quick, silent steps took me where I needed to go. As I went down to my stomach, I unslung my rifle and pressed it into the snow, covering it up. If it came to a fight, it was going to be close quarters work. Better to use my pistol. I had just enough time to draw my Beretta and hide my hands before the man turned around.

He didn't go back toward the house immediately. He took a few slow, strolling steps, casting his eyes around the surrounding trees, probably looking for infected. Not seeing any, he gazed upward through barren limbs at the moon above. It was three-quarters full, only marginally visible through high, fast-moving cloud cover. The freezing wind whipped one end of his scarf behind him and rattled the branches overhead.

"This is some bullshit," he muttered, shivering. "Waste of goddamn time. Got us out here freezing our asses off for nothing."

He coughed a few times, spit into the snow, and walked toward the porch. I waited until he was two steps past me before I stood up. At this range, there was no way he wouldn't hear me, so I had to move fast.

One hand drew my dagger, while the other gripped the Beretta. My target had just enough time to turn his head in my direction before my knife was at his throat. I pulled him against my chest with my forearm, pressed the knife into his esophagus, and then touched the end of the suppressor to his temple.

"Don't move. Don't make a sound. If you call for help, I'll kill you. Do you understand?"

"What the fuck are you-"

The knife bit deeper, cutting into his skin. A thin bead of crimson began to run down the edge of the blade. "I said *quiet*."

"Okay, okay. Ease up."

"Put your hands behind your back."

"What?"

"Do it now," I said, tapping the gun against his temple.

"All right, all right, Jesus."

Working one handed so I could keep the blade pressed to his throat, I holstered the pistol, tugged a zip tie from a pouch on my vest, and bound his hands. Finished, I patted him down and found a folding knife and a Glock pistol. I tossed them away before putting the gun back to his head.

"Who sent you?" I asked.

"What are you talking about? Christ's sake, why are you doing this? Look, I have food and stuff inside, okay? You can take whatever you want, just don't hurt me."

I dragged him a few steps back to keep his voice from carrying into the house. "Nice try. I know you're lying, and I already know why you're here. Now I'm going to ask you one last time, and if you want to live, you will tell me the truth. Who sent you?"

His breath was coming in panicked gasps, raising a cloud of vapor around his face. I felt his pulse hammering against my thumb. His body shuddered, and not just from the cold. If I pushed a little harder, I could probably make him cry.

He said, "Please, I don't-"

"I'm going to count to three, and if you don't answer me, I will slit your throat." I pressed the knife a little harder. "One. Two."

My elbow came up, the blade tugging hard against his skin. He gasped and stood on the tips of his toes.

"Okay, okay, *stopstopstopstopstop*. Just stop, please. Look, I don't know who the guy was, all right? Just some guy. We never met him before. We were passing through town and he offered us a job."

"Who is 'us'? How many of you are there?"

"Four. Me and three other guys."

"Where are they?"

He hesitated, swallowing hard. I cocked the hammer on the Berretta. "Where?"

"They're in the house. S-sleeping."

"All of them?"

"Yes."

"Good. Now I want you to listen to me very carefully, okay? Pay attention like your life depends on it, because it does. Are you listening?"

"Y-y-yes."

"I didn't come here to kill you. You're not the man I'm after, so there's no reason for you to die today. If you do as I ask, if you tell me the truth, I'll let you go."

"Okay, okay. Ask me anything, man. I'll tell you whatever you want to know."

"Of that, I have no doubt. First question: were you sent here to capture someone?"

He hesitated a few seconds, voice growing high-pitched. "Yes."

"What's his name?"

"Garrett. That's all the guy told us, just Garrett."

Suspicion confirmed. "You do this kind of thing often?"

"No way, man. We do protection. Caravans and shit, guarding cargo. Sometimes we collect debts for people. This is the first time we took a job like this."

"So you and you're friends are mercenaries?"

"Y-yeah. I guess so. Something like that."

"A man was murdered not far from here. Tortured to death. Someone carved my name into his back. Did you have anything to do with that?"

No answer. I leaned my face closer and asked him again. His shuddering turned to sobs, tears began to drip onto my forearm. "Yes," he said miserably. "I didn't hurt him, okay. I just helped catch him. Mike was the one who tortured him. He's fucking sick in the head, man. He get's off on that kind of shit."

"Why did you do it? That man had a family. A wife and children."

"I'm sorry. I'm so sorry, I-"

"Fuck your apologies, just answer the question. Why?"

"It wasn't our idea. The guy who hired us told us to do it. Said it was important we do it just like he wanted. He even wrote down instructions."

"Why the farmer? Did the guy who hired you tell you to kill him specifically?"

"No. Mike found him walking alone on the highway. I guess he was hunting, or something."

Wrong place, wrong time. Poor bastard. "The man who hired you, what did he look like?"

"I don't know. He looked like a regular guy, I guess."

I raised the Beretta and rapped him on the ear, drawing a hiss of pain. "Race? Age? Eye color? Tall? Short? Be specific."

"Uh…he was about my height, I think. Brown hair, brown eyes, big beard. He was a white guy. Told us to call him Marco."

I was silent for a moment, thinking. That description didn't sound anything like who I thought was after me, and I didn't know anyone named Marco. He must have been working through hired agents. But why? Why go through the trouble of hiring someone to do his dirty work for him? He knew good and well that sending amateurs after me was as good as sending lambs to the slaughter. So why do it? It didn't make any sense.

Briefly, I debated what to do next. The man under my knife might know something that could help me, but I couldn't interrogate him with the other mercenaries nearby. If I hurt him too badly, he would just scream for help, and unsuppressed gunfire this close to Hollow Rock would draw attention I couldn't afford. I didn't have time to knock him out and carry him far enough away so the others would not hear him scream, which left me with only one option.

Killing someone in a fight is one thing, but cold-blooded murder is something else entirely. Not that I haven't done it. I have, many times. But it never sits well with me. Of all the things that plague me in the night, those memories are the worst. The times when I had the option to walk away, to let someone live, and chose not to.

But then I thought about Sean Montford's reanimated corpse dangling from a tree not far from where I stood. I thought about the fingernail in his mouth, and the parts of him that were missing, and the gruesome wounds left by his torture. I thought about what he went through before he died, the pain and fear he must have felt. I thought of a wife bereft of her husband, and children orphaned because their father was in the wrong place at the wrong time. I thought about the sheriff, and how I lied to him because I wanted to keep my sins dead and buried. How I couldn't let him bring these men to justice because they knew too much. I thought about all these things, and I made a decision.

I asked for the names of the other three men.

He told me.

I asked him to describe the layout of the house, and which room each man was sleeping in.

He did.

I holstered the Beretta and shifted my weight to my right leg.

"Wait, what are you doing?"

"Don't move," I said.

"Please, I-"

"Do you want to live?"

"I...yes."

"Then hold still." I raised the hand holding the dagger and slammed the pommel into the back of his neck. He dropped, his body going limp.

I took a few moments to bind his ankles, hogtie them to his hands, and drag him around the side of the house. Once he was well hidden, I cut away strips of his jacket to make a gag, stuffed it in his mouth, tied it off, and rolled him onto his side so he wouldn't suffocate. Confident he wasn't going anywhere, I retrieved my rifle and moved to the front of the house. The porch steps creaked under my boots as I slowly climbed them, leveled my rifle, and opened the door.

I didn't see anyone in the room beyond. A couch, a couple of chairs, and a long-disused television occupied a living room to my left. There was a dusty kitchen to my right, as well as a small dining room. On the floor of the dining room lay the jumbled bones of a human skeleton, dead long enough for all the flesh to have rotted away, body fluids soaking into the floor. A faint scent of decay hung in the air, clinging to my throat as I breathed it in. The bastards didn't even have the decency to bury the remains. Just left them there.

Sick fucks.

I switched my goggles to night vision mode and stepped inside. I could hear snoring coming from behind two doors in the hallway ahead of me. Staying low, I moved to the first door and opened it. There was a single bed inside, along with the usual bedroom furniture. It looked like an elderly person's room. Old fashioned painting on the wall, scratched up furniture from several decades ago, transistor radio on the windowsill. But the person in the bed did not look old. He looked to be in his late twenties, bearded, gaunt, lying under a pile of blankets. There was a rifle propped in the corner and a pistol on top of the dresser.

"Jason?" he muttered sleepily. "Mike has the next watch, dumbass, not me. Go away."

It was dark in the room, nearly pitch black. A set of blinds lay over the lone window, covered by a pair of thick curtains. The weak moonlight outside did not reach into the cramped little space. Even with NVGs, the mercenary's outline was dim. I stepped closer to the bed, looming over it, waiting to be noticed.

"Dude, what the fuck?" He reached for a flashlight on the table beside him and clicked it on. The dampeners built into my goggles toned down the sudden glare, keeping it from blinding me as he shined it in my face. When he saw what was standing over him, his eyes went wide with fear.

"Holy sh-"

I clamped a hand over his mouth and shoved him down onto the bed. He struggled to get out from under me, but I was twice his size. He wasn't going anywhere. I shifted my weight and put a shin across his thighs to keep him from kicking.

"This is what happens when you murder innocent people."

His muffled screams intensified. With my free hand, I drew my pistol and aimed it at his heart. He went rigid, eyes bulging, shaking his head. His hands came up in a warding gesture.

"Whatever price he offered you, it wasn't worth it."

I pulled the trigger twice.

The suppressor was a good one. Military grade. There was the clank of the slide going back and forth, but nothing else. The man convulsed a few times, spit blood between my fingers, and then died. His last breath rattled out when I took my hand from his face. I left him there and moved on.

Back in the hallway, I thought I heard something moving and stopped, ears straining. A few seconds passed. Nothing, just the sound of my own breathing. I kept walking to the next room and reached for the door handle. Just as I did, it opened from the other side.

Shit.

I stepped back, going still, blending in with the shadows. Another man about the same age as Jason stepped out and glared around dazedly. He was taller, heavier built, shaggy hair and beard. A pistol dangled loosely in his right hand.

"Jason? Rick? What the hell is going on over th-*hrrggk*"

The blade went in under his sternum, angled upward, piercing his heart. At the same time, I wrenched his pistol out of his hand. His mouth worked around a couple of hitching gasps, face slack, eyes bulging with pain. I leaned close and whispered a single word in his ear.

"*Murderer.*"

Withdrawing the knife, I caught him and eased him to the floor.

One left.

SEVENTEEN

I cleaned the blade on the dead man's clothes and sheathed it before switching to my rifle. The last door lay ahead, still closed. There was a possibility the man behind it had heard the commotion, and if he had, he was no doubt awake and wary. Not a good situation for me. If I had flashbangs and a ballistic shield, I might have tried a room entry. But I didn't, and I wasn't in a hurry to test the durability of my body armor.

Instead, I left the hallway and put my back against the wall between the kitchen and the living room. I removed the suppressor from the Beretta, aimed out the kitchen window, and fired a single shot. The report was deafening in the enclosed space. There was a thump and a muffled curse from the back of the house.

"Mike, get out here." I yelled, raising my voice to sound like Jason. "This fucker killed Tommy and Rick."

The door slammed open and I heard footsteps pounding down the hallway. Mike, the man who had tortured Montford, stopped and stared down at Tommy's dead body.

"Son of a bitch. Jason! Where are you?"

He moved into the living room, rifle in hand. "Jason?"

I took two steps and came down on the back of his neck with the butt of the pistol. He went to his knees with a surprised grunt, rifle clattering to the floor. The blow had dazed him, but he was still conscious and struggling to get back to his feet. Another blow to the brachial nerve put him on his face. After checking him for weapons, I folded his arms over his chest and dragged him outside.

He lay in the snow for a minute or two, breath coming in gasps, snoring like a man with sleep apnea. Finally the cold got through to him and woke him up. He rolled onto his stomach with a groan and staggered to his feet, barefoot and shivering in the cold. I stood and watched him silently, blade in hand, unmoving. When his eyes cleared enough to see me in the dim starlight, he jumped.

"Who the fuck are you?"

I responded by unclipping my folding knife with one hand and tossing the Ka-bar at his feet with the other. "You know who I am."

He glanced warily at the knife, then back at me. "You're him, aren't you? You're Garrett."

"My friends call me Gabe, not that it makes any difference."

His eyes darted around looking for help, looking for escape, tensing as though he might try to make a run for it. I moved aside my ghillie suit so he could see the rifle in my hand.

"You're thinking about running, aren't you? Totally understandable, given your current situation. But I wouldn't try it if I were you. As it stands, you have a fighting chance. If you run, I'll just kneecap you and leave you for the infected."

He went still. "What do you want from me?"

"I want you to pick up that knife."

"If I do, you'll just shoot me."

"If I wanted to shoot you, I would have done it already."

No answer.

"Okay, fine." I said, and dropped the M-6 to the ground behind me, followed by the Beretta and falcata. Taking a few steps closer, I interposed my body between the mercenary and the weapons.

"These are yours if you can get past me."

He didn't move.

"Are you still thinking about running? I bet you are. I know how I must look right now. Big guy, ghillie suit, night vision goggles. Pretty intimidating, huh? Well don't let that scare you. Underneath all this, I'm just a man, same as you. I have bones and organs and blood, and I can be killed just like anybody else."

Slowly, I started walking toward him. He stepped back, not making a move toward the Ka-bar.

"I'm going to start cutting you whether you fight back or not. Your choice."

For a while there, he had me convinced he was frozen with fear. I thought I would have to cut him a few times to anger him enough to fight back, but the clever bastard surprised me. When I was four steps away he reached down, snatched up the knife, and threw it straight at my face.

The throw was a good one. He gripped the handle in the correct spot and gave the blade just the right amount of spin as he sent it flying. The blade crossed the distance in less than a second, whistling through the air. If I were a little slower, it might have hit me.

I am a lot of things, but slow is not one of them.

By the time the blade was in his hand, I had already shifted my weight forward to the balls of my feet. As he drew his hand back to throw it, my knees were already bent, shoulders lowered, torso falling to the ground. When the blade cut the air where my face had been, I was in the middle of a forward somersault that ended with me standing in front of him.

With surprising speed, he launched a punch at my midsection. I could have dodged, but I didn't. I let it land and folded with it, dissipating the shock. The mercenary grunted as his fist impacted the thick barrier of my MOLLE vest and the layered ceramic body armor beneath. I whipped my knife out and caught him across the upper arm, laying open a deep gash. A shout of pain tore loose from him as he stumbled backward.

"Hurts, doesn't it?"

"Fuck you."

I laughed and stood up from my fighting stance. "Looks like you lost your weapon."

He glared, gripping the cut on his arm. "Fuck you."

"Is that all you have to say? These are your last words, my friend. Maybe you should come up with something a little more creative."

"You're a coward. Drop that knife and we'll see how tough you are."

"Says the guy who tortures and murders innocent farmers."

No answer. The fear left his face, eyes growing cold.

"Your boy Jason told me how you get off on hurting people. On murder. Doesn't feel so good being on the receiving end, does it?"

He dropped into a fighting stance, lips curling back from his teeth. "Like I said. If you're such a tough guy, why don't you drop that knife and see what happens."

I pulled back the hood of my ghillie suit so he could see my face.

"Okay," I said, and smiled.

The knife hit the snow at his feet.

"Go for it."

He aimed the first slash at my legs, trying to open me up, maybe make a follow up pass at my face or throat. Instead of hopping straight back, I circled to his weak side and cracked him on the jaw with a straight right. He stumbled few feet away, shaking his head to clear the cobwebs.

"You're going to have to do better than that."

He came on again, feinting and jabbing, blade flashing in the moonlight. He faked a slash at my throat, then reversed his feet and diverted the blade toward my groin. I deflected the attack with my forearm, caught his wrist, and pulled him off balance. With my free hand, I locked his arm out straight, then stepped in, twisted my shoulders, and forced him down to his face.

"The groin? Really? That's not very nice."

I put a boot on the back of his shoulder, peeled the knife out of his hand, reached down, and sawed at his ear until it fell away from his head. His screams echoed out into the forest.

217

When I let him up, he pressed his hand against the side of his head, blood dripping between his fingers, jaw clenched with rage. Once again, I stepped between him and the pile of weapons.

"Here," I said, tossing the blade at his feet. "Try again."

He picked it up.

We kept going like that for a while, him trying to kill me, and me busting him up. Sometimes I let him keep the knife, while others I disarmed him and cut him before throwing the blade at his feet. Each time I did, I issued the same challenge.

"Go on. Try again."

After four cuts, I could see fear in his eyes. His attacks grew sloppier, more desperate. He had thought himself a competent knife fighter up until then, but he had never faced anyone like me. Desperation began to take hold. At eight cuts, the pain and blood loss made him tired and weak. His attacks devolved until they were just shy of feeble, like a toddler attacking a lion.

At twelve cuts, he started begging for mercy.

"Don't waste your breath," I said. "You didn't show that poor farmer any mercy, so don't expect any from me."

His eyes hardened and he launched himself at me one last time. I let him get within a few inches of stabbing my leg before I caught his hand. Unable to free the blade, he tried to punch me, but I caught that hand as well. He bared his teeth and lunged at me, panting and dripping blood, a mix of anger and fear in his eyes. A head butt to the bridge of his nose dropped him to his knees. He kneeled there in the snow, hands falling to his sides.

"That all you got? I didn't even break a sweat."

"Fuck you," he said, spraying blood from ruined lips.

I laughed at him and kicked snow in his face. "You feel that emptiness in your chest? There's a word for that feeling. It's called hopelessness. You feel that burning in your stomach? It's called defeat. Tastes like a shit sandwich, doesn't it? Tell me something, Mike. How does it feel to know you're about to die?"

"Fuck you. Just get it over with."

"You think this is bad? You think I've hurt you? I saw that man's body, you sick fuck. I saw what you did to him. This is nothing. This is downright merciful. You're lucky I'm short on time, my friend, or I would burn you at the stake."

I walked over to my weapons and picked up the Beretta. Screwed the suppressor back on. Pointed it at his head. "Any last words?"

His ruined face split into a smile and he laughed, high and hysterical, leering at me through bloody teeth. "He begged me to stop, you know. He begged and begged and begged. They all do that. It's like they're reading from a script or something, like there's a process to it. First there's the outrage. *What are you doing, what's wrong with you, you don't have to do this.* It takes a while for the reality of it to sink in. They think these things only happen to other people, it can't be happening to them. I always tell them the same thing, then, and I smile when I do it. I tell them that before it's over with, they'll thank me. From then on, I don't say a word. No matter what they do, I just keep working."

I lowered the pistol. A dark red tinge began to creep into my vision, crackling at the edges. My stomach began to burn with a low, smoldering fire.

"Then comes the begging. *Please don't, please stop, please don't do this.* They tell me about their families, their kids, their husbands and wives. As if I'm supposed to give a shit. I don't talk then either. It unnerves them, you see. Builds up the tension. The excitement."

The red tinge became a mist, obscuring my vision. The fire in my gut began to spread outward, growing hotter, searing into my chest. My hand grew tense around the grip of the Beretta. I took a step forward.

"Then they start trying to bargain. *I have this, I have that. I'll give you whatever you want. I'll do whatever you want. Just please don't kill me. I swear I'll never tell anyone.*"

I kept walking, step by step, finger slipping over the trigger. *He's baiting you. Trying to make you angry, trying to make you slip up. You're smarter than this. Don't fall for it. Stay alert.*

"Near the end, they start begging again. Not to let them go, but for death. You see, once you maim someone to a certain point, once the damage is disfiguring and permanent, they don't want to live anymore. They give up. They want you to kill them. And when you finally put a gun to their head and tell them it's over with, they thank you. They thank you from the bottom of their heart, and they fucking mean it. That's the part that makes me cum. The surrender. The acknowledgement. And just before I kill them, I always tell them the same thing. A conclusion to the ritual, so to speak. I say, *I told you so.*"

Something was wrong with the NVGs. There was a shimmering, a mirage effect in front of my eyes. My vision had gone completely red despite the green glow of the imager. My body felt hot, like lying on pavement in Baghdad in the summer, waves of heat boiling over me, the angry sun blinding me. I felt light and delicate, like a strong wind could come along and blow me away. I stepped to within a few feet of the man kneeling in the snow.

No more talk. Kill.

His last attempt was quick. Quicker than I would have expected. Perhaps he had been moving slower than he could have during the last few exchanges, trying to make me think he was weaker than he was. Not a bad strategy. In his place, I might have done the same thing. But even at his fastest, he wasn't as fast as me.

I caught his hand as the blade came up and squeezed with everything I had. A high, girlish scream erupted from his lips as his bones broke and ground against each other. I raised the Beretta and touched it to his forehead, watched his eyes roll up, glazed and staring. Agonized. Terrified.

"His name was Sean Montford, you murdering fuck. You think you're about to die now, but you're wrong. You've been dead this whole time. You died the moment you laid a hand on him."

And with that, I pulled the trigger.

*****

It took me two hours to search the house.

I tossed the place from one end to the other, leaving no proverbial stone unturned. When I was done, I stood in the living room staring at the mess I had made. Couch cushions ripped open, upholstery cut from its frame, cabinets torn down from the walls and dismantled, barely more than a few square feet of sheetrock left on the walls. I had emptied the closets, dumped out the drawers, cut open the beds and picture frames, everything I could think of.

Nothing.

Just the usual stuff you find in a house except for the mercenary's clothes, food, and equipment. The only remarkable discovery was a laptop to which they had been streaming video from their surveillance cameras. The laptop's hard drive was clean, save for a single software application. When I opened it, it showed four views around the tree where Sean Montford was murdered and two more watching the front and rear entrances to the house. Evidently, they had kept one man on watch at all times in case I tripped a sensor or showed up on camera. I could only assume that once they detected me, their plan had been track me down and capture me on foot. Clearly, they either did not know who they were fucking with, or had been warned and chose to ignore it. Either way, it was sloppy. Amateurish. Not what I was expecting.

The heat signature I had seen earlier turned out to be a kerosene heater, which was still burning in Mike's bedroom. The liquid in its tank bore the unmistakable odor of jet fuel. JP-8, unless I missed my guess. There was a steel gerry can nearby

221

with about a gallon of foul smelling liquid sloshing in the bottom.

Perfect.

I dragged the two dead bodies outside and lined them up next to where I had left Mike's lifeless corpse. Jason was where I had left him, still weeping with fear and shivering. I carried him over to where his three dead partners lay and tossed him so he landed on his side, his face a few inches from the gaping hole in the back of Mike's skull. When he realized what he was looking at, he began thrashing and struggling against his bonds, eyes nearly bulging out of his head. I gave him a sharp kick to the ribs.

"Stay quiet and behave yourself while I'm gone. Unless you want to end up like these three."

Muffled sobs followed me as I left.

I made my way to the crime scene, removed the four infrared sensors, and switched them off. That done, I turned my attention to the tree where Montford's body was found and the cameras mounted to its trunk. They were small, about half the size of a man's thumb, and very high tech. Zoom lenses, night vision, RF transmitters, the works. The kind of thing you rarely see outside high-level intelligence services.

Services like the CIA.

Back at the house, I searched the woods until I found the other two cameras, which were the same model as the other three. All very useful pieces of equipment, but they might have been fitted with bugs. I piled the sensors, the cameras, and the laptop next to the kerosene heater and went back outside.

Jason stared in tearful horror as I dragged the bodies of his friends back into the house one by one, put them back in their beds, posed them as if they were sleeping, and positioned their weapons exactly where I had found them.

One last thing to do.

A set of sheets I found in the course of my search was just long enough to suit my needs. I cut them into thin strips, soaked them in jet fuel, and wrapped them around the top of the kerosene heater where it was hottest. As I stepped off the front porch, I heard the *whoosh* of the fabric catching fire.

Jason redoubled his efforts to break loose from his restraints as I drew near, shouting at me through the gag in his mouth, tears dripping from eyes squeezed tightly shut.

"Relax," I said.

The eyes opened, fearful and hopeful at the same time. I said, "I told you I wasn't going to kill you, and I meant it. I just have a few more questions. If I cut away that gag, are you going to start screaming?"

He shook his head emphatically.

"You better not, or you'll regret it." I reached down and did as promised. He spit the gag out and drew a few relieved breaths.

"Listen, man, I-"

"Save it," I interrupted. "I only want to know one thing. Where did you meet the man who hired you?"

"A place called the Irisher. It's a tavern over in Blackmire."

"Blackmire? Never heard of it."

"It's in the old Chickasaw Wildlife Refuge, right on the banks of the Mississippi."

I felt my brow come together. The Chickasaw Refuge was a known hideout for slavers and marauders, the kind of place you only went when you had something unsavory to trade. Quasi-honest businessmen like myself never went near the place. The fact that Jason had met his employer there said a great deal about his character.

"Jason, what's your last name?"

"Ross."

"Jason Ross, I'm going to let you go, but I need you to do something for me first, okay? I need you to deliver a message to the man who hired you. Do you think you can do that?"

"Yeah, man. Anything."

"Very good. Now repeat after me: The past is dead. Let it go. You knew the rules when you signed on, and if the situation had been reversed, you would have done the same thing. If you dig those two graves, make sure one of them is for you. This is your only warning."

He got it wrong on the first try, so we went through it again, slowly, phrase by phrase. It took a while, but finally he memorized the message well enough to repeat it ten times without error. Satisfied he was sufficiently coached, I stood up.

"Wait here," I said, as if he had a choice.

"Hey, where are you going? Are you going to let me go?"

"Be quiet. If you want to live, I don't want to hear another word."

He went silent.

Around the back of the house was an old tool shed. I rooted through it until I found a suitable implement—a woodcutting axe—and carried it back to the front yard where Jason lay shivering in his restraints. Stopping a few feet away from him, I swung the axe into the trunk of a maple tree, the rusted blade biting deep.

"That's yours," I said, cutting the zip tie binding his ankles to his hands. "Here's what you're going to do. You're going to leave this place, and never come back. Do you understand?"

"Yes. Fuck, man, I never want to see this place again."

"That's the right attitude. Now when I cut you loose, you're going to take that axe and you're going to make your way back to Blackmire. I know it's a long way, but you can do it. Do you know the way?"

"Yes."

"Good. That axe will be both survival tool and self-defense until you can find a place to scavenge some food and weapons. You should avoid contact with other people at all costs unless they seem like legitimate trade caravans. Anyone you meet on the road travelling alone or in small groups will probably be slavers or marauders. The kind of people that will kill you for your shoes. Stay out of their way. Understood?"

"Yeah, I got it."

"When you get back to Blackmire, you find the man who hired you and give him that message, word for word. If you don't, I will know about it and I will come looking for you. Are we clear?"

"Yes."

"What did I just tell you to do? All of it."

He repeated back my instructions, and I nodded in satisfaction. "Excellent. Now, one last thing. You ever seen that movie, *Inglorious Basterds*?"

"Uh…no. I don't think so."

"That's too bad. It's a good one."

I clamped a hand over his mouth, put a knee on his chest to hold him down, and opened my pocket knife. He struggled, screaming against my hand and kicking his feet, but bound as he was, there was nowhere for him to go.

"You see, Brad Pitt's character, Aldo the Apache, he hated Nazis with a passion. Slaughtered as many as he could find. But with every group, he always let one go. He wanted word to spread about what he was doing, build a reputation for mercilessness and brutality, strike fear into the hearts of his enemies. But the ones he let go, he didn't release them unscathed. He marked them, you see. Carved a swastika in their foreheads so that every time they looked in the mirror, they would be reminded of their sins."

I touched the knife to the mercenary's forehead and pressed down until the tip settled against the hard surface of his skull. He squeezed his eyes shut and moaned pitifully, tears streaking down the sides of his face.

"But you're not a Nazi, are you? I don't think a swastika would be appropriate. I need to give you something more relevant to your crimes. Something everyone can see and know what you've done."

I twirled the knife around on its tip, drilling a dark little circle in the flesh around it. The whimpering turned to shuddering sobs. Leaning closer, I dropped my voice to a whisper.

"How about...M? For murderer."

When I was done, I sat back and admired my work. Nice straight lines cut all the way to the bone. Without stitches, he would carry the scar for the rest of his life, assuming he didn't get an infection and die. I just hoped he made it to Blackmire before then.

After tying a loose bandage around his head, I cut his bonds, leveled the Beretta at his face and backed off. The mercenary stood up on shaky legs, staring fearfully at the gun.

"Go on. Get out of here. Don't forget your axe."

He grabbed it, tore it from the tree, and started running. I let him get a few steps before raising my voice. "One last thing."

He turned around, face slack with pain and terror.

"If I ever see you again, you're a dead man."

I watched his silhouette fade into the night until I was sure he was gone. Behind me, the blaze inside Mike's bedroom had spread to the rest of the house, flames curling around the roof and licking at the night sky, casting long shadows in the darkness. It was far enough away the guards back at the wall wouldn't see it, but they might notice the smoke. If they did, there was little chance Sheriff Elliott would send anyone to investigate until morning, which gave me plenty of time to cover my tracks.

Before I left, I took off my goggles and looked up at the moon. It shone dimly through iron grey clouds high overhead, reminding me of another night eight years ago. A night in New York when the bright city lights shined against nearly identical looking clouds, obscuring the sky on a summer evening. A night when I had followed protocol and let a man die.

Or so I thought.

I remembered the last time I had seen the big city, with its teeming angry masses and its wealth and pretentiousness. I remembered its brutal beauty, and the way the light bled together under the haze of a good liquor buzz at Raines Law Room on the trailing edge of Chelsea. I remembered her tall towers, her glaring neon, and the retina scarring brightness of Times Square on a boiling night. Closing my eyes, I could feel the smooth stone of the simple, poignant 9/11 memorial under my fingertips. I could recall the smell and texture and richness of a city with so many layers no one could ever truly know it, never delve all its mysteries. She had been a gorgeous lady, once upon a time.

But then came the infected, and the panic, and the fires, and the chaos in the streets. The riots. The boats fleeing the harbor so packed with people they were falling over the sides. The bombs and the gunfire and the millions dead in the span of a few days as the military suffered its worst defeat of the Outbreak. I thought about what must be left of her, that crown jewel of the Empire State. The skeletons of world famous buildings gutted and collapsing, the moans of over ten million corpses echoing through the blood-stained streets, the skyline of Manhattan reaching its dead hands toward an indifferent sky.

I remembered all this, and I thought that even three years after her death, she must make one hell of an impressive corpse.

EIGHTEEN

Eight years ago,
New York City

Tolliver arranged my reservations at the Four Seasons, eight blocks from the Waldorf Astoria. I was on the sixth floor in a room designated as a Terrace Deluxe, whatever the hell that meant. My window overlooked the frenetic ants marching on 57th street, the honking, waving, bustling masses with their blank eyes and standoffish attitudes and the merciless superiority endemic of nearby Park Avenue. I felt my shoulders tense just looking at them.

At least it wasn't SoHo.

I showered, ordered room service, and sat in a chair, legs propped up on a polished mahogany table, waiting. There was a polite knock at the door, and a short Hispanic woman rolled a cart into the room bearing a covered tray. Her age could have been anywhere from thirty to fifty, her nametag said Maria, and her wedding band was a humble strip of thin silver. I gave her a twenty-dollar tip and said *muchas gracias, señora Maria.* Her smile went from servile to genuine, and she said, *no hay de qué, muy amable señor,* with a Mexican accent.

You would think, with this being the big city, the hotel staff would be accustomed to generous tips, especially at places like the Four Seasons.

You would be wrong.

In my experience, the wealthier the clientele, the worse they tended to treat the hired help. I didn't want to be that guy, so I always tipped well.

Maria left, and I sat down with my breakfast. As expected, the eggs Benedict was superb. New York may have had its many faults, but the food wasn't one of them. The city boasted some of the best eateries in the world.

Once finished, I set the tray in the hallway, opened up an Elmore Leonard paperback, and continued waiting. At a quarter after noon, there was another knock at the door. Not gentle and polite like Señora Maria, but authoritative and loud, like the cops wanted in. When I opened the door, Tolliver stepped past me uninvited, gave a dismissive greeting, and crossed the room toward the table by the window. The man behind him was far more expressive.

"Holy shit! If it ain't the fucking Wolfman himself!" Rocco stepped in, shook my hand, and pounded me on the back, laughing the whole time.

Five-foot eight and built like a fireplug, he was every New Jersey Italian stereotype brought to life. That said, he looked a far cry from the young man who had spilled blood with me on the streets of Fallujah. Gone were the fatigues, and the smooth face, and the crew cut. His once-boyish frame had filled out by at least thirty pounds, he had let his hair grow long and slicked it back, and a neatly trimmed goatee covered his chin. He looked like a well-groomed pit bull in a Brooks Brothers suit.

I said, "Been a long time, Roc. Good to see you again."

"Good to see you too, brother."

He turned and looked over his shoulder at the man standing in the doorway, eyes hardening, finger wagging back and forth between the two of us. "So we're gonna be working together, right? You see this guy? Me and him, we go way back. He's like a brother to me. You should remember that."

He was smiling when he said it, but there was a hint of warning in his voice. It told me two things: Rocco knew this guy, and he didn't like him.

The third man nodded in acknowledgment, expression unmoved. He was tall, nearly my height, and looked to be about the same age. Very Scandinavian. Stringy hair somewhere between brown and blonde, high cheekbones, aristocratic nose, eyes the color of glacier ice and about as warm. With a jolt, I realized I recognized him. He held out a rather large hand.

"You must be Mr. Garrett."

"Well hell, if isn't Sebastian Tanner. Never thought I'd see you again. How have you been?"

He froze mid-handshake, confused. "I'm afraid you have me at a disadvantage. Have we met before?"

"Yes, at Quantico, about nine years ago. You and a few other spook types were going through sniper school. We crossed paths a few times during training, even shared the range a few days. If I remember correctly, you graduated top of your class."

His eyebrows came together, and after a moment, recognition dawned on his face. "Oh, right, I remember now. You're the guy all the instructors used to talk about. Seemed they were worried you were going to take their job. What was that nickname they gave you? Quick something…"

I grimaced. "Quick Killer."

"That's it." Tanner snapped his fingers. "Quick Killer. Yeah, I remember everyone seemed to think you were something special." He gestured at my expensive suit, and the obvious fact I was a CIA operative. "Looks like you've done well for yourself since then."

I thought about my ex-wife, and the life I had left behind, and shrugged. "More or less."

"Now that introductions are out of the way, can we get down to business?" Tolliver said, opening a briefcase on the table.

I shut the door and moved to sit at the foot of the bed. Rocco and Tanner took the other two chairs. Tolliver arranged a few file folders on the table and set the briefcase aside.

"I assume the room has been swept?" he asked, not bothering to look up.

"Of course."

"Very well. Mr. Tanner, Mr. Rocco, these are for you. Gabriel, you already have your copy."

The other two operatives opened their files and began looking them over, coming to the same conclusions I had the previous night. Narco. Money laundering. Investor conference. Small private army. Rocco's face grew concerned. Tanner seemed excited.

"So let me ask a question here," Rocco said. "Why is the CIA handling this? Guy's a fucking narco, right? Doesn't the DEA normally handle this kind of thing?"

"Normally, yes," Tolliver replied. "However, the circumstances here are a little…different."

"Different how?"

The control agent's eyes narrowed. "Has anyone ever told you that you ask too many questions, Mr. Rocco?"

"Hey, this isn't Iraq, and I ain't no grunt. If I'm gonna risk getting my ass shot off, I wanna know why."

Tolliver sighed. "Very well. Villalobos' father used to work for the Medellin cartel. MAS for a while, then he got noticed and went to work for Escobar personally. Carried out a few assassinations against Columbian officials who were outspoken supporters of the extradition treaty with the US."

Rocco blinked. "Jesus Christ."

"Indeed. In light of his achievements and innate talent, Escobar set the elder Villalobos up in Guadalajara and financed his business operations there. Villalobos saw the potential opportunities presented by the porous Mexican border, and wanted to expand production to Ciudad Juarez. A rather prescient business plan, in retrospect. Anyway, when Escobar was killed in '93, the Medellin cartel fell apart, leaving Villalobos twisting in the wind. He managed to keep his operation running for a few years, but was eventually assassinated by a rival cartel. The younger Villalobos took the reins shortly thereafter, and has had a great deal more success building the family business than his father did."

"Okay, that still doesn't explain why we're here."

Tolliver frowned. "I was just getting to that part. You see, Villalobos blames the US government for his father's death. The actions of US Special Forces and CIA operatives were critical to the destruction of the Medellin Cartel. If they had never gone out of business, his father's enemies would never have gone after him. Or so Villalobos believes, anyway."

Rocco snorted. "Sounds like pretty fucking thin logic to me."

"I concur. However, it is not merely his hatred for the United States which precipitated our mission, but his, shall we say, extracurricular activities."

"What kinds of activities?"

"The kind that involve financing attacks on U.S. personnel and interests in Mexico and South America. The kind that involve two attempts to mastermind coordinated bombings in D.C. and Los Angeles. Attempts that were thwarted, thankfully, by a joint operation between the FBI and NSA."

"Fuck me. How'd they catch 'em?"

"Are you familiar with the Patriot Act?"

"Gotcha. NSA, right? Tracked their web activity?"

"Something to that effect. Which brings me to my final point. The CIA is involved because our operatives, meaning you three, are the most qualified for this type of operation. Normally, the administration frowns upon us violating our mandate by operating domestically, but in these troubled times, they're willing to make a few exceptions. Miguel Villalobos crossed a line, gentlemen. A line from which there is no going back. His operations pose a threat to the national security of the United States, and he has attempted to attack and kill innocent civilians on American soil. This cannot stand. We need to send a clear message to the cartels that while they are powerful, they are not invincible. We have more money, more power, more resources, better operatives, and better technology. If they attempt to harm our people, we will come for them. If they make too much of a nuisance of themselves, there is a cell waiting for them at Guantanamo Bay. As my father would say, these boys are getting too big for their britches. They have forgotten how foolish it is to make an enemy of United States Government. The task has fallen to us to remind them. Does that answer your question, Mr. Rocco?"

Roc tossed his file folder on the table, looked at me, and pointed at Tolliver. "Is he always like this?"

"No." I said. "Usually he's worse."

*****

Tolliver left us to our work.

We began sorting through the dossiers on the people Villalobos would be bringing along with him. The first file we reviewed was for Anja Renner, a very attractive, very German personal assistant. Mid-twenties, nice rack, blonde hair in a tight bun, classic naughty librarian look, eyes the color of the North Atlantic in winter. She was the distraction, the smoke screen, the arm candy to draw attention away from the dead-eyed little man who employed her. While most of the work she did was on the up and up, the people investigating her strongly suspected she had helped Villalobos rid himself of more than one annoying business rival.

The pretty ones are often the most dangerous because you never see them coming. I would have to keep an eye on her.

Next was Ian Hargreaves, formerly of the British Army's Special Air Service and Villalobos' head of security. He was dark haired, dark eyed, obviously fit, and gazed out from his photograph with eyes like flecks of obsidian. Looking over his service record, I couldn't help but let out a low whistle. He had made quite a name for himself in Basra and Helmand Province, earning a Conspicuous Gallantry Cross and racking up a body count that would have made Joseph Stalin raise an eyebrow. Anytime someone has the letters SAS associated with their name, they are a force to be reckoned with. But even among so highly-trained a group of soldiers, there are the elite of the elite. Those who stand out as being especially deadly, regarded with fear and respect among their fellows. Soldiers who usually wind up working for their respective country's clandestine services. Hargreaves was just such a man, but rather than landing in the quagmire of MI6, he had gone private.

And now, he was in my way.

Blow up that bridge when you get to it.

Next was Conner Hughes, a former commando in Her Majesty's Royal Marines who had seen action in Iraq and Afghanistan. Nothing to write home about, just your standard ex-soldier gone mercenary. More of a visual deterrent than anything else. A big ugly hostile presence to warn others against trying anything foolish. I had faced a hundred guys like him.

Then there was Gustavo Silva, a battle-scarred former BOPE officer from Rio de Janeiro's military police. That one would bear extra caution; anyone who could survive as long as he had against the drug gangs in Rio's *favelas* was a tough customer indeed. That said, I couldn't help but wonder what would drive a man who had spent so many years fighting the cancer of the drug trade to go over to the dark side. Maybe he decided if he couldn't beat 'em, he'd join 'em.

Additionally, we could count on Villalobos to contract out some of the local talent, the kind that specialized in protecting wealthy, dangerous people with lots of enemies and keeping it off the books. Cities like New York had armies of them. Ex-soldiers, ex-cops, former federal agents, the works. We had our work cut out for us.

I heard rattling and a pouring sound behind me, and a few seconds later Rocco appeared at my shoulder holding out a drink. "Knob Creek and tonic, just the way you like it."

Tanner looked up from his dossier and frowned disapprovingly. "You know it's only one in the afternoon, right?"

The Jersey boy shrugged. "Who cares? We're off the clock, and the drinks are on Uncle Sam's dime. Take it where you can get it, right?"

I accepted the drink, feeling a familiar dread at Rocco's statement. *Take it where you can get it.* The 'it', in this case, was a single word that encompassed a vast array of things. Relaxation. Pleasure. Good food. The taste of a quality drink. The little things you might regret passing up if an operation goes south and you find yourself breathing your last. "Damn right," I said.

Rocco gave me a light punch on my shoulder. "You see? This guy gets it."

"Just don't get drunk." Tanner went back to his reading.

After we finished getting to know our enemies, we reviewed the mission briefing. As usual, we were the last stage in an operation that was years in the making, as evidenced by the volume of information on our target, and the numerous assets planted amongst the staff at the Waldorf Astoria. It was stacking up to be a run of the mill snatch-and-grab operation. Tolliver wanted Villalobos alive, and he wanted it done with a minimum of noise. Our job was to separate him from the herd, incapacitate him, and get him to any one of the hotel's service exits. From there, one of several government SUV's staged nearby would take custody and the rest of us would make our escape. Later, a report would be leaked to the press exposing Villalobos' ties to the *Las Sombras* cartel and blaming his disappearance on rival drug lords. A likely enough story.

When we had finished, Rocco held up a finger. "I got a question."

Tanner rolled his eyes.

"What's that?" I said.

"Why do this at the Waldorf? I mean, there's a lot of eyes in a place like that. Guests, security cameras, you name it. Wouldn't it be easier just to snatch him off the street or something?"

"That would be too high-profile," I said. "The kind of thing that gets attention from the media and local law enforcement. It's better to set up a controlled environment where we have assets in place and plausible deniability if something goes wrong. Keeps things quieter that way."

Tanner nodded and added, "Not to mention that with as much security as Villalobos has following him around, any attempt to take him on the street would result in a firefight. A situation where civilians could get caught in the crossfire. The last thing you want on an op like this is collateral damage."

"Also," I continued, "the investor conference is the perfect cover story. It lures Villalobos away from his home turf to somewhere with a strong Homeland Security presence. Makes it easy to put the right people in the right places."

Rocco scratched the back of his head and stood up. "Yeah, I guess you have a point there."

He walked over to a mirror next to the door and began fussing at his suit. Fixing his hair. Straightening his tie. "Since we have time to kill, I'm gonna go downstairs and see if I can't score some ass. All the bored Park Avenue housewives love to get shitfaced in the middle of the day at places like this. Makes for easy pickings."

Tanner glanced at him in disgust. "Didn't Tolliver tell us to keep a low profile?"

"Fuck Tolliver. He's not the one risking his ass. If he has a problem with me getting my dick wet before a job, he can hire someone else to do his dirty work for him."

After one last glance in the mirror, Rocco shot us a wink and left. Tanner looked at me as the door clicked shut. "How do you put up with him?" he asked.

"He's delightful in small doses. We don't cross paths very often."

"Lucky you."

"You two have worked together before?"

"Yes, several times. I'll admit he's good at his job, but he lacks discipline."

"He just sees the job for what it is."

"And what's that?"

"Fleeting. This is a young man's game we're in, Tanner. Guys like us are nearing the end of our shelf life. Pretty soon, somebody younger and hungrier and more daring will come along and put us out to pasture. Rocco's just enjoying the ride while he can."

Tanner stared at me, his posture becoming strained. After a long moment, he faked a smile and began gathering up files. "Speak for yourself, Mr. Garrett. I plan to be on top of my game for many years to come. Is there anything else we should discuss regarding the mission?"

"I think we about covered it."

"I'll be in my room if you need me." He scooped up his paperwork and crossed the room with irritated haste, back straight, head down, wingtip shoes thumping on the thin carpeting. He opened the door faster than needed and stepped out, not casting a backward glance. The door shut on its own.

Guess I struck a nerve.

NINETEEN

The guards saw the smoke.

The sheriff's investigation uncovered a cabin burned to the ground with three dead bodies inside. I had hoped Walter would take the scene at face value and assume a trio of wanderers had taken refuge there. That they had been careless with a kerosene heater, and died of smoke inhalation before being consumed by the flames.

Unfortunately, the old man was not so easily fooled.

He had the bones bagged up and hauled back to town for further examination. While he was no forensic anthropologist, the sheriff had investigated a few murders in his time and knew bones could tell a great deal about how a person died. Within two days, he declared the skeletons were the remains of three Caucasian males, two dead of gunshot wounds, and foul play suspected in the third. His report indicated a notch found on the underside of the third victim's sternum that appeared to be a tool mark of some kind. Possibly caused by a knife. The report went on to state that there were currently no suspects, but the investigation was ongoing.

I kept to myself and awaited the inevitable.

It happened on a bitterly cold Monday night as I was eating dinner alone at Stall's Tavern. A biting, sub-freezing wind had sent most of the townsfolk scurrying for shelter, leaving the place mostly empty. I was seated at the bar picking disconsolately at my stew and thinking about how distant Elizabeth had been the last few days, and how our intimacy had grown stale in the wake of Sean Montford's murder. She rarely came to see me, and the few times she did, an uncomfortable silence took hold, making the usual affectionate touches and gestures awkward and insincere. Every time she looked at me, I could see the questions stirring in her eyes, the doubts, the fear. She had seen my name carved into that poor farmer's back, and she wasn't willing to believe I knew nothing about it any more than Sheriff Elliott was. As I ruminated over this, I heard the door to the tavern open behind me.

A familiar clomp of boots approached, the slow, heavy gait of a man who saves all his hurrying for the times when it really counts. There was the creak of leather and the slight jingling of metallic accoutrements, the shiny distinguishing insignia of a solemn office. The steps grew closer, landing steady and purposeful, the unflinching pace of sureness and authority. They stopped behind me as an aged, slightly liver-spotted hand pulled back the barstool next to me and the wide-brimmed hat with the sheriff's star appeared in my peripheral vision.

"You mind, Gabe?"

I gestured with my spoon. "Not at all, Walt. Take a load off."

He sat down, taking off his hat and laying it on the shiny surface of the bar, brim facing up. The aging hands clasped together in front of him, long fingers layering over one another as he looked down and considered his warbled reflection in the polyurethane. Mike came over and said Mattie Wallace had made her famous venison stew, and there was plenty left in the pot if he was interested. The sheriff declined, ordering only a cup of herbal tea. Mike went back to the kitchen, leaving the two of us in silence.

"You know why I'm here."

I nodded. "Figured you'd be coming around sooner or later."

"Is there anything you would like to tell me?"

I turned my head and looked him in the eye. "Nope."

There was a pause. "I don't suppose you can tell me where you were night of March seventh between midnight and three AM?"

"At my warehouse, doing inventory."

"Is there anyone who can corroborate that?"

"It was cold, Walt. Folks stayed in that night."

"So no one saw you?"

"Not that I know of."

"What about Elizabeth?"

"She was asleep. I didn't get home until two in the morning."

One of the hands came up and rubbed at the stubble on his chin. "That's awfully damned convenient, Gabe."

I let out an exasperated sigh and dropped my spoon into the half-eaten bowl of stew in front of me. It was good, but my appetite had been suffering lately. "Just come out with it already, will you? I know what you're thinking."

The watery blue eyes were frank and searching, hunting for deception like a hawk over a field. "Did you do it?"

"It doesn't matter what I tell you. You're not going to believe me anyway."

"That's not an answer."

I pushed my bowl away and shouted for Mike to put it on my tab. The sheriff remained motionless as I gathered my things to leave. "If you're going to charge me with something, Walt, do it. Otherwise, stop wasting my time."

I made it five steps before his voice stopped me. "They killed him, didn't they? The three people we found dead. They were the ones who murdered Sean Montford."

I stood motionless, not saying a word.

"Dragonfly. Two graves. Garrett. I was right, wasn't I? It was a message. Someone wanted you to know they were out there. Wanted to draw you out."

I stayed silent.

"Vendetta is a powerful force, Gabe. I've seen it drive people to do the craziest things. But you would have to be pretty damned angry to track somebody to a little place like this, especially with the world being the way it is. Whatever you did to them, it must have been terrible."

I turned around and looked at him. He still had his back to me, head down.

"I can't say I'm terribly broken up about it, not after what they did to that poor man. But my father always said two wrongs don't make a right. It's a rule I've lived by my whole life. Something I've tried to uphold as a lawman."

He swiveled around on his stool and stood up, face haggard, one hand idly flicking at the yellow-stitched star on his jacket. "I know there ain't much law and order left in the world, but I've tried to make sure Hollow Rock doesn't wind up like so many other places out there. Places where murder and thievery happen as sure as the sunrise. Things are different here. *People* are different here. They understand how much better life is when you have sensible laws in place, and someone to enforce them. It's why they keep electing me."

"That's very moving, Walt. Is there a point to this little speech?"

He dropped his hand and gave me a wan smile. "Sorry. I tend to ramble in my old age. My point is, you lied to me, Gabe. You looked me in the eye and you deliberately and knowingly withheld information pertinent to a murder investigation."

"You can't prove that, Walt."

"Even worse," he continued as if I hadn't spoken, "you went vigilante and killed the men responsible. I'm not going to stand here and say it wasn't justified, but that's not how we do things in Hollow Rock."

"Again, you have no proof. This is pointless."

"Just because I can't prove it doesn't mean you didn't do it. You need to know this changes things, Gabe. How am I supposed to trust you from now on knowing you lied to me?"

"Like I said, Walt. You've already made up your mind, so nothing I say is going to make any difference. Just know I'm still on your side, and I'm going to keep doing what I can to protect this town, same as you."

He shook his head. "No, Gabe. Not the same as me. I wouldn't have killed those men unless I had no other choice. I would have brought them in and made them stand trial. I would have given them a chance to defend themselves."

"And what if there wasn't enough evidence to convict them? What would you have done then? Let them go?"

He stared at me, lips set in a hard line. He didn't answer.

"Would you have let them get away with murder? I don't think so, Walter. I think you would have fortified yourself with a few shots of bourbon and paid me a visit."

He let his eyes drop, confidence draining.

"You would have come to me half-drunk and bitter, complaining about all the ways your badge ties your hands, about all the times you had to let someone walk because you didn't have enough evidence to try them. You would have cursed those men for what they did to Sean Montford, and you would have suggested someone ought to do something about it. Maybe let slip the location where they were released, where I could start tracking them. Arrange something with the guards at the main gate so I could come and go unnoticed. Tell me I'm wrong, Sheriff."

He didn't say anything.

"If you had put them on trial and convicted them, they would have stood in front of a firing squad. If they were acquitted, you would have asked me to hunt them down. The end result would have been the same regardless. So why come to me now and piss in my ear about it?"

He offered no response.

"Law and order is fine for the good people, Walt. It's fine for the petty criminals. But some people are smart and know how to manipulate the law. How to use it against you. That's where I come in. If someone wants to operate outside the law, I make sure they understand the consequences. Because if a person can't obey the law, they don't deserve its protection."

I took a few steps closer so that we were less than a foot apart, voice low, bending down to make him meet my gaze. "You know I'm right, Walter. You've been a cop too long to believe otherwise. So before you go throwing stones, I suggest you take a good hard look at the world beyond that wall out there. At the infected, and the marauders, and slavers, and

242

insurgents, and the war that could break out any day now. You take a good look and tell me how your dime-novel morality is going to protect this town from all the monsters out there, living and dead. You think about that, Sheriff. You think long and hard."

With that, I turned and left.

Later, Mike told me the sheriff had stood there for a long time, head down, hands trembling a little. After a while, he had come back to the bar and ordered a double whiskey. Then he'd ordered three more. Mike cut him off and watched as he staggered his way to the door, mumbling something about going home. A week later—about the right amount of time to let things simmer down—he announced he was closing the investigation due to a lack of evidence.

He never asked me about it again.

*****

That night, as I lay awake in bed feeling the cold hollowness of Liz's absence, I thought about what the sheriff had said to me. How it would take a hell of a lot of anger to track someone to an out-of-the-way place like Hollow Rock, especially three years after the end of the world. I thought about that mission in Manhattan, and Miguel Villalobos, and Anja Renner, and how it all went wrong. I thought about protocol, and rules, and the risks people take, never believing they will be the ones to fall. I thought about a choice I made, and how I could have sacrificed a mission to save a life.

I lay there with the moonlight streaming into my window, arms crossed behind my head, and I remembered those words again, that haunting, searing, prophetic turn of phrase burned indelibly into my heart. I thought again of Karen's sad eyes as she shut the door and left my life forever.

You are what you are, Gabriel. And you always will be.

TWENTY

Eight years ago,

New York City

To people around the world, the Waldorf-Astoria was a symbol of old world beauty and elegance. Upon entering the lobby, I could understand why they felt that way. Mosaic tile floor, smoothly polished marble on columns and walls, carpets that cost as much as a Mercedes Benz E class, a bouquet of flowers on a central table the size of an SUV, chandelier as big as a train car, soaring ceilings, gleaming lines of glass and metal on tables, overstuffed sofas and loveseats in corners and waiting areas—the place was the definition of grandiose. More money had gone into the lobby alone than a hundred real people might earn in their entire lives. I doubted, however, that many of them would realize the décor was not a relic of a bygone era, but rather the result of extensive renovations in the 1980's and 90's by Lee S. Jablin, a preeminent New York architect. I think if they had known this, it might have diminished the hotel's charm just a bit. I know it did for me.

I followed Tanner to the check-in counter while trying my best to look bored and uninterested. For Gabriel Garrett, a man from the wide open spaces of Kentucky, the press of wealth, breeding, ego, expensive perfume, heels clicking on marble, accented speech from a dozen nations, barely noticed physical contact, and casual indifference for personal space was enough to send him running for an exit. But for Thomas McGee, Chief Operations Officer of Mjolnir International, a private security firm out of Phoenix, it was just another day rubbing shoulders with the well-heeled, the old money, the captains of industry. He kept his face a mask of vague contempt and irritation, the don't-fuck-with-me façade endemic of a city where eye contact was verboten.

Beneath that mask, Gabriel Garrett was quietly swearing to himself that the next motherfucker who bumped into him was getting an elbow to the face.

Tanner greased the wheels by giving the pretty receptionist a high-wattage smile and complimenting the Tiffany necklace resting against the hollow of her throat. She smiled back, just a little warmer than professional courtesy required, manicured fingernails click-clacking on her keyboard. I presented my fake Arizona driver's license when asked, confirmed the company credit card information for incidentals, and proceeded with the other two operatives to Oscar's Brasserie, birthplace of eggs Benedict and the Waldorf salad.

A well-dressed, smiling, perfectly polite young woman stepped in front of us at the entrance and asked in her most solicitous tone if she might see our invitations. Tanner, playing the part of the fabulously rich senator's son, presented all three and hit her with the same practiced, flirtatious smile he had given the receptionist. She accepted it, and our invitations, with remarkably more aplomb than the girl at the check-in counter had. Inwardly, I applauded her judgment. If she was half as smart as she looked, she could probably detect the faint predatory glimmer behind those Scandinavian blues.

Most of the other invitees were already milling around in the dining room, sampling the gourmet spread, quietly assessing one another, and accepting the advances of Jerry Pritchard, Director of Investor Relations at Citadel Capital Management, with forced enthusiasm. The atmosphere was as welcoming as a chum-ridden pool of tiger sharks.

Pritchard eventually made his way over to us, with his artificially whitened teeth, impossibly expensive suit, and rimless Gold and Wood eyeglasses. He shook hands with Tanner, who was clearly the leader of the group, then turned to Rocco who introduced himself as Giovanni Palacio. When Pritchard asked him what company he represented, Rocco smiled broadly and said, "I'm in construction."

Pritchard's smile went brittle as he withdrew his hand. In New York, saying you were in 'construction', was as good as saying 'mobster'. The slimy gentry of hedge funds and private equity happily accepted their money, but they washed their hands afterward.

Last, he turned his fake plastic smile toward me. "Let me guess, you must play for an NFL team, right? You certainly have the size for it. A bit too lean for offensive line, so I'm thinking…maybe…defensive end? Middle linebacker?"

I faked an aw-shucks chuckle and shook my head. "Afraid not, sir. Football was never my sport. My stature is the result of good genetics, high-protein diet, and an affinity for the weight room." When I shook Pritchard's hand, I squeezed a little harder than I needed to. His barely restrained wince brightened my day. "Tom McGee, COO, Mjolnir International."

"A pleasure to meet you, Mr. McGee." He flexed his hand a few times when I released it, obviously relieved. "Just wanted to introduce myself to you gentlemen and remind you the presentation starts at four-thirty. I look forward to seeing you there."

The little man walked away, still flexing the compression out of his knuckle joints. Rocco leaned closer to me, voice low, faking a bad Southern accent. "Well ain't you just the most precious little country bumpkin."

"Can it, Roc."

"Seriously, man. How do you turn it on and off like that? Five seconds ago I'd have let you marry my daughter. Now you look like Charlie Manson after a sterno bender."

"Mr. Palacio…" Tanner said, a warning in his tone, staring pointedly across the room. We both turned at the same time. At the restaurant's entrance, showing their invitations to the polite receptionist, were Miguel Villalobos, Ian Hargreaves, and Anja Renner.

Rocco and Tanner gave them a quick, professional appraisal and dismissed them, exactly as they had been trained to do. Ordinarily, I would have done the same, but a pair of smoldering, storm-cloud eyes lanced across the room and caught my gaze, rooting me to the spot.

Her beauty was enhanced by mulberry lipstick and smoky eye shadow, tastefully applied. Her suit was perfectly fitted, hugging her slender curves. Her head tilted a little to the side as she looked at me, a stray lock of golden hair falling across her sculpted face. A dark heat began to burn low in my stomach and I started breathing harder, my heart a hammer in my chest. Anja stood equally still, equally enthralled, lips slightly parted, cold eyes glistening with animal curiosity. Her hand, which had just a moment ago handed over her invitation, went suddenly limp, dropping slowly, its purpose forgotten as I watched her chest rise slowly, the swell of her breasts lifting under her blouse.

A second ago she had been a programmable thing, a machine of efficiency and digitized calculation. But as she stared across the room at me there was a change in her, transforming her from a robot into woman in less time than it takes to say the words. My professional calm crumbled, fell apart, disintegrated to dust. I felt an understanding pass between us, a recognition of like to like, an elemental fascination pulling us together, demanding that we touch, that we feel sparks crackle on our skin under entreating fingertips. I started to take a step toward her, a little voice in the back of my mind screaming a warning, a voice I ignored.

Then Hargreaves tapped her on the shoulder.

She looked away and released me, breaking the spell. I stopped, took a deep breath, and turned away, the shadowed edges of tunnel vision fading, the color coming back into the world, vise loosening from my chest. In a second or two, I felt like myself again, good old reliable Gabriel, possessed of his faculties, the searing heat of attraction receding, mission coming into focus. I checked to make sure Rocco and Tanner hadn't caught that little exchange. They had not. Good.

I cleared my throat and joined my companions, wondering what the hell just happened. I had seen plenty of pretty women before, but I had never reacted like that. Never lost control so quickly, or with so little prompting. Then I remembered Anja's face as our eyes met, the blush that traveled from graceful neck to elegantly curved cheeks, the way she seemed to get a little trembly in the knees. The heat came back all over again, and I had to shake my head to clear it.

Stay focused.

We made the rounds a while longer, introducing ourselves to other potential clients, asking questions, rehearsing our carefully memorized lines. Oh, Phoenix isn't so bad. It's a dry heat. Nothing we do is all that terribly glamorous. Most of our work is overseas. Guarding valuable cargo, riding in trucks from one place to another, that sort of thing. Honestly, you could put most of our employees in cheap uniforms and an armored truck, and their job description wouldn't change a bit. Ha-ha-ha.

All the while, I kept sneaking glances at Anja, already thinking of her by her first name. The photograph in her dossier didn't do her justice. She was stunning. I wondered what her hair would look like if she let it down, how much brighter the eyes would be if she took those glasses off, if her body was as strong and firm as the lines of her suit indicated. The gaggle of paunchy, pasty, middle-aged men around me noticed her as well, some ogling her surreptitiously, others staring openly. I had a primeval urge back them all in a corner and start smashing heads together.

Knock it off, idiot. What is this, junior high? You're not trying for second base with Jenny Landon under the bleachers. You're on the clock. These people are dangerous. Get it together.

Words slipped past me as I went from one person to another, exchanging pleasantries, trying to focus on what they were saying. I must have seemed dull and just a bit distracted to the people I met. Sometimes I caught Anja staring at me when she thought I couldn't see her, and felt my blood heat up all over again.

There is a mind trick I do when I need to split my attention. It works in much the same way as my speed-reading trick, but it is supplemented by a library of stock social responses to the predictable patterns of polite conversation. The words go into my ears, are processed and catalogued, and the shiny surface of sub-conscious thought chooses the correct response, facial expression, and mannerism of body. In this manner, I can perform impressive feats of cognitive agility whilst pretending to be engrossed in some idiot's story of how his yacht ran over a submerged log off a remote section of some Bahamian island and the harrowing three days of second-rate food and lodging ashore before the engineer could get it fixed.

Dreadful, I tell you. They didn't even have room service. I had to stand at the counter and order fried plantains and shredded pork with common laborers. The dining room was this dingy, stinking little place with swarming flies and no air conditioning. Honestly, how do those people call themselves civilized?

While part of me resisted the urge to shake these stupid people by their throats, the rest of me focused on staying centered. I concentrated on my breathing, responses, expressions. Tanner was slowly maneuvering us closer and closer to Villalobos, and soon, I would have to look Anja in the eye from less than three feet away, shake her hand, feel her skin against mine, and do it with no visible reaction. To do that I had to suppress the animal part of me, the hairy, bone-cracking mammal of the ancient savannah.

Carefully, gradually, I started melding the two sides of my mind together again. The pragmatic, analytical core, and the automatic, software-like surface entity. The primal, unpredictable part got shoved down, suppressed, boxed up, filed away for future examination. I didn't need it for the time being. What I needed was control. Precise, unyielding control.

Just as the last vestiges of carnal heat slid rippling beneath the cerebral waters, Tanner reached out a hand and a smile to Villalobos.

"Hi there, I'm Rowan Marshall, Mr..."

"Villalobos." His voice was deep and heavily accented, and just as cold as his eyes. "This is Ms. Renner, my personal assistant, and this is Mr. Hargreaves."

"This is Giovanni Palacio and Tom McGee, old college buddies of mine."

We made the requisite round of introductions. I started with Villalobos, who barely glanced at me as he offered a limp noodle of a handshake. Then there was Hargreaves, strong and assertive, black flecks of iris scrutinizing me and, by their slight narrowing, not liking what they saw. Last was Anja, more petite than I had thought, head barely cresting my chest, face like porcelain, shoulders rigid, eyes avoiding mine like the plague. There was the faintest tremor in her hand as she reached out, making me wonder how she would react when our skin made contact. Just as we were about to touch, we were saved by a fork ringing against a crystal glass.

"Ladies and gentlemen, if I could have your attention for just a moment." Pritchard said, standing on a chair. "I hope everyone had a chance to sample some of the fine cuisine provided for us this afternoon by the talented folks here at Oscar's. I know I certainly did, and I don't mind telling you the desert bar is to die for."

A pause, a polite round of chuckling.

"The presentation will be starting in ten minutes, so if you don't mind, we should all begin making our way to the Conrad Suite on the fourth floor. Each group has its own table set aside, and the hotel staff will be available to answer any questions you might have. Please feel free to take a plate or a beverage with you, and if there is anything you would like once we're upstairs, don't hesitate to ask."

People began moving toward the exit clutching champagne and little plates of spinach quiche. Villalobos and company excused themselves, rounded up a few cups of coffee, and departed for the elevators. On his way out, Hargreaves took a moment to stop and level a stare at me, eyes hard, lips as thin as paper. I offered a friendly smile and lifted my drink, engaging the resonant Southern drawl. "See you up there, partner."

The corners of his mouth twisted in what might have been a fake smile. His eyes scanned the room, darting from one end to the other, deeply ingrained suspicion pouring off him in waves, the tireless alertness of a man who lived his life inches from death. He looked as though at any moment he might lift his employer bodily, draw some hidden weapon, and flee the building in a hail of bullets. A tough customer to be sure.

I hoped I wouldn't have to discover which one of us was tougher.

*****

The presentation was as painfully boring as I expected it to be.

The three of us got through it by sipping ice water, faking a measure of solemn interest, and speaking to one another in low whispers. Anyone watching us might have thought we were debating the relative merits of the various funds Citadel had to offer. In truth, we were casing the room for a good spot to divert Villalobos and strategizing how to separate him from Hargreaves.

"Why don't we just kill the limey fuck?" Rocco asked. "Wait till he goes to the John, or something. I'll do it myself, quick and quiet. Prop him up in a stall with his pants down. By the time Villalobos misses him, he'll be in the back of a suburban."

"That's a last-resort option," Tanner said. "Besides, we still have to worry about Renner."

"Leave her to me," I said.

Tanner looked quizzical. "What's your plan?"

"She's attracted to me. I'll ask her out for drinks after this, take her back to my room. You stay close to Villalobos and find out if he's serious about investing in any of these funds. If he is, call Tolliver and tell him to have Pritchard set up a private meeting with one of his salespeople. Be there when Villalobos arrives, tell him you were invited. Go through the motions, then have the sales guy make up some excuse to leave the room. That's when you grab him."

Tanner thought it over for a moment. "It's not a bad idea, as long as Villalobos doesn't show up with any of his security people."

I shrugged. "If he does, take them out quietly and put them in the suburban with Villalobos. Our assets on the hotel staff can clean up the mess."

Tanner paused again, considering. "I like it. I'll have Tolliver send weapons to our rooms. You guys okay with .22's?"

"Integral suppressors? Sub-sonic ammo?" Rocco asked.

"Of course."

"Works for me."

I said, "Just don't let it become a firefight. You'll be outgunned."

As I sat back in my seat, the dimmed lights brightened and the last presenting hedge fund manager smiled and gave a slight bow to the mutely applauding attendees. Pritchard stepped up and announced the beginning of cocktail hour, and encouraged the audience to come to him or any of the fund managers with any questions they might have. To keep up appearances, the three of us approached the manager of a commodities and currency arbitrage fund and asked some drill-down questions about his methodology. He babbled some vague references to a proprietary computer program his staff had developed, and how it worked in much the same manner as a search engine to monitor import and export data from a vast array of companies to predict minor shifts in commodity prices and currency rates before they could self-correct. Minor fluctuations, really. A few basis points here and there. But if you get out ahead of them and use a modest amount of leverage, you can reap a tidy profit. Thirty-six percent annualized over the last four years, far ahead of market returns.

While Tanner broached the subject of the minimum required investment, I cast a glance over my shoulder and once again caught Anja staring at me. This time, however, she did not look away as quickly. Her gaze held mine for an extra few seconds before she lowered her face demurely, the corners of her lips curving in a faint smile. Her left hand came up, fingers tracing a line down the side of her neck.

Now would be a good time.

I excused myself and made my way over. Anja didn't look up, but I could tell by her body language she was aware of my approach. When I reached her, I leaned close and spoke softly.

"Ms. Renner?"

She turned and looked up, face angled slightly to the side, blasting me with the full effect of those storm-colored eyes. "Mr. McGee, I believe? Is there something I can do for you?"

I could think of a few things. Her voice was rich and clear with a slight Bavarian accent and impeccable pronunciation. "I was wondering if you would join me at the bar for a drink."

Her smile became challenging. "You are very direct, Mr. McGee. Are you not supposed to flirt with me first? Brag to me about your wealth and influence, your chalet in Switzerland, your collection of cars?"

"I don't own any chalets, and a car is just something to move a person from one place to another. Something in your manner tells me you aren't terribly impressed by those sorts of things. I thought you might find a little directness refreshing, a break from all these fake smiles and clever maneuvering. Am I wrong?"

She tilted her head the other way, giving me a view of the curve of her neck. "No, you are not. A moment, please."

She turned to Villalobos and tapped him on the shoulder. He held up a finger to the man speaking to him and turned his dead brown eyes our way.

"Miguel, will you be needing me for the next few minutes?" she asked in perfect Spanish.

He looked at me, then back at her. Gave a little chuckle. *"You like them big, don't you?"*

There was a familiarity in his voice I might have almost called friendly. Perhaps Anja was more than just a mere personal assistant.

"And you like them young. We all have our preferences. Please, Miguel, it's been weeks. A woman must enjoy herself

now and then, or she will go mad. Perhaps he will scare away all these flabby little men bothering me."

"Fine. Take the rest of the night off; get it out of your system. Just don't stay up too late, young lady. We have much to do tomorrow."

"Of course. Thank you, Miguel."

She turned back to me and linked her arm in mine. "It would appear my schedule has suddenly opened for the evening. Perhaps we should have our drink somewhere more...appealing." She cast a disparaging glance at the attendees, almost all of whom were men, and none worthy of her approval.

"Nothing would make me happier."

We walked arm in arm toward the elevator, every eye in the room turning to follow us. The expressions of those we passed ranged from simple jealousy to outright hostility. I caught Tanner's eye on the way out and gave him a slight nod. He blinked twice in acknowledgment.

"So where would you like to go?" I asked.

"Are you staying here at the hotel?"

"I am."

"I assume your room has a mini-bar?"

"It does."

"Then that is where you should take me."

She stepped closer when she said it, the warm curve of her hip pressing against my thigh. I pressed the button for my floor, trying not to let my hand tremble or the heat in my stomach spread to my face.

With any luck, I could enjoy an evening with the lovely Ms. Renner while Tanner and Rocco took care of the dirty work. They would no doubt give me a metric ton of shit about it, but right then, I could not have cared less.

As the elevator doors hissed shut, I noticed Hargreaves watching us. The look on his face was not a happy one.

TWENTY ONE

There are times in life when you have to swallow your pride and make amends.

Two weeks passed after speaking with the sheriff, and during that time I received no word from Elizabeth. No visits, no runners bearing messages, not even a note stuck to my front door. Lacking any better ideas, I paid a visit to Eric and Allison and asked them what I should do.

"Why don't you just go see her?" Eric suggested, his wounded leg propped on an ottoman. The leg was healing nicely, but he would be walking with a limp for at least a couple of months. Allison also informed me Private Fuller was out of the hospital, but confined to bed rest for another two weeks. She anticipated a least a month before he would be fit for duty.

"I don't know if that's such a good idea. I kind of...lied to her about something."

Allison perked up, and I could swear her ears grew little points. "Lied about what?"

"It's kind of a long story."

Eric gestured to his recently perforated appendage. "Do I look like I'm going anywhere? Come on, out with it."

I let out a sigh. "Okay, but this conversation doesn't leave this room, you hear? It would be bad for all parties involved if this hits the rumor mill."

"Gabe, this is us you're talking to," Eric said. "If you want us to keep it a secret, then we keep it a secret. End of story."

I looked across the room at the best friend I had, a man I had been to hell and back with, who had been stalwart and steadfast through thick and thin. The old reluctance was still there, that miserly hoarding of information to ward off the judgmental eyes of the world. But sitting there looking at his concerned face, and that of the pretty young doctor sitting next to him holding his hand, I just couldn't find it in me to hold back anymore. Secrets are a heavy burden, and you don't realize how much they weigh you down until you let them go.

So I told him.

I gave them the abbreviated version of the mission in New York, and who I thought was after me. I told them about the words carved on Sean Montford's back, and the events that followed. I told them about my argument with Sheriff Elliott at Stall's Tavern, and how that information had most likely made its way back to Elizabeth. When I was finished, Eric nodded silently, unsurprised by any part of the story. Allison, on the other hand, looked visibly shaken.

"Jesus, Gabe," she said, barely a whisper. "How could you just…kill those men like that? The way you made the serial killer guy suffer, it's…"

I sank deeper into my chair, feeling tired and empty. It wasn't the first time someone had balked when they learned of something I had done, but it still didn't feel any better. Especially coming from someone whose opinion I held in high esteem. "Allison, I've done worse things than kill a bunch of murderers in cold blood. The only thing I can say in my defense is they got better than they deserved after what they did to Montford. His only crime was being in the wrong place at the wrong time. Now his wife and children have to get along without him. Maybe I settled that account with more prejudice than necessary, but don't expect me to apologize. They certainly didn't apologize to their victims. Montford wasn't the only one, you know. God knows how many people those sick fucks tortured to death."

"I understand that, but still, I'm a doctor, Gabe. What you did, it's anathema to everything I stand for."

"Listen," Eric said, turning to look at her, face darkening. "Life isn't all rainbows and sunshine anymore, okay? Things are different now. Sometimes good people have to do bad things."

"I know that, Eric, but…"

"No you don't, Allison," he said with a sudden heat in his voice. Allison stiffened as if she'd been slapped. "You don't know. You've treated the wounded and the sick, but you've never had to do the fighting. You've spent every day since the Outbreak here, in Hollow Rock, where life is relatively sane. But the world beyond that wall outside is not sane. Not even a little bit. It hellish and dangerous and damn near everyone you meet wants to kill you, rob you, or worse. And that's not even counting the infected. Gabriel and I have not survived by wearing kid gloves and playing by the rules. There are no rules anymore. We might have law and order here in Hollow Rock, but for everyone else, it's survival of the fittest. What Gabe did was rough, I won't deny that. But it's not nearly as bad as what others have done, including the men he killed. At least Gabe did what he did for the right reasons, and in defense of the right people. I suggest you remember that before you go passing judgment."

Allison's mouth worked a few times, face growing red, trying to come up with a response. Nothing came out.

"Listen," I said, trying to keep the peace. "I'm not trying to start an argument here, okay? Eric, I appreciate you defending me, but you really shouldn't talk to Allison like that. She deserves better."

The look he shot me was defiant for a few seconds, then regretful. "You're right. Allison, I'm sorry I snapped at you. I didn't mean it."

Her hand covered his. "No, you're right. It's not my place to pass judgment on Gabe, or you, or anyone else. I *have* spent too much time behind the wall. Being a doctor has kept me protected from the worst of what's out there. I guess it's easy to throw stones when no one is throwing them back at you, right? You guys have been through so much. I just..." Her eyes became red and leaky, her lower lip beginning to quiver.

"Hey, hey, none of that," Eric said, drawing her into a hug. "You've been crying a lot lately. Are you all right? This isn't like you."

Her head was tucked under Eric's chin, so he didn't see the warning look she shot me. "I'm fine. I guess the stress of everything is getting to me. You know how it is."

"Yeah. I do."

They sat holding each other for a few moments, eyes closed, taking comfort in one another's warmth and presence. I remembered all the times Elizabeth and I had done the exact same thing, clinging to each other silently in the cold and the dark. There was a hollow ache in my chest, in the place that grew warm when Liz was around.

You have to fix this. Find a way.

I cleared my throat, bringing Eric and Allison back into the room. They smiled at each other and separated, hands clasped, momentary unpleasantness forgotten.

"So what do you suggest I do about Elizabeth?" I asked. "Maybe one of you could talk to her for me?"

"Gabe, I think Eric's right," Allison said. "I think you should go talk to her yourself."

I grimaced. "I was worried you were going to say that."

She smiled. "It would be best to see her early in the day, right around seven. She's a morning person, she'll be more receptive. Oh, and bring a peace offering. Instant coffee would be my recommendation."

"Coffee I can do. That part will be easy, if expensive. Explaining myself is going to be the hard part."

"Just tell her the truth, Gabe. It's not up to you if she forgives you or not, it's up to her. All you can do is offer your honesty and love, and hope it's enough. Life will go on either way."

I nodded, head down, feeling defeated. Eric asked if I wanted to stay for lunch, but I declined.

"What, you got something better to do today?" he asked.

I looked at Allison and shared a conspiratorial smile. "Yeah. Gotta head over to the warehouse and scare up some coffee."

Elizabeth didn't look very good when she answered the door.

"Good morning," I said.

She pulled her robe tighter around her and brushed her hair out of her face. "Come on in, Gabe. It's too cold to talk on the porch."

I stomped the snow off my boots and did as asked. The living room was warm, heated by a woodstove I had found on a salvage run a few weeks ago. I hauled it back to town and enlisted the help of Tom Glover to install it in Liz's house, along with a chimney. Looking at it, I realized it was the only gift I had ever given Elizabeth. For a guy with a genius IQ, sometimes I am not very bright.

"How have you been?" I said. "I haven't seen you in a while."

Her eyes were red around the edges, the lines of her face deeply etched, hair loose and tangled. She looked as if she had not been sleeping much lately. "I've been busy. The feds finally decided what they want us to do with those insurgents you captured."

"Really?"

She nodded. "They want us to hold a trial."

"What's the charge?"

"Charges. Plural. There's a whole list of them, you'd have to ask Walter."

I winced. "Probably not a good idea. I'm not exactly his favorite person right now."

"I know. You're not mine either."

I accepted the comment with a nod, understanding where it came from and why she felt that way, even though it hurt like hell to hear it. I reached under my coat and produced the jar of instant coffee. Gift number two.

"Would this help?"

Her eyes widened. Coffee, even the vile instant stuff, is a rare and precious commodity. The jar I held still had the vacuum seal on it, making it valuable enough to buy a month's food and lodging at any trading post along the Mississippi. As the beneficiary of many of my reports on the subject, Liz understood this.

"It sure as hell wouldn't hurt," she said. "Let me put some water on."

I handed her the jar and took a seat on the sofa, hands crossed in my lap, remembering what Allison said to me about honesty. It took Liz a few minutes to boil the water, add a couple of carefully measured spoonfuls of grains, and hand me a steaming mug. I held it close to my face and blew coils of vapor from the top, relishing the warmth if not the smell. Liz took a seat across from me and pulled a blanket over her legs.

"So what do you have to say for yourself?"

My shoulders sagged as I put the mug on the table. "I should probably start with an apology."

She tipped her head to the side. "Not the worst idea you've ever had."

"I'm sorry, Elizabeth. I'm sorry I lied to you. I'm sorry I didn't come to you with this earlier. I'm sorry for this whole damn mess. Sean Montford was murdered because of me. Because of something I did a long time ago."

"And you went after his killers." A statement, not a question.

I nodded. "I thought I could take care of it quietly. No fuss, no questions."

Liz tilted her head again, dark eyes staring out from beneath hooded lids. "Setting a house on fire isn't exactly low profile, Gabe."

"No. It isn't. I don't know, maybe on some level I wanted to get caught."

"But you didn't, exactly. Walter couldn't find any evidence linking you to the deaths."

"No, but he wasn't fooled. He knows how to put two and two together. I was stupid to think he wouldn't figure it out."

"He told me about your argument at Stall's Tavern, about all the things you said to him. You were right, you know. He wouldn't have let those men get away with murder, not even if they were tried and acquitted. Nor would I, for that matter."

I looked up, surprised. "What do you mean?"

"It's entirely possible they would have walked. There may not have been enough evidence to prove they murdered Sean. Their hideout's proximity to the crime scene is purely circumstantial evidence, probably not enough to convince a jury even in these troubled times. Speaking of, how exactly did you know they were guilty?"

She was dodging my question, but I let it go. "I...interrogated one of them. He confessed things only the perpetrator would know. I didn't want to take action until I was sure. They killed him, Liz. I'm sure of it. One of them was...I don't know if serial killer is the right word, but he was something close to it. Before he died, he bragged about how many people he had killed and the things he did to them. Disturbing shit, even for me."

Liz was quiet for a moment, contemplating. "But why? It doesn't make any sense. Why did they kill Sean just to get your attention?"

"Someone hired them to draw me out and capture me. I'm thinking they wanted to do it away from town in case I was missed and someone came looking. It would give them a head start."

"But why capture you?"

"I think whoever hired them is very angry with me and wants me alive. There were actually four of them, by the way. I let one live and told him to go back to his employer and give him a message."

"And what message was that?"

"To leave the fuck off. To cease and desist, and the consequences for failure to do so."

"Do you think it will work?"

"I don't know. Probably. If he was truly dedicated, he would have come here and settled things personally. But he didn't. I'm not sure what to make of that."

Liz paused again, taking a sip of her coffee. After a few seconds, she stood up and came over to sit beside me.

"I have a lot more questions I'd like to ask. Like who sent those men and why, and what you did to make that person hate you so much. I'd like to know how you managed to get in and out of Hollow Rock without anyone seeing you, and where you learned to do things like that. I'm willing to bet it wasn't part of your training in the Marines. I'd also like to know how you got all those scars, and the stories behind them. And maybe someday I'll ask you those questions. Maybe someday I'll feel strong enough and anchored enough. But it won't be today."

She let the last few words hang in the air, baiting me. "Okay," I said cautiously. "Why not?"

"Because it doesn't matter. Because I'm happy when I'm with you, and right now, that's all I care about. You gave me something back I thought was gone from my life forever, and I don't want to lose it again. When you're with me, I feel like life is worth living. The way the world is now, that's a precious thing."

I put an arm around her and kissed her on the temple. "I could say the same thing about you, pretty lady. I should have said it a hundred times by now."

She smiled at me, and I felt hope began to burn again. "I was angry for a while that you lied to me," she said. "That you didn't trust me enough to tell me the truth. Eventually, the anger went away, and I was just sad. I cried a lot. Then one day I woke up and realized I was being a hypocrite. I certainly wasn't squeamish when you killed Ronnie Kilpatrick and his gang, or during the fighting with the Free Legion. It seemed wrong of me to trust you when the town was in danger, but doubt you when it wasn't. I've never been a fair-weather friend, Gabe. If you don't want to tell me why you went after Sean's murderers, you must have a very good reason."

I smiled and bowed my head. "It makes me sad to say this, but that's probably the nicest, most understanding thing anyone has ever said to me."

She laughed and shook her head. "It's been a lonely couple of weeks, sweetie. I held out hope you would visit, but days kept passing and you didn't come. Honestly, I was starting to think you had given up on me."

I reached for her hand, watching her fingers slip through mine. "Not on your life, lady. I just didn't know what to say, you know? I was ashamed of myself. I didn't want to stand out there on your porch sputtering like an idiot."

"I'd rather see you sputtering like an idiot than not see you at all. You should have come sooner."

"I know."

Her hair tickled my chin as she shifted and laid her head in the crook of my shoulder. My arms went around her of their own volition, squeezing tight. I breathed in her scent and swore to myself I wasn't going to screw things up this time. Not with a woman this perfect.

"I'm in love with you, you big dope. You know that right?"

A smile spread across my face, and words that hadn't passed my lips in ten years tumbled free. I had wanted to say them before, but never did. I was worried they would not come, that they would remain lodged in their self-imposed imprisonment forever, never to be released. But as I sat there with that good woman, and knew she loved me despite everything, I couldn't keep them to myself anymore.

"I love you too, Liz."

And I meant it.

TWENTY TWO

March slowly declined toward April, and the coming of spring. Unfortunately, winter didn't get the memo.

The day of transition from one season to the other came and went, but there was no warming of air or melting of frost and ice. Instead, gunmetal clouds darkened the sky, the temperature plummeted into the high twenties, and a gentle snow began to fall on Western Tennessee. Not a blizzard like a few weeks ago, but a slowly descending gauze of fluffy white stuff. It came down like oversized dust, gentle and tame, seeming to hang in the air for hours before settling to the earth.

There are bad snowfalls that make life difficult, and there are good ones that demonstrate nature's haunting beauty. This was one of the latter.

Liz and I walked along the wall in the pale bluish light that comes just before sunset. Her hand was in mine, and we were letting our appetites grow sharp before heading over to Mijo Diego for venison tacos and slow-cooked beans. The guards nodded politely and offered muffled greetings from behind scarves and balaclavas as we passed. Liz responded in kind, calling each guard by name even though she couldn't see their faces, a fact not lost on the people she addressed.

"No wonder you always win elections," I said when we were alone. "You know everybody in town."

She shrugged. "I pay attention to some groups more than others. The town guard, for instance. It pays to know who's protecting you while you sleep. Makes it easier to spot minor problems and deal with them before they become major problems. The last thing we need is someone getting killed because a watchman has a weakness for strong drink, or falls asleep on duty because he was up all night arguing with his wife. Little things like that keep me awake at night, so I make an effort to stay informed."

"Good thinking."

"It's what I do."

We walked a little farther in amiable silence, happy to be on solid footing again. The walkway turned southeast at the corner of Dodd Street and Highway 70, leading toward the south wall. To our left was a row of houses, and beyond that, the central part of town. VFW hall, sheriff's office, clinic, and the building that housed Liz's offices. If we took a staircase to ground level, we could be there in five minutes' walk. Not that I was in any kind of a hurry.

"Allison finally told Eric she was pregnant," Liz said, stopping to look out at the rolling fields on the south side of town. An undulating blanket of white rippled gently toward the treeline in the distance. There were a few walkers shambling along, drawn to the sounds of life behind the wall, but even they couldn't detract from the quiet beauty of the scene.

"You knew about that?"

"Yes. I was the first person she told. We've been friends since before she left for med school, you know."

"Actually, I didn't know that. How did Eric take it?"

"He picked her up and spun her around, and shouted at the neighbors he was going to be a father. Then he started crying. Allison said it was very sweet."

I laughed quietly. "Wish I could have seen that."

"They're planning to visit you tomorrow to break the news. Allison asked if you could please pretend to be surprised. Eric probably wouldn't like it very much if he knew you found out before he did."

"I'll do my best."

Liz walked to the edge of the battlement and rested her hands against the rail, smile fading. Her neck creaked as she stretched it from one side to the other, eyes clouding with the dark veil of introspection. I stepped closer and rubbed the strong muscles between her shoulders. "Something on your mind?"

She lifted one boot and absently tapped the toe against a plank beneath her. "I spent an hour on the phone yesterday with an assistant director for Homeland Security. The new administration is calling around to all the outposts to reassure us of their continued support. In our case, they offered to provide additional troops and artillery since we're so close to Alliance territory. The Phoenix Initiative is sending two doctors and a dozen nurses, and starting next month, we'll be getting increased allotments of fuel and medical supplies."

She turned her head to look at me, voice lowering in pitch. "They're also sending aircraft and tanks."

I nodded, understanding her fears. "Which is to imply they think we need it. With resources as stretched as they are, they never would have offered otherwise."

Liz stood up straight, hands going into her pockets. "In exchange for all this, they asked to requisition Fort McCray. They want to turn it into a forward operating base. That's going to be a lot of mouths to feed, and a lot of bored soldiers making trouble in town. I'll have to establish some ground rules with the commanding officers."

"What about the Ninth? Where are they supposed to go?"

"They'll garrison with the Army. Since they know the area, they'll be used mostly as scouts and guides."

"They're not going to like that."

Liz shrugged. "It's a volunteer militia. They can quit whenever they want. We can always call up new recruits; there are enough people in place to train them, now."

I frowned at her. "That's a bit dismissive, don't you think? That militia has fought hard to keep this town safe. They're good people, and they deserve better than that."

Liz closed her eyes and nodded, a quaver entering her voice. "I know. But having a large Army presence will make Hollow rock a safer place, and if we have to lose a few militiamen to make it happen, then so be it. I don't like it any more than you do, Gabe, but it's what's necessary. Being mayor means making the hard choices. If the militia takes exception to their new circumstances, I'll do my best to make them understand. Short of that, they can take their leave. Sheriff Elliott is always looking for guardsmen, and Lord knows there'll be plenty of work in the fields once the weather turns."

She was right. I didn't like it. But I couldn't argue with her logic, and I knew very well how difficult of a situation she was in. In her place, I would do the same thing. I told her as much, and she smiled over her shoulder at me. "Thank you. I'm glad you understand."

She took my hand again, and we walked a little farther, stopping to take in another angle of Tennessee vista. There was a buzzing sound to my left as a transplanted streetlight came to life, its faded bulb casting a sickly orange glow on the fortifications outside the wall.

"Well I'll be damned," I said. "Looks like Jutaro finally found enough cable to hook up the perimeter lights."

"Yeah, he's making great progress," Liz replied. "Did I tell you Central Command sent a Phoenix Initiative rep not long ago to see how things were coming along?"

"No, but I heard about it. Seems like the Phoenix Initiative is all anybody talks about anymore."

"Can you blame them?"

"Not really."

I opened my mouth to ask another question, but was cut short by a shrill whirring that rapidly increased in volume until it culminated in a sudden *THACK*, loud and hard, like someone throwing a rock against a tree with incredible velocity.

I knew that sound. I had heard it many times.

Half-panicked, I looked where the impact sounded from and saw a support post a few feet away. There was a splintered hole in it about as big around as my thumb, and in the air between, a faint red mist drifted to the ground.

Then I heard the report.

Moving on instinct, I grabbed Liz and lifted her up like a child, breaking into an all-out sprint. A distant part of my mind analyzed the sound of the shot, doing a few calculations. By the volume, pitch, and timbre, I knew the round was most likely a 7.62x54. Judging by the time between impact and when I heard the report, it had traveled from five to six hundred yards before impacting the post. More than enough time had elapsed for the shooter to shift aim and draw a bead on me. The shot could come at any moment.

I had to get off the wall.

As I ran, Liz let out a cough that sprayed my chest and the left side of my face with blood and spittle. An agonized sound somewhere between a scream and a moan bubbled from her throat, and she struggled in my arms.

"SNIPER!" I screamed. "Sound the alarm! Take cover!"

A guard patrolling nearby heard me and, to his credit, did not hesitate. He crouched and dashed to the closest bell, seized the ringer, and began frantically swinging it back and forth, splitting the air with a cacophony of bronze clanging. An answering bell came from the next station down, then another, and another, until bells all over town were ringing the signal for an attack.

"Hang on Liz, I'm getting us out of here."

"Gabe...*nghk*..." She started coughing again.

"Don't try to talk, you'll make it worse. Just hang on, baby, hang on. We're not far from the clinic. You're going to be all right. Just hang on..."

I kept repeating it, over and over, a mantra against my own fear. I had caught a glimpse of Elizabeth's back as I grabbed her and saw a jagged, blossoming red spot on her coat, right about where the lower portion of her left lung would be.

Open pneumothorax, better known as a sucking chest wound. A penetration of the chest wall that allows air to pass freely between the pleural space and the atmosphere. I could hear her gurgling breath whistling in and out of her torso.

The proper first aid would be to place sealing bandages front and back, leaving one side of the front bandage unsealed, thus plugging the punctures on inhalation and allowing air to escape on exhalation. Once the holes were covered, the next step would be to insert an endotracheal tube to help her undamaged lung continue to breath, then insert an IV in her arm and start pumping in fluids. None of which was going to happen, of course, because I had left my first aid kit at home, I didn't have an endotracheal tube, and I sure as fuck didn't have an IV.

A guard dashed up to me as I approached the staircase shouting something about helping me carry Liz. I roared at him to get the fuck out of the way and nearly knocked him over as I passed.

"Take cover you idiot!"

There was a prickling feeling in my back, a tingle I had felt many times before. The expectation of impact, the buzzing, panicky anticipation of a bullet slamming into me at immense speed. I shrank down, trying to stay as low as I could without slowing. The staircase ahead of me grew closer and closer, and with every step, I waited for that sledgehammer feeling followed by burning and howling agony. Then would come the report, the miniature sonic boom, the sound of air slamming back together after a small object passed through it faster than the speed of sound. Last there would be the fall, and the encroaching cold, and the slow descent as the world grew smaller and smaller until it went black, and then there would be nothing …

Stop it. Just keep moving.

Finally, my foot came down on the first stair. My shoulders were still visible above the battlement, still vulnerable. I let my knees go almost limp, barely touching the boards underfoot, pumping my legs for maximum descent. The second stair passed, and the third, and the fourth. Now it was just my head above the line. If the bullet came, I would never feel it. My boots hit the fifth stair, the sixth, all the way down to the eighth and the landing where the stairs double backed on themselves. I was out of danger, and could finally stand upright, move faster, gain momentum. In my arms, Liz tried speaking again.

"I…I can't…*hgk*…"

"Liz, please, don't talk. I'm taking you to the clinic right now. You're gonna be ok."

The effects of a gunshot wound to the lung began scrolling through my head like the credits at the end of a movie. The first problem was airway. It is hard to get sufficient oxygen to support life with only one lung, which is why we have two of them. One of hers was damaged and inoperable. The next problem was bleeding. The lungs are full of blood-rich tissue and arteries that bleed profusely when damaged. With every step I took, with every ragged breath as I charged toward town, her lung was filling up with blood.

Faster. Move faster.

The only thing I had going for me was the bullet hit the left lung and not the right one. Due to the asymmetrical shape of the human heart, the right lung is larger than the left, with three lobes instead of two. The left lung is longer than the right one, which explained how the bullet had penetrated it despite hitting so low. Since her right lung was still intact her chances of survival were better, but she was still in a lot of trouble. I had to get her to Doc Laroux and get her on an operating table, and I had to do it *now*.

My feet hit the pavement of Dodd Street as I sped along, wounded love bouncing in my arms, head down, mouth open wide to feed as much oxygen to my muscles as possible, stride opened up to its maximum. I barely felt Liz's weight in my arms. She was tall and muscular, and well fed. She should have weighed more.

Adrenalin. Use it. It won't last much longer, and when it's gone, you'll start slowing down.

Reinforcements for the perimeter guards sped past me, barely more than streaks at the edges of my vision. I screamed at them to move, to make way. Some stopped, eyes wide, shouting things I couldn't understand. I ignored them and focused on pushing harder, on breathing deeper, on getting everything I could out of the fear response before the chemicals faded and I was running on willpower alone. I remembered thinking a few minutes ago that the clinic was a five minute walk away. I hadn't asked myself how quickly I could make it there at a dead sprint.

The answer was about ninety seconds.

A nurse saw me coming and opened the door, shouting for the guardsman at the desk to get Doctor Laroux. I sped through the entrance, slowing just enough to turn sideways and ease Liz through the gap. The guard opened the door to the clinic's interior, raising his voice at a passing orderly to get the doctor. I pushed past him and headed for the two marginally well-equipped rooms that serve as the closest thing Hollow Rock has to an ICU.

"Mr. Garrett, wait!" a nurse shouted as I passed her.

"Just follow me. Where's Allison?"

"I'm right here," she said breathlessly as she rounded a corner and began peeling off her white coat. "Oh my God, Elizabeth. What happened to her?"

"She's been shot. Rifle round, through and through. Penetrated her lower left lung."

"How long?"

I turned her sideways again and squeezed into the room before placing her gently on an operating table. Her eyes were half closed with shock, face pale from plummeting blood pressure, breath coming in hitching gasps. "Not more than three minutes ago."

Allison turned to her nurses. "All right. Ellen, Dave, scrub in and do it quickly. Brett, get a chest tube and an IV and fluids in here right now. Amanda, cut her clothes off and get a dressing on those punctures. Laura, go to the storeroom and bring me a vial of Propofol. Carrie, get an IV started, then check to see how much A-negative blood we have left. I have to go scrub in. Move fast, people. We don't have much time."

I stood over Liz and took her hand, the noise and motion of the nurses around me growing dim. All sound faded except for the rasp of my own breathing and the *hush-thump* of my heartbeat. Liz's eyes fluttered and went blank, rolling up into her head. My voice came to me from a distance, as though my ears were underwater. A big hand that looked remarkably like mine started slapping her frantically on the cheek.

"No, no, no, Liz, stay with me now, come on. Wake up baby, wake up."

Then hands were tugging at me, strained voices imploring. "Gabriel, come on, you have to leave the room. Please, we're going to take care of her. Let's go, you're in the way."

The rational part of me knew they were right; I couldn't help her. I didn't want to leave her there, but I stepped back anyway, letting the grasping hands and gentle voices lead me away.

"It's going to be okay, Gabe, we've handled wounds like this before. We know what we're doing, all right? Stay right here in the waiting room. Allison will come and speak to you once we get her stabilized. No, honey, I don't know how long it's going to take. You just wait right here, and we'll be back as soon as we can, okay? Your clothes have blood on them, sweetie. You'll need to change. Is there anyone who can bring new ones for you? There's a runner on duty, he can go and find them."

Without thinking, I said Eric's name. An automatic response to the stress, the shock, my subconscious mind falling back on the one person in the world I felt I could rely on. The nurse said they would send for him. Just wait here, sweetheart. I have to go now. Don't worry, we'll take good care of her.

I sat down and put my head in my hands.

Not Liz. Please, not Liz.

TWENTY THREE

Eric showed up within half an hour.

He limped into the waiting room, sweating and clutching his cane. "Gabe, what happened?"

"Elizabeth's been shot," I said, voice a hollow monotone. "Sniper, out past the wall on the east side. We were walking along the catwalk. Must have been five, six hundred yards away. I didn't catch a muzzle flash. We were close to the clinic. I carried her in."

There was a long silence. I could hear the dim echoing of Allison's calm commands and the more elevated chattering of nurses in the ICU. My hands were sticky with blood. Liz's blood. I could smell its coppery scent above the vinegar the nurses used to clean the floors.

Eric sat down heavily in the chair to my left, facing me from the L-shaped wall of the waiting room. He stretched out his injured leg and leaned close. "How bad is it?"

"Lung. Left side, through and through."

"Jesus. Is she going to be okay?"

"I don't know. Allison's working on her right now."

Another pause. "How...who do you think did this?"

I sat up and leaned my head against the wall behind me, eyes closed. A great, yawning emptiness had opened in my chest, the flesh excavated and the air drained out, leaving only a vacuum. A cold feeling had started in my stomach and was slowly emerging outward, crawling like frost into my arms, my hands, my face. My lungs and throat felt like they were filled with sand. My biceps and the muscles in my lower back screamed from the adrenalin-fueled abuse of carrying a hundred and forty pounds of woman a quarter-mile at a dead sprint. I focused on that pain, reveled in it, let it fill up my mind. Anything was better than the encroaching emptiness.

"It's my fault," I said.

"What do you mean?"

"I know who shot her. They did it because of me."

Eric put a hand on my shoulder, gripping tightly. "Gabe, what are you talking about? You're not making any sense."

"It's the same person, Eric. The one who sent those men to capture me. The one from the mission in New York."

The hand withdrew. "Tanner?"

I nodded.

I heard him sit back, and opened my eyes to look at him. He was holding his chin in one hand, brows knitted.

"There's no way to be sure about that, Gabe. Remember those insurgents we captured? They were Alliance troops. This could be retaliation. Maybe they sent a sniper team to harass us. Maybe they targeted Liz specifically because she's the mayor."

"It's possible, but I doubt it. The Alliance would gain nothing by killing Liz; the town would just elect another mayor. And if the sniper is captured and confesses, it could provoke open war with the Union. They don't want that, at least not yet."

I stood up and began pacing the room. "I should have known this wasn't over. I told myself what I wanted to hear, and like an idiot, I believed it. And now Liz is paying the price."

Eric caught my arm as I went by, stopping me. "Hey, calm down and think for a minute. You don't know for sure who the shooter was, so don't jump to conclusions. It could have been anyone."

"No, it couldn't. That shot came from half a kilometer away."

"Lots of people could make a shot like that."

"When it's snowing and visibility is shit? When there's no place to set up an elevated firing position? That shot came from the forest, Eric. You know how hard it is to hit a target through limbs and branches, even when they're bare. Whoever did this knew exactly where to be, and exactly when to be there. They knew Liz and I go for walks in the afternoon. They watched us, they gathered intel, and they waited for the perfect opportunity. This wasn't just some random retaliation by the Alliance. This was the work of a professional."

Eric lowered his forehead into his hand, voice growing insistent. "Gabe, do you have any idea how many soldiers and special forces types have defected to the Alliance? Thousands of them. How many snipers do you think they have? I would say at least a few hundred."

"Then why didn't they shoot me too, Eric? They could have, easily. But they didn't. Why is that?"

Eric opened his mouth, but nothing came out. After a second or two, he deflated, sinking back into his chair.

"One of the many lessons I taught you, Eric, is that the simplest answer is most often the correct one. Remember?"

"Yeah. I remember."

"So what's the simple answer here? The Alliance stands to gain nothing by assassinating Elizabeth, but a lot of people know who I am. They know I played a key role in defeating the Legion last year. They know I bring a lot of trade to Hollow Rock, and that I oppose the Alliance. So bearing all that in mind, why kill Liz and not me?"

It was a long instant before he spoke. When he did, his voice was barely audible. "They wanted to send you a message."

"And?"

"They wanted to hurt you."

"What does that tell you?"

He leaned forward, clasping his hands. "That someone is very pissed off at you. That they watched you for a while to figure out how to hurt you. They found out about you and Liz, and then they spotted a pattern—your afternoon walks. They figured out the best place to strike from, and waited for you to show up."

A silence hung between us for a while, the two of us staring off into space. Orderlies and nurses walked by in their scrubs carrying tubes, gauze, and a suture kit. They glanced through the opening to the waiting room, faces curious. I imagined what they must have seen—one of us seated and sweating despite the cold, and the other grim-faced, fists clenched at his sides and covered in blood. A smallish man with Arthur on his nametag finally worked up the courage to step gingerly into the room and offer a nervous smile.

"Mr. Garrett, sir? I, uh, need to take your clothes. Do you have something you could change into?"

I looked at Eric, who unwound the strap of a messenger bag from his shoulders and held it out to me. "Undershirt, bush jacket, pants, and a coat just like the one you're wearing," he said.

"That'll do."

As I turned toward the bathroom, Eric stood up behind me and leaned on his cane. "What are we going to do about this, Gabe?"

I spoke over my shoulder. "What do you think?"

*****

It was nearly two hours before Allison stepped out of the ICU. She took a few minutes to clean herself up, and then joined Eric and me in the waiting room. Her expression was not encouraging.

"How is she?" I asked, a ball of ice where my stomach used to be.

"She's stable for the moment. We got the worst of the bleeding stopped and re-inflated her lung. The bullet missed her ribcage, and it looks as though it didn't tumble or deform as it passed through. Small miracle, that. If it had struck a rib going

276

in, things would have been much, much worse. That being said…Gabe, you should probably sit down."

It is never a good thing when a doctor asks you to sit down. The flesh of my cheeks began to tingle, and my vision narrowed a bit, going gray at the edges. I took the doctor's advice.

"How bad is it?"

"It's a good thing you got her here as fast as you did. You increased her chances significantly by doing that."

I waved the comment away, growing impatient. "Again, how bad is it?"

She sighed, pinching the bridge of her nose between two delicate fingers. "Under ordinary circumstances, she wouldn't be in very much trouble. If I had all of the equipment and drugs of a pre-Outbreak hospital, I could have her back on her feet in a few days. But my resources are severely limited. It's not the wound itself that worries me; we can treat that. It's all the complications that go with it. You see, a wound like hers could result in-"

"I know the complications you're talking about," I interrupted. "I've been shot through the lung before."

She paled a bit. "Oh."

"What are her chances, Allison?"

She spread her hands in front of her, palms up. "If I can somehow get the supplies I need, her chances are very good. If I can't…I don't know. Maybe seventy-thirty, if that."

"In favor?"

Her face fell, eyes brimming with unshed tears. "No, Gabe. Against."

I don't know how long it was before I moved again.

Allison kept speaking, but her voice was muffled, traveling a vast distance to reach me. Absently, I noticed a strong grip on my shoulder, but I couldn't figure out who it belonged to, nor did I care. My eyes tracked down to my hands, and the small streaks of blood caked there. I had cleaned them in the bathroom, but some of it had stuck stubbornly, refusing to be scrubbed away. It was dry in some places, and wet and sticky in others, adhering to the creases between knuckles and the little black hairs between finger joints. I watched my hands spread out on my knees and turn vertical as my legs extended, standing me up. A red tinge had obscured my vision, and a voice boomed in my head.

Don't be the hunted. Be the hunter.

I walked to the bathroom, barely feeling my legs. The water from the sink was ice cold and came out in a trickle. There were a few tiny flecks of black in my palm as I splashed a handful over my face and rubbed it into my eyes. It felt good, so I did it again. The roaring in my ears faded until it was just a far-off rumble, like crashing waves on a distant shore. The color came back into the world and I could see clearly again, the gauze of red receding. I stood up straight and heaved in a deep breath, staring into the mirror. A grizzled, scarred man with close-cropped hair, a heavy brow, and luminescent gray eyes stared back. The eyes were red around the edges, black rings circling underneath. I looked like a weary, hunted thing.

As the numbness faded, a lancing pain tore through my stomach, doubling me over. I gasped raggedly, clutching my waist and stumbling against the wall. The agony was intense, ripping into me as if it were a living thing. I had a strong urge to curl around it and crawl into a corner, to find a dark place and sink down to its farthest depths and never come out. I wanted to kill something with my hands. I wanted to tear the flesh from my face. I wanted to break myself against an ocean wall. My knees gave out, dropping me to the ground. I sat hunched and miserable, odd little pained noises ripping loose from my chest.

It was too much. Every time something good came into my life, something always shattered it. Every time I found hope and light, something snuffed it out. Every time I tried to build something, fate found a way to burn it down. And I had no one to blame but myself.

And Tanner.

"Tanner," I whispered.

The knife of agony in my gut burst into a thousand shards, unleashing fire in my chest, in my arms and legs. Its heat burned behind my eyes, ached in my teeth. I stood up and trembled with the power of it, fists clenching until blood squeezed through my fingers.

Did he think there would be no consequences? Did he think it was going to be that easy? That I would meekly accept my punishment and let it go?

The simplest answer was clear.

I'm coming for you, Tanner. And hell is waiting.

TWENTY FOUR

Eight years ago,

New York City

Anja's fingers traced a dime-sized circle of scar tissue on my ribcage. It had a larger twin on my back, roughly the diameter of a golf ball, where a 7.62mm projectile had extracted several ounces of meat and bone on its way out.

"You have many scars, Tom McGee," Anja said, raising her head from my shoulder. Her blond hair cascaded down her face, curving along the line of her cheek. With her glasses off, the effect of her eyes was startling.

"I haven't always been an executive."

"You were a soldier?"

I nodded without saying anything, seeing no point in denying it. Best to let her come to her own conclusions and not give up any information. Play the part of the recalcitrant, traumatized war veteran. It wasn't much of a stretch.

"You must have been in combat. These are bullet wounds, and this looks like shrapnel. How did you get them?"

"I fell down the stairs at church."

Deep, velvety laughter followed me as I got out of bed and crossed the room to the windows, stopping along the way to tug my pants back on.

"You do not like to speak of the war, do you?"

I crossed my arms and remained silent, staring down at the bustling humanity along Park Avenue. Several hours had passed since we retired to my room, and we had made very productive use of that time. Her body had turned out to be every bit as strong and pliable as it looked, possessed of delicious flexibility and stamina. We explored each other until our energy flagged

280

and we lay exhausted on rumpled sheets, bodies intertwined in the fading afternoon light.

"I have heard that those who have seen real fighting do not like to talk about it. That you have nightmares and flashbacks. Is this true?"

"You ask too many questions, Miss Renner."

The sheets rustled as she climbed out of bed and walked up behind me, feet padding quietly on the floor. When she reached me, her lips traced a tingling trail up my spine, soft tongue brushing against my skin.

"Perhaps I like you, McGee. Perhaps I would like to know you better. We have had a very pleasant time these last few hours."

"I'm going back to Phoenix on Monday."

"And I am going back to Guadalajara. That does not mean we cannot meet again. Perhaps in Paris or Milan next time?"

I turned around and pulled her into my arms, putting on my best contented smile. What I felt at the moment, however, was pretty damn far from contentment. There had been no word from Tanner or Rocco, and I was beginning to worry about them. They should have taken Villalobos into custody by now. I had hoped Anja would fall asleep and I would be able to slip quietly out of the room and find them, but apparently, my efforts to fatigue her had fallen short.

She reached up and traced her fingers over my lips, head tilted back for a kiss. All thoughts of the mission faded as I accommodated her, pulling her against me and feeling her hands slide down the front of my pants. Warm fingers closed around me and began stroking gently, drawing an involuntary moan from my lips.

"Again?" I whispered.

"It has been a long time. I am hungry."

We kissed again, and I was about to start edging her back to the bed when a garish ringtone cut through the room. Anja broke off the kiss and released me.

"*Scheisse*."

She walked over and snatched her iPhone from the foyer table, frowning at the display. I leaned against the windowsill and admired the firmness of her breasts, the trimness of her waist, the muscular curve of her rump. She was, without a doubt, one of the most stunning women I had ever seen. As she ran her finger across her phone's screen to unlock it, I heard the simple chime of my own device on the bedside table.

"Shit."

I picked it up and saw Tanner's call sign on the display. *About damn time.* I walked to a corner and answered it.

"McGee."

Tanner spoke quickly. "We've been compromised. Kill Renner. Track me on your locator app and find me as soon as you can. Acknowledge."

I almost answered with a simple 'acknowledged', but stopped myself. An efficient, single-word response dripping with militant familiarity would give me away. Instead, I kept my voice jovial and said, "Don't worry, Marty, I'll take care of it. You just enjoy your vacation, all right? I'll see you in two weeks."

He hung up.

I stood still for a moment, unable to move. Behind me, Anja spoke into her phone. "Are you sure? Yes, he is. But I don't understand… All right. I will be there shortly." Her thumb stabbed the disconnect icon as she stomped over to her purse. Her posture was agitated, shoulders stiff, movements hurried. Alarm bells rang in my head.

"I am sorry, McGee, but I have an unexpected problem to deal with." Her hand dipped into her purse, rummaging around. I began to edge closer, shortening the distance.

"And what is that?"

"You are not who you say you are."

Her hand came out of her purse and I caught a silhouette of something long and cylindrical with the unmistakable curve of a trigger guard underneath. She raised it and pointed it at me, the lines of her body stark and beautiful in the moonlight. There was a roaring in my ears, and the world seemed to slow down, making Anja's movements painfully slow. A pale silver beam shone through the window on her face, illuminating her eyes in sparkling, piercing blue, all the warmth and passion now gone from them. They were the eyes of a shark, a crocodile, a predatory thing.

The muscles of her right forearm shifted as her finger tightened on the trigger. I had less than half a second to live.

The cellphone.

My hand whipped forward, snapping at the wrist, sending the phone streaking across the room. One of its rounded corners caught her squarely in the left eye and she cried out, hand clapping to her head. The gun shifted slightly and let out a single chuffing sound along with a small metallic clank. There was a faint tug at my arm, and behind me, I heard a *whap* of lead bursting into wood paneling. By the time Anja regained the presence of mind to line up another shot, I had closed the distance and lashed out with a kick. The ball of my foot caught the inside of her wrist and sent the pistol flying across the room.

Without hesitation, Anja launched a punch at my groin. I tried to dodge, but wasn't fast enough. Her fist grazed my testicles and a burst of liquid fire erupted in my lower abdomen. Gritting my teeth against the pain, I countered with a reverse elbow that snapped her head back and sent her reeling. She swayed drunkenly and fell on her butt, eyes rolling back in her head, jaw already swelling. I staggered away until I hit the wall, struggling not to fall to my knees and vomit.

"Anja, just stop for a minute. There's no need to do this. Let me take you in. No one will hurt you."

Her eyes cleared, and she scrambled to her feet, fists clenched, eyes welling up with tears. "You lying piece of shit! I gave myself to you! How could you do this to me? I trusted you!"

"Anja, I-"

The tears vanished as she came at me again, pivoting into a spinning back kick. Her heel nailed me in the solar plexus, driving the wind out of my lungs. I let out a startled *oof* and doubled over, struggling to draw a breath. Anja followed up with a right hook that caught me on the chin, and then an uppercut that I managed to dodge. The miss threw her off balance, giving me a chance to lunge forward, wrap my arms around her, and lift her in a tight bear hug.

"Anja, for Christ's sake, just stop!"

She gnashed her teeth and slammed her forehead into the hollow of my throat. When I didn't react, she did it again, and again.

"This is pointless. It's over, Anja. Give it up."

She responded by throwing her legs back, turning her hips, and planting a knee squarely into my balls. A broken roar of agony tore loose from my chest, but I managed to keep my grip and shift her over to my right side, pulling her up higher. The idea was to keep her from kneeing me again, but I had forgotten about her head. The miscalculation became painfully obvious when her teeth clamped down on my ear.

Screaming with renewed agony, I released her and grabbed her around the throat, vision blurred, squeezing with everything I had. The world went red as I dug my thumbs into her larynx, all thoughts of sparing her life evaporating. Something gave way under my fingers, and she stopped biting me to tear at my hands, eyes bulging, strangled little croaking noises breaking loose from her throat. Before I knew what I was doing, I had released her with one hand, clamped down on her thigh, and lifted her high over my head. She tried to kick free, but my grip was too strong. I twisted her in the air until she was upside down and slammed her to the floor with all the strength I could muster. There was a sickening crack, like breaking a handful of carrots in a towel, and Anja Renner went limp.

I stood over her, chest heaving, until the world turned back to its normal colors.

"Anja?"

She lay awkwardly, buttocks in the air, limbs piled like discarded sticks. Her head rested on her back at an impossible angle, the elfin point of her chin nearly touching her spine. Those storm-colored, North Atlantic eyes stared blankly at me over her shoulder, all the light gone out of them. My stomach twisted, intensifying the burning cramps clawing at my stomach.

I made it to the toilet, but just barely.

*****

Tolliver answered on the first ring.

"I already spoke to Tanner," he said without preamble.

"What happened?"

"Worry about that later. Are you near your tablet?"

"Yes."

"Enable the remote connection and bring up the hotel's schematics."

I pulled the tablet from my suitcase and did as asked, first bringing up the settings and giving Tolliver remote access, then opening an app that displayed an interactive diagram of the Waldorf-Astoria's floor plans. Once connected, Tolliver shifted the display to the third floor and hovered a small cursor over a stairwell near 49th street.

"Villalobos and Hargreaves are holed up in this stairwell. Rocco has them boxed in from the third floor, and our assets on the hotel staff are covering the other entrances. Our surveillance team intercepted a call from Hargreaves to the rest of Villalobos' security team. There are at least eight hostiles in play, including Connor Hughes and Gustavo Silva. I sent Tanner to deal with Silva and his crew. I need you to proceed to Rocco's location and take out Hughes, then find a way to get Hargreaves out of that stairwell. Is it safe to assume Renner is dead?"

I had to clear my throat before answering. "Yes. You'll need to send a cleanup team."

"I'll take care of it. Now get moving, Garrett. The clock is ticking."

I dressed quickly, taking a moment to put on a shoulder rig and arm myself with a handful of flashbang grenades and a specially manufactured Ruger Mark III. The Ruger was chambered in .22 long rifle, loaded with sub-sonic ammunition, and boasted a seven-inch integrally suppressed barrel, meaning I did not have to screw on a silencer. Once armed, I grabbed my cell phone and activated its GPS locator app. Tanner, Rocco, and I all had encrypted GPS transmitters that gave us the ability to locate each other virtually anywhere on the planet. The trackers were small devices, no bigger than a nickel, implanted under the skin of the shoulder.

After stuffing three spare magazines in my shoulder rig, I untangled Anja's corpse, turned her head until it was facing the proper direction, composed her hands over her chest, and covered her with a blanket. Although she was far from such concerns, I wanted to spare her the indignity of being found in a broken heap. It was the least I could do.

The hallway outside my room was empty. Waiting for the elevator would take too long, so I sprinted for the stairs and flew down them two at a time until I reached the third floor. The door opened into a broad, open square connecting several hallways. I activated the two-way radio function on my phone and selected Rocco's call sign.

"What?" he said angrily.

"Need a sitrep."

"Hargreaves and Villalobos are still trapped. Fucking limey bastard killed one of his own security people and took his gun. Shot one of our assets on the ground floor and damn near got me too. Tolliver says we got company on the way."

"Affirmative. How many people do we have blocking the other entrances to the stairwell?"

"Two each. It's got all our people tied up, that's why I'm here alone."

"Not anymore."

I turned off the radio and called Tolliver. "Do we have eyes on Hughes or Silva?"

"Caught Silva on a security camera. He's headed for the stairwell entrance on the fourth floor. Tanner is moving to intercept."

"What about Hughes?"

"Hargreaves ordered him to proceed to the third floor entrance and take out Rocco. If they get past the two of you, our people on the ground floor won't stand a chance. You have to take Hughes out at all costs. Leave the channel open, I'll keep you posted."

I plugged in an earpiece and stuffed the phone in my jacket's breast pocket. There was a large urn with some kind of broad-leafed plant growing from it at the corner of the hallway. I moved over to it and crouched down, pressing myself into its shadow.

If Hughes wanted to avoid drawing attention to himself, this was the best route to take. Attempting to get past the guards at the other stairwell entrances would be loud and bloody, and draw the attention of the NYPD. Not the best way to make a clean getaway. In all likelihood, Silva would discover the same problem at the fourth floor entrance and take the elevator to ground level, then try to circle around the back of the building: exactly what we wanted him to do. Tanner could follow them, and with any luck, take them out in time to help me deal with Hughes and his team.

Seconds seemed to stretch on forever as I waited, respiration increasing with the anticipation of combat. Hughes' people would be well-armed and well-trained, and would not hesitate to kill me if I gave them a chance. I had no plans to do so. Another minute or two went by until finally my earpiece crackled. Tanner's voice came over the channel.

"Rocco, Garrett, acknowledge."

I spoke first, in accordance with protocol. In the background, I could hear the low whump of suppressed fire, and the pitter-patter of bullets striking walls. "Ten four."

"Loud and clear," Rocco said. "Sounds like you're under fire."

"I'm in the 49th Street alley. The two agents with me are down. Silva has three men with him, armed with suppressed pistols. I'm pinned down and low on ammo. Request immediate backup."

"Acknowledged," I said. "I'm on my way."

Just as I gathered myself to stand, Tolliver's voice cut in. "Negative, Garrett. I have visual on Hughes. He's on his way to you, coming down the northernmost corridor. There are three hostiles with him. Stay on station and take them out."

"Fuck that," Rocco cut in. "Gabe, go help Tanner. I can take care of Hughes and his little bitches."

"That's a negative," Tolliver shouted. "Rocco, you will follow protocol, or so help me God I will sanction your ass. Garrett, stay on station until Hughes is taken care of. Tanner, I'm sending one of the extraction teams to back you up. ETA two minutes."

Tanner's voice was panicked. "Goddammit, Tolliver, I don't have two minutes."

Tolliver ignored him. "Garrett, you are to stay on station. Acknowledge."

I hesitated, eyes on the opposite stairwell. "Rocco can handle Hughes and you know it, Tolliver."

"Garrett, you will follow protocol. That's an order. You are to remain on station until you take out Hughes and his men. We can't afford to lose Villalobos. You know the rules. The mission takes priority."

I stayed where I was, staring at the stairwell. With each second that passed, Tanner's chances grew slimmer. I could acknowledge, then render assistance anyway. But Tolliver was tracking us and he would know if I left my post. If Hughes managed to get past Rocco, the agents at ground level were dead men. If I didn't help Tanner, so was he. I ground my teeth in frustration, debating what to do.

I thought about Villalobos' case file, and the cartel he ran, and the money he funneled into terrorist cells. I thought about all the effort and money and resources that had gone into this operation. I thought about all the people whose deaths Villalobos was responsible for, innocent or otherwise. I thought of all the damage he could do if he made it back to Mexico, all the people who would die if this mission failed. When measured against that, Tanner's life became expendable. He knew the risks when he took the assignment.

I closed my eyes, let out a breath, and spoke. "Acknowledged. Remaining on station."

Tolliver sounded relieved. "Good. I just caught Hughes on camera again. He should be there in less than a minute. Tanner, give me a sitrep."

No answer.

"Tanner, acknowledge."

Nothing.

"Tanner, are you there?"

Static. A leaden weight settled into my stomach.

Tolliver sighed. "All right people, stay focused. The extraction team is en route, ETA one minute. Garrett, Rocco, all bets are off. Silva could show up anywhere, I'll keep you posted. Do whatever you have to do, just don't let Villalobos escape. Am I clear?"

"Crystal," I said.

Rocco's voice was a snarl. "You're a miserable fuck, Tolliver."

Around the corner, I heard the sound of hurried footsteps.

TWENTY FIVE

The clinic's front door nearly came off its hinges.

A crowd of worried townsfolk was gathered outside in the parking lot shouting questions at Sarah and Sheriff Elliott. The two officers had hastily positioned a semi-circle of wooden sawhorses as a barricade, desperately trying to block people from entering the clinic's lobby. The din of voices subsided as I approached the crowd, their eyes widening, jaws hanging slack in worried surprise. Whatever they saw on my face sent them scrambling to get out of the way.

"The clinic is off limits," I said, rage flooding my voice. "Anybody goes in without permission, I'll break you in half. Now go the fuck home."

They stared after me as I walked away.

No one said a word.

My left hand went to the piece of paper in my pocket, fingers running over its edges. On it was a list of the things Allison needed to save Elizabeth's life. I was going to make sure she got them, or tear the world apart trying.

When I reached Town Hall, another door flew open and slammed against the wall behind it, nearly startling the poor woman at the front desk out of her chair. I was five steps into the building before I remembered it was supposed to open outward.

Ahead of me lay my destination: the communications room. In that room was a satellite phone with a direct link to the office of General Phillip Jacobs, head of Army Special Operations Command, a man who attended weekly meetings with the Director of Homeland Security, the Joint Chiefs of Staff, and the President herself.

The communications room was important enough to be under twenty-four hour guard, and the guard on duty at the time happened to be Quentin Reid. He stepped in front of me, one hand on his baton, the other outstretched, palm up.

"Hold it right there, Gabe."

"Get out of my way."

"Gabe, I can't let you in there. You know the rules."

"*Fuck your rules,*" I shouted, stopping an inch from his face. "The mayor was just shot, you idiot. She needs medical supplies the clinic doesn't have. Every second you stand here wasting my time is another second she comes closer to dying. Now you *will* get the hell out of my way, or I *will* put you through a fucking window. What's it gonna be?"

Reid paled, hand easing off his baton. "Okay, Gabe. Just take it easy, all right?"

"Don't you tell me to take it easy, boy. Give me the keys."

"I'll open the door for you."

Before I could say anything else, he turned and walked to the communications room fishing out a set of keys with trembling hands. After two attempts, and a growled threat to take the keys from him if he didn't have that door open in exactly three seconds, he turned the lock and stepped aside.

"Go ahead, take whatever you need."

"I don't remember asking for your permission."

I went to step forward, but Reid stopped me with a hand on my shoulder, eyes hardening. I turned and glared at him, rumbling deep in my chest.

"I know you're upset, Gabe. And I'm sorry about what happened to the mayor. She's a good woman, and I don't know what this town would do without her. But this room is under guard because Mayor Stone wanted it that way. So whatever you take out of here, you be careful with it and make sure you bring it back. It's what she would want you to do."

I glared for a moment longer, fists clenching. Reid held my gaze, not backing down, young face firm and honest. Just a good man doing his job. A tightness in my shoulders I hadn't been aware of began to ease, leaving me tired and drained. I let my head drop, looking away.

"I'm sorry, Quentin. I shouldn't have talked to you like that. Would you mind bringing me the sign-out log?"

"Not at all."

"Thanks."

I stood in the doorway and waited. Reid brought me the little book and a pen, and indicated where to sign.

"It's on the charger over there," he said, pointing.

"I'll only need it for a little while."

"Keep it as long as you need it. I'm off duty in half an hour, but I'll let my replacement know to expect you."

"Thanks, deputy."

"Anytime." He smiled sadly and started to walk away, then stopped. "Hey, uh…how's she doing?"

I shook my head. "Not good. She's stable for the time being, but…" Suddenly I had a hard time talking. Something squeezed inside my throat, cutting off my voice.

Reid looked away. "Right. Well, if you get a chance, give her my best, will you?"

I answered with a nod, not trusting myself to speak.

Once outside, I crossed the square to the VFW building and climbed a ladder to the roof to get better reception. The little phone felt dense and heavy in my hand, as if its mass had multiplied on the short walk from town hall. A frigid wind picked up, sending the once gentle snow sideways, skittering and clattering across the ice under my feet. Leaden banks of clouds obscured the sky to the west, dampening the sunset in shades of crimson and copper. I put on my goggles and stared at the phone in my hand, thumb poised over the send key, remembering all the times a single conversation had altered the course of my life, and not for the better.

Without Elizabeth, there is no life. Not anymore. Do what you have to do.

I pushed the button.

An impersonal female voice answered without introduction. "Identification please."

I spoke the appropriate alpha numeric sequence, given to me by the general himself just before he left town last year. He had tried several times to entice me into rejoining the military, but I had steadfastly refused, saying nothing he could offer would convince me to go back. Now, I wasn't so sure.

Amazing how things change, isn't it?

"How can I help you?" the voice said.

"I need to speak with General Jacobs."

"The general is not available at the moment."

"Tell him it's Gabriel Garrett. He'll make himself available."

"I'm sorry, sir. He's in a meeting I can't interrupt. Would you like to leave a message?"

I sighed, pinching the bridge of my nose. "The mayor of Hollow Rock has been shot. She's badly wounded, and in need of medical equipment we don't have. In light of a recent attack by insurgents, and their pending trial, her death could jeopardize relations with loyalists in the region and potentially destabilize the Union's tenuous peace with the Midwest Alliance. You get all of that?"

There was a long pause. "Yes, thank you, sir. May I repeat the message for verification?"

"Please."

She did, word for word, getting it right on the first try. I wasn't surprised. Jacobs was the kind of man who did not tolerate incompetence.

"I'll notify the general as soon as he is available," the woman said. "Is the number you're calling from the best way to reach you?"

"Yes."

"Thank you, sir. General Jacobs will be in touch with you soon." The line went dead.

I sat down on the edge of the roof and listened to the wind, waiting. Darkness slowly began to fall over the town, casting long shadows and bathing rooftops in desolate shades of blue. Across the street, I could see the clinic.

The crowd in the parking lot was gone.

*****

It was an hour before he called back.

"Mr. Garrett, I'm sorry to hear about Elizabeth. Is she going to be all right?"

"It's not looking good, Phil. The bullet took her through the lung. Doctor Laroux can treat the injury, but she needs additional supplies to treat the complications. I have a list in hand."

"Just a moment." The phone rattled when he set it down. There was a shuffling sound, and then Jacobs came back on the line.

"Go ahead."

I read the list. Some of the items I recognized, others I didn't. Jacobs stopped me a few times and asked me to spell some of the more outlandish sounding medications. When I was finished, he went silent. I could hear him tapping a pen against something, probably a notepad.

"Gabriel, it's going to be very difficult to get all of this to Hollow Rock on such short notice. You have to understand, medical supplies are in high demand. The things we ship to communities like yours come from warehouses and vaults scattered all over the country. Every bean, bullet, and bandage is earmarked long before it ever leaves the shelf. It's against regulation to divert a shipment once it leaves storage."

I ground my teeth, feeling the rigid plastic in my hand start to bend. "Yeah, and you're doing it every fucking day, Phil. Don't hand me that bureaucratic bullshit. This is Elizabeth Stone we're talking about. You know her personally. She served you a chicken dinner on your first visit to Hollow Rock for Christ's sake. If you don't help her, she could die."

I heard him heave a weary sigh. "And if I divert those medical supplies, someone else in some other town could die. I'm sorry, Gabe, but I can't place her life as a priority over anyone else's."

I spoke through gritted teeth, fuming in frustration. "Are you kidding me? Do you think I'm stupid, General? You're fucking stonewalling me."

His voice took on an edge. "Gabriel, you need to remember who you're talking to."

I took the phone away from my head and snarled a curse. *Deep breaths. Deep breaths. Count backwards from ten. This is not the time to lose your temper.*

After a few moments, I was back in control. I raised the phone back to my ear. "What do you want, Phil? What's it going to cost me?"

"I'm not sure what you mean, Gabriel."

"Yes you are."

Another pause. "You remember that commission I offered you?"

I closed my eyes, heart sinking. "Yes."

"It's been filled. The man I put in charge of your region is doing an excellent job."

My right hand balled into a fist. *Steady, Gabriel.* "General, I know you're a powerful man, but believe me when I say you do *not* want to play games with me. Not over this."

"I'm well aware of your capabilities, Mr. Garrett, and I assure you this is not a game. What I meant to say is I don't have an opening of sufficient importance for someone of your talent. That's not to say I couldn't use you in some other capacity."

"Such as?"

"One that doesn't require a uniform."

I closed my eyes, head bowed. "Which is to say, one that does not officially exist."

"You know, it really is a pleasure to speak with someone who doesn't need me to hold their hand and draw them a picture. I understand you spent a few years with the CIA. Is that correct?"

I went still, a cold feeling spreading from the bottom of my gut all the way to my face, like being splashed with ice water. Several seconds went by before I answered.

"You've been doing your homework."

"I'm a diligent man, Mr. Garrett."

"What did you have in mind?"

"You remember the information I shared with you about the Flotilla and the Republic of California?"

"Yes." *You have no idea how well.*

"We managed to get to someone inside their central leadership. They've been feeding us intel for some time now. The President is ready to act, but the plan we've put together requires more operators of sufficient skill than we currently have available."

I spoke without hesitation. "Count me in."

"I'm glad to hear that, but I'm afraid it's not enough. Tell me, does Eric Riordan still reside in Hollow Rock?"

"He does."

"What are the chances of bringing him on board?"

I let out a breath and scraped a cold palm over my face. "I don't know, General. He's recovering from a bullet to the leg right now."

"Do you think he'll make a full recovery?"

"His doctor thinks so."

"Then I repeat the question."

I scratched at my chin, considering. Eric would never admit it, but when it came to action, he couldn't help himself. He was never so alive, nor so in his element, as he was in a fight. He liked to consider himself a peaceful man, but I knew better. The more danger he faced, the brighter the fire in his eyes burned. Convincing him to work for Jacobs would depend upon presentation, on how noble and important I could make being a black-ops killing machine sound. With a little additional training, Eric would make one hell of an operative.

Wait, are you really considering this? Are you willing to bring Eric into that world just to save Elizabeth? You know that road. You know where it leads.

No, it wasn't like that. I would not force him into anything. I would not tell him Elizabeth's life was the price of admission. I would inform him of the stakes. I would tell him what he was getting himself into, and his participation would hinge upon informed consent. It would be his call, not mine.

"I can't make any promises, General, but I'll try. Either way, I'm in."

I heard the pen tapping again. "Is there anyone else you can think of? Anyone who might be a viable candidate?"

I almost said no, but then remembered a certain tall, wiry, scarred young man from Texas. A man who had displayed uncanny intelligence and combat proficiency. A man who worked hard to make people see him as less than he really was, to dim their expectations. When people do things like that, they usually have very good reasons. Reasons I knew all about it.

"Maybe. I'll have to get back to you."

"In that case, I might be able to pull a few strings."

"How soon?"

"The day after tomorrow, most likely. Will she last until then?"

"Does it matter? It's not like she has a choice."

"Good point. Before I send those supplies, Mr. Garrett, I want your word you will hold up your end of the bargain. Because if you don't, you and I are going to have a very serious problem."

In spite of the implied threat, his voice sounded regretful. I wondered how many conversations he'd had exactly like this one, bargaining human lives against holding what was left of his nation together. He may have been hanging me over a fire, but I still felt sorry for the old man. His burden was a heavy one, and I did not envy him the weight of it.

"You have my word, General. When the time comes, I'll answer the call."

"And you'll talk to Eric?"

"Yes. And whoever else I think can help."

"Very well, then. You have a deal. Keep that satellite phone in your hand close by. My secretary will call you in the morning with an update."

"Understood. Thank you for your help, General."

"No, Gabriel. Thank you."

He hung up.

There was something in his voice in that last sentence. Something I didn't like. If I had to put a name to it, I would have said it was sorrow.

I climbed down and went back to the clinic.

TWENTY SIX

I waited three days.

On the morning of the first day, Jacobs' secretary called me back as promised. She politely informed me the equipment Elizabeth needed was en route, and we would have it by the next day. Relief is not a strong enough word. I had to sit down for a long while after I spoke with her, hands trembling on my knees.

Allison kept her stabilized and sedated, saying it was necessary because of the pain, and because too much movement could aggravate the damage to her lung. I stayed by Liz's side as much as possible, holding her hand, speaking to her in low, gentle tones. Every few hours, when her meds began to wear off, her eyelids would flutter and she would smile at me, hand squeezing mine. At those times, I told her everything was going to be okay and buzzed the nurse's station for more sedative.

The supplies came on the second day, a cloudless Monday morning, brilliant sunlight shining on an endless sea of reflective white. The kind of day if you didn't wear sunglasses you had a migraine by eleven in the morning. Any other time, it would have put the town in a festive mood. People would have crowded the streets, shopping, talking, trading, going about their business. Instead, I found myself standing alone in a crowd, the people around me keeping their distance. When they weren't darting nervous glances my way, they shaded their eyes and watched a Chinook drop a cargo net in the clinic's parking lot.

Allison and her team moved quickly unloading the supplies and carrying them to the ICU. While they worked, I sat in the lotus position on the floor of the waiting room, eyes closed, hands curled atop each other, concentrating on my breathing. I could feel the stares of the clinic staff on my back, but right then, I could not have cared less. The meditation was necessary if I wanted to get through the day without causing someone grievous bodily harm.

The day before, I had noticed that when I spoke to people they wrung their hands and slowly edged away from me, as if stumbling upon a bear in the woods. A minute spent standing in front of a mirror enlightened me as to why.

My face was a gaunt roadmap, scars standing out angrily, jaw set in a hard line, eyes burning with the eerie light of the mentally unhinged. As a consequence, Eric sat close to me while Isaac Cole strained the legs of a chair on the other side of the room. Next to him lay a taser, charged to its highest setting, along with a bundle of heavy-duty zip ties. Upon arriving, he had jokingly asked me if I thought the precautions were really necessary. I gave him a level stare and told him I couldn't make any promises. His ever-present smile stayed fixed in place, but it was about as sturdy as porcelain.

Not long after sunset, when my legs felt like disconnected rubber tubes and my lower back had taken as much as it could stand, I stood up and moved to a chair. The ensuing pins and needles would have been maddening at any other time, but at that moment, I welcomed them. The pain gave me something to fixate on other than the churning tornado where my stomach used to be. Finally, the door to the ICU opened, and a short time later, Allison joined us in the waiting room.

"She's doing much better, Gabriel."

I nodded and remained seated. It would have been impossible to stand up even if I had wanted to. "What's her long-term prognosis?"

"Very good, I think. We have everything needed to properly treat her. I can't rule out further complications, but I don't think she's going to throw anything at me I can't handle. I don't know how you managed to get those supplies, Gabe, but it probably saved her life."

Allison surprised me by leaning down, wrapping her arms around my neck, and squeezing tightly. "Thank you so much. You have no idea how much this means to me. I won't forget it."

And that was when I finally broke down.

*****

Cole went back to his barracks.

It did not take a genius to figure out his services would not be necessary. Eric stayed at the clinic with me, occupying a bed in an unused recovery room.

I slept on the floor of the waiting room, propped upright in a corner. I didn't want to sleep too heavily, lest Elizabeth wake up and the nurses couldn't rouse me. At just past five in the morning, I felt a hand on my shoulder.

"Hello? Mr. Garrett?"

I opened my eyes and patted the hand. "I'm awake. Laura, is it?"

The nurse smiled. "That's right. I'm surprised you remembered."

There was a lot I could have said about that. "How is she?"

"She's awake."

If I had been a cartoon, I would have left a smoke outline.

Elizabeth was sitting upright, the nurses having adjusted her bed to aid her breathing. The skin of her hand was cold and dry as I held it. "Good to see you again, pretty lady."

She smiled and curled a finger for me to come closer. I did, and she kissed me softly. "How are you?" she said.

"Shouldn't I be asking you that?"

"You could, but I would just say I feel like I've been shot, and then you would roll your eyes and groan."

"That's a very good point."

"I notice you conveniently neglected to answer the question."

I sighed, sitting down in a chair next to her bed. "I've had better days. That's for damn sure."

"All of this must have been very hard for you."

I stared at her for a long moment, unable to speak. Here she was lying in a hospital bed with a bullet hole in her lung, after nearly dying, and she was worried about how hard it had been on *me*. I squeezed her hand tighter, voice coming out as a choked whisper. "I couldn't stand it if I lost you, Liz. You're all I have."

She smiled chidingly, shaking her head. "Now that's not true and you know it. You have Eric, and your business, and the Glover family, and all your other friends, and half the women in town chasing you around with stars in their eyes. It's a good thing I snatched you up when I did. These frontier girls around here would have eaten you alive."

With a pang of regret, I realized that at least the first half of her statement was correct. I may have been in love with Elizabeth, but she wasn't the only person out there who cared about me. There was Tom and Sarah and Brian, not to mention Miranda, the guys on my crew, Mike Stall, and the regulars at the now famous Saturday Night Texas Hold-Em Poker League. When I thought about it, the list was actually pretty long. And I had neglected every single one of them the moment I hit a bad patch. Liz saw the shame on my face and patted my hand.

"Don't worry, sweetie. I'm sure they'll forgive you if you've been ignoring them. You've had a very stressful couple of days."

"There you go again, comforting me when you're the one who got shot."

Her eyebrows came together and her eyes cleared, gaze growing intense. "Speaking of, has the sheriff made any headway in his investigation?"

"I have no idea. Haven't talked to him. I imagine he'll be stopping by very soon when he hears you're awake."

"I hope so. I would very much like to know who did this to me." There was a heat in her voice I had not heard since the fight with the Free Legion. With a sinking heart, I took her hand in both of mine and braced myself.

"Liz, I think I might know the answer to that."

She had been looking away, pondering, but now her head snapped around. I could practically see the cogs and gears grinding their way to the obvious question. "You don't think this was related to Sean Montford's murder, do you?"

"I'm pretty sure it is."

"How do you know?"

"Remember I told you those men I killed were sent to capture me?"

"Yes."

"I think I know who sent them."

She sat back, her face darkening. "Who?"

"His name is Sebastian Tanner. We worked a mission together about eight years ago."

"A mission?"

"For the CIA."

I could have grown a beard in the time it took her to speak again.

When she finally gathered herself, I felt as if an invisible distance had sprung up between us. Invisible, but very real.

"You...worked for the CIA?"

"Yes."

"I thought you were a Marine?"

"I was. I joined the CIA after I got out."

Another long pause. "Okay. So...what did you do for the CIA?"

I released her limp fingers and passed a hand over my face, scrubbing at my eyes. "A lot of things. Sometimes it was surveillance, sometimes I was a messenger, sometimes I helped with investigations. Mostly, though, I was just hired muscle.

Someone smart and capable enough to capture people or, when necessary, make them disappear."

Her voice dropped to a whisper. "You were an assassin?"

"When they needed me to be, yes. But that wasn't my only job."

Liz digested this new information, eyes distant, clearly not liking what she was hearing. The urge to kick myself for not telling her all of this from the beginning was very strong.

"So this Tanner fellow," she said finally. "He's the one you think might have shot me?"

I nodded.

"Why would he do that?"

"If you're half as smart as I think you are, you already know the answer to that."

"I want to hear you say it." Her tone was sharp.

I winced as if she had slapped me. A real slap would have hurt less. "He did it to get back at me. To hurt me. To punish me for something I did."

"And what was that?"

I sighed and sat back in my chair, closed my eyes, and told her the story. When I was finished, I opened my eyes again. Liz's color didn't look so good, but her voice was gentle.

"Gabe, you did what you had to do. I know it must have been a difficult decision not to help him, but you were under orders. What would have happened to you if you had disobeyed?"

"Nothing good. If I did that and Villalobos got away, I could have been facing criminal charges. The penalty for insubordination and dereliction of duty is a stiff one."

"Imprisonment?"

"At least."

"And at worst?"

"Execution. And not the long-term, death row kind. A bullet to the head and an incinerator was the usual method."

I did not think Liz could get any paler, but she proved me wrong. "Then why is Tanner doing this? He has to know you were just following orders. It's not like it was anything personal."

"In my experience, when you deliberately allow someone to fall into enemy hands, regardless of the circumstances, they tend to take it personally."

"Touché."

The conversation lulled for a while, and we sat not looking at each other, lost in our own thoughts, an uncomfortable tension hanging between us. I couldn't blame Liz if she was upset with me; I had withheld information from her I shouldn't have and she had nearly died because of it. The crippling guilt I had been feeling for the last two days returned in a rush, threatening to smother me. The room seemed suddenly too small, as if the walls had grown close and were trying to crush me.

"Gabe?" Liz said.

"Yeah?"

"Are you okay, sweetie? You're breathing really hard."

I turned my head toward her and saw concern on her face. It broke the spell immediately. The room went back to its normal size, and the blood rushing through my ears receded. I gave a weak smile.

"I'm fine."

Her hand found mine again. "Okay. Just making su-" Her sentence was interrupted by an expansive yawn, stifled on the back her hand. She winced at the end of it, hand going to her chest.

"Ow. That did not feel good at all."

I was on my feet before I realized it. "Want me to get a nurse?"

She fluttered a hand, shaking her head. "No, no. It's not that bad. I'm just tired, and I think my pain meds are wearing off. I hate to do this, but I should probably take another dose. Whatever they're giving me, it's strong. I doubt I'll be awake for much longer."

I sat back down and clasped my hands together. "Okay. Listen, before I go I want to ask you something."

"All right."

"What do you want me to do?"

She thought it over before answering. "I'm not sure. What would you have done if I hadn't made it?"

My voice came out like ground glass. "I would have hunted him down."

Liz nodded. "Just out of curiosity, what makes you so sure it was Tanner?"

"Do you remember what was carved into Sean Montford's back? Garrett. Dragonfly. Two graves. There is no way anyone else could have known the name of the operation. Only Rocco, Tolliver, Tanner, and the investigating agents knew that."

"It couldn't be one of them?"

"I sincerely doubt it. What would be the motive?"

She considered it, and finally shook her head. "I suppose you're right. Still, you shouldn't just assume it was Tanner. Like Walter always says: pursue the evidence, but make no assumptions."

I opened my mouth to disagree, but stopped. In all honesty, she had a point. Assumptions had a nasty way of getting people killed. "Okay," I said. "I'll keep my eyes open. Now are you going to answer my question?"

"I thought I did."

"You're not Socrates. You don't get to answer a question with another question. I say again: what do you want me to do?"

"What do you think you should do?"

I hissed a breath through my nose and glared.

"I'm serious," she said. "You're the super-soldier secret agent. I'm just a small town mayor. You tell me."

"I think I should go after him. He might be satisfied with his revenge, or he might not be. He might try something like this again, especially if he finds out you're still alive."

She tilted her head to the side, eyes narrowed. "Is that the only reason?"

"No, it isn't," I said, not bothering with a denial. "I want to punish him for what he did to you."

"Gabe, I don't want you getting yourself killed trying to avenge me. Maybe you should just let Sheriff Elliott deal with it."

"He's not trained to handle someone like Tanner. Even if he does manage to find him, which he won't, Tanner will make mincemeat out of him. I'm one of a very few people in the world skilled enough to take him down."

Liz sighed, her gaze dropping to her hands. "It sounds to me like you already made up your mind."

"I won't go if you tell me not to."

She laughed, throwing her hands in the air. "And if I do that, what will it do to you? I know you, Gabriel. You'll never feel right about it. It will eat at you, and eat at you, until you get so filled up with anger you won't know what to do with yourself. No, Gabe. I won't tell you not to go. If I'm honest, there is a very large part of me that hopes you find the son of a bitch and you kill him. But there is an even bigger part that hopes you don't."

I leaned down and kissed her cheek. "I'll find him. Don't worry about that. And when I do, I'll make sure he never hurts anyone again."

She grabbed my face and kissed me, hands slowly caressing my cheeks. "Just be careful, Gabe. Come back to me."

"Count on it."

There was a knock at the door, and a nurse with a vial and a needle came in. "Mayor Stone? It's time for your medicine."

"I was just leaving," I said, and turned to walk out the door.

"Gabe?"

I stopped and turned.

"I love you," she said.

"I love you too, Elizabeth. I'll be back soon."

I left the clinic and headed for the armory.

TWENTY SEVEN

Eight years ago,

New York City

Connor Hughes and his goons came around the corner like a herd of buffalo, showing no concern for what might be waiting for them. As a result, it took them almost a full second to spot me hiding behind the urn.

It was all the time I needed.

Hughes was the biggest threat, so he died first. My little pistol clanked twice, and a pair of thirty-eight grain lead projectiles entered his skull at nine-hundred feet per second. His body went rigid, seizing up before it began to topple over. As he died, his trigger finger squeezed involuntarily, putting a nine-millimeter round through the foot of the man standing next to him. The man screamed, making the cardinal sin of dropping his weapon as he collapsed to the floor.

It would have been easy to kill him right then, but he wasn't the most dangerous target. There were still two armed, able-bodied thugs to worry about, both still recovering from the suddenness of the attack. I knew what they were feeling: the cold electric rush, the stopped breath, the deadened limbs, the hot tingling of the face, the shocked synapses struggling to process the sudden influx of information. I swear I heard their brains click the moment they realized that, in less than two seconds, I had reduced their fighting force by half. One of them switched his gaze from Hughes' collapsing body the large, disheveled man pointing a gun at him. He had a fraction of a second to register alarm before I squeezed off another double tap.

And then there was one.

I couldn't get a bead on him before he raised his weapon, so I did the next best thing—I moved. Even at close range, it is difficult to hit a moving target. I was gambling that because I was calm and he was jolted, my aim would be better. The gamble paid off when he squeezed the trigger and a burst of plaster erupted behind me, wide to the right. It was the only shot he had time for, and he missed.

I didn't.

The last man, realizing that he was on his own, reached for his weapon. A swift kick to the base of the skull knocked him out, his outstretched hand just short of the pistol. I raised my gun and fired four times, using up the rest of the magazine. Two would have done the job, but there was no sense in taking on Hargreaves with only two rounds in the stack. Once I reloaded, I dragged the bodies down the hall and around the corner, out of sight.

Just as I finished, Tolliver's voice rattled my earpiece. "Garrett, how about a sitrep?"

"Sorry, I've been kind of busy, here. Hughes and his men are taken care of."

"Where are the bodies?"

I told him.

"Good," he replied. "I'll send a cleanup team."

"Any sign of Silva?"

"None. I think he may have fled the hotel."

"Let's hope so."

"Indeed. All right, time to finish this. What's your plan?"

"In these situations, I usually prefer the direct approach."

"Fine by me. Just be careful, that Hargreaves is a cagey fucker."

"Understood."

I ran down the hallway and around another corner where Rocco waited, weapon in hand. I stacked up on the other side of the door and took out a couple of flashbangs. "Here," I said, handing them to him. "You throw, I'll take point. Once we're inside, I'll stay low so you can lay down covering fire over my head."

"Works for me."

I checked my weapon one last time, and then took a deep breath. "Okay, on three."

Rocco counted off, and on three, he turned the door handle and tossed in the stun grenades. No sooner than the door opened than did a round ricochet off the metal frame just above his head sending Rocco ducking backward, snarling a curse.

A second later, the flashbangs detonated, deafeningly loud in the narrow confines of the stairwell. I heard a pair of screams as Hargreaves and Villalobos were rendered temporarily blind and deaf. Pushing the door open, I hurried down the steps toward them, pistol raised, eyes searching. As I rounded the landing, I saw them. Villalobos was on his back, one hand raised defensively, eyes wide with terror. Hargreaves was on one knee, looking in my direction, blinking rapidly. I knew the effects of the flashbang would wear off quickly, especially on someone as highly trained as Hargreaves. There would be time for only one shot, so I had to make it count.

The Ruger appeared in my line of sight, rear aperture lined up with the blade on the front of the barrel. I lifted my thumbs, let out half a breath, and focused on the front sight, putting it on Hargreaves' right arm. Slowly, I squeezed the trigger, careful not to pull the gun one way or the other. When the shot surprised me, I knew I had done it right.

Hargreaves snarled in shock and anger, gun clattering from nerveless fingers. The bullet had taken him through the deltoid and smashed into the shoulder joint, rendering his arm useless. Most people would have fallen down, unable to function through the pain.

Hargreaves, however, was not most people.

The ex-SAS commando reached down with his good hand, still trying to clear his vision. I shifted my aim and put another bullet into his right kneecap. This time, he went down.

Rocco stayed close behind me as I descended the stairs, gun trained on Villalobos. "Don't you fucking move, you little cunt," he shouted. "I may have to take you alive, but that doesn't mean I can't kneecap you."

I moved in, keeping my weapon aimed at Hargreaves' head. His eyes had cleared enough that he could see me. They traveled to the Sig Sauer nine-millimeter lying on the stairwell next to his feet. I stepped up and kicked it down the stairs.

"Huh-uh," I said. "Don't even think about it. I need the old man alive. You're expendable."

Hargreaves glared daggers for a moment more, then let out a sigh. "Fuck you, you bloody wanker. Go on then, get it over with."

"Only if you misbehave."

The earpiece came to life again, startling me. I had forgotten that Tolliver was listening in.

"Nicely done, gentlemen," he said. "Extraction team is en route."

"What about Hargreaves," I asked. "Do you want him alive, or what?"

Tolliver was silent a few beats, considering. "Yes. Maybe he knows something we can use."

"Copy."

The door opened at the bottom of the stairs and two men dressed in porter's uniforms climbed up, guns drawn. Neither one of them looked to be a day over twenty-five. I couldn't help but wonder where the people at Langley did their recruiting.

"Are these the targets, sir?" one of them asked, looking at me.

"Affirmative. Let's get them downstairs."

The two young men holstered their weapons and helped me drag Hargreaves down the stairs, cursing and spitting the whole way. Villalobos followed us with his hands on his head, Rocco's pistol only inches from the back of his skull.

At the bottom of the stairwell was an exit door with a big red handle that read EMERGENCY EXIT ONLY, ALARM WILL SOUND.

"Hey Tolliver, has anyone shut off the alarm on this door?"

"One moment," he said. I heard the clattering of a keyboard. "And...done. All right, the extraction team is waiting. Make it quick, gentlemen. We've got a hell of a mess to clean up as it is. I don't want you adding to it."

I kicked the door open and stepped outside, listening to Hargreaves make a few pointed comments about my lineage, upbringing, intelligence, and the dubious circumstances of my conception. To my right, barely six feet away from us, was a large black SUV, the rear hatch open and two men in suits standing by.

"Come on," I said. "Help us get them inside."

The two men moved, first seizing Villalobos and handcuffing him, then Hargreaves. Within seconds, both prisoners were restrained, gagged, black hoods cinched over their heads, and the taillights of the SUV fading from sight. When they were gone, Rocco and I looked at each other and spoke at the same time.

"Tanner."

*****

Tolliver tracked his GPS signal to an alley three blocks away.

We found his clothes in a dumpster, along with his weapon, empty magazines, and a small plastic bag smeared with blood. The bag contained Tanner's tracker, still smudged with gore, and was stapled to a piece of paper. On the paper was a note written in Tanner's blood consisting of only two words.

NICE TRY.

"Motherfucker," Rocco swore. "The son of a bitch cut it out of him."

I stood silently, watching the end of the alley. Behind me, a cleanup team was bagging the evidence and preparing to move out. Tolliver stood with them rattling off instructions and admonishing them to hurry. As the team finished up and drove away, Tolliver made his way over to us.

"Well that was a clusterfuck," he said, lighting a cigarette. I wrinkled my nose at the smell.

"Would someone mind telling me just what the hell happened back there?" I said, glaring at Rocco. "This was supposed to be a simple snatch-and-grab, not a goddamn bloodbath."

My old friend closed his eyes and rubbed a hand across his forehead. "Fucking Hargreaves, man. That's what happened. Everything was going fine. We had the Citadel guy set up a meeting with a fund manager, just like you said. We showed up in the middle of it, pretended we were supposed to meet some other manager there. The fund guy says there must have been a mix up and leaves to make a call. Hargreaves is watching us the whole time like he's about to jump. As soon as the civilians were out or the room, we moved. There were five of them, Hargreaves, Villalobos, and three guys that must have been mercs. I took out one of the mercs and double tapped Hargreaves right in the heart, nice and neat. The guy goes down. Tanner pops one of the other mercs, but the last one knocks the table over and starts shooting. Tanner draws his fire while I'm flanking, and the next thing I know I'm waking up. Turns out Hargreaves was wearing a vest. The two shots I took at him hit his piece; he couldn't use it. Fucker popped me from behind, grabbed Villalobos, and ran for the door. Tanner tried to take him out, but he was out of ammo. We chased them into the hallway, and Hargreaves pulls a knife and kills his own security guy, takes his gun, and bolts for the stairwell. You were there for the rest. Now I got a question for you, you slack bastard. Was Renner as good a piece of ass as she looked? She must have been. You were with her for four fucking hours. Care to explain to me how a well-trained CIA operative like yourself can't find an excuse to ditch a girl in a hotel room? If you had been there for the takedown, shit might not have gone sideways."

I glared angrily, fists clenched at my sides. At any other time I would have said something in my defense. But the truth was, Rocco was right. I could have just killed Renner and returned to assist with the mission. Or I could have spent an hour or two with her, then pretended I had to meet with someone and slipped out. But I didn't. I let the wrong head do my thinking for me, and now Tanner was paying for it.

"All right, that's enough," Tolliver broke in, sensing the tension. "There's plenty of blame to go around, so let's not waste time pointing fingers. The important thing is the mission was a success. Our people managed to get rid of all the bodies with the public none the wiser. We got Villalobos, and as we speak, he and Hargreaves are both getting a one-way, all expenses paid trip to sunny Guantanamo Bay, Cuba. Missions don't always go off without a hitch, gentlemen, and this was one of those times. Everyone did their jobs and we got what we came here for. Our job is to get results by any means necessary, and that's what we did. End of story."

Rocco's glare could have cut diamonds. "How about you tell that to Tanner's family, huh?"

"Tanner knew the risks," Tolliver said flatly. "This isn't the minor leagues, gentlemen. You're playing with the big boys. And in this game, you lose people. It happens. When it does, you count your losses and you move on. Unless, of course, you don't have the stomach for it anymore."

Rocco glared a moment longer, then looked away. "Whatever. Let's just get the fuck out of here."

"Best idea I've heard all day."

Tolliver drove us to La Guardia and stopped his car in front of the departures terminal, then informed us that our plane tickets and government IDs were in the glove box. "Get some rest," he said to both of us. "Your payment will be wired to your accounts by tomorrow morning. I'll have more work for the two of you very soon, assuming you're interested."

"Count me in," I said, taking my plane ticket.

Rocco left the car without a word.

We walked together as we passed through security and proceeded to our gates, a withdrawn silence hanging between us. When it came time to part ways, Rocco's flight headed for Florida and mine to DC, he reached out a hand.

"I wish I could say it's been nice working with you again, Wolfman."

I smiled at the old nickname. "Same to you."

He returned my smile briefly as we shook hands, then gave me a mock salute and walked away.

I didn't know it at the time, but I would see him again a few months later. Except instead of teaming up for a mission, I would be flat on my back in a hospital bed, and it would be the end of my career with the CIA.

TWENTY-EIGHT

Sheriff Elliott was waiting for me on the wall.

The old man had developed a knack for knowing where to look for me, as if he knew what I was going to do before I did it. Rather than search for me, he simply went to where he thought I might show up next and waited. You can argue with a lot of things, but you can't argue with results.

There was a thermos in his hand, and I caught the scent of herbal tea as he raised it in greeting. I nodded to him as I approached. "Morning."

He yawned, covering his mouth. "It certainly is. How's the mayor?"

"Doing much better. Allison says she should be on her feet in a week."

"I'm glad to hear it. Don't know what this town would do without her."

I smiled, gazing out over the snow-covered field beyond the battlements. "That seems to be the prevailing sentiment."

We stood for a few moments, no words exchanged, watching the sun turn the eastern sky from pale gray to burnished yellow, an arc of red corona just beginning to blush to life beneath low-hanging clouds. Walter offered me a sip of his tea, but I turned him down and waited for the old man to work up his nerve.

"You're going after them, aren't you?" he asked finally.

"Him. Singular."

He nodded, thoughts confirmed. "So you know who did it, then?"

"I do."

"How certain are you?"

"As certain as a man can be of anything in these uncertain times. What's your real question, Walt?"

One corner of his face curled up, about as close to a smile as the lawman ever got. "Not so much a question as a confirmation of suspicion."

He waited, expecting me to feed him a line—an old cop tactic. I didn't bite. Sensing I wasn't going to volunteer anything, he pressed on. "One of the things you learn in thirty years of law enforcement is how to look for patterns. You see, human beings are creatures of habit and tend to behave along predictable lines. Take our conversation here, for instance. How exactly did I know you were going to show up on this particular section of wall?"

My eyes tracked involuntarily to a splintered post a few feet away, still stained with Liz's blood. "Because you're capable of elementary logic?"

He chuckled, raising his thermos. "That's part of it. But mostly it's because when you get to know somebody, when you spend a few months talking to them on a regular basis, break up few bar fights with them, haggle over the price of office supplies, you start to get an idea of what makes them tick. Patterns begin to emerge, little by little. And I think I've figured yours out."

Again, the pregnant pause. Again, I remained silent.

"You know what I think?" he said, conceding. "I think there's a hell of a lot more to you than you let on. You go around with your slow walk, and your Kentucky drawl, and your backwoods diction, and people think you're just another good old boy. And you do nothing to dissuade them from that notion, do you? But you see, it's all a little too careful, a little too manufactured. People are multi-faceted creatures, Gabe, and I can't think of anyone who displays quite the consistency of personality you do. You're never too mad, or too happy, or too anything because it might draw unwanted attention. It might lift the veil and let people catch a glimpse of the real man hiding under all that hill-country charm. Except the other day, when you came out of that clinic like the wrath of God himself, for a second there, I didn't recognize you. There was your face, and your scars, and the same clothes you wear every day, but it was a whole different man under that disguise. He didn't look slow, or lazy, or mild-mannered. He looked like he might kill me with a swipe of his paw and not break stride doing it. And now here you are again, not ten feet tall with lightning bolts coming out of your eyes, but just an ordinary mortal, same as me. I don't feel like I should back away slowly and avoid sudden movement. Now why is that, do you suppose?"

I shifted my feet, wondering what all those people in the parking lot thought of me now. Was it as bad as that long-ago block party, and the months of strained greetings and forced, queasy manners that followed?

"I was pretty upset, Sheriff," I said. "I'm sorry if I scared anyone."

"Gabe, scared doesn't quite cut it. Those people survived the end of the world, and you had them shitting their pants."

"All I can do is apologize, Walt."

He let out a hissing exhale, raising a cloud of vapor. "You see that town down there? Those people walking down the streets? It's my job to protect those people, Gabe. They elected me to be their sheriff, and they trust me to look after them. But that's hard to do when there are unknown quantities involved. When a man in my position sees the things I've seen from you, and hears the stories I've heard, it brings an unavoidable question to mind. Just exactly what kind of a monster do those people have living amongst them?"

I turned and faced the sheriff then, waiting for the inevitable flood of anger. I braced for it, ready to fight it down when it emerged. We stood there, the two of us, squared off, both wondering what was going to happen next.

But the anger didn't come.

Confused, I broke eye contact and took a step back. My temper had always been my go-to, my ready response, the way I dealt with anything I didn't want to sort through or talk about. It was always easier to make a fight of things and let it run its course, especially as I had a tendency to win those fights. But now, of all times, it refused to show itself. I leaned against the railing, feeling a yawning emptiness in my chest where the rage used to live.

"I'm not a monster, Sheriff. But you're right, I am dangerous."

I turned my head and saw him watching me, hand resting lightly on his revolver.

"I'm dangerous to insurgents who show up with bombs and a horde of ghouls."

I pushed away from the rail, voice growing in strength.

"I'm dangerous to murderers who torture innocent farmers to death and hang them from trees."

My feet moved of their own volition, stopping an arm's length from the sheriff. My hands went to my hips and I stood firm, looking in the eye.

"I'm dangerous to the son of a bitch who shot the woman I love out of misdirected hatred and spite. And I when I find him, he will regret the day he was born."

The sheriff's expression shifted, like a ripple passing over still water. A whirl of emotions crossed his face, settling somewhere between wary and regretful. His hand eased away from his pistol and hung loosely at his side.

"But those people down there, Walt? I'm not dangerous to them. Or to you, for that matter. You want to know who I am? Fine. I'll tell you. I was once an eight-year-old boy who lost his father to an accident. That little boy grew up into an angry young man with cunning, immense physical strength, and a mean streak a mile wide. He wanted so much to be like his old man that he joined the Marines. Somewhere along the way, it occurred to him that if the Corps could turn ordinary men into killing machines, what could it do for a motivated, dedicated, hard core motherfucker like himself? So he set out on a mission to find out. The man standing in front of you is the result of that mission. And he is on your side, Walter, whether you choose to acknowledge it or not. So here's what's going to happen next.

You're going to tell me everything you turned up in your investigation. Then, I am going to use that information to track down the man responsible. When he is dealt with, I am going to come back here and live as peacefully as I can until the next crisis hits. And when that happens, I'll be the first man stepping up to defend this town. Is that acceptable, Sheriff? Do you think you can live with that?"

He measured me for a long moment, eyes steady, searching for the faintest hint of a lie. I waited patiently, holding his gaze, not worried in the slightest. There is no need to control your facial muscles or carefully monitor your mannerisms when you are telling the truth. Eventually he looked down slightly and gave a little nod.

"I suppose I can." He put his hands in his pockets and looked westward toward a stand of trees peeking over the back of a gentle hill. "I'm afraid the investigation didn't turn up much, but I think I know where the shot came from. Let's get going, we got a long walk ahead of us."

*****

The sheriff's idea of a long walk turned out to be about five-hundred and fifty yards, but I guess when a man hits his sixties and has lived a hard life, a half kilometer walk through knee deep snow can seem pretty long.

I followed behind the sheriff, rifle held loosely, sling adjusted for fast engagement. Walter carried a stick he poked into the snow as he walked, prodding for dead bodies lying dormant. In powder this deep, when it wasn't quite cold enough to immobilize the undead, one had to stay on the lookout for crawlers.

As Sheriff Elliott crested the hill ahead of me, he stopped suddenly and scrambled backwards, clawing frantically for his pistol. Hampered by the snow, his feet became entangled and he fell onto his butt, cursing like a drunken sailor. I took four running steps and brought my rifle up. Ahead of me, just below the rise and less than five yards away, was a small horde of over two-dozen walkers headed straight for us. A ghoul near the front spotted me and sent up a ragged howl, answered quickly by the corpses behind it.

"Shit." I raised my rifle.

The first two were recently dead, as evidenced by the fact that they were still wearing shoes. I lined up the little red dot on the first one's forehead, let out half a breath, and pulled the trigger. A crimson splash burst from the back of its head like someone tossing a cup of red wine. The blood hit the snow, followed closely by a shuddering body. Without willing it, my hands took over and shifted the rifle, giving the second closest walker the same treatment.

"Walt, you all right?" I said, pausing for a moment.

"I'm fine," he said, flustered. He had landed at a decline, rear end deeper in the snow than his feet and shoulders. I snuck a glance at him as he flailed about, reminding me of a large, spindly turtle.

Another line of walkers closed in, drawing me back to the task at hand. Shifting my aim, I drew a bead on the closest one. It was older, long-dead, resembling a ghoul in the truest sense of the word. Massive gobbets of flesh were missing from its abdomen, allowing swollen gray loops of intestines to show through. It reached for me, mouth creaking open, ragged tongue swirling in a mouthful of black teeth.

"Not today, sweetheart." My rifle bucked, ending its existence.

I took out three more, finally clearing enough space to help Walter to his feet. Once up, he drew his pistol, stepped to the edge of the hill, and fired one handed. To my surprise, a walker fell, the bullet striking it squarely between the eyes. Double action revolvers are not the easiest guns in the world to fire accurately, which is why most people use automatics. But Walt had carried that pistol for years, and put quite a few rounds through it. Despite its size and weight, he handled it as deftly as illusionist handles a deck of cards.

The big frame moved a few inches to the left and boomed again, the report echoing far into the surrounding countryside, claiming another walker.

"Walt?"

"What?" he said, half turning toward me.

"You're not helping our situation." I raised my M-4 and tapped a finger against the suppressor on the end of it. The sheriff looked down at his weapon and shrugged sheepishly.

"Sorry. Fuckers pissed me off."

"I understand completely. But we should probably make a tactical retreat, don't you think?"

"Right." He gestured with his pistol. "Lead the way, Captain America."

I took the lead as we skirted the edge of the horde, plowing a path for the sheriff. When we had a hundred yard lead, I motioned for Walter to take point again. He raised an arm and pointed ahead, breathing heavily. "It's not much farther, up at the top of that rise. See the yellow tape?"

I squinted and searched carefully. After a moment, I saw what he was talking about. "Got it."

"That's where we're headed."

He followed me up the incline, huffing and puffing along. I set an easy pace, making sure to clear as much snow out of his way as possible. The last thing I needed was the old fellow having a heart attack this far away from town.

A couple of minutes later, we stood outside the yellow crime scene tape. I slipped under it and looked around. The bare limbs of trees were thinner ahead of us, providing an unobstructed view of the wall. Taking out a small pair of field glasses, I lay down on my stomach and peered through them, adjusting the focus. Sure enough, I had a clear, unbroken line of sight directly to the section of parapet where Elizabeth was shot.

"Son of a bitch."

I stood up and looked around again, trying to find some evidence of the shooter's passing. There was none that I could see.

"Walt, how did you find this place? There have to be a couple hundred acres on this side of the wall. It's like a needle in a haystack."

The sheriff allowed himself a small, smug smile. "You ain't the only Marine around here, you know."

"You?"

He nodded. "There was a time when I used to run around in a little patch of jungle over in Southeast Asia. Me and a friend of mine had a good old time huntin' Viet Cong and busting up ambushes. Up until Tet, that is."

"Tet? Jesus. Where were you?"

He grimaced. "Huê."

Enough said. "So I'm guessing you took a vector from where the bullet hit the post?"

Walter accepted the change of subject smoothly. "That's right. I put a straw in the bullet hole and lined my old hunting rifle up with it, and it pointed right at that slope up ahead. At first, it didn't make any sense for the shot to come from there, but when I got here, I realized if the shooter belly crawled to this spot, he would be just low enough not to skyline himself. If he was camouflaged, he'd be practically invisible. Then I found this."

He rooted around in a breast pocket of his heavy Sheriff's Department jacket and produced a shell casing. I took it from him and looked it over. The brass was unpolished, and the cartridge stamp indicated 7.62x54 rather than the 7.62x51 used by the US military.

"Russian," I said.

"Looks that way. I'd bet the beer money it came from a Dragunov, or a PSL."

I thought about the Flotilla, and the crates of Russian ammo Eric and I had found at the Legion's supply caches, and felt my heart sink. Walter reached for the shell casing. "You thinking what I'm thinking?"

I sighed, and kicked at a pile of snow. "Yeah. This just got a lot more complicated."

TWENTY-NINE

"I'm going with you," Eric said.

I sighed, and laid the upper receiver of my M-6 on the table. The rifle was in pieces, lying among wads of oil soaked cloth and bottles of solvent. "No, Eric, you're not."

"Gabe, I'm not letting you go after this guy alone. You know it takes at least two people to survive out there."

"I'll be fine."

"Really? Okay then, tell me something. How are you going to keep the walkers away while you're asleep, huh? What happens if you're spotted by marauders? You remember what happened with Ronnie Kilpatrick's gang, right? If you run into something like that on your own, you're a dead man."

I began reassembling the M-6. It was a 5.56mm version, a weapon that had travelled with me from North Carolina. I chose it over my 6.8 SPC because its ammo was lighter, and with the distance I would be traveling, I needed to pack light.

I said, "That's not going to happen."

"You don't know that." Eric ran his hands through his longish hair and gripped it, face tense with frustration. He limped over to the counter and leaned against it, taking some of the weight off his sore leg. The wound was mostly healed, but it bothered him if he used it too strenuously. It would be at least another month before he could return to work, and the leg might never be a hundred percent again.

"It's suicide to go out there alone, and you know it," he said.

"Eric, you can barely walk. What are you going to do, crawl to Blackmire?"

He ground his teeth, head leaning to one side. I knew that expression well; it was the one that said, 'you're right, but I don't like it'. "Okay, fine. Take someone else with you."

I stood up and pulled back the rifle's charging handle, peering into the chamber. "Like who?"

"Maybe Sanchez, or Flannigan."

I shook my head. "No can do. They're good soldiers, but they're not cut out for what I'm up against."

"Okay, what about one of Ethan's guys? Maybe Cole, or Hicks."

"They're regular Army. I'd have to get permission from their CO, and that's not going to happen. He won't risk any of his men to settle a personal vendetta, not even for me."

"But Gabe-"

I cut him off with a swipe of my hand. "No buts, Eric. I'm doing this alone. That's it. End of discussion."

He opened his mouth to lodge a protest, but it died on his lips. Whatever he saw on my face forestalled any further argument. He shook his head sadly.

"Will you at least let me help you pack?"

*****

There is an old adage every soldiering man lives by, and it goes like this:

Ounces equal pounds, pounds equal pain.

Fortunately, if you are six-foot five and weigh in at around 240 to 250 lbs (depending on your diet over the last few days and whether or not you have stayed properly hydrated), you can carry a lot of pounds without inflicting a lot of pain. There is another adage I live by, not necessarily as popular as the aforementioned one due to the fact that I made it up, and it goes like this:

You can never have too much ammo.

Or the foreshortened version:

Ammo is your friend.

But before one packs those heavy little murderous miracles of chemistry, metallurgy, and engineering into the large MOLLE pack, you have to decide what implement of death you will be firing them out of. Or not firing, if all goes well, which in my experience it usually does not.

The urge to pack the six-eight was strong; it doesn't have much more range than 5.56, but it packs a hell of a wallop. Not as powerful as a .308, but if you double tap someone in the chest at three-hundred yards, chances are pretty good they're not getting back up. But as previously mentioned, 6.8 SPC is heavier than 5.56, and if I used the smaller cartridge, I could carry more rounds for the same amount of weight.

Physics and arithmetic, two areas of study which, when one learns them, are really quite synonymous. And they are subjects at which I am well studied.

So I went through the routine, roaming here and there through the warehouse armory, filling in the slots, choosing the best tools for the job. The NVGs, optics, body armor, and blades were a no-brainer, as was the primary firearm. The only question marks were the secondary firearm and the long-range tool of the trade.

The Sig .45 was a temptation, but again, heavy ammo, low capacity magazines, and I was down to my last couple of hundred rounds. No go.

Then there was the Beretta: battle proven, venerable 9mm, but still a lot of weight to carry. If there had not been a higher capacity, lighter, equally serviceable option to which I could fit a suppressor, I would have gone with it. But, sadly for the Beretta, there *was* a higher capacity, lighter, equally serviceable option to which I could fit a suppressor. Eric's favorite, the Kel-Tec PMR 30: Lightweight .22 magnum ammunition that packed a surprisingly hard punch, thirty-round magazine capacity, and it even had good quality sights. It may not have been mil-spec, but I had used it enough to know it was reliable.

That settled, I had to pick a sniper rifle. Weight of ammo was less of a concern, since I would only be carrying fifty rounds, but the rifle itself was a different matter. I had three options by order of weight: Desert Tactical SRS configured for .338 Lapua magnum, M-110 semi-automatic chambered in 7.62x51 NATO, or a Savage Weather Warrior in .300 Winchester magnum.

The SRS was by far the most powerful, but it was also the heaviest, and its ammo, while readily available from my Army trade contacts, was exorbitantly expensive. I left it on the shelf.

The Savage was a good option, being that it was the lightest of the three, and .300 Win-mag is an extremely powerful cartridge. However, I only had twenty-six rounds for it, and the gun did not technically belong to me. It was Eric's, although we had a standing agreement that all weapons in the armory were essentially community property between the two of us. But I had decided on a fifty round load out, and there was barely half that number on the shelf. No go.

By process of elimination, I took down the M-110, cleaned it, dry-fired it on a dummy round, and when the little firing pin dent appeared at the appropriate place on the inert primer, lashed it to my pack.

"Hey, you have room for a couple more boxes of five-five-six, or another packet of goat jerky," Eric said, looking up from the metal table where he was packing my gear for me. He knew me well enough he didn't have to ask what to include, except when he arranged the required items with sufficient skill there was room leftover. "Which one do you want?"

I pondered for a moment, then said, "Ammo. You can-"

"Yeah, yeah. You can never have too much ammo. I heard you the five-hundred and sixty-sixth time." He grabbed two more boxes of cartridges and stuffed them into one of the modular side pouches. That done, he zipped it up, fitted the rain cover over it, and hefted it, keeping his weight on his good leg.

"Okay, you have a change of clothes, ghillie suit, first aid kit, multi-tool, toilet paper, paracord, one-man tent, rain poncho, bed roll, five pairs each underwear and socks, cleaning kit, mess kit, head lamp, six days' worth of food, a bar of soap, washcloth, towel, fire steel, tinder bundle, two canteens, water purification tablets, half a liter of bleach, hunting knife, machete, hatchet, steel wool, nine volt battery, one unopened pack of double-A batteries, portable solar charger with an adapter for your NVGs, Sig Sauer Mosquito, four spare mags, a five-hundred round brick of .22 long rifle, two-hundred rounds .22 magnum still in the box, and ten pre-loaded P-mags with thirty rounds each, giving you a total of three hundred five-five-six rounds ready to go and oh my God this thing is heavy as shit."

I laughed. "It's not that bad."

"Gabe, between this and your weapons, you'll be carrying over a hundred pounds of gear."

"It's no worse than what I had to do in the Marines."

"Yeah, but you were, like, twenty years younger then."

My smile disappeared. "I'll be fine."

Eric watched as I made a show of reaching across the table, grabbing the pack with one hand, lifting it up with my arm outstretched, and giving it a little toss in the air as I slipped my arms through the straps.

"See?"

"Whatever, dude."

Once I was armed, armored, and otherwise geared up, Eric limped along beside me to the north gate. I told him not to, that I could find my way on my own, and that he was just being a stubborn asshat. He told me he did not recall asking my opinion on the subject, and to shut the hell up and walk.

I got a lot of strange looks from the guards, but my reputation was such that they didn't bother asking questions. After I signed out, the guards opened the pedestrian gate and waited impatiently, guns trained through the opening.

I took a moment to turn and offer Eric a hand. He shook it, but did not smile. "This is stupid, Gabe. You should let me talk to Lieutenant Jonas. There's no need to do this alone."

I shook my head, and let out a sigh. "Trust me, Eric. It's for the best. Too many people have gotten hurt as it is. I'm not dragging anyone else into my problems."

"Sir, you should get moving," one of the guards said. "We can't keep the gate open much longer."

I nodded to him and clapped Eric on the shoulder. "Look in on Elizabeth for me, will you?"

"Of course."

"And look after that wife and baby."

"Allison's not my wife."

"You sure about that?"

He blinked, and stood rooted to the spot, the color draining from his face. For once, he had nothing to say.

THIRTY

After the defeat of the Free Legion, a few people from Hollow Rock had the bright idea to set up a trading post just north of nearby Huntingdon.

When I first heard about it, I wondered what the hell they were thinking. After all, why set up a trading post less than ten miles from a town that is itself, ostensibly, a gigantic trading post? However, once word got out that Hollow Rock was safe again and trade picked back up, the wisdom became clear.

It is about a hundred miles as the crow flies from Hollow Rock to the Mississippi River. You can make it there on foot in about four days if you're in shape, eight if you're not, and three days on a good horse. But there isn't much civilization between the Mississippi and Hollow Rock, and by the time people get there, they are usually tired, sore, and ready for a home-cooked meal and a good night's sleep. For many of them, given the choice between stopping or pressing on another ten miles, they choose to take a rest. Which is where the outpost gets its name, Traveler's Rest.

And that was where I was headed.

There would be several days of hard living between Hollow Rock and Blackmire, but I saw no reason to spend my first night on the road sleeping on a rooftop or wedged in the boles of a tree when there were better accommodations available. It was already one in the afternoon by the time the north wall of Hollow Rock disappeared behind me, and I had no desire to be caught in the open after dark. So I set a hard pace and covered nine of the ten miles required by the time the sun began to dip below the western sky.

I stayed within a stone's throw of Highway 70 for most of the way, traveling due west, and was just about to turn northward again when I heard the unmistakable sound of a woman's scream.

I stopped and went still, ears straining, eyes darting left and right. The scream repeated itself, farther ahead on the highway, then abruptly stopped. After making sure there was no threat in my immediate surroundings, I dropped my pack, donned my ghillie suit, and set out to locate the source.

The highway cut a broad curve until it ran parallel to a set of railroad tracks—an old CSX line that crossed the south side of Hollow Rock—and stretched past a large clearing amid a ring of burned out buildings. Spotting it, I dropped down and crawled on my belly, trusting my ghillie suit to keep me hidden in the deep snow. When I was a hundred yards away from the clearing, I could see a disorderly knot of people struggling around a campfire, their shapes outlined by the flickering light. Moving very slowly, I brought my rifle up, adjusted the scope to its 4x setting, and peered through it.

At a quick count, there looked to be fifteen of them in all. Five were either bound, or in the process of being bound, two were tossing things out of a large wooden wagon, one was trying to keep a pair of horses calm, three were standing outward from the violence as lookouts, and the rest were casually brutalizing the people they had tied up. I lowered the rifle, knowing I had a decision to make.

There are various levels of criminal scum in the world, and they generally fall into a few broad categories. The two most common are raiders and marauders: people who rape, rob, pillage, and kill anyone who gets in their way, including each other. These two groups are differentiated by their methods: raiders are constantly on the move, never staying in one spot for very long, whereas marauders are territorial, much like gangs or organized crime. Then you have the various categories of swindlers, con men, thieves, and other petty criminals that seem to persist everywhere in the world, but are not necessarily violent. Beneath them are the pimps and the hustlers, those who ensnare and sexually exploit other human beings for personal gain. And at the bottom of the dung heap, deep down with the sludge and the maggots and the worms, where the sun never shines and all is stench and rottenness, are the dregs, the scum of the earth, the lowest of the low, those for whom the mere mention of their name will incite people to sneer and curse and spit on the ground.

Slavers.

They are never difficult to spot. Raiders and marauders have simple, predictable methods. First, they kill the men. All of them, young or old. Then they usually try to take the women alive for reasons which do not require explanation, but if they put up too much of a fight, they kill them too. Then they make quick work of sorting their victim's belongings, decide who gets what with the biggest share going to the leader, and move along.

However, three of the five people on the ground ahead of me were men, fully grown and healthy by the look of them. If this were the work of raiders or marauders, those men would be dead, not tied up. As for the women, they were not in the process of being raped just yet, but it was only a matter of time. Slavers like to sample their wares before selling them.

Where the slave markets were, I could only guess. I had heard rumors of massive auctions being held up north in Mt. Vernon and Jasper, but no one seemed to know for sure. It was well known, however, that slavery was allowed in Alliance territory so long as the slaves were not Alliance citizens. Which meant anyone traveling the roads in Missouri, Kentucky, and Tennessee did well to travel in large, well-armed groups, and in sufficient number to dissuade slavers from attacking them. Evidently, the people on the ground ahead of me were either not aware of this danger, or dumb enough to think they could slip by undetected. Not a very wise thing to do.

Under other circumstances, I might have moved on. I was outnumbered ten to one, and although I hate criminals as much as the next guy, I understand and accept that I cannot save everyone. There are some fights you just can't win, justified or not. But the putrid bags of shit ahead of me were not merely thieves, or bullies, or thugs, or even marauders. They were slavers.

And I fucking hate slavers.

Working slowly, I retreated and edged my way back to the woods, staying low to keep from being spotted. When I reached the trees, I got back to my feet and moved toward thicker cover closer to the campsite, maneuvering so I had the sun at my back. The slavers continued their work, unaware that death was closing in on them.

Near the edge of the treeline, I spotted a fallen maple that looked as if someone had felled it, cut off a few large limbs for a campfire, and left the trunk to rot. Offering a silent thanks to the erstwhile lumberjack for his hard work, I belly crawled to the tree and set my rifle on its bipod.

Through the reticle, I picked the order in which they would die. There was a man standing apart from the others I pegged as the leader. He had that look about him, the straight posture, the hands on the hips, the placid calm as if his every word would be obeyed without question, a man accustomed to authority. For anyone who has ever served in the military, these people stand out like a sore thumb. And when they go down, when you cut off the beast's head, chaos ensues. Chaos is good. A frightened enemy in disarray is much easier to defeat than a confident, organized one.

He did me the favor of turning his back and standing still, the accommodating bastard. To thank him, I adjusted my grip on the M-6, let out a little air, and squeezed the trigger. There was a clank and a thump, and through the magnified view of my scope, I watched a gout of brain matter splash the snow in front of him, blood pouring from the wound like a ruptured barrel. He went stiff and tipped over face first, landing in a spattering of his own gore.

One down, nine to go.

Before the leader hit the ground, I shifted my aim to the three lookouts. They were still facing away, unaware of the danger they were in, rifles held loosely, eyes more preoccupied with the loot coming out of the wagon than on locating threats. I took them out quickly with a single head shot each, firing with the sureness of long practice—tap, tap, tap. Six to go.

A slaver sorting through the wagon noticed the guards falling and raised a shout of alarm. All heads swiveled toward him, then to the dead body of their leader. One of them unslung his rifle—an AK-47, surprise surprise—and let off a quick burst in my general direction. None of the rounds hit anywhere close to me, but I didn't want the other slavers finding their spines and following suit. A double tap to the face ended his onslaught and sent the others scrambling for cover. Two of them bumped into each other as they scurried around the wagon, the smaller one rebounding from the larger one and landing on his side in the snow. My rifle coughed twice, and he did not get up again.

The clatter of another rifle rang out, followed by a hail of bullets hammering away at the trees over my head. I dropped down, head below the top of the fallen maple, and waited. More rifles joined the fracas, their reports shockingly loud in the still twilight. Very quickly, as I knew they would, the shots died off when the slavers ran out of ammo.

Looking through my scope, I risked a peek over the top of the tree, and in the square of space beneath the wagon, I saw several pairs of legs shifting back and forth. Switching the M-6's selector to three-round burst, I pulled the trigger twice, a grin stretching across my face as a chorus of agonized howls rewarded my efforts. Two more slavers hit the ground, hands clutching at the shattered bones in their legs. There was a quick adjustment of the reticle and a couple of muted thumps, and their suffering ended.

Two left.

They were both huddled in the back of the wagon, staying low where I couldn't see them. For a moment, I almost felt sorry for them. They probably didn't realize that the wooden planks comprising the wagon's sidewalls were not sturdy enough to stop a bullet. I aimed center of mass, and let off another burst. A slaver screamed, raised his rifle over the side, and fired blindly at the forest. Again, I waited until he was out of ammo, and then raised my head.

"There is no escape. Drop your weapons and come out with your hands up."

No response.

I fired another burst. There was a bit of frantic shuffling, but no screams. "Last warning. The next burst is going to be full auto, and I will not stop until you are both dead. You have five seconds. One. Two. Three. F-"

"All right, all right!" a voice shouted. "We're coming out. Don't shoot."

Two men emerged from the wagon, hands in the air, one of them with a bloodstain expanding rapidly down his left leg. From the tear in his pants, I guessed one of the rounds I fired through the wagon grazed his thigh. The two men stared at the carnage around them, faces slack, eyes bulging with disbelief. I stood up and approached them, rifle leveled.

"Turn away from the sound of my voice."

The slavers hesitated, gaping at the hulking, white-clad figure coming toward them. I stopped and took aim. "Do it now."

They obeyed.

"Down on your knees, hands on top of your heads. Good. Now cross your feet. Stay where you are, and do not move. You move, you die. Nod if you understand."

They both did.

"You will not speak unless given permission. Is that clear? Nod if you understand."

Another silent affirmative.

I crossed the campsite to one of the men tied up on the ground. He was older, maybe mid-fifties, staring at me with a mixture of fear and hope. I unsheathed my Ka-bar, cut the rope from his wrists, and offered him the hilt of the knife. He grabbed it, but I held on for an extra second.

"Stay where I can see you, you hear? Don't try anything cute. You won't live to regret it."

He nodded quickly. "Yes sir."

"Go help the others."

He complied, not saying another word until the other four victims were all free. They huddled together in a little group and slowly edged toward me, the older man in front. "You," I said, pointing at him. "Do you have any rope, duct tape, zip ties, anything like that?"

"Y...yes, we do."

"Grab it and follow me."

He did as I asked, retrieving a roll of nylon twine from the detritus around the wagon, and then joined me by the two surviving slavers. "That one," I said, gesturing to him with my rifle. "Tie his hands and feet, and make it tight. We don't want him getting loose."

"Hey, listen man-" The slaver began, but I interrupted him by placing a bullet in the ground less than an inch from his knee.

"Shut up. Open your mouth again, and it'll be your last words."

He was very compliant as the old man tied him up. Very humble.

"Hey, what's your name?"

The old man looked at me. "Me?"

"Yes."

"Um...Harold. Harold Nelson."

"Okay. Harold," I said, keeping my voice calm and friendly. "I need you to go back over there with the others."

As he walked away, I hog tied the second slaver and laid them both on their sides. "Don't try to move," I said. "And no talking. This is your last warning. Disobey, and you die."

By the looks on their faces, I didn't have much to worry about.

THIRTY-ONE

It would have been nice to sit down and have a chat with the people I rescued, but as usually happens when a bunch of idiots let loose with unsuppressed rifles, the goddamn infected showed up.

The first moan sounded from the east, where the sky had already faded from cobalt blue to a lurid purple. It was quickly answered by dozens of others, converging from all directions. I let out a stream of curses that would have set a drill sergeant's hair on fire and stomped over to the prisoners, knife in hand.

I knelt in front of them. "Do you want to live?"

They made the appropriate noises.

"Then you will do exactly as you're told." I cut the rope binding their ankles and helped them stand. "Wait here," I said, and walked back over to Nelson and his group.

I said, "You have to get out of here. Every walker within five miles is headed this way."

The old man spoke up, clearly the leader of the group. "We were headed for Hollow Rock. I understand we're not far from there."

I shook my head. "Hollow Rock is ten miles that way." I hooked a thumb over my shoulder. "I just came from there."

The old man's face fell, and a woman who I guessed to be his wife stepped forward. "Then where should we go? It's almost nightfall. We were going to build a camp fort and spend the night here, but now there's no time."

I raised a placating hand. "There's a place about a mile north of here, it's called Traveler's Rest. You'll be safe there. If you want to keep any of this stuff, I suggest you get it on the wagon and get ready to move."

The old man turned around and looked at his group's scattered possessions. A little of the fear left his face and he seemed to gain confidence. "He's right. Estelle, you get up on the wagon. Leo, Ernie, Jenny, y'all help me pick this stuff up. Come on now, we got to move."

I lent them a hand, moving swiftly, not trying to stack or organize anything, just throwing it in the wagon. We were done in less than two minutes, but already there were infected close enough to be a problem. Regretting the loss of ammunition, I put down a dozen of them in rapid succession, then made my way back to the wagon.

"Listen to me," I said, as Harold took up the reigns. "Take the highway back the way you came. The first road you come to, take a right. Follow it until you see a water tower on a hill. At the bottom of that hill is another road. There's a big wooden sign, you can't miss it. That road will take you to Traveler's Rest. If anybody gives you trouble at the gate, tell them Gabriel Garrett sent you. Okay?"

Harold nodded. "Okay."

"Go on," I said. "I'll catch up with you."

I started walking back to the prisoners, but heard Harold's voice behind me. "Mr. Garrett?"

I turned and looked over my shoulder.

"I just…" he struggled for words, not sure how to thank a man who had just saved him and his family from being sold into slavery.

"You can thank me later," I said. "Now get moving."

He gave a single nod, shouted at the horses, and slapped the reigns.

*****

There exists in the wastelands a burgeoning subcategory of society, created by circumstance, necessity, and the natural

340

proliferation of effective survival techniques, and they are commonly referred to as Runners.

They are a very useful people, and make their living by a combination of scavenging, trading, and transporting things from one place to another.

Got a letter for a trade contact on the other side of the river but don't feel like making the expedition?

Hire a Runner.

Found out your uncle is still alive in Colorado and want to send him a message?

Hire a Runner.

Can't sell something where you live, but know it will fetch a good price somewhere else?

Hire a Runner.

Most folks think Runners are lone wolves who live in the forests and sleep in trees every night, and because of this, some people have taken to calling them Rangers, although they generally dislike that term. But what I have learned through extensive buying of drinks and generous trade negotiations is that Runners are not as aloof from one another as most people think they are. I would not call them a community, per se, but they definitely have a sort of loose association and rules of conduct.

Rule number one: If you take a contract, you fulfill it, or you die trying.

It takes a long time for a Runner, or a group of Runners, to establish a good reputation. The more dependable people perceive them to be, the more they can charge for their services. But it only takes one failed contract to spoil things for everyone, and you do not want to be that guy.

Rule number two: Runners are not hired muscle. Which means no assassinations, no robberies, no vandalism, no leg-breaking for debt collectors, no kidnapping—basically no involvement with vice, racketeering, or general thuggery.

Rule number three: Never reveal the location of a campsite without a consensus of the community.

And that is, without a doubt, the best part of being on good terms with Runners—the campsites.

The rules regarding campsites are simple, but strictly enforced. It boils down to three things: leave the place cleaner than you found it, don't be greedy, and leave something behind for the next guy.

To keep track of who uses the campsites and when, every Runner has two names. There is the normal name used for interaction outside your Runner association, and then there is the name known only to your fellow Runners. This name is not chosen, it is given by someone else based on any number of things. Maybe you have a tattoo, or a distinguishing physical feature, or you are seen engaging in some activity that is, for whatever reason, memorable.

Or in my case, a walker jumps a Runner out of nowhere on the road to Hollow Rock, I peel the thing off the guy before it can bite him, toss it away, grab the first weapon close at hand— which happens to be a sawed-off shotgun in a holster on said Runner's back—and disintegrate the walker's face. Then the Runner, in his elation at not dying, gleefully screams, "This. Is. My. BOOMSTICK!". And from then on I am known and referred to exclusively by that moniker.

Boomstick.

It can be anything really, but once an association decides on your name, you're stuck with it whether you like it or not. Each Runner makes a symbol for their name, which only people in his or her association can identify.

And so it was, I found myself on a wooden platform, built among the struts of a water tower near Traveler's Rest, leaving a pound of goat jerky, five MRE packets of instant coffee, and a twenty-round box of 5.56 ammo, drawing a circle around it with a piece of chalk conveniently left there for the purpose, and then scratching a crude pictogram of a shotgun with a backwards B on the stock.

Boomstick was here. And he was generous indeed.

Considering the messy purpose I was using the site for, I thought the donation—which would have been considered excessive, albeit welcome, by most Runners—appropriate.

Finished leaving my mark, I walked back to the edge of the platform and peered downward. It was after nightfall, but the sky was clear and the moon was nearly full, allowing me to see the two men dangling from the platform by their feet.

It had taken a lot of effort to retrieve my pack and then hightail it to the campsite with the two slavers in tow, but I had pulled it off. And now, the two would-be kidnappers hung upside down from a platform thirty feet in the air, suspended by lengths of para-cord, their heads less than five feet from the grasping hands of a hundred or more ghouls. The smell was atrocious, and I was much further from the source than they were.

"How you boys doing down there? Ready to talk yet?"

"Fuck you!" one of them shouted, the man I had dubbed Pig Face, because ... well, he kind of resembled a pig. The other I called Smart Guy, because he didn't seem nearly as dumb as his partner.

After reaching the tower, I had made use of a four-in-one pulley system some enterprising soul had installed above the platform. The prisoners hadn't cared much for it, being that I tied the rope around their ankles and hauled them to the platform upside down, but they had nonetheless cooperated. I can only assume that being held captive was a better option than being left for the infected, so they had not given me any trouble. I think for just a few brief moments they entertained the hope I was not going to hurt them, maybe take them back to Hollow Rock to stand trial.

That hope was to be short lived.

"You know, you're not giving me much reason to let you live," I said, cupping my hands around my mouth to be heard above the din of moans.

"I ain't telling you shit, cocksucker," Pig Face said. "You're just gonna kill me anyway, so go ahead and do it."

I shrugged, put in my earplugs, and leaned down with my knife. "Okay. Suit yourself."

The blade sawed back and forth and the cords holding him up popped—one, two, three—and with a cry of dismay, he plunged down into the waiting arms of the infected.

I walked back to my bedroll and stretched out, letting my back relax after the day's efforts. My pack had felt a lot lighter when I was nineteen.

The screaming went on for a while, first from Pig Face, and then from Smart Guy as he watched his friend being eaten alive, then eventually subsided into ragged sobs only barely audible through my earplugs.

If it had been anyone but a slaver, feeding someone to the undead would have seemed an extreme punishment. But kidnapping people, raping them, and selling them into a life of brutalization, sexual exploitation, and hopelessness, is hands down the worst sin a human being can commit. So no, I did not feel the least bit bad about it. Had the situation been reversed, he would have done the same to me in an instant.

I let the last slaver marinate for a little while, staring at the promise of a hideous death, before I tried again.

"I'm thinking you must have a hell of a headache by now. I'm also thinking you don't want to go out like your friend there. It's no trouble at all the haul you back up here, but I'm gonna need some answers first. What do you say?"

His voice was hoarse, trembling with terror. "Please, I'll tell you whatever you want. Just don't feed me to those things."

"Excellent." I hauled on the line until his head was above the platform, where he could look me in the eye, then looped the rope around a cleat bolted to the floor. "First question. Where do you slavers take your merchandise?"

Smart Guy's face was beet red, and his eyes had turned dark and bloody. He spoke rapidly. "There are markets in Mt.

Vernon, Jasper, Red Blade, and Blackmire. Other places too, but I've never been there."

"Hmm. I'm familiar with Mt. Vernon, Jasper, and Blackmire, but I've never heard of Red Blade. Where is it?"

"It's the old Southern Illinois Airport, but the people there renamed it. You can find it on any highway map."

"Good to know. What's it like, this Red Blade? Where'd the town get its name?"

"I don't know where the name comes from. Place is a fortress, kind of like Hollow Rock but smaller. It's an Alliance outpost."

"That's interesting. I didn't know the Alliance had claimed territory so far south. Usually they stay behind the border. Except for scumbags like you, of course."

"Listen, man, I-"

"Shut up. Let me think for a minute."

I put my chin in my hand and pondered the events of the last few weeks. From what Smart Guy was telling me, Blackmire was associated with the Midwest Alliance, or at least with its slave trade. Then there were the AKs the slavers had been carrying, and although I didn't get a chance to look at them, I was willing to bet if I checked the manufacturers stamps they would be written in Chinese, just like the weapons of the men sent from Blackmire to capture me. I was also willing to bet that if I went back to Hollow Rock and hung a few of those insurgents awaiting trial over a horde of ghouls, they might also be able to tell me something about Blackmire. Now that I thought about it, their appearance occurring shortly before Sean Montford's murder, in light of other evidence, no longer had the feeling of a standalone attack.

Blackmire.

That name was popping up far too often to be a simple matter of coincidence. And its proximity to Hollow Rock did not fill me with a sense of ease. As much as I wanted to stay focused on tracking down Sebastian Tanner, I couldn't ignore the threat posed by the Alliance if they had influence over a community that close, especially one composed of thieves, slavers, marauders, and other assorted scum. Much like when Sheriff Elliott handed me that Russian-made sniper cartridge, I realized my situation was far more complicated than previously thought.

I gave Smart Guy a little shove on the chest, sending him swinging back and forth. "Tell me, have you ever been to Blackmire?"

"Yeah, lots of times."

"How long ago was your last visit?"

"Not long. A couple of weeks."

"Okay. Here's what's going to happen," I said. "I'm going to cut you down, and give you a pen and a notebook. You will draw a map, as accurately as you can, of the layout of Blackmire and the surrounding area. When you are done, you will tell me everything you know about the place. And if I detect any hint of deception," I held up my knife, "I'm going to start cutting. We'll start with your fingers and toes, and work our way from there. Do I make myself clear?"

His Adam's apple bobbed as he swallowed hard. "Yes sir."

We talked long into the night, the two of us. Once, after he finished drawing the map and I was re-tying his hands, he tried lunging for my pistol. I caught his hand and snapped a few finger bones, then stomped on his ankle. Rather than scream, his face went pale, his eyes rolled up in the back of his head, and he passed out. I finished the job of restraining him, woke him back up, and informed him any further unpleasantness would result in me tossing his sorry ass over the side and smiling while I did it. He gave me no further problems.

When I had wrung as much information as I could out of him, making him answer the same questions many times, in different orders, and worded differently every time, I slapped my hands on my knees and heaved an accomplished sigh. "Well, I guess that concludes our business for the evening. It's been a pleasure speaking with you, Smart Guy, but I'm afraid, like all things, our conversation must come to an end."

Standing up, I grabbed him by the scruff of his jacket and began dragging him toward the edge of the platform.

"Hey, wait! Stop! Please, don't throw me to those fucking things."

"Don't worry, I'm not going to let the infected eat you alive."

I positioned him so he was sitting on the edge, facing the horde. "Then what…what are you doing?"

I drew my pistol and touched it to the back of his head. "The federal government recently passed new laws and regulations. Do you know what the penalty is in Union territory for kidnapping with intent to enslave?"

He tried to speak, but only a strained croak came out.

I leaned down and lowered my voice to a whisper. "Summary Execution."

And then I pulled the trigger.

The infected spared me the trouble of disposing of his body. I guess the poor disgusting things have their uses after all.

THIRTY-TWO

I only planned to stop in Traveler's Rest long enough to pick up a few things, but when I walked into the general store I quite literally ran into Harold Nelson.

He was walking by with a large jar of pickled eggs, studying a list in his hand, and didn't see me come through the door until he hit me in the chest and bounced away. I reached out a hand and grabbed him before he could topple over.

"Mr. Garrett," he said, face brightening. "I'm so glad to see you're all right. After you didn't show up last night I...well, we feared the worst."

I stepped farther inside the store, unblocking the entrance, boards creaking under my feet. "There were a lot of walkers out there. I didn't want them to follow me here, so I led them off and doubled back. Took me most of the night." It was technically true, but not the whole story.

"What, uh, what happened to those fellas you captured?"

I shook my head. "I had to make a choice between them or me. They lost."

Now I was lying, but it was better than saying, 'I fed them to the walkers, spent the night at a Runner campsite, then threw chunks of rusted metal at a tree until enough infected wandered away to escape.' It was bad enough he had watched me kill eight people, I didn't want to regale him with tales of torture and murder. Furthermore, there were a few people in Traveler's Rest—namely the constable—who might take exception to the way I disposed of those last two slavers.

"I guess I can't say I'm sorry to hear that," Nelson said. "Not after what they tried to do to my family and me. You know, it's strange to me I feel that way. Before the Outbreak, what happened yesterday would have had me curled up in a corner like a scared kid. But now...I guess I'm just glad I'm still alive and they're not. I slept fine last night. No nightmares or anything. What does that say about me, do you think?"

"It means you're human, Harold. When you survive enough bad things, you grow callouses. It's a common affliction."

The old man smiled weakly, and nodded. I let an appropriate length of silence pass, then said, "Is everyone in your party all right?"

He let out a shaky sigh and ran a hand through his thinning hair. "They're a little shook up, but they'll be fine. Listen, I can't thank you enough for helping us. When those men came out of the woods, I thought we were done for. Then when I realized they were slavers…"

I smiled. "I'm just glad I could be there to help. In the future, you might want to think about joining up with a larger group before you get back on the road. It's not safe out there."

He looked down, watery eyes regretful. "Yes, I realize that now. I was a damn fool to think we could make it all the way from the river without running into trouble. I won't make that mistake again."

I patted him on the shoulder. "I'm glad to hear it. Listen, I hate to cut this short, but I have somewhere I need to be."

He reached out to shake my hand. "I understand completely. If you ever find yourself in Fort Holloway, come and see us. Ask anybody around town, they'll tell you where to find me."

I had heard of Fort Holloway, and had a general idea where it was, but had never been there. "I'll be sure to do that. You take care, Harold."

An hour later, I had traded the slavers' gear to replace the items I left at the Runner camp, and was back on the road.

*****

One of the effects of over ninety-nine percent of the world dying off is that once you leave the trade routes behind, you can travel a very long way without seeing another living human being. You do, however, see a lot what *used* to be living human beings.

The infected were everywhere, maybe a hundred or more per square mile, traveling in hordes of varying sizes. I avoided them as much as possible, but due to their acute hearing and eerie ability to triangulate noise with lethal accuracy, I was frequently forced to set a running pace in order to outdistance them. The problem with this was every time I shook off one horde, another stood poised and ready to take its place.

The first night, I slept in a large farm equipment storage building surrounded by a copse of cedars. There was a pile of charred detritus nearby that had once been a house, and a Ford pickup truck with dry-rotted tires and smears of blood on the windshield. The surrounding land had once been a sprawling farm, but was now just flat squares of undisturbed snow stretching between patches of gray, leafless trees.

The building before me consisted of two walls supporting a pitched tin roof with a couple of steel support columns in the middle. A rusted, disused combine sat dejectedly on one side of the columns, while a bevy of attachments occupied the other space, slowly sinking into the dirt. Despite the high winds, the scene had that quiet, hushed feeling a place gets when it is abandoned long enough. It was a feeling I was very familiar with, as were all Outbreak survivors. Much like fine wine, I had learned to appreciate its diverse and particular flavors.

Looking behind me, I spotted the horde that had been dogging my trail all day. Under other circumstances, I would have left them far behind. But being that I was traveling in more or less a straight line, all they had to do was keep walking and eventually one of them would spot me. It would be dark soon, and the storage building was the only shelter available. There was no loft above me, but the top of the combine was large enough to sleep on. It would have to do.

Working quickly, I gathered some firewood, dug an old Weber grill out of a snowbank, and set up my distraction system.

Anti-walker survival technique number 43: Cut a length of string (or para-cord, or twine, or dental floss, or vine, or whatever you have on hand) about eighteen inches long, tie it in a loop, and then attach some cans, sticks, and other rattly things to it. Run another length of para-cord (or whatever) through the loop, then string it out a good distance from where you will be sleeping. In this case the side view mirror of the pickup truck with the cans dangling against the metal fender. Then run it back to camp and tie it off next to your bedroll so it is close at hand. When you wake up in the morning, stay where the infected can't see you and tug the string vigorously. The cans will make a God-awful racket and attract the undead. When enough of them leave to investigate, untie the para-cord, reel it in, and make your escape. You will lose the rattly thing, but you can always make another one later. One thing there is no shortage of at the end of the world is garbage.

With the can-laden para-cord in place, I dragged the Weber grill atop the combine then followed up with a few armfuls of firewood. I would have liked to gather more, but the arrival of the infected forestalled such efforts. Settling in for the night, I broke the legs off the grill, set it down on the combine's roof, and made a small fire. I wasn't worried about being spotted; the two walls of the storage building and the surrounding evergreens provided excellent concealment. Someone would literally have to step around the corner to see me. The smoke might be detectable farther away, but without a telltale orange glow, it would be highly difficult to locate.

The infected surrounded the combine while I ate my meager dinner, so I kept my eyes down and focused on what was directly in front of me. Long experience may have inured me to the terror the ghouls can inspire, but looking at them still kills my appetite.

Finished, I added a couple of sticks to the fire and stretched out on my bedroll. I couldn't seem to get comfortable, so I used my knife and a few well-placed strikes from the hilt of my falcata to remove the windshield from the cab. The leather covering driver's seat was a little cracked, but the padding underneath was still remarkably intact. I cut it out and placed it under my ground mat. That did the trick.

The next morning, I used the distraction system for the purpose for which it was intended, then set out due west. I kept a brisk pace, walking forty steps then running forty steps, over and over, until the undead were a speck on the horizon. I was safe for the moment, but I knew there would be more. There always were.

When the sun reached its zenith, I climbed on top of an overturned tractor-trailer and ate a quick, cold lunch, then continued on. My path took me through a patch of forest where I ran afoul of a walker lying dormant under the snow.

I was jogging along, counting off my twenty-sixth running step, when the toe of my right boot hit something and I went pitching over onto my face. I was up in an instant, but it was enough time for the walker to raise its head and get a grip on my pants leg. Not for the first time, I marveled at the strength of the rotten thing. It would have been easier to cut its hand off than attempt to pry it loose. As it was, I simply leveled my rifle, lined the barrel up with its forehead, and pulled the trigger. The walker went limp.

"Rest in peace, you poor bastard."

The rest of the day passed quietly enough, wearing on toward nightfall. A low bank of steel-colored clouds moved in from the north like an invading army, and the temperature dropped about fifteen degrees. Before long, I began passing frosted deadfalls of walkers, frozen where they stood and toppled atop one another. As I passed, the only thing that moved was their eyes. Even covered in a milky white film, I could still see the hunger in those mindless gazes.

I checked my rifle for the umpteenth time and picked up the pace.

It was well after dark before I finally found a place to take shelter: the roof of an old utility shed. I tried picking the lock, but even with a spritz of rust-breaking compound, it was too deteriorated to turn. Cursing my luck, I tossed my pack on the roof, pushed an old wooden cable spool the size of a dinner table next to the wall, and climbed up.

Around midnight, I felt the soft, tickling caress of snowflakes on my face in the pitch darkness, prompting another round of vicious cursing. Moving in the dark, I set up my pup tent by feel and climbed in. Normally I preferred to sleep without it, as it obscured my view of the surrounding terrain. But if I didn't take shelter, I would wake up soaked to the skin. Not an acceptable option in sub-freezing conditions.

It continued getting colder until, even huddled in my sleeping bag and fully dressed, I couldn't stop shivering. If I slept more than two hours that night, I would be amazed. I was awake when the sun broke the horizon, and not wanting to prolong my misery, I packed my things and got moving.

So far I had not encountered anything too difficult to endure, but nearly ten months of easy living in Hollow Rock had softened me. I longed for the feeling of a soft bed and a warm woman to share it with. The image of Elizabeth lying next to me sent an ache through my chest so intense that, for a moment, I could have sworn I had been stabbed. Thinking about her lying in that hospital bed, probably wondering if I was still alive, made me seriously contemplate turning around and going home. Liz had made it clear she would not think less of me if I did.

Too late for that now. You have to end this.

Shoving aside all thoughts of home, I plodded onward.

THIRTY-THREE

After a night spent in shivering agony, and dreading the prospect of a repeat performance as night fell over Tennessee, the gabled roof of an abandoned house in the distance was a welcome sight. The other houses I had passed for the last few miles were nothing more than piles of charred rubble, which struck me as odd, because while it is not unusual to see a few burned out structures here and there, finding so many on one lonely stretch of highway was very strange indeed.

According to my map, I was just a few miles north of I-40 and closing in on State Highway 70, headed northwest. If I went about ten miles further north, I would run into a thin stretch of greenery known as the Tennessee Safari Park, and if I turned southward, there was the Hatchie National Wildlife Refuge. Neither destination interested me, however, as my path lay straight ahead to a place just over twenty miles away, in what was once the Chickasaw National Wildlife Refuge—a den of thieves, raiders, slavers, marauders, and other assorted scum, all lorded over by a man who ruled the place with an iron fist, a man who had dubbed the town by the only name he ever gave.

Blackmire.

There was a man there named Marco who had hired a group of half-assed mercenaries and sent them to draw me out and capture me. Those mercenaries tortured and murdered a good and decent man and, for that, Marco was going to pay.

If my theory was correct, Marco was working for Tanner, and if I found him, he might be able to point me in the right direction. Not exactly the most well-thought-out plan, but it was all I had to go on. If Marco couldn't lead me to Tanner, I would be back to square one.

But that was a problem for tomorrow.

Night was fast approaching, and I needed to rest.

The house was still in relatively good condition, save for peeling paint, sagging porch steps, and a few broken windows. A quick recon around the perimeter revealed no signs of recent habitation, but there was a shed in the back—about the size of the trailers I used to see at construction sites—with a rusted chain and padlock holding the door shut. Oddly, the shed had no windows, with the chained door being the only way in. A few raps on the door, ear pressed against the cold wood, revealed no noise from within. I briefly considered chopping my way in with my axe, but decided against it. It was only mild curiosity that made me want to know what was inside, not necessity, and doing so would make a hell of a lot of noise. I was pretty sure I had shaken the last horde that spotted me from my trail, and had no interest in attracting them again. With a last curious glance, I left the shed be.

The back door to the house was unlocked, so with rifle leveled and ears straining, I pushed my way inside. There was enough light to see by, revealing a ransacked kitchen and pantry directly in front of me. It looked as if someone had long ago found this place and picked it clean. The living room was empty except for a broken lamp lying listlessly in one corner, as was a bathroom in an adjacent hallway. Why someone would remove a toilet and sink was entirely beyond me, but that was what happened.

Weird.

The first eight stairs had been pried away from the staircase and the supporting structure beneath had been savaged with an axe; a common defense against the undead. I tossed my pack onto the next floor, grabbed the edge so my back was to the staircase, did half a pull-up, and swung my legs over my head. I finished up lying flat on my stomach.

The upstairs portion of the house, consisting of three bedrooms and a laundry room, were in much the same condition as the downstairs rooms. Even the carpets had been taken, revealing the tightly fitted plywood beneath. My boots sent up little spouts of dust as I walked along the creaking floor, searching for signs of habitation. There were none. I was alone.

355

Lowering my rifle, I stepped into the bedroom with the best view of the downstairs area.

"As good a place as any."

After laying out my bedroll and eating a quick dinner, I scattered broken glass and a few handfuls of rocks beneath the windows, tied a rattle alarm across both doors, and opened all the interior doors of the house. Doing so improved the house's acoustics, allowing me to hear any sounds coming from downstairs. Finished, I stretched out on the floor to get some rest.

Sleep was not long in coming.

*****

I awoke to the sound of crunching glass.

My first thought was the infected had found me and somehow gotten inside, but I quickly dismissed that idea. Both doors were locked, and they would not have been able to get through the windows without making a hell of a noise. Which lead to only one conclusion.

I was not alone.

Moving slowly, I donned my NVGs, grabbed my M-6, and crawled toward the door. Reaching it, I gazed toward the living room, scanning the gray and white thermal image for heat signatures. Nothing. Unconvinced, I adjusted the goggles' FLIR to its highest setting and looked again. At the window closest to the kitchen, just before the wall on that side cut off my view, I saw an outline. It was faint, barely detectable, but there. And definitely man-shaped.

If I had to guess, I would say the individual at the window had crept to it, checked for movement, then stepped slowly over the sill. To his dismay, when he put his weight down, his boot crunched a mess of glass, rocks, and dirt, and he had stepped quickly back. I imagined him crouching in the dark, heart racing, eyes wide, ears straining for the slightest sound. It's what I would have done, anyway.

If I stayed quiet and gave him no reason to run, maybe he would try again. I just had to hope he was alone, or things could get very ugly, very quickly. Backing off a few feet, I assumed a seated firing position, elbows resting on my knees, and waited.

To give credit where it is due, he was patient. He did not panic and run. After several minutes, he stood slowly, head appearing around the edge of the window. I kept my sights on him, remaining still as a statue.

Gradually, carefully, he lowered one foot over the threshold. This time, rather than stepping down, he gently nudged his boot from side to side, brushing away the glass and debris with barely a sound. When he had his foot planted, he brought the other leg in and repeated the process. Now inside the room, he took one more cautious step and was clear of the countermeasures.

His next obstacle was crossing the floor without making the boards creak. Very quickly, I realized he had a great deal of practice at this. His footfalls were precise and deliberate, going to places he knew would not groan under his weight. In less than a minute, he was standing under same lip I had climbed a few hours ago. I watched him reach his hands up, grab hold, and lever himself to the second floor in the same manner I had, albeit with more grace and stealth.

Finally, he was standing and doing his tip-toe creeping routine down the hallway, headed for my room. The fact that he knew which one I was in meant he had watched me arrive, a revelation I found not at all comforting. As he approached, I realized he was a large man, maybe six-foot two or three, and probably around two-hundred twenty pounds, give or take. Judging by the way he moved, he was fit and knew how to handle himself.

Oh well. Nothing a bullet won't fix.

Drawing closer, his hands went into his pockets and came out clutching two small objects. One of them was obviously a gun, but I couldn't tell what the other one was. It was about a foot long, and seemed to have a bit of flexion to it. With dull dread, and blooming anger, I realized it was a blackjack—basically a coiled spring with a large lead weight on the end encased in braided leather. I had used weapons like that a few times, and knew very well how deceptively deadly they could be. Hit someone straight on like you are swinging a baton, and it won't do much damage. Swing it in a whipping motion, giving a little flick of your wrist at the end, and you can knock a hole in someone's skull with minimal effort. Nasty little things.

As quietly as I could, I stood up and crept into a corner where I would have a clear shot at his back as he stepped through the door. Rifle leveled, I focused on my breathing and waited, seconds ticking slowly by. After what felt like an hour, but was probably only a minute or two, I saw his head appear through the doorway, looking around. A balaclava covered his face, making his features indistinguishable. He took a few tentative steps in, head leaning forward as he squinted at my bedroll. There was a hesitation in his stride, as if he were beginning to realize something was wrong with the dim, rumpled outline of my sleeping bag.

"Don't move," I said.

Without hesitation, he whipped his head in the direction of my voice and started to raise his weapon. In a situation like that, you have to make a split second decision. I wanted to question this guy, but if he fired that gun, it would bring every walker in a square mile down on my head. Worse, he might actually hit me. There was no choice at all, really. I squeezed the trigger three times, all three rounds punching holes through his forehead in a space the diameter of a half-dollar. The pistol dropped from nerveless fingers as he fell, legs twitching in death spasms. I began to walk closer, but stepped back in disgust as his bowels loosened.

"Jesus…"

Not wanting to run into any more surprises, I put two more rounds through his chest, then climbed out the same window the intruder used and conducted a perimeter sweep. Once I felt confident the intruder had acted alone, I followed his tracks into the forest. They led to a cleverly camouflaged hunting lodge, situated in the saddle of two hills, surrounded by tall pines. It was covered in camo nets, and the walls of the lodge itself were painted in swirls of white, green, and brown. As I stood next to the window, I had a clear view of the house in the distance.

"So that's how you spotted me, you sneaky son of a bitch."

Inside the lodge, I found a pair of binoculars hanging on a nail by the window, a bed, a small table and chairs, a grill connected to a makeshift ventilation hood, a pile of blankets that reached up to my waist, and a large trunk. The trunk had a padlock on it, but I easily defeated it with my lock pick. Within it was a random collection of weapons and personal items, including jewelry, figurines, knives, pistols, rifles, and a few boxes of ammunition. In one corner, there was a Crown Royal bag full of what appeared to be human teeth. By the smell, some of them had been removed recently.

"What the fuck…"

Putting the bag down, I felt a strong urge to wash my hands. Back at the house, I removed my NVGs, hung a blanket over the window, removed a small wind-up survival lantern from my pack, and turned it on. The light allowed me to see the intruder's face clearly when I pulled off his balaclava.

Other than his larger than average stature, there was nothing overly remarkable about him. Caucasian, mid-thirties, thinning hair the color of mud, pale hazel eyes, average features on the face, the kind of guy you pass on the street a thousand times and never notice. A quick search of his clothing yielded no clues to his identity, but around his neck, I found a small brass key on a thin nylon cord. The kind of key sold with padlock sets. My mind immediately went to the shed out back. On a hunch, I went outside and tried it. Sure enough, the key fit perfectly and the lock clicked open.

With NVGs in place and leading with my pistol, I stepped into the shed and then immediately stepped out, overwhelmed by the stench of the place.

"*Motherfucker.*"

Recovering quickly, I tied my scarf over my face and went back inside. There were tables lining both sides of the room with lumpy shapes on top of them. I looked closer and nearly jumped in horror when I realized the shapes were hands, feet, and an assortment of arms and legs neatly cut apart at the shoulder, knee, and elbow joints. I took a few dazed steps backward and looked above me, seeing more shapes dangling from the ceiling. Instead of limbs, these were headless, limbless torsos in varying states of decomposition. At the back of the room, carefully arranged on shelves like bowling balls, were close to a dozen severed heads.

Heart pounding, breath coming in gasps, struggling against the bile rising in my throat, I edged out of the shed, closed the door, and attempted to lock it. It took me a few tries because my goddamn hands would not stop shaking.

After moving my gear to another room away from the dead man, I spent the rest of the night sitting propped up in a corner, NVGs at the ready, ears straining, rifle clutched tightly in my lap. I did not move from that spot until the first pale glimmers of dawn brightened the window.

Before I left, I stared at the dead intruder's body and considered dragging it into the shed before I torched the place. Deciding it was too much effort, and knowing I would rather shoot myself in the foot than look upon that reeking horror again, I took the path of least resistance and burned the house down around him, then set fire to the shed. Just for good measure, I marched back to the hunting lodge and burned it down too.

After a cold, tasteless breakfast eaten near the warmth of the inferno, I turned northwest and trudged away into the frozen morning. Behind me, tall black plumes marred the clear morning sky.

I did not look back.

THIRTY-FOUR

Barely five miles from the border of the Chickasaw NWR, I reached the edge of a large patch of forest and was confronted with a snowbank nearly ten feet tall. It was piled up against ranks of maples, cedars, and pine trees, most likely blown there by strong prevailing winds out of the north. I tested it with a few hard shoves and found it was packed tightly enough to climb over.

So I scrambled up the bank, slipping one step for every two I took, and at the summit, launched myself over the other side, sliding down like a human sled and letting loose a giddy laugh. At the bottom, I wiped off my goggles, looked up, and felt my heart freeze in my chest. Across the road in front of me, populating a broad clearing for as far as I could see, was a horde of at least a thousand ghouls.

There was a brief pause, a moment of confusion among the undead as they stared at me, rotten brains trying to process whether or not I was food. The closest one was maybe a hundred feet away, and I swear I saw his eyes flicker with recognition just a split second before his mouth opened and he let loose with an ear-splitting howl. Within seconds, the other walkers took up the call, the noise becoming so loud I could feel it rattling my sternum.

Scrambling to my feet, I looked left hoping there were less of them that way. No joy. They wrapped all the way around the edge of the field and into the forest. To my right, the situation wasn't any better, just more ghouls. Looking ahead, I realized the walkers were not densely packed, maybe twenty or more feet between them. I drew my falcata and stood rooted to the spot, trying to figure out what to do.

Option one: Turn tail and run. If I put enough distance between me and the horde, maybe I could circle farther south and get around them. But that would add a day or two to my journey, something I did not want.

Option two: Go right through the fuckers. If I kept a fast pace and relied on my axe and short sword, there was a good chance I could clear the horde. It would mean I would have to set a hard pace for the rest of the day to outdistance them, but it would save a lot of time.

I scrambled back up the snowbank and stood up, surveying the terrain. From there, I could see the edge of the horde about a quarter-mile away, near the edge of a barren field.

Ah hell, I've fought through worse than that.

After taking a moment to unlimber my axe, I slid back down the snowbank, tied my scarf around my face, and set off at a jog.

The snow was much thinner once I crossed the highway, probably because most of it was piled behind me at the forest's edge. The ground beneath me was frozen, making for solid footing and allowing me to avoid buried obstacles.

I angled away from a knot of six ghouls, but my path took me toward two more I couldn't dodge. When I reached the first one, rather than break stride to kick him out of the way, I sidestepped left and hit him with a backhanded slash from my falcata. The top of his head went spinning away, flinging a trail of reddish-black blood as it flew. Before the walker's body hit the ground, I attacked the dead woman behind him and smashed her skull with the axe, causing one of her eyeballs to fall out of its socket. A spinning shoulder-check freed my weapon and sent her tumbling limply away.

By this point, the call had spread throughout the entire horde, and I could hear moans coming from all directions. The noise was deafening, like being in some kind of hellish stadium filled with screaming undead fans. Cursing myself for not putting in my earplugs, I sprinted another fifty yards or so and engaged the next set of walkers.

The lead one was short, incredibly fat, and had been dead a long time. Like most ghouls, a great deal of the flesh on his face, chest, and arms had been eaten away, and one leg dragged behind him, the flesh almost too destroyed to support his weight. He reached for me as I drew near, eyes bulging wide, mouth open and gnashing, hands grasping. I spun my sword in a figure eight pattern, severing both his arms at the elbow, then finished him off by continuing the motion into an overhead slash. Before he could fall, I booted him in the chest and sent him rocketing back into the ghouls behind him, bowling them over like tenpins. Several became stuck under the obese walker's tremendous weight. A few running steps and a strong vault carried me over them to hit the ground running on the other side.

For the next couple of hundred yards, I managed to serpentine my way through the walkers' ranks without having to fight, but as they pursued me from all sides, they were starting to pack in more tightly. Estimating I was about halfway through, I increased my speed to an all-out sprint.

For the last couple of hundred yards, technique went out the window. If a ghoul got close, I smashed it, favoring my falcata over my axe. At one point, confronted with three ghouls I couldn't dodge, I swung the axe too hard and it lodged in the sinus cavity of what had once been pre-adolescent girl. Unable to wrench it free, I grudgingly released it and kept moving.

Now I could see the edge of the horde about fifty yards away, growing closer, the thinnest section packed two ghouls deep with only inches between them. There was a clear patch about ten yards around me, but the pocket was closing quickly, and I knew I would not be able to clear the last line with just my sword. Stabbing it in the ground in front of me, I reached back for my rifle, switched it to semi-auto, and went to work.

Breath in, hold it just briefly, halfway out, squeeze the trigger and wait-

-crack-

-for the shot to surprise you. Now do it again, breath in...

-crack-crack-crack-

Four down. There's a big one, two more on his heels. Drop him, and you'll have the gap you need. Breathe in, aim, and...

-crack-

Now grab your sword and go, go, go!

A hand brushed my jacket as I sprinted clear of the horde, leaping over the pile of tangled limbs I created with my last shot. I came down hard and kept running, lungs heaving, mouth wide open to draw in as much oxygen as possible. When I had gone a hundred yards, following the road just past the treeline, I slowed down and risked a look over my shoulder. The horde was well behind me, converging into an arrowhead formation as the faster, less damaged walkers outdistanced their slower competition.

Unwinding my scarf, I leaned over, put my hands on my knees, and drew big, deep breaths, trying to slow my heart rate. Once recovered a little, I took a moment to clean the gore from my sword with a few handfuls of snow and dried grass. Taking out my compass, I took a quick bearing and referenced the map in my head. If I turned a little to my left, that would lead me on a northwest vector directly toward Blackmire. With any luck, and barring further hordes, I could be there by nightfall. After a quick check of my gear to make sure I hadn't lost anything other than my axe, I set out at the same forty-steps-walking, forty-steps-running pace I had kept up for the last few days.

An hour later, the sound of the horde was a faint echo in the distance.

THIRTY-FIVE

Walking into a place like Blackmire is all about attitude.

It is a den of vice and greed, populated by a host of nefarious characters who would just as soon kill you as look at you. So if you show up and appear nervous or frightened, it is like blood in the water, and the sharks come a-runnin'. But if you maintain the proper thinly-veiled aggression, the fuck-with-me-and-I'll-kill-you glower, head slightly tilted forward, eyes burning beneath hooded brow, mouth set in a contemptuous sneer, hands dangerously close to your weapons, then the snuffling curs will keep their distance. The smart ones will, anyway.

The three men standing between me and the main gate were not smart ones.

"I don't think I've seen you around here before," one of them said, probably the leader. He was a little shorter than me, strongly built, glaring with mean little black eyes, head shaved down to stubble, thin beard, yellow teeth, dirt caked in the creases of his neck. The two men on either side of him were even uglier, one a tall skinny fellow with his front teeth missing, long hair tied back under a head scarf, and a beard that hung down to his chest. The other one was nearly seven feet tall, shoulders as wide as a doorway, and obviously accustomed to intimidating people with his size.

I said, "If you don't get out of my way, I'll be the last thing you ever see."

He chuckled, unimpressed. "You got a mouth on you, I'll give you that. But you see, the thing is, there's three of us and one of you. So I'm thinking if you want to get in that gate over yonder," he pointed at the wooden palisade behind him, broken by a narrow opening just wide enough to permit a horse-drawn wagon, "your gonna have to pay a little entry fee."

I made a show of looking over his shoulder and pointing. "That's funny. I could swear that guy in the black outfit over there is the town guard. You assholes don't look like guardsmen to me. You look like a bunch of inbred, sister-raping dumbshits."

The little grin disappeared. He raised a hand and jammed a finger into my chest. "Listen up, smartass, here's what's gonna happen. You're gonna put down that pack and all your guns, and your boots, and that fancy pig-sticker you got there, and if you're real nice about it, we might not take turns stomping a mud hole in your ass. And if you don't, then me and my two friends here are gonna-"

I'm sure he had some dire threat in store for me, but he never got it out. Instead, he emitted a spray of spittle and blood as my pocketknife slashed his throat open, showering the men on either side of him with arterial spray. As he stumbled backward, I took advantage of his friends' temporary shock by whipping my falcata out of its sheath and swinging it in two quick strokes. Both men's eyes went wide with shock as my blade passed through their necks, just a split second before their heads tumbled from their shoulders. They collapsed in a heap, followed not long after by their dying leader.

Stepping back to avoid the blood, I cast a glare at the small crowd of onlookers. "Anybody else?"

The looks on the faces around me ranged from amusement to wide-eyed awe. There were a few seconds of silence as they regarded the dead men at my feet, then it was as if the crowd collectively shrugged their shoulders and carried on, dismissing the incident as unimportant.

Must be one hell of a rough town.

Stepping around the pile of bodies, I continued on toward the main gate. Once there, a smirking guardsman dressed from head to toe in crudely-dyed black combat fatigues held up a hand.

"Hold up a minute, fella. You been here before?"

I shook my head, fingers dangling close to my pistol.

"All right then, there's a few rules you need to know about. First, ain't no fighting allowed inside the wall. Kill whoever you want outside it, but once you go through that gate, you mind your fuckin' manners. Got it?"

I gave a single, silent nod.

"Second rule: thieves hang. So don't go gettin' sticky fingers."

A shrug. "Fair enough."

"Last rule: you make a trade or take a contract, you stick by it. Somebody stiffs you, take it to the magistrate. But if you do, be aware that any ruling the magistrate makes is binding and final. Understood?"

"Perfectly."

"One more thing. You break the rules, you get punished. Up to and including ten lashes from a scourge. You know what a scourge is?"

"It's a whip with little blades braided into it."

"That's right. You ever seen what one of those things can do to a man?"

I shook my head again. "No."

"It'll take the skin right off your fuckin' back. Right down to the bone. Most men don't survive it. It's a shitty way to die, fella. Believe me when I tell you, you don't want that."

"I'll keep that in mind. Anything else?"

The guard stepped back with a smile and made a grand gesture toward the entrance. "Welcome to Blackmire, my friend. May God have mercy on your soul."

*****

The layout of the town was exactly as the slaver I captured, Smart Guy, had described it. Four-sided wooden palisade wall surrounded by a trench, steep berm, catwalks and guard towers, archers and riflemen, interior trench bristling with stakes, wooden fence to keep drunks from stumbling into it, signs posted here and there with the town's few rules clearly on display, taverns, stalls, livery, and other assorted businesses laid out in a concentric grid around a wide central plaza, and within the plaza, a large raised dais complete with iron rings and manacles.

The slave market.

It was empty now, but according to the nearby wooden sign, painted black and scribbled over with chalk, there would be an auction held in three days' time. Gritting my teeth, I kept walking.

According to Smart Guy, Blackmire had only been around for a year or so, and while not officially affiliated with the Alliance, they did a lot of business with them. The town's leader, who was also its namesake, rarely appeared in public, but was nonetheless well known to all permanent residents and business owners. Most of the population on any given day consisted of visitors looking to trade their ill-gotten gains, re-supply, or just indulge a few vices frowned upon by more prudent communities. For a price, a man could get just about anything he wanted in Blackmire, including slaves, which were the main source of municipal income. Slaves weren't cheap, and the tribune, as Blackmire's despotic leader styled himself, got a percentage of all sales. Typical auction house setup.

Since it was getting late, I spent the remaining daylight hours casing the place, committing the layout of the narrow, muddy lanes, locations of gates and guard towers, and the number of black-clad guardsmen to memory. If the mercenary I mutilated a few weeks ago survived long enough to make his way back here, there was a possibility I could be recognized. A remote possibility, but a possibility nonetheless. Should that happen, having a detailed mental map would greatly increase my chances of escape.

The largest building in town had a large, hand-painted sign above the entrance proclaiming it as Blackmire Office of the Tribune and Magistrate. To my surprise, I saw the top of an antenna array jutting up behind the building. A walk around the block and a quick trip through a series of alleys, and I found myself peering around the corner at the space between the Tribune's office and the surrounding structures.

Two large military vehicles were parked there, one painted traditional olive drab, and the other the dun brown of desert camouflage. The green vehicle was a tanker truck with a massive, oblong cylinder of fuel mounted to the rear frame, while the brown vehicle was a flatbed upon which sat a portable antenna tower and a generator the size of a small car. Looking closer, I noticed there were bullet marks on the armor along the sides of the vehicles, and smears of blood on the interiors and door handles. Even the big generator was stained red. Realizing the implications, I had to fight the urge to level my rifle and exact retribution. If these guys were raiding military convoys, they must have some very serious firepower. The Army needed to know about this place.

But first, I had work to do.

Just past sundown, I finished reconnoitering and headed toward one of the less sleazy-looking taverns on the south side of town. The tavern was, like most other buildings in town, built entirely of rough-hewn wooden planks. Asphalt shingles on the roof, shutters over glassless windows, and the light of oil lanterns burning within. Under other circumstances, the place might have looked inviting. But between the listless, jaded, scantily-clad whores out front, the leering, lascivious men they catcalled with insincere enthusiasm, and the shaved gorilla standing by the door with a shotgun in his hands, there was not the faintest presence of hospitality or charm.

As I approached, I noticed that while the men fondling and negotiating prices with the prostitutes were permitted on the wide porch, they stayed well clear of the doorway and the massive, armed man standing next to it. Figuring he was there for a reason, I stopped a few feet away and nodded to him.

"Looking for a room and a hot meal," I said.

He gave me a quick up and down appraisal before grunting, turning his head, and firing an impressive arc of spittle to his right. "Place ain't cheap, but we got the nicest rooms and cleanest girls in Blackmire. Fresh food, pre-Outbreak whiskey, the whole nine. What you got for trade?"

I patted my weapon. "Spare rounds. Maybe a few other things."

His eyes took in the loaded mag carriers on my vest and the sword hanging from my hip. "I reckon so. Come on in, then. Head for the bar and talk to Slim. He'll set you up."

I nodded once and stepped through the door. The tavern's interior was a wide dining room with a collection of wooden tables and chairs, a staircase, a balcony that covered three walls, and tightly spaced doors lining the second floor which, I assumed, were the guest rooms. There were maybe a dozen or so people sitting at the tables, some of them in various states of drunkenness, others eating silently, and a few playing exceptionally loud games of chance. All the place needed was a guy in shirtsleeves and a waistcoat playing a piano in the corner, and the effect would have been complete.

At the bar, I was greeted by a tall, reedy bartender with a perfectly bald head, close-set, hostile little eyes, and a nose that looked to have been broken with a frying pan, reset, allowed to heal, and then broken again. I nodded to him as he approached. "You Slim?"

"Last I checked. What can I do for you?"

"Need a room."

"How long you staying?"

"Not sure. Couple of days maybe."

"What are you trading?"

I pulled a P-mag from its carrier and held it up. "Thirty rounds, five-five-six. I keep the mag. How long will that get me?"

He ran his tongue across his teeth and appeared to consider it. "Let's say…ten rounds a night. That'll get you a room and one meal per day. Drinks are extra."

"How about four?"

The bartender chuckled. "Fella, that won't even get you a lice-ridden cot in the bunkhouse. We'll call it nine."

"Six."

"Eight."

"Seven. Final offer."

Slim tapped his fingers on the bar, faking an inner debate. I knew for a fact seven rounds was a fair price, and I could tell he was a little disappointed I was not proving easy to fleece. "Fine," he said finally. "Seven a night. But you pay every day in the morning, in advance. And since you're too late for supper, I'll let you have tonight for six. Fair enough?"

"Fair enough."

I removed the P-mag's dust cover and counted out the necessary cartridges. "Tell you what," Slim said, pointing at the magazine. "Those are pretty popular around here. Hard to find. You part ways with that one, and I'll let you have a night with any one of my girls you want."

I stared at him, trying very hard not to let disgust show on my face. It would have been extremely satisfying to grab him by the throat and introduce his face to the surface of the bar. But I had a cover to maintain, so I kept it in. "No thanks. Like you said, these things are hard to find."

"You sure about that?" he asked, an avaricious sparkle in his eyes. "These girls are well trained. You can have nice hot bath, a massage, and then they'll do whatever you want them to."

I shook my head again, feeling my temper begin to rise and struggling to keep my voice level. "Sorry. Pass. It's cheaper to jerk off, and I don't have to worry about cock-rot."

His beady eyes narrowed a bit. "You got a problem with girls, or something?"

I leaned forward, lowered my voice, and twisted my face into a sneering, licentious grin. "Let's just say my tastes run to the...exotic. The girl wouldn't be much use to you by the time I got done with her."

Looking at me, Slim paled and took half a nervous step back. When he spoke, there was a tremor in his voice. "Well…all right then. Just, uh, let me know if you change your mind. Offer stands." His hand shook a little as he handed me my room key.

"One last thing," I said, reaching into my pocket and taking out an MRE pack of compressed toilet paper. Slim's gaze locked to it instantly, calculating its worth. "I'm looking for someone. Goes by the name Marco. Medium height and build, brown eyes, longish hair, bushy beard. Seen anybody like that around?"

"This must be your first time in this town, my friend. Everybody knows Marco. He's Tribune Blackmire's right hand man. Carries out his business for him, collects taxes, that sort of thing."

Interesting. "Good to know," I said, handing over the toilet paper. As I turned to walk away, the bartender spoke up behind me. "Hey, you need any other information, you come see me first, you hear? Ain't much happens around here I don't know about."

I looked over my shoulder and nodded. "See you in the morning, Slim."

With that, I climbed the stairs, entered the door with the appropriate number, and locked it behind me.

*****

Dinner. Water.

Lay back on the bed and listen to the debauchery swell and stretch until it rattles from every room in the creak of bedsprings, thump of headboard against wall, fake moans and gasps and shouts of encouragement from the working girls, grunts and laboring and cries of release as the Johns finish their business. Drunks hoot and howl and bellow for more booze, serving girls fake-squeal, drinking songs slur in disjointed attempt at harmony, stomp of boots on wooden planks.

Forget a little while you're living at the end of the world, ye of broken faith. Find comfort in the warm burn in the gut, throw off the yoke of inhibition, indulge the flesh with grasping, desperate hands until your breath is like kerosene and about as flammable. Raised voices, sound of furniture toppling, dull meaty thuds of fists, duller meatier thuds of clubs, shouts of bartender and patrons, guards snarling through the press, offenders protesting all the way out the door.

Put in the earplugs and doze.

Wake up. Check the watch. Seven-thirty in the morning.

Time to find Marco.

Time to get some answers.

THIRTY-SIX

Finding Marco turned out to be easy.

I came downstairs, picked a table where I could watch the door, and when the serving girl came around, ordered a bowl of venison and potatoes. The food was surprisingly good, flavored with salt and fresh herbs, which was probably why it was so expensive.

The tavern had been cleaned since the night before, tables and chairs put back in their rows, drunks dragged outside to sleep it off. A young woman no older than twenty, sporting a fresh black eye, diligently mopped the floor behind the bar and then began refilling empty bottles and water pitchers. I wondered how she had come to be in this place, and if she was here willingly or in bondage. Just as I was about to cross the room and strike up a conversation with her, there was a forceful pounding at the front door.

"Slim, wake your lazy ass up," shouted a muffled voice.

The serving girl dropped what she was doing and hurried around the bar, sprinting for the door. When she reached it, she threw the bolt and opened it wide, staying well behind it, eyes down, not saying a word. A man who fit Marco's description walked in, flanked by two large, black-clad guardsmen.

"Slim! Get the fuck out here, I ain't got all day." He stomped inside, headed toward the bar. The girl came out from behind the front door and disappeared into the kitchen area. She was gone for maybe a full minute, then came back following a bleary eyed, cursing Slim.

"Sorry 'bout that Marco," he said. "Goddamn drunks kept me up half the night."

If Marco heard him, he gave no indication. "What's your take this month?"

"Come on back, I'll show you."

The men walked into the kitchen while the girl went back to her chores. A few minutes later, Marco's men emerged with a small barrel with the word WHISKEY painted on the side, a quiver of arrows, and a cloth bag containing the heavy, unmistakable rattle of ammunition. Slim was smiling when he and Marco re-entered the room, but it was a sickly smile, and it came nowhere near his eyes.

"Nice take, Slim," Marco said mockingly. "Tribune Blackmire sends his sincere thanks for your contribution to the community."

The scrawny man bobbed his head nervously. "Always glad to do my part."

The two guards shared a chuckle over that as they carried the goods outside where a horse-drawn cart waited. I watched them put their haul into the back and then trundle off to extort the next business down the street.

"Son of a bitchin' taxes," Slim muttered as he came back inside and shut the door. "How the hell am I supposed to turn a profit with these bastards bleeding me dry?"

As he walked past, he noticed me at my table and stopped short. "Well, you're up early Mister…what did you say your name was, again?"

"I never said."

"So what do folks call you?"

"Meyer," I said, remembering a character in an old mystery series I used to read.

"Just Meyer? No first name?"

I shot him an irritated glare. "You ask a lot of questions, barkeep."

He offered his greasy smile and held up his hands. "Just curious is all. I have to call you something, right?"

I let the glare linger for a moment, then went back to my meal.

*****

Marco made it nearly to the other side of town before I caught up with him.

He worked quickly, going into each business like a storm and shouting for the owner to show himself. In most cases, his two henchmen loaded a few items into the cart, Marco offered his condescending thanks on behalf of Tribune Blackmire, and they proceeded on. In a few cases, however, the tribute paid to their protector and benevolent dictator for life was insufficient, prompting the guardsmen to administer a savage beating with large, flexible sticks. All in the interest of public safety and the common good, of course.

I trailed them from a distance. Sometimes I let them out of sight, but never out of earshot. By four in the afternoon, they had hit every bar, brothel, eatery, and tradesman in town, then headed back to the Tribune's office. Their cart was laden with everything from booze, to weapons, to horseshoes. There was even a frantic, squealing piglet in a dog carrier. I wondered if the Tribune would be dining on roasted pork tonight.

The two guards drove the cart around back while Marco entered the office through the front door. Seeing no reason why he wouldn't leave by the same way, I crossed the street to a low-slung building proclaiming itself The Red Rooster, ordered a beer and a roasted chicken quarter, and waited. The beer was hand-crafted, and surprisingly good. When I asked the man serving it where he got it from, he proudly proclaimed he brewed it himself. I offered him my compliments, and slowly put away two more until, finally, I saw Marco emerge from the office building. Finishing quickly, I paid for my meal and headed out.

The part of town I followed him to was one I had only briefly explored the day before. It was nestled against the western wall, not far from the gate on that side, and there was a palisade around it, lower and less heavily fortified than the one surrounding the town, complete with two hostile-looking guards manning the entrance. They stood a little straighter as Marco approached, and made an odd fist-over-chest gesture I assumed was some sort of salute. Marco returned the gesture and waited as one of the guards knocked on the heavy door and shouted to someone on the other side. The door opened immediately, and Marco went through without a backward glance. A moment later he was out of sight, the guards relaxing and resuming their vaguely aggressive boredom.

Looking above the low wall, I could see three of what were, without a doubt, the most well-constructed houses in town. Most of the other buildings in the squalid residential areas were little more than hastily built bunkhouses and shacks. The three structures across from me actually looked like proper houses, the largest one boasting a carving of a stylized B surrounded by laurels above the front door. The residence of Tribune Blackmire, no doubt. It was logical to assume that one of the houses belonged to Marco, him being the instrument of Blackmire's will, but the other one I had no idea. Probably some other element of the town's leadership. Captain of the guard, maybe.

As I watched, a light flared to life in an upstairs window of the house to the right of the Tribune's mansion.

So that's where you sleep, Marco. Good to know.

On the way back to Slim's Tavern, I began formulating a plan. First, I would need a distraction. A fire would do, somewhere on the other side of town. Get the guards' attention, then a quick bit of rifle work from a nice dark alcove, scale the wall, take out the guards on the other side, and pay Marco a little visit. Get some questions answered, send him to his final reward, and slip silently into the night. But the timing would have to be perfect, and I would have to wait until long after nightfall when the livers were booze soaked and the debauchery was beginning to wane. Then strike, take them off balance, create a panic.

But first, rest. Once Marco was taken care of, there was no telling how far I would have to run to escape Blackmire's wrath. Better to save my energy and start the evening's festivities refreshed from a long nap.

I felt no trepidation as I walked through the door to Slim's, just a dim excitement and smug confidence that Marco had no idea what was about to hit him. So when I looked up and found myself surrounded by ten armed, grim-looking men, to say I was surprised would be an understatement.

Stopping in my tracks, I looked around, cursed my own hubris, and wondered where I had screwed up. My hand began to inch toward my pistol.

"I wouldn't do that if I were you," a voice said.

With a sinking feeling, I realized the voice was familiar. It's timbre and tone had taken on some of the harshness that comes with age, but the modulation, the amplitude, the inflection and hint of accent were the same. I looked in the voice's direction and saw a man stand up behind the ring of guards. He was tall, broad shouldered, but lean and wiry. Much thinner than I remembered him. He was dressed in the same black fatigues as his men, albeit cleaner and in better condition. As he stepped forward, all I could see of his face was a thin blond beard. The rest was obscured by a dark, flat, wide-brimmed hat. He pushed the hat up and stopped a few feet from me, regarding me with one blue eye and one milky white one. A scar bisected the blind eye, starting at his hairline and running all the way down to his chin, curling one side of his mouth in a permanent sneer. He grinned, revealing a few missing teeth.

"What's wrong, Gabriel? Aren't you glad to see me? I'm the reason you're here, after all. You seem…what's the right word? Nonplussed."

I remained silent, too stunned for speech. He stepped closer. "Did you really think you were just going to walk in here, in my town, and no one would recognize you? Please. Every guardsman, barkeep, hash-slinger, and whore has had your description for weeks. I've been expecting you, Gabe. You took your sweet time, though, didn't you? I was beginning to think you weren't going to show up. But now here you are, in the flesh. And I am so very, very happy to see you."

A coldness started in my stomach and spread quickly to my limbs and face. I couldn't even bring myself to be angry. I had blundered into this place like a blind mouse in a room full of hungry cats and started sniffing around for cheese. My only consolation was knowing there was no way I could have guessed Blackmire's true identity. Although, in retrospect, I had made no effort at all to learn more about him. Only then, when it was far too late, did I realize what a mistake that was.

And now, there was only one thing left to do.

I'm sorry, Elizabeth. I tried, but I came up short this time. Had to happen sooner or later.

I moved quickly, more quickly than Tanner expected. He barely managed to duck and roll, my first shot going over his head and striking a guard behind him. Heart pounding, counting out the last seconds of my life, I tried to adjust my aim. But he was moving quickly, shouting at his men, dodging between tables. I felt the prickling expectation of impact, of lead rending through flesh and bone.

Instead, there was a crackle.

Every muscle in my body seized up, the gun fell from my hand, and I went down. For a few seconds I bucked and screamed and twitched in agony. And then, as quickly as it started, the pain stopped. I tried to roll over, tried to reach for my backup piece, but a pair of boots appeared in front of me and there was an explosion in my head.

And then the world went black.

THIRTY-SEVEN

To my surprise, I woke up.

There was an invisible man standing over me, dutifully pounding away at my head with a hammer. I thrashed about trying to locate him, to no avail. As it turned out, he was *inside* my skull, and he seemed to have a special hatred for the backs of my eyes.

I managed to sit up, but then had to hold perfectly still while a wave of crippling nausea ran its course. When I was reasonably sure I wasn't going to start dry-heaving, I opened my eyes and looked around. The room was black, so dark I literally could not see my hand in front of my face. My hands were cuffed in front of me, and I could feel the cold weight of leg irons around my ankles. They had taken my clothes, leaving me naked on the floor.

Standing up, I explored the room, hands waving blindly in front of me. I found a wall and followed it until I counted four corners. The surface of the walls was grainy and splintery, the feeling of rough-hewn wood. Every few inches there was the cold smoothness of nails, and the barest hint of a gap between tightly fitted planks—the work of a skilled carpenter. Same story with the floor.

An indeterminate amount of time passed as I tried to find a place I could grip with my fingers, or jimmy with a link of chain, but there was nothing. Whoever had built this prison, they knew their business. Dejected, I sat back down.

Then came remembrance, and analysis of the last thirty-six hours, and self-recrimination at not casing Blackmire with anywhere near the level of diligence I might have displayed during my CIA days. I had grown conceited and impatient, infatuated with my own track record of operational success and battles survived. There were few who could match me in my pre-Outbreak days, much less after, and outclassing the competition for so long had made me complacent. Sebastian Tanner—AKA Blackmire—evidently did not suffer from such an affliction. And now here I sat, naked and in chains, awaiting what was going to be, without doubt, a painful, humiliating death.

No. Do not accept that.

I got up and searched the room again. Hours passed. Still nothing. No way out.

So sit down, and stew and simmer and boil, until sleep eventually comes. Then wake up with a dry throat and an aching belly, and start the process all over again.

No bucket. Pick a corner and ignore the smell.

Fumble about in the dark, whisper curses, get tired, rest, ruminate, let the imagination run wild with all the painful things they are going to do to you. Then locate your spine again and start pounding the walls. When that doesn't work, sit down and silently vow you will not let them torture you. They made a mistake cuffing your hands in front of you. Whoever comes through that door is in for a fight to the death.

Then sleep.

Wake again. Same agenda as yesterday. Hear voices. Sharp scent of oak as you press your ear to the door, listening. Can't make out what they say. Smile in the dark and decide to force the issue. Sooner or later, the screaming and pounding and door rattling on its hinges will bring them, and that will be your chance. But they never come, and your palms and feet are torn and bleeding, and your voice grows hoarse, then goes away altogether. Flop exhausted to the floor. Let out a hitching sob of frustration.

Remember the Saudi, and the month spent at Guantanamo, the gurgling and firecracker curses, refilling the water bucket again and again and again. No dice. Too tough. Time to change tactics. Then the dark room, and the night vision camera, and the waiting. It took a week of living in complete darkness, soiled in his own piss and shit, no human contact, no food, barely enough water to sustain life, and he finally broke. They hauled him howling and gibbering from that room, and for two weeks he sang like a dove. The interrogators never had to lay another finger on him.

Feel the dawning realization that this is not just retribution. Tanner is not doing this for the sole purpose of making you suffer. Hear the click as the mental gear turns and falls into place.

The Alliance's expanding territory, the attacks, Hollow Rock, the Free Legion, Chinese rifles, Russian ammo, Korean ships, an ex-CIA operative with a hatred for his former agency. Why not hate the country while he's at it? And if he gets a shot at payback for a long ago judgment call that didn't go his way, then so much the better. Because the only thing more valuable than armed men anxious to carry out your will is information, and a gold mine just walked right on in and made himself at home.

It's only been two and a half days.

How much longer?

*****

Five days.

The answer was five days. No food. Maybe two liters of water. Wake up, pain and rage, back to sleep. Repeat. Repeat. Repeat.

Then they came for me.

They took no chances. They made sure I was asleep when the door slammed open and three men rushed in, all bearing plastic riot shields. Behind them came four more, piling on, batons swinging, feet kicking. I was already weak from hunger and exhausted from constantly pacing and trying to tear the room apart. A well-timed headbutt crushed one man's nose, but other than that, it wasn't much of a fight.

After re-cuffing my hands behind my back, they hauled me up and dragged me down a hallway. Wooden floor. Plank walls.

382

Artwork, mostly impressionist prints. I caught a glimpse of a doorway with a few desks beyond, but it was gone quickly.

We emerged into a wide lobby with a receptionist's desk at the front. Although the windows were shuttered, I could tell it was early morning. My feet barely hit the ground as they rushed me up the staircase and through a door at the top. Then I was dragged into a room with oil lanterns hanging from hooks on the walls, more artwork, heavily-laden bookshelves, and a low table to my right. On the table lay my weapons, pack, and equipment. They had even folded my clothes in a neat pile. The urge to fight loose from the hands gripping me and make for my rifle was strong, but I kept it in check. What good would it do? It's not like I could operate an M-6 with my toes. Tearing my gaze away, I looked to the center of the room and at the man sitting behind a massive, ornate desk.

Tanner.

His men shoved me forward until I was standing just in front of the desk, then forced me to my knees. I felt the cold barrel of a pistol press into the back of my neck.

"You don't look so good, old friend. Not much fun hanging out in the hole, is it?"

He was leaning back in his chair, fingers steepled, hat tilted low, milky left eye glittering in the lamplight. My brain was addled from starvation, exhaustion, and the beating I just took, so I kept it simple. "Fuck you."

"Now that's not very nice. Ron?"

A steel-toed boot slammed into my kidney, driving the air from me in a hissing gasp. If not for the hands gripping me, I would have fallen over. Tanner stood up and crossed the room, stopping in front of the low table where my gear lay.

"It looks like you've done well for yourself since the Outbreak, Gabriel. These are very nice things you have." He picked up my falcata and slipped it from its sheath, turning it slowly in front of a lamp. "This sword alone is worth a small fortune. It's a beautiful weapon; very well made. Where did you get it?"

It took me a moment to recover enough breath to respond. My voice came out in a thin wheeze. "A friend gave it to me."

"Hm. Must be a very good friend." He held the sword up to the wall, as if measuring where he wanted to hang it. "I think I'll keep it. In fact, I think I'll keep all of this stuff. Put it on display, maybe build a little shrine. Your skull can be the centerpiece. I'll put it over a little stand with your sword on it. That would look very intimidating, don't you think? Put people in the correct frame of mind when they walk in here. Inform them of who they're dealing with."

As the pain in my side faded, so did my fear. I was suddenly very tired of kneeling on the floor while this gloating asshole listened to himself talk. "Why are you doing this, Tanner?"

He sheathed the sword and put it back on the table, then slowly stepped closer until he was barely an arm's length away. Kneeling so he was eye to eye with me, he pushed back his hat and showed me a gap-toothed grin. "There are several reasons, but at least one should be obvious. You left me to die, Gabriel. Needless to say, I took it personally."

"It was a mission. You knew the risks. You would have done the same to me."

Lights exploded in my head as he struck me a backhanded blow. "NO!" he roared, hands coming up and gripping the sides of my face, the one good eye barely an inch from mine, gleaming with feverish brightness. "I would have helped you! I would never have abandoned a fellow agent. Not like you did. That was *unforgiveable*."

A tear began to snake down his cheek below the ruined eye, catching in the channel of his long scar. He absently flicked it away and stood up, gathering himself with a few deep breaths.

"Did you ever wonder what happened to me after your betrayal, Gabe?"

Betrayal? We barely knew each other. We were on a mission. He knew as well as I did that when an order comes down from your control, you follow it. End of. I opened my mouth to explain this, but when I looked up and saw the iron conviction on Tanner's face, the words died on my lips. No point in arguing with a madman.

"I figured they killed you," I said finally.

Tanner walked back behind his desk and took a seat. "Obviously not. But I tell you, Gabe, there was a long time there when I wished they had."

He reached into a desk, took out a bottle of dark brown liquid and a glass, and poured himself a drink. "You see, we didn't know it when we took the mission, but Gustavo Silva was already well on his way to taking over as leader of *Las Sombras*. He had been plotting and maneuvering for years. He was a careful man. Exceedingly clever and utterly ruthless—a dangerous combination. After we took care of Villalobos for him, it was a simple matter of ordering a few executions, and he was in." He leaned forward, turning to stare with the good eye. "You're probably wondering how I know all this, right?"

Play along. "The thought did occur."

He sipped his drink and smiled. It traveled no further than his lips, and I noticed a muscle twitching under his blind eye.

"Silva told me all about it, many times. He always laughed when he did, and thanked me. He told me the CIA capturing Villalobos was the greatest favor anyone had ever done for him. And every year, on the anniversary of the day he captured me, he took another tooth."

Putting his drink on the table he said, "Count the gaps." Then hooked fingers into his cheeks and pulled them wide, turning his face to the light so I could see better.

There were five.

Releasing his face, Tanner said, "He loved trophies, that man. There were hundreds of them, but I was always his favorite. He kept me in a cell in the basement of his mansion. Five years, Gabe. Five years of beatings, and torture, and starvation, and hopelessness. Five years of listening to him laugh. He kept it dark. The only times when the lights came on was when they fed me, which was not very fucking often. I never got water two days in a row. Sometimes he would bring

385

people down and show me to them, and say, 'This is what happens when you cross me. You do not want to be this man.'"

Tanner leaned forward and ran a finger down the length of his scar. "He gave me this. It was a punishment, you see. Shortly after we reached Mexico, I got my hands on one of his men and killed him. Ripped his throat out with my bare fingers, but not before he shouted for help. The others found me and held me down while Silva cut into me. Worst pain I've ever felt, and that's saying something."

Leaning back, he picked his drink up and sipped again. "It's not easy getting around with impaired depth perception. Common tasks become much more difficult. Take shooting your woman, for instance."

His smile returned, and I felt a burning heat growing in my chest. If he noticed my rage, he gave no indication.

"That was a tough couple of weeks I spent watching you, sleeping in the cold, dodging the infected and those pathetic morons your people call guardsmen. But everything finally lined up, and I can't tell you how satisfying it was to see the look on your face when you realized what happened. It was a thing of beauty."

His eyes went distant and he let out a contended sigh. I strained at my handcuffs, teeth clenched, vision clouding over in crimson. The pistol at my neck shoved farther in, forcing my head forward. The men around me tightened their grips and growled warnings. Tanner went on as if nothing was amiss.

"The guy who brought me water used to piss in it," he continued, studying his drink. "Then he would laugh when I drank it anyway. I'm quite certain I lost my grip on reality. I tried to kill myself a few times. Silva had doctors working for him. They kept me alive for his amusement. I almost reached the point I accepted I would spend the rest of my life in that stinking shithole, but then, lo and behold, a miracle happened."

He stood up and cast his gaze to the ceiling, smiling rapturously, hands upraised, voice rebounding in the small room. "The Outbreak! May its glorious name forever echo through the pages of history, forever and ever, world without end, amen."

Sitting down, he drained his glass, placed it on the table, and began filling it up again. "He starved me for ten days. Gave me barely enough water to live. He wanted me nice and weak. The day he and his men fled the city, he came down and unlocked my cell. I couldn't even stand up. He said to me, 'I am not doing this out of kindness, my friend. The world is a bad place now. I do not think you will last long. I think you will die screaming.' And then he left."

The room was silent for a long moment after that. Tanner's men seemed fascinated by the story, gazing with rapt attention. He ignored all of us and sipped thoughtfully at his drink, lone functioning eye clouded with faraway memories. Just as I began to wonder if he was falling asleep, he finally came back to himself.

"So how did I survive, right? That's what you're thinking; I can see it. It was simple, really. I found the strength to drag myself upstairs and searched around until I found the kitchen. The power was out, but the food in the fridge was still cold. Silva's men hadn't bothered bringing the perishable stuff with them. So I ate, drank some water, and a few hours later, my strength started coming back. I explored the place, and let me tell you, I will never understand why he left. It wasn't just a mansion, it was a goddamn fortress. Silva's bright idea of killing me consisted of leaving the front gate open—not the most clever idea he ever had. I didn't know anything about the infected back then, but I knew the screams and explosions and raging fires in the distance were not a good thing, so I shut the gate and locked it. When the undead showed up, they couldn't get in. I stayed holed up in there, rationing what little food I could find until a few days later the Mexican Army showed up. They informed me I was in Juarez, and stuffed me in a truck with a few dozen other survivors. Took us all the way up to Colorado. I was admitted to a hospital there, a proper one, fully equipped. The doctors were appalled at my condition, as you might imagine, so they took very good care of me. Once I was healthy again, I took a job as a caravan guard and set out for

Missouri to find out if my family survived. I'm originally from Poplar Bluff, did you know that?"

I shook my head, thinking about all the ways I would like to kill him.

"It's true," he said. "Less than two hundred miles from here. Place isn't there anymore. I guess some marauders took up residence and the Army burned them to the ground. That was in the early days, back before the Alliance started getting organized. The Union wouldn't try that now."

He stood up and strolled to a window, brushed a curtain aside, and stared out at the first light of morning. "It's hard, finding out you have no home left. You feel uprooted, like the compass is spinning and there's nothing to hang on to. So I headed south to this place, the Chickasaw Refuge. When I was a kid, my father used to take me canoeing not far from here. Lots of fond childhood memories." He paused, smiling ruefully. Through the window, I heard the first chirping of songbirds welcoming the sun.

"Those memories were quickly shattered," he continued. "The whole forest was crawling with infected. I barely survived the first night. On the third day, on the very spot where this building now stands, I ran afoul of raiders. Two of them spotted me and came after me. I was out of ammo, but so were they. I killed one of them and hurt the other one bad enough to run him off. A few hours later, he and his friends tracked me down. I took up my weapons and readied myself to die like a man, but they weren't there to fight. Much to my surprise, they offered me a spot on their crew. Their leader, who you know as Marco, said if I was tough enough to handle two of his men, I was tough enough to be one of them. Lacking any other opportunities, I agreed. Long story short, we had a successful career, I took over the reins of leadership, and we built this fine community you see around you…" He spread his hands in a grand gesture, grin broadening. "Blackmire."

I laughed, drawing an angry look from Tanner's men. "What's with the stupid name? Why do you call yourself Tribune instead of something normal, like governor or mayor?

Is Sebastian too pussy of a name for these shitbirds around here?"

One of the guards raised a fist, but Tanner forestalled him with a hand. "Those are reasonable questions. To answer the first one, Blackmire is my mother's maiden name. You see, my father was a useless drunk who beat us for entertainment, and I hated him almost as much as I hated my first name, Sebastian." He said it like it tasted bad, and gave a little shiver. "That's something you name a cat or a goldfish. Not a child. The Tanner family name meant less than nothing to me, and as far as I was concerned the man who had once been Sebastian Tanner died in that dungeon in Mexico. So I took the name of one of the very few people in my life I have ever loved. It seemed fitting the town should be named after her as well."

Against my better judgment, my shoulders began shaking with laughter. "Great," I said. "I'm being held prisoner by an egomaniacal lunatic with mommy issues. Maybe you should have changed your name to Norman Bates."

This time, when the guard raised his fist, Tanner did not stop him. It hurt like hell, but I kept laughing. Tanner's frown deepened as he continued.

"To answer your second question, I call myself the Tribune of Blackmire because I am the protector of these people. You see, in ancient Rome-"

"I went to school, dickhole," I interrupted. "I know what a tribune is."

Another blow, this one hard enough to make my ears ring. A dark blob appeared at the top of my vision, growing and expanding until it broke free and trickled down my face. Several more followed it until I had a thin, steady stream of blood obscuring my left eye.

"Then you know why I call myself Tribune," Tanner said, and sat back in his chair. He knocked back another drink and closed his eyes, savoring it. When he spoke again, his tone took on a businesslike quality.

"You can't imagine my surprise when I heard you were alive. Your exploits against the Free Legion made quite a stir last year. You're practically a celebrity, although it's probably not the kind of attention you would wish for."

Noting my surprised expression, he chuckled and leaned forward. "Come on now, Gabriel. You didn't really think all your good deeds would go unnoticed did you? You're Gabriel Garrett, strong and mighty and feared throughout the land, the high protector of Hollow Rock. Did you know there is a price on your head? The president of the Alliance himself issued the warrant."

"I'm flattered."

"You should be. It's quite a sum. Which brings me to why I've gone to so much trouble and expense to bring you here." He pushed his chair back and kicked his feet up on the desk. "As much fun as I'm going to have repaying you for abandoning me to die, you are not my primary target."

I shook the blood out of my eye and looked up. "Let me guess. Silva."

He nodded. "Thus far, he has proven elusive. I know he is alive, and I have a few men pursuing his trail in Nevada, but unfortunately, such endeavors are quite costly. I have the necessary equipment to stay in touch with my men, but providing them with supplies and resources is difficult in the extreme. However, with the reward I'm going to get for turning you over to the Alliance, I'll have the necessary working capital to mount a larger expedition. If my agents are as good as they claim to be, then Gustavo Silva should be enjoying my hospitality before the end of the year." He sighed and rubbed his hands together, expression wistful. "That will be a most enjoyable reunion indeed. But in the meantime, you and I have some business to settle. Douglas, if you please?"

One of the men holding me left the room and came back with a large wooden box. He set it on the ground in front of me to make sure I had a good look at its contents. There were chains, iron eye-bolts, and a variety of torture instruments.

No fucking way.

I surged upward, catching my captors by surprise. The one standing closest to me caught the top of my head against the bottom of his chin. I heard a crunch and saw a tooth spin past me. Wasting no time, I heaved to my left and drove the crown of my head into another man's face, racking up my second broken nose of the day. He went down, giving me the opening I needed to bend down, pop my handcuffs below my butt, and leap into the air. My hands came up in front of me as my feet touched the ground. Turning around, I saw the other men had recovered and were rushing me as one. I sidestepped right and clubbed one of them on the side of the neck, sending him stumbling into the others and causing them to trip over one another.

Your weapons!

I turned and ran for the table as fast as my hobbled legs could take me. Just as I reached a hand down to grab my pistol, I had a flash of thought—one of those realizations that passes through your mind so quickly it is immeasurable as a span of time—and realized that in the last few furious seconds I had been so focused on fighting the guards, I had completely forgotten about Tanner.

The crackle was familiar.

So was the pain, and the fall, and the flash of light.

I caught a dim outline of Tanner standing over me holding a blackjack, and just before the darkness took me under, I felt a pang of concern my skull might be shattered.

Then nothing.

THIRTY-EIGHT

I was back in Fallujah.

The sun beat down hot and angry, determined to kill us all. I was sitting in a chair, rifle propped on a bench-rest improvised from a crib and a sandbag. There was a wall in front of me with a hole large enough to climb through. The building around me had been taller, once, but a few insurgents had decided to use its rooftop as a sniper hide, sealing the structure's fate. A few rounds from an Abrams reduced the building from five floors to three, and reduced the insurgents from human beings to meaty paste.

The remnant of the third floor's outer wall rose up in front of me, concealing me from the column of insurgents advancing just over three-hundred yards away. I peered through a scope mounted atop an M-40, mentally cataloguing information to relay back to two companies from the First Marine Expeditionary. In the reticle, I watched angry, bearded young men serpentine from building to building, weighed down by heavy bandoliers of ammunition, AK-47 rifles, RPGs, and RPK light machine guns.

Rocco's voice sounded beside me. "You want to call it in?"

"Naw," I replied, accent much thicker than it should have been. Life in the military eroded my Kentucky drawl until it was almost gone, but that happened much later. In my early twenties, I may as well have been fresh off the farm. "You go on ahead. Don't wanna come off my point o' aim."

Rocco's voice monotonously detailed the enemy troops' number, armament, disposition, and location. It took him maybe ten seconds, a sterling example of military brevity. The response came a few seconds later.

"Copy Echo Six. Are you in position to engage? Over."

I could hear the grin in Rocco's voice. "Like a motherfuckin' boss. Over."

"Acknowledged. Echo Two and Echo Four are en route, ETA six minutes. You are weapons free, clear to engage. Happy hunting, gentlemen. Acknowledge."

"Copy that, Echo One. Engaging now. Just make sure the cavalry knows where we are; I don't want to catch a TOW to the face. Over."

"Wilco. Echo One out."

"Here we go," I said, letting out half a breath and lining up on the first target. He was very young, maybe eighteen, not even old enough to grow a proper beard. He was short and painfully thin, even under his billowing dishdasha man-dress. The kefiyah on his head was torn and dirty, and his sandals looked like he found them in a roadside ditch. I might have felt sorry for him under other circumstances, but the bandolier of loaded magazines, the rifle in his hands, and the murderous determination in his dark eyes made him an enemy. There was a universally known maxim most of the world understood, but these insurgents had evidently never heard. It was a simple statement, boiling down to nine easy words:

You don't fuck with the United States Marine Corps.

My finger tightened on the trigger. The reticle rested steadily, aimed center of mass. No headshots today. This was serious business, and American lives were on the line. No room for showing off in that equation.

The shot surprised me, letting me know I was doing it right. I saw the projectile's faint, shimmering vapor trail as it sped towards its victim, crossing the distance at incredible speed. The young man in my sights jerked from the impact, his mouth forming a little O of surprise as he slumped over.

"Nice one. Got him in the heart. Didn't know what hit him."

As Rocco spoke, I was already shifting my aim, working the bolt to chamber another round. The insurgents heard the report, and could see their dead comrade leaking blood onto the dusty street, but they could not pinpoint where the shot came from. At this distance, the noise was low, and with all the identically ruined buildings between us, from their vantage point, Rocco and I were nearly impossible to spot.

The next target was a little older than the first one, full black beard, checkered kefiyah, clutching an RPK, eyes wide with alarm. Another trigger pull, and he joined his comrade on the ground.

That one got them moving. Rather than the orderly advance I had been watching moments ago, they broke into a panicked scramble to find cover. I caught another one on the run as he tried to slide behind a parked vehicle. The impact caused him to miss a step and pitch forward, landing on the car's trunk, then slide limply down.

I was just about to carve notch number four when Rocco spoke. "What the fuck?"

My head lifted from the rifle as I looked up, blinking at the sudden change of parallax. "What?"

"Down there, where you shot the first guy."

I looked through the scope again and swiveled to the body of the dead insurgent. Only instead of lying in the dirt, he was on his feet, eyes locked in my direction. I could swear he was looking straight at me.

"The fuck…"

After adjusting the scope's magnification, I peered through it again and got a much enlarged view. The insurgent's mouth hung open, eyes vacant, skin a ghostly shade of gray. He had dropped his rifle, and seemed not to notice the heavy belts of ammo hanging from his gaunt shoulders. Shifting focus to his face, I saw that one of his eyes, the right one, was normal. But his left eye had gone milky white, a deep, livid scar bisecting it from forehead to chin.

"Shit," Rocco said. "There's another one."

On instinct, I moved to the body of my second victim. He too had risen, same pale skin, same slack jaw, same dead eye, same scar. I checked the third insurgent. Same result. Then the rifle's magnification shifted, and in my peripheral vision, I saw Rocco's hand making an adjustment on the knob.

"Gabe, look at them. What are they doing?"

Through the wider field of view, I could now see that all the insurgents had stopped and stood still, eyes locked in my direction, weapons held loosely. As if on command, they canted their rifles into their chests, directly over the heart, and in unison, pulled the trigger. More than a hundred plumes of red splattered against walls, vehicles, doors, and other insurgents. They collapsed like marionettes with the strings cut.

I tried to move but couldn't. I was frozen, limbs locked into place, utterly immobile. I watched as, a few seconds later, the insurgents rose and began shambling toward me, all of them bearing the same scar and clouded eye. Hours passed. They filled the streets, flowing like water through alleys and around houses, their moans filling the air like the winds of a storm. Finally, I heard them coming up the stairs, feet dragging and kicking aside broken bricks and other detritus. In the distance, I heard the distinctive whine and boom of a mortar shell detonating.

"We deserve this you know," Rocco said.

I found I could talk. "What? Deserve what?"

Whiiiiinnne boom. Closer this time.

Against my will, my head rose, the rifle fell from my hands, and I turned to look at Rocco. His spotting scope stood forgotten in front of him as he sat with his head down, boonie hat obscuring his face, thumbs spinning around each other. There was something wrong with his skin tone. As I watched, it shifted from dark olive to pale pink, and finally to the dull gray hue of the grave.

Whiiiiinnne BOOM. Less than a hundred yards away.

"That." The skin of his hand peeled apart as he gestured toward the door, reminding me of a hardpan desert drying after a rain. "It's what waits for all of us you know. We think we've stabilized, that we're holding the line, but it's not true. We're in decline. All of us. It might be slow, but a slow decline is still a decline. A hundred years from now, there will be nothing left. Just crumbling skyscrapers, and nuclear hotspots from long-dead reactors, and all the garbage we left behind."

WHIIIIIINNNE BOOM! The floor beneath me shook, dust cascaded from the ceiling. The impact was right outside the building.

Rocco looked up at me and I felt my heart go still in my chest. His face was the same mottled color as his hands, and his left eye stared blindly ahead, scar standing out purple against the dead flesh around it. When he smiled, I counted five missing teeth.

"But for us? After all the harm we've done, and all the blood on our hands," he raised his palms, and there was crimson liquid smeared from the tips of his fingers all the way down to his elbows. "Retribution comes much sooner."

My head moved again of its own volition. My hands came into view, covered in the same gore as Rocco's. Behind me, I heard the door smash inward and the amplified cries of the undead. Unable to control my actions, I looked back at Rocco just in time to see him lunge for me, mouth open wide. Suddenly, the spell was broken and I was in command of myself again. I reached out and grabbed him by the throat as he slammed into me, bearing us both to the ground. His fingers dug into my shoulders like iron hooks, ripping a cry of pain and fear from my throat. I struggled to hold him back, but he was too strong. His mouth grew slowly, inexorably closer. I gibbered incoherently, begging him to stop, screaming for help, but the only response I got was another long whine, and then, as if right on top of me, the world exploded in a blinding flash of orange and white.

I felt cold, then hot, and then-

*****

I woke up.

The invisible man with the hammer was back, working as diligently as ever. I tried to sit up, but my hands were cuffed behind my back. Scuttling around on the floor, I exhaled strongly, tightened my abs hard enough to make them cramp, and with a grunt of effort, slipped my wrists down to my thighs. That done, I pivoted until my back was against the door and passed the chain beneath my ankles.

Should have killed me when you had the chance, Tanner.

Behind me, I heard raised voices. I pressed my ear against the door and listened. I couldn't make out what they were saying but they sounded agitated—frightened even. Then there was a tremendous WHOMP, followed by a shockwave that knocked me away from the wall hard enough to rattle my teeth. As I scrambled to my feet, I realized the mortar rounds I heard in my dream were not figments of my imagination.

Blackmire was under attack.

There was little chance Tanner's men would take the time to let me out, so I crouched in the center of the room, fingertips in my ears, mouth open so another shockwave wouldn't knock my teeth together and break them. I didn't have to wait long until the next blast. It came from the other side of the building, powerful enough to rock the floor and send me stumbling.

Recovering my balance, I stepped back to the center of the cell and waited. A full minute or so ticked by, but there were no further blasts. I decided it was worth the risk and went back to the door, listening. I strained my ears and closed my eyes, concentrating hard. There was nothing. The voices were gone.

Then, echoing through the wall on my left, I heard the unmistakable sound of a light machine gun. In half a second I was flat on the floor, trying to make myself as small as possible. When bullets start flying, you never know where they are going to hit. People don't always aim so well when they are enthusiastically trying to kill one another. If you're a non-combatant, the best thing to do is take cover, keep your head down, and stay the hell out of the way.

I listened to the sounds of combat grow and become more heated. A volley of bullets thunked into the wall behind me,

397

high over my head. The lack of shrapnel peppering my back told me they didn't get through, which made me feel just a tiny bit less exposed and vulnerable. Several minutes passed as I lay there, hoping against hope no bullets found me and no one blew up the building I was in.

And then I heard a fist pounding against the door.

"Gabe? Gabe, you in there?"

For a second, I was too surprised to move. Then I was on my feet and shouting. "I'm here! I'm in here!"

"Hang on, step back, the door's locked. Gotta set a breaching charge. Get to the back of the room and stay low."

I did as ordered and lay flat, eyes squeezed shut and facing away from the door, arms covering my head. A few seconds later, there was a deafening *POP,* and the door to my cell shivered open.

"Gabe? You all right?"

I stood up and walked to the doorway. The figure standing in it was framed by the firelight of the Red Rooster across the street as it burned to the ground. Through the broken shutters over the windows, I could see several other buildings nearby were on fire. I stepped closer to the man, peering at his face.

"Hicks? That you?"

A set of white teeth appeared in the darkness. "Never thought you'd be so happy to see me, did you?"

If not for the cuffs, I would have hugged him. "What are you doing here?"

"Long story. I'll tell you later. For right now, we need to get you out of here." He clicked on a red-lens flashlight and looked me over.

"Damn," he said, wrinkling his nose at the smell, taking in my battered face and general deplorable condition. "What did they do to you?"

"Nothing good. Don't suppose you have any water, do you?"

He responded by dropping his pack and taking out a clear plastic bottle. "Here you go. I knew they were holding you prisoner. Figured you might need it."

I took a few sips, careful not to drink too much and make myself sick. As dehydrated as I was, too much water could be just as painful as not enough. The effect was immediate, like pouring water on a sponge. I've had sex that didn't feel as good.

"Can you do something about these?" I said, holding up my cuffs.

"One sec." He rooted in his pack again and produced a set of picks. "Let me see your hands."

He worked swiftly, turning the picks with deft, practiced fingers. The cuffs snapped off my wrists, then my ankles. Total time: maybe ten seconds.

"You are full of surprises, Caleb Theophilus Hicks."

He smiled again. "You have no idea. Come on, let's find you some clothes. Can't have you runnin' around here in your birthday suit."

Remembering my gear in Tanner's office, I said, "Follow me."

As I turned down the hallway, Hicks stopped me by grabbing my shoulder. "Hold up, take this."

I wrapped my fingers around the grip of a Beretta M9. "Thanks."

"No problem. It's got one in the hole, ready to rock."

Flipping the safety off, I headed for the staircase. The door was locked, but it was nothing a hard kick couldn't handle. Hicks and I poured into the room, weapons up, him breaking left and me breaking right. The office was empty, but my gear was right where I hoped it would be.

"Shut the door," I said, nodding to Hicks. "Try to make it look normal."

He complied, working quickly and quietly. If someone took a close look, they would see it had been forced open. But from the ground level, as long as we didn't make too much noise, someone could come in the lobby and be unaware of our presence.

There was a washbasin and a towel under the window behind Tanner's desk. I soaked the towel and wiped myself down as best I could, then splashed the remaining water on my face. When the worst of the congealed blood was washed away, I felt like a new man.

"Might want to hurry," Hicks said, peering out a window at the street below. "They might start coming back this way. Don't know how much longer Cole and Thompson can keep the guards occupied."

"Cole and Thompson are here?"

He nodded. "Sanchez too. He was the one firing the mortars. We're supposed to meet up with him at the rendezvous point in an hour. Cole and Thompson are keeping the guards attention so I can get you out of here."

I had about a hundred questions, but figured it wasn't the best time to ask. Crossing the room, I threw on my clothes, donned my MOLLE vest, and checked my weapons. They were in good working order, mags still loaded, blades in their sheaths. Once re-armed, I slipped on my pack and motioned to the door.

"Okay, I'm ready. What's the plan?"

Hicks shrugged. "Honestly, I'm surprised I made it this far."

"You're kidding, right?"

Another shrug. "I saw some guards on horseback. Maybe we could requisition ourselves some equine transportation."

Transportation ... I slapped myself in the forehead and cursed myself for an idiot. In my defense, starvation has a way of addling one's memory.

"Come on, I have a better idea."

*****

The trucks were exactly where I last saw them, parked behind the building.

Unlike before, however, they were now surrounded by a ring of guards. Peering over the sill of a window, I counted eight of them. I turned to Hicks, who was crouched behind me, and explained the situation with hand signals. He acknowledged by patting his rifle, and then patting my shoulder, essentially saying, *let's do this.* His hand went to a pocket on his vest and produced a frag grenade. I took it, and adjusted my rifle so I could get to it quickly once the grenade was out.

We crept a few steps to the back door, staying low so the guards wouldn't spot us through the windows. At the exit, I did one last check to make sure I was ready. Safety off, round in the chamber, same story with my pistol, tactical sling in the proper position. Reaching up, I tested the doorknob and found it unlocked. I turned it slowly until the door just barely began easing back from the jamb. Then I gripped the grenade, pulled the pin, counted to two, and hurled it out the door.

Hicks and I went flat, waiting for the blast. There was a hoarse shout, and then the windows shattered, dousing us with broken glass. I felt the power of the explosion in my chest, but despite the blow, I wasted no time getting to my feet. Surprise was our only chance, and we both knew it.

As I cleared the door and broke right, I noticed the grenade had killed two guards and wounded a third. The rest were still picking themselves up from the ground.

Perfect.

I took aim at the nearest one and squeezed off four rounds, center of mass. He stopped trying to get up. To my left, I heard the suppressed clanking of Hicks' M-4, and a strangled cry that ended quickly.

Four down.

My running feet carried me close to the guard wounded by the grenade. His left arm was missing from the elbow down, and the only thing keeping him from screaming was the metal confetti lodged in his lungs. A double tap to the head put him out of his misery.

A flash of movement ahead of me caught my attention. I looked up to see a man leveling his rifle, stock against his shoulder and sighting in. I zigged right, taking myself out of his line of fire as he pulled the trigger. A hail of supersonic lead zipped past me, but not by much. The gunman turned, following my movement, but it was too little too late. Firing on the run, I stitched him from groin to throat with a full-auto burst. His rifle fell from nerveless hands and he went down.

Reaching the communications truck, I did a quick scan to make sure there were no bad guys on my side, then took cover behind the engine. I heard a burst of fire on the other side, but rather than the high clang of metal impacting metal, there was the thudding *wap* of bullets penetrating wood. Hick's M-4 coughed three times, and then, as suddenly as the fight started, it was over.

"Clear." Hicks called out.

I looked around again, just to be sure. "Clear."

Hicks met me at the driver's door. "You might want to let me drive," he said. "You're lookin' a little woozy."

It was only then I realized I was swaying on my feet. The adrenaline left me in a rush, and I felt my legs begin to tremble. Seven days with no food is not a good way to prepare for sudden combat.

"Sounds like a plan. Let's get the hell out of here."

I climbed in the passenger's side and took a seat. Hicks bashed the lock from the ignition cover, opened it, and touched his thumb to the switch.

"Fingers crossed..."

He pressed down. The engine gave a few high-pitched false starts, then roared to life. I felt my face stretch into a grin. Hicks matched it with one of his own.

"Let's roll."

We rolled.

THIRTY-NINE

"Looks like the cavalry finally showed up," Hicks said.

As we hung a left around the corner of Blackmire's office building, I craned my neck to see through Hick's window. In the distance, backlit by the orange-yellow light of the fires raging all over town, I saw the lurching, moaning silhouettes of walkers.

"That your handiwork?"

The wiry Texan grinned. "Figured I'd give 'em a taste of their own medicine."

I looked at him with a furrowed brow, not sure what he meant, but let it go. It was a conversation that could wait until we were out of imminent mortal danger.

"Turn left up here," I said, pointing. "That'll take us straight to the main gate."

He scowled at me. "You sure we should do that?"

I hooked a thumb southward. "All the fires and fighting seem to be coming from that way. The main gate is on the north side. It'll be easier to fight our way through."

Hicks acknowledged with a nod and hauled on the wheel. I felt the weight of the big vehicle lean to the right as he gunned it around the corner, slinging mud and fishtailing the rear end into a ramshackle clutch of food stalls. The wooden shelters and tables flew to pieces, roofs and strips of tarp and oilcloth clinging to the antenna protruding from the bed. Hicks let off the accelerator, worked the steering wheel until he found traction again, and then stood on the pedal, driving us clear.

"Maybe slow down a little?" I suggested as I hung on for dear life.

Hicks eased off a bit. "Better?"

"Better."

We sped through the streets past fleeing townsfolk, gun-toting guards, and ravening infected. A few walkers wandered into our path, but Hicks simply ran them down. Not far from the main gate, I saw a few guardsmen up ahead take notice of our approach and fan out into defensive positions.

"That's not good," Hicks said.

"Just hand me a grenade and keep driving." I replied, ejecting the mostly empty mag out of my rifle and inserting a fresh one. Hicks handed over the little green pineapple. "Speed up some. When I say the word, duck, and put it to the floor."

Hick's jaw clamped down hard, knuckles going white on the steering wheel as he pressed his foot harder against the accelerator. The truck shimmied side to side in the loose mud, but stayed mostly straight.

I opened my window, shifted so my knees were on the seat, hooked one foot under the dash, and leveled my M-6. When we were in range, I set my rifle for three-round burst and went through the ritual.

Breath in. Let it out slow. Stop. Aim. Put the reticle just above where you want to hit. Compensate for the rock of the truck. Squeeze....

-crack-crack-crack-

And watch him fall. Now for the next one. He was behind a battlement constructed from thick pine logs. I switched to full auto and aimed low, then walked it up until I saw a red cloud erupt from the back of his head. I was about to pick another target when I saw muzzle flashes from the remaining guards.

"*Shit.*"

I ducked back inside just as bullets started pinging and popping against the thick ballistic glass of the windshield.

"This thing ain't gonna last long." Hicks said.

He was right. Already, the windshield was covered in a network of spider-web fractures. *Time to put them on their heels.*

I estimated the truck was going about thirty miles an hour, which meant both me and the grenade in my hand were traveling at the same speed. For this to work, I would have to hurl the grenade with sufficient force to overcome the hard wind resistance it was going to encounter when I leaned out the door. The one advantage I had was the grenade was small, heavy, and round, which would mitigate the effects of wind drag, but not by much.

It's either this, or they kill you. Not much of a choice now, is it?

"No choice at all," I whispered, then pulled the pin, opened the door, leaned out, and with a shout of effort, winged the little explosive with everything I had. The guards at the gate had just enough time to watch it arc through the air, land in the center of their defensive position, and detonate. The blast was bright against the darkness of the night, causing a green spot to appear in my vision. When the smoke cleared, several guards were down with varying degrees of shrapnel wounds. The ones still alive decided the fight wasn't worth it and disappeared into the darkness.

I jumped back in the cab and slammed the door. "All right. Floor it and get down."

The engine roared as the truck hurtled toward the thick wooden planks and tree trunk pillars comprising the main gate. I ground my teeth in anticipation, half expecting the truck to collapse on impact and crush us to death. Instead, there was a tremendous *CRACK,* the clattering of wood over the windshield and along the roof and doors, and the cab reared upward as we drove over the small earthen berm just in front of the gate. When I sat back up, we were bouncing along the dirt two-track leading from Blackmire all the way to Watkins Road. Hicks sat up and gripped the wheel, cranking it to the right to avoid a stand of trees. When we were clear, he picked up speed, flipped on the headlights, and sped off into the forest.

"Nicely done," I said.

"Thanks," Hicks replied. "Hope you don't mind if I take a little side trip."

I reached into the back and rooted through my rucksack, looking for food. "Where are we headed?"

In response, he unplugged an earpiece from a radio on his belt, lifted it, and keyed the mike. "Bravo, Alpha. How copy? Over."

I recognized Cole's distinctive baritone. "Lima Charlie, Alpha. Over."

"How about a sitrep? Over."

"En route to the rendezvous. We busted 'em up good; don't think they followin' us. Too busy putting out fires and fighting the dead. How about you? Over."

"Cat is in the bag. I even managed to arrange us some motorized transportation. Don't suppose you'd be interested in catching a ride? Over."

"Shit yeah. Catch you at the fallback point? Over."

"Works for me. Charlie, you get all that? Over."

"Affirmative." Sanchez this time. "En route. Charlie out."

Hicks put the radio on the console between us and concentrated on the trail ahead. I rolled down my window and adjusted the mirror to reflect the orange glow coming over Blackmire's outer wall.

"Think they'll come after us?" Hicks asked.

I shot him a glance and chuckled. "Does a bear shit in the woods?"

He nodded grimly and drove on.

*****

Seven-year-old corned beef hash never tasted so good.

From the corner of his eye, Hicks watched me wolf down a second packet generously donated from his supply of MRE's.

Already, I could feel my strength returning. "You got any more of this stuff?"

He shook his head. "Sorry. You should probably slow down, you know. How long has it been since you ate last?"

"About a week, I think." I shoved the last spoonful in my mouth and tossed the packet in the back floorboard, then took a long pull from Hicks' canteen. We were parked on the side of the road near the intersection of Watkins and Barr Road waiting for Cole, Thompson, and Sanchez to show up.

"Not to sound ungrateful, but how the hell did you find me?" I asked.

Only one side of his face was visible in the gloom, but I could see the corner of his eye crinkle. "You can thank Eric for that one."

I frowned at him. "What do you mean?"

"He slipped a GPS tracker in your backpack."

My mind shot back to the cold confines of my warehouse in Hollow Rock, the armory within, and Eric standing by my rucksack, loading it up with the things I would need to survive.

"That sneaky little bastard."

Hicks chuckled. "You don't want to know where he got it from."

I climbed into the back and began rummaging through my gear. Sure enough, stuffed in a plastic container of dried peas was a small disc about the size of a quarter. It was clever of him to put it in the peas; he knows I hate the things and would eat them last. The tracker was the same one that had been implanted in Eric when he infiltrated the Free Legion. He must have had it removed and kept it. I remembered it was powered by movement, kind of like an expensive watch, which explained how it was still working.

"I don't get it," I said. "How did you pick up the signal? It's encrypted."

He shrugged. "Lieutenant Jonas called in a favor with Central and got the authorization codes. We've been tracking you on a ruggedized tablet."

My heart sank at the mention of Lieutenant Jonas. He was a good man, but he never did anything for free. I wondered how much of a hit G&R Salvage's quarterly profit margin was about to take. Then I remembered Hicks and his team probably weren't here out of the kindness of their hearts, either.

"How much did he pay you?"

Hicks leaned forward and peered out the driver's side window, eyes searching the treeline. "Fifty rounds of nine-millimeter, a bottle of Pappy Van Winkle 20 year, and this thing." His hand went to his chest rig and produced a suppressor-equipped Beretta M-9. I groaned and climbed into the front seat.

"What about the other three?"

"Not sure. You'd have to ask them."

It may have been my imagination, but my pockets suddenly felt lighter. "I'm gonna kill him. He better hope I don't make it back because if I do, I'm gonna fucking kill him."

A flicker of red light blinked to life in the treeline on Hicks side. He held up his own flash light and answered. "You do realize if he hadn't arranged all this, you'd still be trussed up in that stinky little room back there."

The glare I gave him was daggered, but the points were blunt. In all fairness, he was right. I probably never would have made it out of Blackmire alive. "Touché. So how long have you been following me?"

"Since about two days after you left Hollow Rock. It took Eric that long to line everything up. You were already taken prisoner by the time we caught up with you."

"How did you find out?"

"When we got there, I disguised myself as a raider and went into town. Tracked you to that building, the Tribune's office or whatever. I figured if you were there, and not in one of the

408

taverns, something must have gone wrong. So I took a seat at a busy place and kept my ears open. Overhead a bartender talking about it; I think his name was Slim or something like that." He turned his head to look at me. "That name ring a bell?"

I nodded, thinking about how much I would like to ring Slim's bell. "Yeah, it does. If I ever see him again, he's a fucking dead man. What did he say about me?"

"He was bragging to some fella about what he was gonna do with the bounty he got from turning you in. I guess everybody in town had your description and was on the lookout."

I grimaced. "Yeah. That's how they got me."

Hicks opened his door and started to get out. "Looks like the others are here."

Cole, Thompson, and Sanchez emerged from the treeline, NVGs flipped back on their helmets. Sanchez was in his ghillie suit, hands wrapped around one of the Militia's sniper carbines. Cole carried his customary SAW, while Thompson hefted a suppressed M-4 with an attached grenade launcher. Over the shoulder of all three men protruded the distinctive, round canisters of LAW rockets, complemented by grenades on heavily-laden vests. Their faces were smeared with black paint, along with the exposed skin of their hands and wrists. I noticed there was a muzzle brake protruding from Cole's shoulder next to his LAW canister, and my heart leapt in my chest as I realized what it was.

"Is that mine?" I said, pointing. Cole unslung it and held it out to me.

"Eric said you might want it."

I felt a grin spread across my face as I hefted my customized Desert Tactical SRS .338 Lapua magnum sniper rifle. "He send any ammo along?"

"Twenty rounds. Bought it from Lieutenant Jonas. It's in my pack."

"Outstanding."

"It's good to see you again, Gabe," Thompson broke in. "Looks like you landed yourself in a spot of trouble."

The four of them had a chuckle at my expense. But they deserved it, so I kept my mouth shut and nodded, chagrin showing on my face. "Thanks for busting me out."

Sanchez stepped forward and patted me on the shoulder. "Don't sweat it, *jefe*. Just doing our jobs. You keep getting into trouble like this, and we're all gonna be rich."

I thumped him on the chest. "Asshole."

His grin widened. "I didn't get too close with any of those mortars, did I?"

"No, but it wasn't by much. And where the hell did you get the artillery? Don't tell me you carried it all the way from Fort McCray."

The fiery Mexican shook his head. "Nah. Air drop. Civilian craft. Best Central could manage with all the trouble in Hollow Rock."

I glanced at Hicks, and then back at Sanchez. "What are you talking about? What trouble in Hollow Rock?"

Thompson's smile evaporated as he glared at Hicks. "You didn't tell him?"

The Texan shrugged. "I been a little preoccupied. You know, gettin' shot at and all."

The big staff sergeant sighed and looked down. "All right. I'll fill you in on the way out of here. But for right now, we need to get moving. There's no telling how long before they catch up to us."

I called shotgun and walked around the other side of the truck. As I climbed into the passenger seat, Hicks restarted the motor and stared darkly at the console.

"Trouble?"

He tapped a finger on something and turned on his flashlight. I leaned forward and saw he was pointing at the fuel gauge. The needle hovered a millimeter or two above the big red E.

"Shit."

"Yep."

I turned in the seat. "We got a problem. This thing is low on fuel, and it's only a matter of time until Blackmire gets his shit together and sends his men after us. If we're on foot, they'll catch us. No doubt about it. We need to have an ambush waiting when they do. Thompson, what other hardware did you bring?"

He patted his rifle. "What you see here, grenades, and a few claymores. That's it."

"Okay," I replied, the first drifting images of a plan beginning to form. "Hicks, take us to Highway 19 and head toward Brownsville. There's a settlement there, they might be willing to help."

"With this little fuel, we ain't gonna make it to Brownsville."

"I know. But it'll buy us some time. Unless of course you have a better plan?"

He pursed his lips and tipped his head side-to-side for a moment. "Mmm...sorry. I got nothin'."

"Then let's get moving."

FORTY

All was not well in Hollow Rock.

As we drove, Thompson filled me in on the happenings in my absence. Two days ago, another group of ghoul wranglers attacked Hollow Rock from the south, leading a horde estimated at over two-thousand strong. They hit the wall on that side with RPGs and created a breach, killing four guards in the initial exchange. The wranglers were not content, however, to simply let the undead lay waste to the town. Instead, they went ahead of them as an advance assault force, armed with rifles and light machine guns. The attack occurred at around four in the morning when they expected all to be quiet and the townsfolk to have their guard down.

Evidently, they didn't know much about the people of Hollow Rock.

I remember, many years ago, there was a Navy corpsman in my platoon. He had done a four-year stint on a Ticonderoga class cruiser, and he once explained to me that in much the same way every Marine is a rifleman, every sailor is a firefighter. If a fire breaks out on a ship at sea—every sailor's worst nightmare—the crew can't just run away and call the fire department. They *are* the fire department. There is an old joke in the Navy that a warship is the only place in the world where if a fire breaks out, you see people running *toward* the danger.

After three years of surviving the dead, fighting raiders and marauders, incursions by the Free Legion, and a host of other threats, the people of Hollow Rock had long ago learned to be prepared to fight at all times.

When the insurgents attacked, they expected chaos and confusion. They expected people to stumble blearily from their homes and be cut down like wheat. They did not expect over five-hundred men and women to leap from their beds, grab their rifles, bows, or whatever else they had on hand, and run *toward* the sounds of fighting.

There were twelve insurgents.

They did not last long.

The butcher's bill on our side was six dead and three wounded, at least until the horde made it through. Eric and Sheriff Elliott organized the townsfolk into two assault forces, positioned them on the wall and on rooftops, and tasked them with piling up the dead within the breach. While they did so, Elizabeth had Lieutenant Jonas and his men meet up with the Ninth TVM by the north gate and march southward. Once there, they fanned out in a wide skirmish line and attacked the horde from behind.

Locked between the hammer of the soldiers and militiamen, and the anvil of hundreds of people fighting to defend their homes and children, the walkers had nowhere to go. The horde was reduced by half, then half again, and when they were down to just a few hundred, Lieutenant Jonas called a cease fire and had his men move in with hand weapons.

It was over in less than an hour.

All told, we lost nine people. Six civilians in the initial assault, two soldiers who got bit fighting the horde, and one woman who slipped off a rooftop and landed on her head. All tragic losses to be sure, but it could have been a hell of a lot worse.

I've said it before, but it bears repeating. There is no substitute for readiness and competent leadership.

As soon as the bodies were cleared away, Elizabeth gathered volunteers and put them to work repairing the breach in the wall. Thompson heard radio chatter earlier in the day that the repairs were complete and Elizabeth had beefed up the patrols, sending them out farther afield.

"Needless to say, Central is pissed," Thompson concluded.

"What are they planning to do about it?"

He shrugged. "Not sure at this point. With all the insurgents dead, there's no way to know who they were working for. The Alliance has already denounced the attack and denied involvement."

"That's their story and they're sticking to it, huh?"

"Something like that."

I ran a hand through my hair and breathed a heated sigh. "I tell you, the Alliance is about to get on my last motherfucking nerve."

"You're telling me."

As he said it, the engine—which had been sputtering and hesitating for the last couple of miles—finally gave out with a sickly wheeze. Hicks applied the brakes and rolled us to a gentle stop.

"End of the line, amigos."

We piled out and distributed the gear. Thompson, Cole, and I took the heavy stuff while Hicks and Sanchez loaded up with the food and lighter equipment. That done, I retrieved my NVGs from my pack, replaced the batteries, climbed atop the truck, and looked around. The only heat signatures I caught were from a small herd of deer about a mile away, headed away from us. There were no walkers in sight, but it was only a matter of time before they showed up. As much noise as the truck made, they would definitely be coming.

The area surrounding the stretch of road we were on consisted mostly of flat, snow-blanketed fields. The ground rose steadily upward to the east, topping out at a sloping ridge about three hundred yards away. At the crest of the ridge, winding southward and terminating at the highway, was a long stretch of pine trees. Lots of places to set up a sniper hide in there.

To my left, an intermittent fence of thin young trees lined a shallow ditch, stretching as far as I could see. The field beyond was visible, but obscured, leading to another treeline. I ranged it with my scope, figuring it at about two-hundred forty yards. Sanchez could set up over there, and we would have them in a crossfire.

To my right, there was an abandoned house set back far from the road, roof sagging under the weight of heavy snow. A cluster of farm buildings were spread out over a several acres beyond. I spotted old tractors, attachments, a Chevy pickup, and a variety of equipment I couldn't identify. Beyond them were a couple of squat aluminum grain silos. Plenty of places for Cole to set up his SAW.

As for Thompson and Hicks, there was an abundance of places within a hundred yards of the truck where they could dig in and conceal themselves. It would be hard work in the frozen ground, but it could be done. All in all, not a bad spot to set up an ambush. Higher ground would have been nice, but one works with the tools they are given.

Climbing down, I motioned to the others to gather round. "Okay, here's how we're gonna do it…"

I laid out the plan, making sure everyone knew their place and what signals to wait for. When everyone was up to speed, Hicks and Thompson picked their spots and started digging. There weren't enough entrenching tools to go around, so Sanchez and I searched the shed behind the farmhouse and requisitioned two shovels and a mattock. Once the foxholes were dug and properly camouflaged, Sanchez volunteered to head down the road and watch for approaching riders.

"How's the battery on your radio?" I asked.

He squinted at me and tilted his head. "I charged the batteries for all the radios in the truck, Gabe. You watched me hook them up to the dash outlets."

I blinked a few times, and did indeed remember him connecting the chargers to a multipronged adapter, then slipping the radios' blocky little batteries into them. "*Tienes Razón, amigo.* I'm not on top of my game today."

"You look like shit, *ese,*" he said flatly. "It's going to be a while before those *putos* get here. You should try to get some rest."

To my dismay, I noticed I was swaying on my feet again, and at the mention of sleep, my legs went shaky. "That's not such a bad idea. Hicks, do you mind helping me clear that house?"

"Not at all."

The house was empty save for a family of birds in a broken patch of drywall in the living room. I informed them if they left me alone, I would extend the same courtesy. The biggest one chirped and ruffled its wings at me, then settled down and closed its eyes. I took that as a yes.

After looking over my M-110, cleaning my .338, and donning my ghillie suit, I laid out my bedroll and settled my head against my pack. Approximately four seconds later, a hand on my shoulder shook me awake. I opened my eyes and saw Hicks squatting next to me, a shaft of early morning sun highlighting his dark blue irises like iridescent glass.

"Sanchez called in," he said. "They're coming."

*****

One of these days, I'm going to search through the hard drive and tally up how many hours of my life I have spent lying on the ground peering through a scope. I'm willing to bet it is a depressing number.

The riders came into view less than five minutes after Sanchez hustled to his hide. I counted twelve, the familiar bearded visage of Marco leading the way. They rode in carefully, spread out on both sides of the road, hooves kicking up snow in their wake, faint jingle of weapons, creak of leather in the cold dry air, each man with one hand on the reins, the other gripping a rifle. They approached the truck with wary eyes and nervous mounts, the perceptive horses picking up on their riders' tension. If they saw any sign of us, they gave no indication. The wind had done the job of covering our tracks, but the twin grooves carved by the truck's tires were still plainly visible. Further working in our favor, with the exception of Hicks and Sanchez, the sun was at our backs.

I keyed my radio. "Hold tight, everyone. Let's wait for them to bunch up. Cole, how's your line of sight?"

"Good to go," he said. "Sanchez, if they get on your side of the truck, they're all yours."

"Roger."

I scanned where Sanchez was waiting, but couldn't pick him out. He had done a fine job of concealing himself. Cole was off to my right, lying in the bed of a pickup truck under a snow-covered tarp. A section of the tarp was folded over against the cab, allowing him to see the road without being spotted. His SAW lay next to him, bipod deployed, ready to bring to bear at a moment's notice.

Marco rode a circle around the truck, keeping several yards between his mount and the vehicle, shining a flashlight around, probably searching for traps. I could have told him he was wasting his time, but that would have defeated the purpose. Satisfied nothing was going to blow up, he motioned one of his men closer. The man was leading a pack mule with four gerry cans strapped to its harness and a large funnel dangling near its neck. Grinning, I keyed my radio. "You boys seeing what I'm seeing?"

Cole answered first. "You talking about the soon-to-be-dead bitches, or the diesel strapped to that donkey?"

"It's a mule, actually. And yes, that's what I'm talking about. Careful what you shoot at—I want that fuel."

"What's the difference?" Cole replied.

"What?"

"You said it's a mule, not a donkey. What's the difference?"

I pinched the bridge of my nose and laughed silently. Here we were, about to do murder, and Cole wants a primer on the finer points of the animal husbandry. "It's the sterile offspring of a male donkey and a female horse."

A moment of silence, then, "That's kind of specific, ain't it? Why's it got to be a male donkey and a female horse?"

I clenched my teeth, suppressing the urge to growl. "It's genetics, Cole. Now in case you didn't notice, we're about to start a firefight. Can we focus on the task at hand? Pretty please, with a fucking cherry on top?"

"Hey man, you brought it up."

"Cole…"

"All right, man, chill out. I got this."

"Thank you."

Marco's men began gathering closer as the truck was refueled. There was a slackening in their posture, hands loosening on weapons, small conversations picking up, the easy energy of men beginning to relax. *If someone was going to attack they would have done it by now, right? Those Union assholes are probably scared shitless. I bet they're running with their tails between their legs. There's only five of them, after all, and one of them is probably too starved to fight. They would have to be crazy to take us on. I bet they're miles away by now.*

"All right, Cole. Get ready."

"Copy."

I pressed my cheek against the cold stock of my M-110, slipped a finger over the trigger, and sighted in. Marco would be first. Cut off the beast's head, and the body dies. I estimated him at about six feet tall, taking up just shy of eight mils on the reticle. So figure it at 7.8 mils, and apply the formula. Two yards times a thousand equals two thousand. Divide that by the number of mils, and you get 256.41 yards. Adjust for error and call it two-fifty—better to hit him low than high. Make a slight windage adjustment, settle in, let the breath ease from the lungs, and squeeze.

The recoil was hard, but oddly comfortable. The report was immensely loud, as I had forgone the use of a suppressor. I wanted that shock factor, that moment of panic when men suddenly realize someone is shooting at them with malicious intent, and they are exposed.

Marco doubled over as the round took him low in the chest, face going rigid with shock, disbelief in his eyes as he slumped to the ground, the look of a man who has seen others die but lived with the fervent conviction he was invincible. Other people died, not him. Not Marco. But then there is the noise, and the impact, and the burning pain, and the blood, and the heat in the face, and the panicked, racing thoughts. *No, no, no, this isn't happening. Wait! Just wait! Maybe it's not that bad. I need help. I need to get to my horse, get back to Blackmire, find a doctor…*

And then all is darkness.

I shifted aim to the guy pouring diesel. The men around him had the same reaction I have seen hundreds of times—the surprise, the moment of rigidity, the heads swiveling in the direction of the reverberating kill-crash. Then my second shot split the air, and another of their number hit the ground with a burst red melon where his upper cranium used to be. A bit showy on my part, but nothing inspires panic like the sight of a comrade's shredded cerebrum.

In the seconds it took me to kill the first two men, Cole threw aside the tarp covering him, leveled his saw, and opened fire. He did it properly, firing in six-to-nine round bursts, aiming through an ACOG scope, spraying bullets into the stunned enemy with lethal accuracy. Aided by the 4x optical sight, the weapon's high rate of fire, and the big gunner's steady hands, he killed three of them before the rest could break for cover.

All but one of the remaining riders abandoned their horses and scurried around the other side of the truck. I shifted my point of aim and caught one of them as he rounded the corner, the bullet punching dead-center between his shoulder blades. He pitched forward onto his face and did not move again.

The one who didn't run tried to use his horse as cover and return fire at Cole. Just as he was aiming his rifle, the sheet of plywood covering Thompson's foxhole lifted a few inches and the barrel of his M-4 poked out. He took a moment to aim before firing a full-auto burst. The gunman died before he had a chance to pull the trigger.

On the other side of the truck, I heard panicked shouting as Sanchez's rifle began taking its toll. At the same time, Hicks popped up from his foxhole—cleverly dug just beyond the other side of the trees lining the road—and fired two quick bursts. Releasing his rifle with one hand, he keyed his radio. "Cease fire, cease fire. Looks like they're surrendering."

The clatter of rifles died immediately. "How many left?" I asked.

"Three."

"All stations, move in."

Hicks kept the prisoners covered while Thompson and Cole approached. The two soldiers spent a few moments firing headshots into the fallen guardsmen to ensure they were well and truly dead, then searched the survivors and bound their hands with zip ties. By the time Sanchez and I arrived, the prisoners were kneeling by the side of the road.

One of them was older, maybe early fifties, dark hair, beard streaked with gray. He kept his eyes down, mouth pinched in anger. The other two were young, barely more than kids. They looked remarkably similar, and I realized they must be related. Brothers, probably. I put one at twenty, and the other at maybe seventeen.

Stepping in front of them, I slung my rifle across my shoulders and drew the Beretta Hicks had loaned me. "There's no need for you to die," I said, holding the gun at my side. "I want information. If you give it to me-"

The squawk of a radio interrupted me. "Raven, this is Eagle. Come in, Raven."

I looked at Thompson and gestured toward their pile of gear. "Which one of them did you take that radio from?"

"That one," he said, pointing at the older man.

I picked it up and motioned to Hicks. "Cut his hands loose."

The man glared up at me, giving me my first good look at his face. Glancing between him and the two boys, I saw they all had the same hazel eyes and shared a similar curvature of face.

Lifting my pistol, I pointed it at the head of the kid next to him. "Let me guess. Nephews, maybe?"

The old man simply stared.

I thumbed back the hammer on the Beretta and held the radio out to him. "I'm going to count to three."

Before I could start, he reached out, took the radio, and pressed the talk button.

"Eagle, Raven. Go ahead."

"Did you find the truck yet?"

"Yes sir. We found it on Highway 19, just like you said."

"I knew it. They're headed for Brownsville, gotta be. You see any sign of them?"

I pressed the gun a little harder to the kid's head, one finger held over my lips.

"No sir. The wind is blowing pretty hard out here, it must have covered their tracks. Do you want me to send out a patrol?"

"Negative, Raven. Powell and his men secured Brownsville last night. I'll have them set up roadblocks and send out riders. You can coordinate with them later. Now how about the truck, is it operable?"

The old man glanced at me. I shook my head. "Negative, sir. They disabled it before they left."

"Figures. All right then, tell Marco to proceed to Brownsville and to be on the lookout for those Union fuckers. Make sure you radio ahead and coordinate your search with Powell's men. I'll send someone out to retrieve the equipment in a few days. I don't think it's going anywhere. Acknowledge."

"Roger, Eagle."

"Copy. Eagle out."

I glanced around at my impromptu squad and saw the same question on all of their faces. Thompson took the radio back and aimed his rifle at the old man's head.

"You can't fight them all," he said as he stared at me, one side of his mouth curled in a defiant smirk. "You have no idea what you're up against."

"You let me worry about that." I reached up to my vest, drew my Ka-bar, and squatted in front of him. The smirk vanished.

"Now tell me. Who is this Powell guy?"

FORTY-ONE

One of us had to ride with the prisoners.

It was going to be cold and miserable, but mercifully brief. Brownsville wasn't far away, and with our newfound supply of fuel, we would make it there with plenty to spare. Maybe even enough to take us back to Hollow Rock, assuming we survived to see another day.

I found a piece of paper in the abandoned house, wrote our names on it, tore it apart, and rolled it into little balls. After a few tosses in his helmet, Cole drew a piece and read it out loud.

Thompson.

The big sergeant cursed fluently as he loaded the prisoners on the flatbed and tied them to the large antenna array. The rest of us piled in the front and enjoyed the warmth as we trundled southeast on Highway 19.

Less than a quarter-mile from the scene of the ambush, we saw the first stumbling figures of the walking dead emerge from the forest. There were only a few at first, but within minutes several large hordes, probably numbering a thousand or more each, populated the surrounding fields. Hicks drove straight through them, only having to run over a dozen or so before we were clear.

"Those things are going to follow us," Hicks said, casting a nervous glance at his side view mirror.

"Don't worry. We'll find a place to circle around and lead them off," I replied.

When we were a little over a mile from Brownsville, I had Cole consult his tablet to find a place for us to await nightfall. He pulled up the most recently updated satellite imagery available and located a large structure ahead of us about a quarter mile off the highway. It was surrounded by a copse of trees, and when the photo was taken, the parking lot was empty.

"Sounds good to me," I said. Everyone agreed.

When we arrived, we found a snow covered, but otherwise none the worse for wear funeral home. Hicks picked the lock while Thompson and Cole helped the prisoners down from the flatbed. Once inside, we conducted a thorough sweep, ensuring we were the building's only occupants. As we moved from room to room, I marveled at how untouched the place looked. Aside from a thick layer of dust covering every horizontal surface, it looked as if the owner had simply finished a day's work, locked up, and never returned.

In a back room, where a mortician had once prepared bodies for their final rest, the tools were neatly laid out, the various machines were clean and ready for their next use, the stainless steel worktable was spotless, and the shelves holding bottles of chemicals were neatly faced and well stocked. We did not find any dead bodies, thankfully, but we did find a bottle of Crown Royal and a Smith and Wesson .357 revolver in the director's desk.

"I can't believe this place hasn't been picked over," Thompson said as he searched the cupboards in a small kitchen. "Look at this."

He held up two boxes of Dixie Crystals sugar, one opened, one still sealed. "This stuff is like gold. Why do you think no one's been in here?"

I shrugged. "I guess even at the end of the world, people still avoid these kinds of places. Must be a psychological thing."

"I don't know about that. Being here doesn't bother me."

"Yeah, but you're on the run and surrounded by enemies. If you could hunker down somewhere else, would you still pick this place?"

He thought about it for a second before shaking his head. "No. I wouldn't."

After allowing the prisoners to relieve themselves outside, we freed their hands long enough to eat a meal, then emptied a small, windowless office down to the carpet and ushered them inside.

"If you want to live," I told them, "you'll take a seat and stay the fuck quiet. Do anything stupid, make too much noise, or even look at me in a manner I find displeasing, and I'll feed you to the walkers. Am I clear?"

"Can you at least cuff our hands in front of us?" one of the boys asked. "My shoulders are killing me."

I stepped further into the room and blasted him with a withering glare. "Let's get things straight between us, sweetheart. You were sent to kill me, and you would have done so if I had given you half a chance. So don't expect any fucking sympathy. You're alive right now because you are useful to me, but you're only useful so long as you remain cooperative. Being cooperative means keeping your fucking mouth shut until I tell you to speak. Which means if I hear anything else about your inconsequential physical discomforts, your shoulders won't be the only thing killing you. Got it?"

He looked down and gave a sullen nod.

I turned to Sanchez. "Keep an eye on them. I'll have someone relieve you in an hour. If the radio buzzes, have the old man talk to them. Make sure he doesn't try anything cute."

The Mexican nodded. "No problem."

I found Cole in the kitchen heating water over a Sterno stove. A handful of little single-serving MRE coffee packets lay on the counter next to him.

"Mind if I borrow your tablet?" I asked.

"Not at all," he said, handing it to me. "What's the plan for tonight?"

"Still working on it."

"Cool. You want some coffee?"

I rubbed my eyes and shook my head to clear it. "More than life itself."

*****

According to the old man we captured, the small but once-prosperous community of Brownsville had, less than twenty-four hours ago, fallen victim to a nighttime assault. The perpetrators of this crime were led by a man known only as Powell, who commanded a force of between twenty-five and forty mercenaries. They called themselves the Crow Hunters, ostensibly because they thought it sounded cool. From the way the old man described them, they were little more than gun-toting thugs.

Unlike Hollow Rock, Brownsville did not enjoy a high level of federal protection. The town's population was less than a fifth of Hollow Rock's, esteeming it as little more than a trading post in the government's eyes. They were still considered Union citizens and identified themselves as such, but did not have a military presence like some of the larger outposts. If they called for help the Army would have responded—most likely drawing troops from Hollow Rock—but the attack had come so unexpectedly the town never had a chance to muster an organized defense, much less request federal aid.

The assault on Brownsville had been planned long in advance, with many Blackmire guardsmen involved in the logistics—including the old man zip-tied in the room next to me. Tanner himself had hired the mercenaries, his intention being to annex Brownsville and expand his small trade empire. Because Brownsville was so small, he did not figure the Union would retaliate.

He figured wrong.

Thompson came into the room and took a seat across from me. "We have authorization."

I nodded. "Good. How about support?"

He held up empty hands. "All assets are otherwise engaged. That's what they told me. There's a big push right now to clear the infected out of Kansas. Central Command wants to send more settlers out there. Colorado Springs is getting overcrowded, and it's taxing the Army's resources."

I ran my fingers through my hair and lowered my forehead to the table. "Figures."

"Listen, Gabe. I heard something else while I was on the radio I think you need to know."

"I don't like the sound of that."

There was a moment of hesitation, then he said, "The Marine Corps has been disbanded."

My head shot up. "What?"

"They've been absorbed into the Army, along with the Air Force. The Marines are now the Army Expeditionary Corps, and the Air Force is once again the Army Air Corps."

"You have got to be kidding me. This better not be a joke."

He shook his head sadly. "Afraid not."

There was a little warm spot on the table when I lowered my head again. "I could give a fuck about the Air Force, but the Marines? What are they thinking?"

Cole chimed in. "They're probably thinking they don't have the resources to manage two armies, and putting everybody under the same umbrella streamlines things. Removes a lot of duplication."

I considered that for a minute or two, and had to admit the big gunner had a point. The country as a whole would probably be better off without all the recent dick measuring and infighting occurring between the three branches' chains of command. But that didn't mean I had to like it. "It still sucks."

I'm not sure which one of them patted me on the shoulder.

After allowing myself a brief but heartfelt pity party over the demise of my beloved Corps, I sat up and consulted the tablet again. Cole, Thompson, and Hicks joined me at the table and sipped their coffee while I worked.

"Okay," I said finally. "There's too much we don't know about Brownsville right now. We've all been there a few times, but we always slept in the caravan quarter. None of us have been inside the town proper. Right?"

I looked up to see them all nodding, then leaned over so I could shout through the doorway. "Hey Sancho, you ever been to Brownsville?"

"Not inside the wall."

"That's what I figured. All right, so the first thing we need to do is recon. We'll wait until a few hours after nightfall, and then Hicks and I will head out. You down, Hicks?"

"You know me, man. I'm always up for startin' trouble."

I grinned. The kid was really growing on me. "Excellent. Thompson, I need you, Cole, and the Pride of Hermosillo over there to keep an eye on the prisoners. I know it's boring, but it's important. We're going to need their testimony if we want the feds to start taking these insurgents around here seriously."

Thompson leaned forward and lowered his voice. "Testimony? What makes you think they'll say a word? Even if we can get them brought up on charges, which is a big fucking *if* by the way, it'll be our word against theirs. They'll keep their mouths shut and walk."

"Yes, but they don't know that. And as long as we don't tell them, that ignorance works in our favor."

Thompson considered it for a moment, then one side of his face began to slowly tilt upward. "If you can get Sheriff Elliott to play ball..."

"I always said you were a smart man, Thompson."

He sat back in his chair. "Okay. I guess we're on prisoner detail tonight."

Cole downed the last of his coffee, grimaced, and picked up his SAW. "I'll go set up a perimeter. Holla if you need me."

"We should probably try to get some sleep," Hicks said. "Gonna be a long night."

I stood up and stretched, spine popping *alla marcia*. "Best idea I've heard all day."

FORTY-TWO

Despite the clouds obscuring the moon, the night was illuminating.

Hicks and I returned just before dawn, the batteries in our NVGs all but spent. The infected had been out in force around Brownsville, making an already tough and dangerous task that much more difficult. My right arm was tired from swinging my falcata, and I had used nearly all of the preloaded rounds for my Sig Mosquito. Hicks and I were both tired, dirty, and more than a little chilled, and I wanted nothing more than to melt some snow, wipe myself down with a cloth, and sleep for ten hours.

But first, debrief and planning.

"It looks like they killed most of the men," I said, after everyone had gathered in the funeral home's little kitchen. The prisoners were asleep, but I had asked Hicks to watch them anyway. He didn't need a mission brief, being that half the plan was his idea. "The teenagers and children are still alive," I continued, "but I think it's only a matter of time until they're sold into slavery, along with the women."

"Jesus Christ," Thompson said, face darkening with anger. The others didn't look any happier.

I found a piece of paper and had the soldiers gather round while I sketched a map. "Most of the hostages are being held here in this gutted-out garage. We counted three guards on duty, rotating in four-hour shifts. These here," I pointed at two squares drawn near the western wall. "are bunkhouses. The Crow Hunters are using them as barracks; it's where most of them sleep. Over here," I pointed to another square in the middle of town. "is where they're holding the town's leadership hostage and storing their generators and communications equipment. Before we do anything else, we need to secure this building. But we have to do it quietly. If the troops wake up, we're going to have a hell of a fight on our hands."

"So how do you want to handle it?" Thompson asked.

"We'll do it in three phases. For the first one, Hicks and I will scale the wall on the western side. I'll take out the guard in this tower here, and Hicks will proceed to where the women and children are being held. He'll take out the guards there, and I'll use Sanchez's sniper carbine to take out the ones posted on the wall. When that's done, I'll radio you three and have Hicks let you in through the western gate. From there, you'll take up position near the bunkhouses. Be on the lookout for stragglers around town, these guys don't exactly enforce the strictest discipline. Some of them might still be out drinking."

Sanchez's dark eyes flashed in anticipation as he nodded. "No problem."

"Once in position, stand by and wait for orders. Hicks and I will assault the communications building and make contact with what's left of the town's leaders. That's phase two. With any luck, I can take this Powell character alive and ... *convince* him to lure Blackmire and his men to Brownsville."

"Whoa, wait a minute," Cole broke in. "Since when is fighting Blackmire and his people the goal here? I thought we were just saving the hostages?"

"We are," I said. "But this Blackmire son of a bitch has a personal vendetta against me, and he's not going to stop until one of us it dead. All the trouble we've been having in Hollow Rock lately—Sean Montford's murder, the burned bodies in that cabin, the ghoul wranglers, the assassination attempt on Mayor Stone—it all traces back to him. And it's not going to stop unless we do something about it."

He was silent for a long moment, then said. "Yeah, I guess you got a point there. But what's this personal vendetta? What's his beef with you?"

I shook my head. "It's a long story, and not relevant to the situation. The bottom line is he's a threat to Union citizens, and Central Command has authorized us to take him out. I'm authorized to render assistance. This is no longer about doing the job Eric paid you for. This is about following orders. Thompson is technically in charge here, but I have more combat experience than all of you combined. You do this my way, and I'll get you all home alive, provided you don't do anything stupid. Fair enough?"

Cole glanced at his fellow soldiers. He got no argument. "Fair enough."

"Good. So anyway, while Hicks and I are taking the comms building, I want you three to keep an eye on the barracks. If it looks like they've been alerted, hit 'em with the LAWs, SAW, claymores, grenades, and the goddamn kitchen sink. Show no mercy. Kill every one of them. Can I assume you're all competent enough to establish your own firing positions without my direction?"

Thompson nodded grimly. "That we are."

"Good. When Hicks and I are finished with the comms building, I'll give the order to commence the assault. That will be phase three. If possible, Hicks and I will render assistance, but I can't guarantee we'll be able to get there in time. Are you three okay with handling the final assault yourselves?"

Sanchez laughed and slapped me on the arm. "Do you even have to ask?"

Not for the first time, I was glad he was on my side.

*****

Different communities survive in different ways.

Hollow Rock is a major agricultural hub. The town survived the Outbreak much more intact than most places in not only Tennessee, but around the world. As a result, the town's population now numbers over a thousand, including original residents and people who have drifted in over the years. With that many people, farming is not only feasible, it is highly profitable.

Brownsville had its share of agriculture, but it was barely enough to keep the town alive. One bad winter, one poor harvest, could mean starvation. So the year after the Outbreak,

431

the town's leaders took a gamble and planted only the grains used in the distillation of alcohol. That winter, they brewed up a massive batch of grain liquor and sent out trade caravans to find customers.

They sold out their inventory in a month.

Although they were out of booze, they were flush with food. More than enough to get the entire town comfortably through the winter. Since then, they had expanded their operations to include grain purchased from other communities, scaled up their distilling operations, and were doing a cracking turn of business distributing booze.

At least until the Crow Hunters showed up.

Consequently, the guards were drunk.

At least three of them were anyway, I wasn't so sure about the other two. As I crouched behind a tree, watching them through my FLIR scope, I had to shake my head at their lack of discipline. What was the point of posting watchmen if they were wasted?

"You ready?" I whispered to Hicks.

"Yep."

"Let's go then."

We advanced slowly, being careful of every footfall. I held my rifle loosely, falcata gripped in my left hand. There were a few infected between us and the wall, and no way to avoid them. I glanced to my right and saw Hick's glaring white heat signature in much the same posture as mine, left hand gripping a short, heavy bladed spear—his preferred weapon for hand-to-hand combat against the undead.

The infected were blind in the darkness, but it didn't stop them from pinpointing us and shambling in our direction. There were six of them, moving in a tight little knot, feet crunching through the hard-packed snow. I raised the sniper carbine Sanchez had loaned me—which was really just a heavily modified M-16—balanced the barrel on the flat of my sword, and sent three rounds downrange. The only sound was the clack of the chamber as spent cartridges were ejected and new ones loaded. All three rounds found their targets, ending the pseudo-lives of an equal number of walkers. Three left.

Hicks advanced ahead of me and speared the closest one with an upward thrust, cleaving it's soft palate and penetrating its brain. Before it could slump to the ground, he jerked his weapon free and fell into a fighting stance. I circled left and hit the next one with a backhanded slash, sending the top half of its cranium spinning away into the night. Just as I was about to go after the last one, Hicks changed his grip on his spear and stepped into a forward thrust. The long blade crunched through the ghoul's sinus cavity with terrific force, an inch or two of blade protruding from the back of the creature's skull. As it fell, Hicks wrenched the blade free.

"Nice one," I whispered. He accepted the compliment, as usual, with a silent nod.

There were more infected around, but none close enough to bother us. We could make it over the wall long before they were within striking distance. At the treeline, we crouched behind snow-covered brush and waited until the closest guard wandered tipsily away. I briefly considered shooting him, but decided it was too risky. Better to take the tower first, then pick them off with impunity.

Hicks twirled a length of rope with a large knot tied in the end and let it fly. Drawing down on the rope, he wedged the knot between two large palisade stakes and went nimbly up. I waited until he was over, then followed.

Once over the wall, I found myself on a narrow catwalk ten feet above the ground. Hicks crouched a few feet away, rifle up, scanning for hostiles. After a moment, he gave me an all clear signal and we proceeded toward the guard tower on the southeast corner of town.

When we were close to twenty feet away, I stopped and aimed the carbine at a man-shaped blaze of white standing with his back to me. The tower was not very high, only five feet above the palisade wall, making for an easy shot. Hicks aimed his weapon as well.

"Ready?" I whispered.

"Yep. On your mark."

"On three. Five, four, three."

Two muted cracks. The heavy carbine in my hands barely twitched. As the guard above me slumped to the planks under his feet, I decided I could get used to this thing.

"Okay, Hicks." I said. "Take off. Happy hunting."

"Will do. I'll let you know when I'm in position."

The ladder was a bit on the rickety side, but held firmly enough for me to climb up. When my head came level with the tower's floor, I found myself staring directly into the face of the dead guard. Even through the pale luminescence of FLIR, I could see the gaping hole in his forehead.

Sorry pal. You picked the wrong team.

I hauled his body upright and placed it in a corner, out of the way. That done, I took a knee and propped the carbine on a handrail, taking aim at the guard on the opposite tower to the northwest. It was the one closest to where the hostages were being held, and I didn't want the guard there sounding the alarm if he noticed Hicks dispatching his comrades. Taking careful aim, I watched him for a minute or two, timing his movements. Like most people, he had a pattern. Probably wasn't even aware of it.

Walk to one side of the tower. Stop. Weight on the left foot. Count to five. Weight shifts to the right foot. Another five count. Turn, walk to the other side, repeat. Always the five seconds per foot. His posture was relaxed, but not wobbly like his intoxicated friends. Not a drinker, then. Not bored or anxious either, just sort of resigned. The look of a man who has not long ago taken the watch and made his peace with the hours of boredom that lay ahead.

Somewhere, deep down in the suppressed part of me that hates what I have become, I felt pity for the man. He had no idea the boredom he felt would be his last emotion. Whatever ponderings drifted through his mind to pass the time, they would be his last thoughts. I hoped they were at least pleasant ones.

After three repetitions, I had his timing down. He turned, walked to the side facing away from me. Left foot. One, two, three, four, five. Wait for the shift, let the air out, squeeze...

-crack-

And down he goes.

Next target. Search the other two guard towers. Both are empty. Shift to the north wall. There, at the corner, turning around, heading back the way he came. Drunken wobble to the gait. Strained tension in his steps, feet falling a little too closely.

I watched him take a guilty look around, then step to the edge of the palisade and begin working at the front of his pants. A moment later, a pale, thin stream of white began to flow from his groin toward the ground. He died with his dick in his hands, tumbling head first over the wall to the ground below.

"Shit..."

Now I had to work fast. The walkers would be on him soon, and the noise was bound to alert the last two guards.

The south wall was clear, so I moved to the western one. Took aim. Fired twice. Watched him fall and lay still. One left. I spotted him on the east wall, walking toward me. I moved to another handrail and sighted in. He was close enough there was no question of my aim. One round did the trick, sending him over backward like a felled tree.

My earpiece crackled. "In position," Hicks said.

"Copy. Engage."

There was silence for a few moments. Then I heard the sighing of wind through trees, the flapping and banging of unlatched shutters in the town below, the rattle of ice crystals skittering over frost-crusted rooftops. I raised my NVGs and looked upward at the night sky, blinking at the change of spectrum. Heavy clouds stretched from one horizon to the other, a half-moon shining through a narrow break in a ghostly halo of silver light. A smattering of stars broke through then vanished again, light from distant celestial furnaces that spent a billion years in transit, only to fall upon a place of slaughter.

Sorry you wasted the trip.

Another crackle. "Targets are down. All clear. I made contact with the hostages. The door is unlocked in case they have to run for it, but they know to stay put for now."

"Copy," I replied. "Commence with phase two."

"Roger."

I climbed down from the tower, reloaded, and headed for the center of town.

FORTY-THREE

I had seen the pile of bodies the night before, but it had been from a distance. Just a large, slowly cooling jumble of white, the outlines and creases only vaguely definable as human beings. I didn't look at them long, then, just catalogued the information and moved on. But now, standing less than thirty feet away, the effect was far more visceral. There may have been as many as a hundred bodies, some large and clearly identifiable as adults, others smaller.

Much smaller.

Rather than the white and gray infrared signatures I had seen last night, they were now bathed in an eerie green glow, and in greater resolution. After finishing my bloody work on the tower, I had switched from FLIR to standard night vision, which is better for the close quarters fighting I expected in the comms building. But now, knowing what lay before me would be indelibly burned into my memory, I wished I hadn't.

"Sons of bitches," Hicks muttered, voice dripping with uncharacteristic venom. It was the most emotion I had ever seen him display.

"Come on," I said. "Let's keep moving."

As we darted from building to building, I heard brief chatter between Cole, Thompson, and Sanchez. After Hicks let them in through the west gate, they proceeded according to plan and set up firing positions around the Crow Hunters' bunkhouses. Between their grenades, Cole's SAW, three LAW rockets, and their rifles, if things got ugly, it would not go well for the enemy troops.

Hicks and I rounded a corner and found ourselves standing a block away from the comms building. I switched back to FLIR briefly and spotted two guards, one posted at each entrance. After a few hand signals to Hicks, we split up and approached from opposite sides. I found a good spot to take my shot from, switched back to night vision, and crouched down, waiting. A few seconds later, I heard the click of a mike being keyed.

"In position. Ready to engage."

"Copy. Three count, then fire."

As soon as I released the mike button, I counted three, two, one, then fired three shots. Being as close as I was, headshots were no trouble at all. The bullets transferred a large section of the guard's upper cranium to the wall behind him just before he stiffened and fell flat on what was left of his face. I heard a faint clacking coming from Hicks' side, then, "Target down."

"Copy," I replied. "Move in."

I tried the door on my side and found it locked. Hicks' voice buzzed in my ear and reported the same on his side.

"Gotta be a key," I replied. After searching the body thoroughly, I came up empty. "Any luck?" I asked.

"No joy," Hicks radioed back.

I cursed, then said, "Don't suppose you brought your lock picks, did you?"

"As a matter of fact, I did."

I crossed over to his side of the building, sticking to the back alley, and waited while he worked on the door. Although I am no stranger to lock picking, I had stupidly neglected to bring my own set along.

Won't be making that mistake again.

The lock clicked. Hicks nodded to me and we stacked up beside the door, one on each side. He pointed to himself and held up a finger, indicating he wanted to take point. I nodded, trusting his abilities would carry him through if someone was waiting on the other side. He held up three fingers and counted down—three, two, one, and we moved.

We entered a small lobby, unoccupied. A quick sweep, check behind the desk, all clear. Two doors in the back and a staircase. I stacked up at the door on my right, tried the handle, found it unlocked. A quick push, and we were in a small bathroom, the kind with just a toilet and a sink. As I shut the door, I noticed the little woman in a skirt, a straight line, then the stick man. Unisex.

The next door led to a short hallway that wound around the bathroom and emerged into a wide open room. Desks to my left and right, support columns down the middle. No sign of anyone. The door at the other side of the room turned out to be the emergency exit. The first floor was clear. Now for the stairway.

On the way up I heard a voice drift down, bleary, groggy, just emerged from sleep. "The fuck is going on down there. That you, Tony?"

On a hunch, I asked. "Hey is Powell up there?"

Sound of feet on steps, thumping downward, coming closer to the landing, still out of sight. "That's Captain Powell to you, shitbird. Fuck that up again and I'll take you up to see him personally. Now what do you-"

The next words never made it out of his mouth. His eyes flashed wide as he rounded the corner and saw two armed men in night vision goggles waiting for him on the stairs. Our rifles cracked four times each, all hitting center of mass. A mess of red blossoms appeared on the front of his shirt. I caught him as he fell, eyes already going blank, and eased him to the ground.

We proceeded up the rest of the way, turning the corner into a long hallway with two rooms to the left, three to the right. Management offices, looked like. The big wigs up here, and the worker bees down below. According to the dilapidated sign over the building's front entrance, this had been an accountant's office once upon a time. The layout supported that claim.

As we crept down the hallway, I heard footsteps coming from a room ahead. The door was open. A voice preceded a pair of hands clutching an AK-47. "Sergeant, what's going on out there?"

The voice had an air of authority, the kind that asks a question and expects a prompt response, accustomed to giving orders rather than receiving them. Shifting my point of aim, I tilted the sniper carbine sideways, aimed through BUIS mounted at a forty-five degree angle from the scope, and fired two rounds. Both hit the rifle's foregrip just inches from the gunman's hands. With a yelp, he dropped the gun, and darted backward. Hicks and I were across the hallway in a heartbeat. I arrived first, weapon leveled. Three men on the ground and one standing, still shaking his hands, all emerging from various states of sleep and reaching for weapons. I took a knee so Hicks could fire over my head. Four seconds later, our mags were empty, and it was just me, Hicks, and the man whose rifle I had shot. He held up his hands.

"Wait, okay? Just wait."

"Are you Powell?"

He hesitated, unsure how to answer. I kept the gun trained on him, not moving an inch. After a few more seconds he nodded. "Yes."

"If you're lying, we'll know soon enough. Now where are the hostages?"

He sputtered for a moment, then finally raised a shaky hand and pointed at the room across the hall. "Over there. They're still alive, I didn't-"

"Shut up. Not another word until I tell you to speak. Hicks, keep him covered. If he tries anything, kill him."

The man swallowed hard, acquiring an acute case of the shakes. Staring down the barrel of a rifle whilst surrounded by dead comrades tends to have that effect on people.

I crossed the hall and opened the door cautiously. The room was empty save for an old-fashioned steam radiator on the opposite wall, and two people chained to the pipes on either side. They were bound and gagged, staring wide-eyed in the darkness, a mixture of fear and hope on their faces. I borrowed Hicks' bolt cutters and cut their chains, then parted their restraints with my Ka-bar.

"Are you with the government?" one of them asked. An older man, early fifties, bald, thick gray beard, stink of body odor and fear. The other was a woman with close cropped hair, early forties, lean and weathered face. As she stood up, I realized she was over six feet tall and built like a distance runner. There was a gold sheriff's star embroidered on her tan shirt.

"Yes," I replied. "Are you all right?"

"We're fine," the old man said as I helped him to his feet. "What about the others? Have you seen them?"

"The ones still alive are safe for now."

"How did you find out what happened here?" the woman asked. "We never even got a chance to send out a distress call."

"I'll explain later. Right now, we need to get you out of here. You're Joseph Steinman, right? You're in charge around here."

The old man looked surprised. "That's right. How did you know? Have we met?"

"And you're Sheriff Ann Tucker, correct?"

It was her turn to look surprised. "Yes. How…"

"The name's Garrett. Maybe you've heard of me."

Her eyes widened further. "Gabriel Garrett? The salvage man over in Hollow Rock?"

A grin. "I haven't always been in the salvage business. Hicks, gag and cuff that fucker and let's move."

"I'm on it."

Less than a minute later, we emerged back onto the street. Checked both sides. All clear. I drew my pistol and held it out to Steinman, motioning for Hicks to loan his to Sheriff Tucker. She immediately flipped the safety off and pointed it at Powell's face.

"You son of a bitch."

He whimpered and went to the ground, eyes squeezed shut, terrified incoherence emitting from behind his gag. Only Hicks' iron grip on his zip-tied wrists kept him from bolting. I put a hand under the gun and lifted it skyward, earning an angry glare from Sheriff Tucker.

"Don't," I said. "We need him alive. Don't worry, he'll pay for what he's done."

The glare lasted a moment longer before subsiding. "He damn well better." The hand came down slowly, finger off the trigger. Turning to Hicks, I said, "Go get the other hostages and lead them out of here. Use the north gate. I'll radio as soon as I can."

I half expected him to protest, or question my intentions, but he surprised me by simply nodding and giving a gruff, "Will do." Then turned and led the others away.

When they were out of sight, I keyed my radio. "This is Garrett. Everyone still in position?"

They answered according to protocol, Thompson, Cole, then Sanchez. All stations standing by.

"All right, then," I said. "Stay put. I'm on my way."

*****

Hope for the best, prepare for the worst.

It is an adage ingrained in me from a young age, and it has never steered me wrong.

When I conducted my recon the night before, I counted thirty-one men including Powell. But that was before the fighting started. So subtract the leader, the five guards on the wall, the three guards watching the hostages, and the six we killed at the comms building, and that leaves 16. Nearly half their original force. Which meant my men and I were now only outnumbered four to one.

Not the best odds, under most circumstances.

But considering most, if not all, of those men were in various states of drunkenness, and sleeping to boot, we had on our side the factor which allows small forces to defeat larger ones, which can turn the tide of even the most desperate of battles.

Surprise.

Two bunkhouses. Sixteen troops. How to proceed?

Hope for the best, prepare for the worst.

Cole was in position on a rooftop, SAW dialed in, two LAW rockets lying next to him. Sanchez and Thompson were with me, stacked up outside the door to the southernmost barracks. I had studied the barracks through my FLIR scope, and by cranking the device to its highest, battery-draining setting, discerned the outlines of ten men. Meaning the other six were in the northern barracks.

So check the weapons, exchange a few terse sentences, evaluate the lanes of fire, check the weapons again—rounds chambered? safeties off? suppressors fitted properly?—and stack up.

The door did not have a lock. Just a simple wooden latch, enough to hold it shut when the wind blew and nothing more. I raised a careful hand and unlatched it, then swung it open. Sanchez was the point man, so he went in first. I followed close behind, Thompson nipping at my heels.

There is a sense of unreality to these things. The progression that comes with time and practice mitigates but does not entirely destroy the giddy adrenaline rush, the sense of crossing a threshold when the first sleeping target is sighted and the trigger is pulled and the blood is spilled, the certainty of it, the finality, the fruition of guile and malicious intent made manifest, to wield the power of life and death and choose death. We moved silently, purposefully. Take aim, head shots, two to be sure. Hear the clacking, the metallic pinging of shell casings bouncing on wooden planks. Hear the death rattles, the spasmodic shuffling of feet under wool blankets.

End of the room. Last target is awake, mouth opening, but the hands are fast and sure and he is dead before the warning comes out. Beat him by a fraction of a second. On such things the fates of men and nations rest.

"Clear."

"Clear."

"Clear."

Our boots left tread-pattern prints in expanding black pools as we left, clinging to soles and souls and leaving gradually fading tracks. We repeated the procedure. Stacked up around the door. Again, I reached out, left handed, palm turned toward the wall.

And then the wall exploded around my hand.

We fell back, rifles up, firing through the wall, backpedaling as fast as we could. *Must have heard us in there*, I thought dimly. My right heel caught something in the pavement and I went over backward, landing with a grunt. When I put my hand to the ground to pick myself up, it occurred to me I couldn't feel it. There was a great pressure there, a numbness, a slowly building heat. It still responded to commands however, so I put it back on the foregrip and kept firing.

Cole's SAW came to life across the street, bright orange fireball around the muzzle, bullets ripping into the barracks like rain. The chamber on my rifle clanged open on the last round. I was slow on the reload, numb left hand fumbling at the mag carrier, unable to get a decent grip. Then something brushed the end of my ring finger and a streak of molten fire shot up my arm. The pain roared to life, blinding, searing, relentless. Not a throb, but a howling torch where my finger used to be. Giving up on that hand, I let my rifle dangle and pulled a mag with my right. Gritting my teeth, I gripped the weapon with my left, shoved home the P-mag, and brought the stock back up to my shoulder. As I began to squeeze the trigger, I noticed that the night had gone silent. The SAW no longer chattered. The distinctive bark of AKs had departed. No clack-clang of suppressed M-4s.

My mouth moved before my brain had a chance to catch up. "Move in. Make sure they're all down."

There was a brief hesitation, a gathering of breath and wits, quick self-pat-downs, making sure there were no perforations. It occurred to me to check my left hand. I decided it could wait.

As I approached the door, a warmness began to spread on my right side, just below the border of the Dragon Skin vest. The muscles felt tight there, twitching, like an overworked hamstring on the verge of a cramp. Whatever was going on down there, it wasn't good.

Thompson went through first, firing at anything that moved. He heard me behind him and broke left, so I broke right. Caught sight of a man trying to stuff his guts back into his abdomen. Ended his misery. Sanchez moved past me with a noticeable limp. Four more bodies on my side. No way they were alive, but I gave them each two in the head anyway.

"Clear."

"Clear."

I cast a look around, just to be sure. "Clear."

Sanchez raised his NVGs and walked over to me. "I'm hit."

"How bad?"

"Not sure. Got me in the lower leg."

"Well, you're still walking, so it can't be that bad."

"Didn't feel it for a while there," he said grimacing. "But I'm getting around to it."

"That's how it usually goes." I reached down and wormed my fingers under my gear down to my undershirt. Warm, sticky blood held the fabric against my skin. I probed it, ignoring the hot agony it caused, and felt a six-inch groove through the flesh, deeper towards the back. The wound was pretty ragged back there, but not life-threatening. Some stitches and iodine and a little fresh air, and it would be just another artifact in the collection.

"Holy shit," Sanchez muttered and clicked on his flashlight. He pointed it in my direction.

"What?"

"Gabe, your hand."

I raised it and looked at it. There was a noticeable gap.

"Well that's not good," I said, and passed out.

FORTY-FOUR

Vague memories of a hand slapping my face, being lifted up, grunt and curses. Jeez, he's a heavy son of a bitch.

There had been warning signs. A man can't just starve for a week and become severely dehydrated and expect to recover in a day or two. The legs didn't move as quickly. There was a little tremor in the hands, a tightness around the eyes. It took a few extra breaths to recover after a sprint. The sweat came quickly from the least exertion and had the close, humid, clammy texture of a fever. I had moments of forgetfulness, which should have been a big red flag flapping agitatedly in gale-force winds.

But I ignored it. It's mind over matter, you see. If you don't mind, it don't matter. This works just fine in theory, but in reality, disrupting the body's processes of breaking down raw materials for nutrients and utilizing those chemicals, enzymes, proteins, and minerals to build new cells has severe consequences. The fat stores disappear. Muscle tissue is cannibalized. ATP is at a premium. There is very little energy on demand, and if you use up too much of it, the body hits the kill switch.

So I lay on a table, and woke up with the sun in my face. Thompson was there, staring at a picture of his family. He had showed it to me, once. Pretty red-headed wife. A baby who was now, as I understood, three years old. Even at six months he bore a strong resemblance to his father. Ethan was different in the picture as well. *Ethan? First name, now? I must be really loopy.*

The kid's name was Aiden. The wife's name was Andrea. They lived in a house, Fort Bragg, four bedroom. Justin Schmidt and his girlfriend Emily and their baby son, Joshua. All under one roof. The ache on Ethan's face could have been one of Rembrandt's famous sketches.

"Hey," I croaked.

He tucked the picture in a clear plastic case, then stowed it safely in a chest pocket. "Hey yourself. How are you feeling?"

"Like shit."

He nodded. "I'm not surprised. How much do you remember?"

"Not much."

He filled me in.

Sending Hicks outside the wall with the hostages turned out to be a waste of time. But they were all safely back now, engaged with piecing together as much of their shattered lives as they could.

While Brownsville's surviving residents cleaned up, Hicks and Sanchez took the truck back to the funeral home, retrieved the trussed-up prisoners, and turned them over to Sheriff Tucker. They were currently in lockup, awaiting their fate.

There had been some radio chatter. Hicks, quick thinking fellow that he is, informed Powell that his continued presence among the living hinged upon his performance convincing Blackmire that everything was five by five. He succeeded, and a contingent from said den of iniquity was inbound. ETA tomorrow morning.

"Is Tanner with them?"

Ethan looked confused. "Who?"

"Sorry. Blackmire, the leader. Is he coming?"

"Not sure. Ask Hicks, he might know."

I lifted myself up slowly, wincing first at the pain in my side, then in my hand as it pressed against the table.

"Shit."

Thompson stood up and crossed the room. "Careful. I stitched it up as best I could, but it's going to hurt for a while."

I held up my left hand and stared silently. The left ring finger started at the knuckle connecting it to my palm just like it always had. It proceeded upward to the second knuckle without interruption. Beyond the second knuckle, there was a bit of an oblong nub swathed in bandages and compression tape, and that was all. End of the line.

"Motherfucker."

"At least you're right handed."

I tore my eyes away and let the hand fall to my lap. "That's something, I guess."

"Be careful with it, Gabe. I cleaned it up, but I don't have any antibiotics. It could very easily become infected. Same with the stitches on your side."

I nodded. "How's the Pride of Hermosillo?"

"He'll make a full recovery. Bullet tore out a chunk of is inner calf, right about here." He tapped a finger against the appropriate spot on my leg. "He'll have a limp for a while, but with a little physical therapy, he should eventually be a hundred percent."

"That's a relief." I pushed off the table and stood wobbling for a moment, then felt a little strength return. "Got any water?"

"Sure." He fetched a canteen from his pack and handed it to me. I drank slowly in little sips until it was empty. Paced the room while I did it, working a little mobility back into my stiff right side, trying to ignore the throbbing in my hand.

"You were awake when I stitched it, you know." Ethan had resumed his seat by the window.

"Was I?"

"Yep. Hicks loaned you his belt to bite down on. Didn't have any local anesthetic. You cursed at me bad enough to wilt flowers."

I searched the hard drive, but came up empty. "I don't remember that."

"You were pretty out of it. The others had to hold you down. You gave Cole a pretty good shiner."

I closed my eyes and pinched the skin between them. "Sorry about that."

He smiled faintly and waved a hand. "Don't worry. I'm sure he'll forgive you. As for me, I've seen a heck of a lot worse."

Looking at the thousand yards between his eyes and where his gaze came to rest, I believed him.

*****

The enemy was inbound, so I made the most of the day.

The first step was a town meeting. I briefed Steinman on the situation and told him what I needed him to say. He gathered everyone in a rough wooden building that served as town hall and did as requested.

While he spoke, I watched the faces of the women, boys, teenage girls, and the younger children. It reminded me of pictures in American history books, the documented history of the old west, photos of lean, hard-faced, unsmiling people in frontier attire. Only now they were not dampened by primitive photography or the grainy texture of a printed page. They were real, vivid, in high definition, every haggard line, puckered scar, smudge of dirt, and dark angry gaze. They listened first to Steinman, then to me. I told them what I needed from them and asked for volunteers.

Nearly every hand in the room came up.

There were a few babies and toddlers too young to understand what was going on, but other than that, I had my army.

"All right then," I said, trying my best to sound confident and determined. "We have work to do."

*****

If Powell was bothered by the demise of his men, he didn't show it.

He stayed on the radio, exchanging chatter with Blackmire, very humble, very servile. Yes sir, no sir, whatever you need sir. I promised him if he cooperated he would not be prosecuted since his men were dead. The relief on his face was nauseating.

The Crow Hunters had brought in generators—likely stolen from a Phoenix Initiative shipment—and plenty of fuel, which we used to power the radio and antenna array on the truck. Hicks parked the big vehicle behind a square of buildings so Blackmire's men would not see it when they rode into town.

When all preparations were complete, I found Sheriff Tucker and gave her a report.

"You seem to know your business," she said, head tilted to the side, intelligent eyes probing mine. She stepped closer, just within arm's reach, taking a sounding. "You know, I don't think I ever said thank you for saving us."

Against my will, my eyes tracked to the other side of town and the frozen pile of corpses that had once been husbands, uncles, brothers, nephews, grandfathers, and sons. "I just wish I could have gotten here sooner."

Her hand was gentle on my arm. "Still. Thank you."

I nodded silently, taking in the firm planes of her face. She was neither ugly not pretty. Sort of severe. Then she smiled, and she was ten years younger. "I put you up in the tavern, over there." She pointed. "The owner's wi-…well, I guess she's the owner now. She'll have her girls draw you a bath. There'll be a warm bed for you tonight."

"You have no idea how much I appreciate that."

The hand squeezed. "It's the least we could do. Come on, I'll walk you over there."

I followed her to the tavern and stepped inside. A fifty-ish woman and several girls in their early twenties were busy cleaning the place. Wiping tables, mopping the floor, restocking the shelves behind the bar, setting overturned chairs upright. The smell of stew wafted from the kitchen, causing my stomach to remind me how long it had been since I last ate. The older woman, who I assumed to be the new owner, came out from the behind the bar and offered me a hand.

"You're him? The one who killed the Crow Hunters?"

I shook the hand and found it surprisingly strong. The eyes behind it were red-rimmed from tears shed not very long ago. I was reminded again of those early pioneers, those hard people who buried husbands, wives, and children by the side of the trail, said a few words over them, then hitched up their horses, slapped the reins, and rode on undeterred. "I had help."

She took me in for a few seconds, looking me up and down. "You look formidable enough."

"I have been accused of that from time to time."

A smile showed itself, albeit a sad one. "Will you have a drink?"

"What do you trade?"

It was a common question, asked far and wide by traders and Runners and everyone with a good or service to purvey. But this was the first time in my experience anyone had ever taken offense to it.

"You drink for free, here," she said sternly. "You and your men. And you eat for free, and whenever you come around, you'll get a room and a bath for free. And if I hear one damn word of argument about it, I whop you upside the head with a frying pan. Do I make myself clear?"

I kept my face neutral and nodded respectfully. "Yes ma'am."

"Penny. The name's Penelope, but everybody around here calls me Penny. You will too."

"Yes Mrs. Penny."

"That's the right attitude. Now have a seat, soldier. I'll go get your drink and have some food brought out to you in just a little while."

She bustled off. I briefly considered correcting her on the distinction between soldiers and Marines, but thought better of it. I have not survived two decades of near-constant violence by being stupid.

I did as ordered.

FORTY-FIVE

The food was good, but the bath was better. I emerged from the tub, then dried, shaved, ran a comb through the no-longer-regulation-length hair, and felt like a new man.

Despite the pain in my side and hand, sleep came quickly. I was out by eight thirty. Consequently, I awoke promptly at four-thirty in the morning, refreshed and as ready for what lay ahead as a man can get.

In the dining room, a single candle burned at a table near the door. If not for that lone pool of orange-yellow illumination, the room would have been pitch black.

Outlined in the light was the figure of a young man, lean, a bit on the tall side, deceptively broad through the shoulders, the kind that looks 180 but is closer to 200. I threaded my way through the rows of tables and stopped, looking over his shoulder. There was a book in front of him. He had opened it to the first page, the blank one before you get to the front matter where autographs go if you happen to meet the author. There was a dedication written in neat, flowing script. I recognized the handwriting.

For my soldier, my heart, my warrior-poet.

Happy birthday.

M.

He noted my presence and closed the book.

"The Collected Poems of Rudyard Kipling."

A nod. "He's one of the greats."

"Where did Miranda get it?"

The blue eyes were startled. "How'd you know?"

"Miranda's a special girl. I make it a point to look after her."

The surprise diminished, replaced by resignation. "It's only been a few months, but things have moved pretty quickly between us."

"Do you love her?"

He looked at the candle, ran his fingertips over the flame, and nodded. "Yes. More than I've ever loved anyone. My old man used to tell me when you find the right one, you just know. I always thought he was full of shit."

"But not anymore?"

"Nope."

I sat down across from him and moved the candle to the left so I could see him better. "Can I ask you a question? Slightly off topic."

"Sure."

"Who trained you?"

He covered it well, but I caught it. A shift in the eyes, a pause in the movement of hands over leather-bound hardcover, a flicker of tension in the shoulders. He gave a casual shrug. "I've been in the Army for over two years now. Along the way, I figured out the guys that work hardest at being good soldiers tend to live longer. So I improved."

The delivery was smooth, but it lacked a certain note of sincerity. Like the kind of thing that is easy because it is well practiced. "Don't bullshit me, kid. This ain't my first rodeo. I can smell it from a mile away."

The eyes shifted again, narrowed slightly. "What are you drivin' at?"

"You move like a guy I used to know in Force Recon. You can sleep sitting up; I've seen you do it. You handle a carbine like a Green Beret. Your knowledge of land navigation is impeccable. You apply camouflage better than most Marine snipers. I've fought with Navy SEALS that couldn't clear a

454

room or execute a dynamic entry as smoothly as you. You shoot as well as Eric Riordan, and that's saying something. You're as comfortable fighting at night, wearing NVGs, as you are in daylight. If I didn't know better, Specialist Caleb Theophilus Hicks, I'd say you've been training since you were old enough to walk."

I leaned forward, then, and lowered my voice. "Or maybe I don't know better."

All pretense evaporated. The eyes became clear and shrewd. The sleepy, lazy expression sharpened, as though carved from granite. He went so completely, utterly still, I began to wonder if he was real, or if I was dreaming the whole thing.

"What about you, Gabriel Garrett?" he said. "I have an inkling as to the training marines get, and what I've seen from you is way beyond that. Why don't you let me in on some of your secrets, huh? You know, since we're sharing."

I smiled and sat back in my chair. "Point taken."

Silence hung heavy between us for a long moment. We made no eye contact, watching the flame flicker and dance atop the little beeswax candle. The wind picked up outside, scraping ice along the walls and shaking the rafters. The tavern protested with a chorus of creaks and groans. A bird began chirping somewhere beyond the front door, a clear, melodious trill in the oppressive dark.

"Gonna be a long day," Hicks said finally.

"That it is. I should probably start waking people up." I stood up and stretched, wishing like hell I wasn't out of instant coffee.

"You ever wonder if this is all gonna end some day?"

I looked down to see Hicks gazing thoughtfully at the cold night beyond a window. "What do you mean?"

"All the fighting and killing. Seems to me we'd all be a lot better off if we just agreed to respect each other's dignity and work together so everyone can get by. That'd be the sensible thing to do. The rational thing."

"That's the problem, Caleb. Reason and sensibility are precious commodities, and in short supply. And every once in a while, in order to keep the folks willing to work for a living safe, guys like you and me have to engage in a little irrationality ourselves. People have lots of words for it. Duty, justice, self-defense, vengeance, murder. But in the end its all the same. It's killing, plain and simple. Whether it's right or wrong is entirely a question of perspective. Kill a man in anger, and you're a criminal. Kill a man for your country, and you're a hero. Either way, the guy on the other side of the equation is just as dead. You want to know what I call it? Necessary. That's what. I care about good people. I want them to live in safety and as much comfort as they can earn. I have no patience for those who seek to take from the hard work of others through use of violence. So today, I'm going to give some bright people a few orders, and an unknown number of men will show up here in Brownsville, and we will kill them. Not because of any high-minded notion of duty or justice, but because it is necessary so people around here can sleep safe in their beds at night. And that's all there is to it."

Hicks let out a bitter chuckle. "And here I thought we were fighting the good fight."

"If it helps you sleep better, kid, keep telling yourself that."

As I walked out the door, a voice followed me, oratory, cultured, completely devoid of accent.

"Though all we knew depart,

the old commandments stand.

In courage keep your heart,

in strength, lift up your hand."

*****

Dawn burned clear and yellow through a cloudless sky.

I looked around at the catwalk, and the guard towers, and the shuffling figures in the town below, and understood why through the course of history, in cultures and armies around the world, warriors have always feared, above all else, being captured and turned over to the enemy's women.

There were only enough outfits for thirty of them, and those had to be hastily laundered and repaired. Thankfully, the generators seized from the now-defunct Crow Hunters allowed for the use of washers and dryers, although the stains were still visible. Considering what their former owners' occupations had been, it was easy to assume the blood was someone else's. At least I hoped that's what Blackmire's men would think, anyway.

Sheriff Tucker was out there among them, a few extra layers of clothing under her disguise to hide her feminine physique and make her look bigger. There were no overweight women in Brownsville—or anywhere else since the Outbreak that I had seen—which made things much easier. Very large breasts were rare, as were exceptionally wide hips, which meant as long as a woman was roughly the right height, was willing to endure the necessary haircut, and wound a scarf around her face to hide her features, she could pull off the disguise by merit of pressing her chest flat with tightly wound strips of fabric. Not the most comfortable solution, but effective.

They carried the mercenaries' weapons, of which I had instructed them in the proper use thereof. I covered the plan repetitively until everyone knew their role and could recite it without hesitation. They were as well prepared as they could be under the circumstances. I just had to hope it would be enough.

As I watched the sun rise, my earpiece came to life. "Alpha, Bravo. I have visual. Over."

"Copy, Bravo. How many are we dealing with? Over."

"I count fifty-two. All on horseback. Over."

I let out a low whistle. Fifty-two was more than I expected. But in a way, it was a good thing. With that many men, maybe Tanner would be among them. The possibility appealed very much indeed.

"Copy. Get yourself back here ASAP. Over."

"Wilco. Bravo out."

'Bravo' was Hicks. I had sent him out an hour earlier to scout the highway leading in to Brownsville. Sheriff Tucker loaned him her horse with the stern admonishment to bring it back safe and unharmed. Hicks promised he would, then swung into the saddle as if he were born there and rode away.

"That boy barely holds the reins," Tucker said. "Guides with his knees. Quite an impressive young man."

I laughed quietly. "You have no idea."

Presently, said soldier came riding back through the main gate, head lowered, legs braced against the stirrups, wind whipping back his hair. He wheeled the horse to a stop a few feet in front of Sheriff Tucker, then hopped down and rubbed the animal's neck, whispering in its ear. It's sweat-streaked flanks continued to heave, but it calmed down.

"All right, Alpha," he radioed. "Gonna take position."

"Copy. Nice work, killer."

He looked my way and offered a mock salute, then headed for the rooftop he would be firing from. He had my M-110, given to him on loan, strapped across his back.

I settled in and waited.

Half an hour later, according to the wind-up watch I acquired in a quick bit of bartering with Penny earlier in the day, the clomp of hooves and jingle of harness made its way to my ears. "All stations, stand by," I said.

As the riders drew closer, I watched them through my little binoculars. They looked relaxed enough, weapons slung, hands on the reins, riding easy in the saddle. I reached for the radio and switched channels. "Hey Sheriff."

"Hey yourself."

"The Pinkertons are coming. Your posse ready to slap iron?"

There was a chuckle in her voice when she answered, and an affected drawl. "Yessir. These gals are fit to kick up a row."

"Sounds good. Rustle up the shitbird, if you please."

"Can do. Any advice as regards the forthcoming conflagration?"

"The Lord created all men, but Sam Colt made 'em equal. In my experience, the same rule applies across the gender lines."

"Understood. Cowboy up, Mr. Garrett."

Tucker climbed a ladder down from the north catwalk and strode into the comms building. A moment later, she emerged with Powell in tow, then resumed her place on the wall. Just as her boots landed on the planks, the first riders came through the main gate.

I'd had a conversation with Powell earlier in the morning which consisted of me showing him my .338 rifle, holding up one of its very large rounds where he could see it, explaining to him what kind of damage such a weapon could do at less than two-hundred yards, and informing him that, when the attack commenced, the crosshairs on my rather fancy Nightforce scope would be focused squarely on the center of his back.

"If you want to know what your spine looks like before you die," I said to him, "then by all means, attempt some foolish fuckery and warn Blackmire's men of their impending doom. However, if you wish to remain among the living for a bit longer, I would strongly caution you against such action. Nod if you understand."

He nodded. Rapidly.

Now he stood in the town square, smiling and waving as if nothing were amiss. The riders streamed in at a canter, laughing amongst themselves, no doubt looking forward to a little quality time with the captured women. I didn't recognize the rider at their head. Both his eyes were intact, and he was not wearing a black, wide-brimmed hat. Searching the others, I felt a surge of disappointment. No sign of Blackmire.

Oh well. Content yourself with slaughtering his men.

As the last rider made it through the gate, Sheriff Tucker strolled casually over, shut it, and locked it. The lead rider stopped a few feet in front of Powell and exchanged a few words. Reaching down, I hit the talk button on my radio.

"Stand by for my signal."

The women pretending to be Crow Hunter guards slowly, nonchalantly wandered away from the north side of the wall, eyes cast toward the fields and forests in the distance, backs turned to Blackmire's men, no conversation among them lest the pitch of their voices give them away. Tucker stayed near the back, rifle over her shoulder, strolling silently along. When they were far enough away, I keyed the radio again.

"All right. Give the signal."

On the other side of town, a young woman named Shelly Moore pointed a rifle toward the sky and fired a single shot. It had the intended effect, causing Blackmire's men to startle and look southward. Powell immediately turned on his heel and ran away as fast as his legs could carry him, much to the consternation of the black clad asshole he had been talking to. With a deep sense of satisfaction, I watched understanding dawn in his eyes. He turned to shout at his men, but it was already too late. In a house a couple of blocks east of where the riders sat astride their horses, Sergeant Isaac Cole picked up a transmitter, opened a hard metal cover, and pressed a switch.

Around the riders, set thirty meters away and aimed slightly upward, four M-18 Claymore mines, each containing 700 1/8th inch steel balls set into epoxy resin and backed by C-4 explosive, detonated.

The effect was devastating.

2800 of the aforementioned steel balls exploded outward at incredible velocity, ripping into the Blackmire guards and their mounts like a steel tornado. The force of the blast knocked over the ones closest to the detonation and sent them rolling. Horses screamed, reared, and collapsed. Shredded sacks of meat that were once men slid limply from saddles. The men on the edges of the group still alive found themselves under assault by powerful tons of agonized flesh and sharp, flailing hooves.

Here, a man tries to stand up, but gets too close to a horse's legs and takes a steel-shod kick to the face. He goes down and does not get up. There, a figure with a savaged red mess where his left side used to be pushes himself partially up, only to have a horse fall sideways and land directly on his head. His legs thrash for a moment, then go still.

As bad as it was, the claymores didn't kill all of them. Only about half the Blackmire guardsmen died in the initial blast, but almost all of the survivors were wounded. They screamed orders at one another, desperately fighting to control their panicked mounts, reaching for weapons, trying to go on the offensive against an enemy they couldn't even see.

"Sanchez," I said into the mouthpiece, "you're up."

In the guard tower across from me, the young militiaman bent down, picked up a long metal canister, took aim, and fired. There was a tremendous *crack*, then the brief hiss of a LAW rocket covering two-hundred yards in less than a second, and then a *BOOM* that whacked me in the chest and shook the tower under my feet. The rocket detonated in the center of the surviving guardsmen, sending men, horses, and pieces of men and horses sailing through the air, many of them landing on porches and rooftops.

The radio button clicked. "Tucker, you are clear to engage."

"Ten-four."

Moments later, thirty women, all disguised as Crow Hunters, descended on the surviving guardsmen from an elevated position, leveled their rifles, and opened fire. Hefting my .338, I joined them.

I started with the ones still in the saddle. There weren't many. A torso appeared in my vision, shirt torn and bloody. I pulled the trigger and watched about of pound of bone and flesh explode from his back. Shifting aim, I found a man trying to return fire at the women and squeezed the trigger again. The top half of his head exploded, the force of the impact throwing him sideways from the saddle.

I worked the bolt, expended the spent cartridge, and shucked another one in. I looked around for movement. Didn't find any. Across the way, Tucker's voice rose above the chattering din of automatic weapons.

"Cease fire! That's enough, they're all down! Cease fire!"

It took a while, but eventually the shooting stopped. In the town below, the few horses who somehow managed to survive the ambush galloped away in blind panic. None of their riders appeared to be so lucky. Where once there had been a neat town square, paved and swept with painted white squares for stalls on market day, now stood what could only be described as the world's largest chum bucket. Steam rose in the cold air from bundles of intestines, glistening organs, and gleaming white bone. Blood quite literally ran in the streets.

The women along the battlements stared at what they had done, mouths hanging open, breath coming in ragged gasps. They had started the day fired up and ready to fight, but now looked a little pale around the gills. A few of them turned away, leaned over the wall, and lost their breakfast. Most, however, simply shouldered their rifles, took a deep breath, and looked to Sheriff Tucker for instructions. I felt an odd sort of pride for them.

"We're all clear, Mr. Garrett," the sheriff's voice said in my ear. "What should we do now?"

The wind picked up the smell of ruptured intestines, carried it to my tower, and dropped it on my face. I grimaced, knowing what lay ahead.

"We made a hell of a mess, Sheriff. Now we have to clean it up."

*****

Some bright day, a long time from now when the walking dead are just a lurid entry in the pages of history, assuming the human race is still around, I hope someone notates that for all the harm they did, the infected occasionally had their uses.

Disposing of dead bodies being chief among them.

The Blackmire guardsmen went over the wall as whole bodies, for the most part. About a dozen or more had been torn apart and eviscerated, and I had a feeling people were going to be tracking down bad smells and finding bits and pieces for weeks to come. The dead horses, on the other hand, were a bigger problem.

I put my falcata to hard use that day, but not against enemies or the undead. Instead, I used it to pare down once-magnificent animals into manageable portions so the meat could be smoked, dried, and preserved. Some of it would be put to more immediate use such as stews and pot roast, while about a hundred pounds or so went into cold storage to be consumed in days to come. The idea of eating the horses of men I had killed was off-putting to say the least, but the women of Brownsville were nothing if not practical. As Penny put it, there was no sense is letting good protein go to waste.

The few horses who survived were rounded up, fed, watered, brushed down, and quartered in the town stables. I asked Joe Steinman if I could have a couple of them, and he said I could take them all as well as their saddles and kit. A light bulb came on over my head, and I mentioned the weapons and equipment and other possessions the Blackmire men and the Crow Hunters had left behind. He said he would talk to the sheriff.

An hour later, there were two piles in front of town hall, a structure I had previously known as the comms building. One consisted of things too mangled and destroyed to be of use, and was scheduled to be shipped to one of a few working foundries along the Mississippi and sold for scrap. The rest, which constituted quite a significant heap—not to mention a sizable fortune—lay piled on the other side. Sheriff Tucker stood with my men and me and told us it was ours.

"Take as much as you want," she said. "You deserve it after all you've done for us."

We looked at each other, the three soldiers, the militiaman, and the aging Marine, and shook our heads. "I'll take a horse and a one-twentieth share. That sound fair to you?"

The younger men agreed. I turned back to Sheriff Tucker.

"My men here will take the same. That's four horses and twenty percent of the spoils. The rest goes to the town. After all this, you're going to need it more than us."

A tension I hadn't noticed earlier faded from the sheriff's face, and she breathed a sigh of relief. "That's very kind of you, Mr. Garrett. Thank you."

We left it at that.

*****

With the division of profits settled, there was one more loose end to tie up. I asked a question of Joe Steinman—who had been a federal judge in his previous life and continued that vocation here in Brownsville—and after a moment's consideration, he gave me the green light.

Powell was where I left him, sitting next to the radio, under guard. He looked at me as I entered the room, much of his previous nervousness faded.

"So what happens now?" he asked.

I turned to Lily Garner, one of Sheriff Tucker's deputies. "Did he radio Blackmire?"

"Yep," she said, staring hard at Powell with dark brown eyes. "Told him his men were safely quartered and currently partaking of the prisoners. Blackmire said he had matters at home to attend to, and would call again in a few days. And not to use the women too badly."

I nodded and seethed. "All right then. Come on Powell. Let's go."

His eyebrows came together, but otherwise, he didn't move. "Go where?"

"You held up your end. You're done. Outta here. Let's go."

He stood up and cast a quick glance around the room. "Um…do I get to take anything with me? Maybe some supplies?"

I got an inch from his nose. "What the fuck do you think?"

He walked in front of me down the stairs and out the front door. We continued on outside the gate and turned west on Highway 19. There were no infected to impede us, being that all of them close enough to be a problem were currently occupied devouring the remains of the Blackmire guardsmen. When we were around a quarter mile from town, I stopped.

"That's far enough," I said, as I drew my pistol and fished its suppressor from my vest. "Turn around."

He obeyed slowly, the glowing relief on his face vanishing. He began to back away, one hand raised defensively. "Wait…wait just wait a minute now. We had a deal. You said if I cooperated nothing would happen to me."

"Actually, that's not true. I said you wouldn't be *prosecuted*." Finished with the suppressor, I raised the barrel and centered the three white dots on his forehead.

"And you won't be."

FORTY-SIX

Clouds rolled in the next day, dragging the temperature from the low thirties to the low twenties. There was no telling how long it would stay cold enough to immobilize the infected, so the town awoke early and got to work.

Among the many items seized from the Crow Hunters, Sheriff Tucker found a dozen Marlin model 60 rifles and an entire crate of ammunition. It consisted of over 60,000 rounds of .22 long rifle, worth a fortune all by itself. The sheriff handed all five of us a rifle and two bricks of ammunition.

"There are a lot of infected out there," she said. "Most everyone in town is going to be digging graves today, and every one of them lost a husband, son, father, granddad, or nephew. The sight of men working amongst them might have a...difficult effect."

I nodded in understanding. "Not to worry, Sheriff. I think we can keep ourselves occupied."

We were a silent crew as we marched out the west gate and turned southward where the bulk of the ghouls had congregated. Cole and Thompson worked as a pair, as did Sanchez and Hicks. But as for me, over their objections, I opted to work alone. As cold as it was, the dead weren't much of a threat, and I had some thinking to do.

From what Powell told me, fifty-two men comprised nearly half of Blackmire's forces *before* Hicks and the others showed up to rescue me. Then there was the ensuing ambush on Highway 19. Deprived of all those men, Tanner's forces were now down to maybe ten to twenty insurgents. Maybe more if he managed to recruit replacements. Either way, he was badly understrength, and not exactly well loved among the people he lorded over. Perhaps I could use that to my advantage.

As we worked, the cracking of unsuppressed rifles eventually became tedious, so I put in my earplugs. It took us three hours to use up all of our ammunition, a good portion of that time being spent reloading.

Even after expending four-thousand rounds, there were still a significant number of infected littering the forest beyond the flat fields surrounding Brownsville. We went back for more ammunition, each of us emptying our pack and filling it up with as much ammo as we could carry. Then we returned to the woods, spread out at five yard intervals, and began walking expanding concentric circles around town.

The noise from the fighting had brought the undead to Brownsville in hordes, to the point where Joe Steinman and Sheriff Tucker were concerned they might breach the wall through sheer force of weight. It was just dumb luck the weather and circumstance conspired to present an opportunity to clear them out with minimal risk. If there really was a God, perhaps he decided to cut the survivors of that small, beleaguered community some well-deserved slack.

I kept my mind blank as I worked, doing my best to ignore the rolling, milky eyes of the dead as I placed the barrel behind their ears and pulled the trigger. The Marlin was small and light enough I could fire it one-handed, like a really long pistol. The pouch where I normally kept my first aid kit made an excellent ammo bucket, which I had to refill every half-hour or so. By the time the sun went down and we called it a day, my left hand was killing me from all the abuse.

That night, just before I went to bed, I peeled the bandage off and surveyed the damage. There was a thin pucker of flesh held together by neat sutures—like the stitching of a jacket— stretched over a nub of bone. The wound must have been pretty ragged, but Thompson did a good job of removing the shattered bone, trimming the flesh, and stitching the viable tissue back together. I could move it, although it was badly swollen. After wiggling it around a bit, I cleaned it and wrapped it up in a fresh bandage.

Next, I checked the wound in my side. A little swollen from the day's exertions, but otherwise not bad at all. I could probably have the stitches out in a week, barring incident.

Lying on my bed, I thought about Tanner, and Elizabeth, and Sean Montford, and Sheriff Tucker, and the women of Brownsville. I thought about the attacks on Hollow Rock, and the Midwest Alliance, and the complex power play between them and the Union, and how the Republic of California fit in to all of it. They had been suspiciously silent, that faction, and I didn't like it one bit. You don't just show up in a giant flotilla, annex a chunk of landmass nearly the size of Texas, declare the people there your subjects under pain of death, and expect there to be no consequences. I sincerely doubted the people of California, Oregon, and Washington went along willingly. In fact, it would not surprise at all me to learn there were still pockets of resistance fighters, quite likely working hand-in-hand with Union forces. Food for thought.

Whatever the ROC wanted, whatever their agenda was, it did not bode well for the Union. And bearing in mind my promise to General Jacobs, I knew it was only a matter of time before I would be embroiled in the conflict. Not exactly a pleasant thought.

But mostly—and I'm not proud to say this—I thought about my finger. I thought about how it was gone, and how I would never get it back. I thought about how when I moved it, it felt like the missing part was still there, as if I could scratch myself with it.

Going forward, wielding two melee weapons at once was going to be tough. With most of my ring finger missing, the strength of my grip on that side would be forever diminished. I just had to hope that over time I could strengthen the hand to compensate. Not like I had much of a choice.

As I drifted off, it occurred to me that if not for Sebastian Fucking Tanner, my left hand would still be whole, Sean Montford would still be alive, the people Hollow Rock lost in the walker attacks would still be alive, the menfolk of Brownsville would still be alive, Elizabeth wouldn't have a hole in her lung, Sanchez wouldn't be sporting a gunshot wound to his leg, and Eric and Private Fuller would not have been wounded. Taken in aggregate, it was a hell of a lot of damage.

And it was not going to go unpunished.

I had been sloppy the first time. I moved too quickly, driven by anger, focused solely on results and not nearly enough on methods. It was a long litany of mistakes I made, but the thing about mistakes is you can learn from them. The lesson had been hard, one I would remember for the rest of my life, but by God, I had learned. And I was not going to make the same mistakes again.

Decision made, I slipped beneath the waves and slept like the dead.

*****

"Gabe, there's no need for you to do this," Thompson said as he watched me pack. "Blackmire is on Central's radar. Cole sent them a video of those bodies. You don't even need Sheriff Elliott anymore, the prisoners took one look at what the Crow Hunters did and flipped. We have their sworn testimony on record. As soon as Pope or FOB Harkin can free up a few air assets, Blackmire is as good as toast."

"And how long is that going to take, Ethan?" I asked, not looking up from what I was doing.

"Not more than a week or two."

"And you think Tanner won't figure out what's going on by then? You think he's going to stick around?"

"What difference does it make? We have his description. It's not like a guy with a ten-inch scar on his face and one fucking eye can go incognito. There are bulletins going out to every loyalist community on record. He has a gigantic bounty on his head. If he shows up anywhere south of the Illinois border, he's a dead man."

"Exactly my point. If we don't get to him in the next few days, he'll flee to Alliance territory and disappear."

"You say that like it's a bad thing."

Before I knew what I was doing, I was an inch from Thompson's face. "Look out that goddamn window Sergeant!

Look to the west side of town! There's about a hundred fresh graves over there with their wives' and daughters' and mothers' tears still wet on the soil. You look at that, you take a *good hard look*, and explain to me why we should let that son of a bitch get away."

He paled, expression brittle as flint. There was a flash of anger, then the well-oiled gears began to turn. I took a step back and watched his eyes fall to the ground, hands clenching and unclenching. A long moment passed, then he rubbed his forehead, passed his fingers through his hair, and walked over to the window.

"Okay. You have a point. I get so caught up in the strictures of things, sometimes...I get a little near-sighted, you know?"

In a rush, I remembered my own days when I was his age and rank, and the weight of guilt when I made a bad call and people died. It was a wound that had never quite healed, and I did not envy the young man his position.

"You have a great deal of responsibility on your shoulders, Staff Sergeant. I understand that. I've been there. I didn't mean any disrespect. You're a good, brave man, and the world could use a hell of a lot more like you. I'm sorry I lost my temper."

He looked at me then, bemusement crossing his face. "I'm sorry. Is that an apology I just heard? From the great Gabriel Garrett?"

Against my will, I smiled. "Yes. I guess I'm evolving, or something. Or maybe just getting soft in my old age."

Thompson crossed the room and laid a hand on my shoulder. "Gabe, when I'm your age, if I'm half the man you are, I'll consider my life well lived." He stepped back, picked up his radio, and clipped it onto his belt. "Meet me in the dining room in an hour. I'll gather the others and we'll see what we can do. Fair enough?"

I gave a grateful nod. "Fair enough."

*****

Sanchez was a no go. A classic case of the spirit being willing but the flesh being weak.

Thompson had to stay in Brownsville to help coordinate relief efforts. With most of the town's defenders interred in the ground, the shattered community was in very real danger of being overrun again. To address this, Central Command authorized a force of forty troops, drawn from both First Platoon and the Ninth TVM, to garrison within the town. But even with both of Hollow Rock's transports ferrying men and equipment back and forth, it was going to be at least a few days before they were at full strength. In the meantime, Staff Sergeant Thompson was in charge of the town's defenses.

"Isaac, I want you to stay here with Thompson," I said.

The big man frowned. "What, you don't think I got enough sneak on me?"

I shook my head. "It's not that. You're a wrecking ball, Isaac. If anyone tries to attack Brownsville before the troops get here, you'll rip them to pieces. I'll sleep a lot better at night knowing you, Ethan, and Sancho are here to protect these people."

"I don't know, man," The Pride of Hermosillo spoke up. "Seems to me like these *chicas* can handle themselves pretty well."

"They're brave enough, that's for sure," I said. "But you three are disciplined, well-trained, experienced professionals. You'll catch things they might miss. You'll see enemy tactics for what they are, and you won't get suckered in by any tricks or traps. You know how to stand your ground when every instinct screams at you to run. In short, you're soldiers, and damned good ones. These people need you until reinforcements get here, and I know I can count on you to protect them. That's why I want you to stay."

There was no chest puffing or immature banter. They accepted the compliment with silent nods—not because they didn't appreciate it, but because they knew it wasn't puffery. Just a simple statement of fact.

I turned to Hicks. "What do you say, Caleb? You in the mood to pick a fight?"

The enigmatic young soldier grinned, and his teeth were all fangs.

FORTY-SEVEN

Having grown up in Kentucky, I've had my share of experience with horses. During the summers, when I wasn't learning the finer points of the barber's trade from my uncle, I was mucking dung out of stalls for extra money.

One of the breeders I worked for took a liking to me and gave me free riding lessons. She was an attractive woman in her mid-thirties, had inherited the farm several years earlier from her deceased husband, and treated me with a great deal more kindness and respect than most of the other people I worked for. I always thought she was just a very nice lady until I showed up for work a few days after my sixteenth birthday—by which point I was already six-foot-three and over two-hundred pounds—and found a note tacked to the barn door informing me she had a present for me, but I had to go inside to get it.

Upon entering the house, I called her name, and heard her answer from upstairs, inviting me up. So I went up and called to her again, and pinpointed her voice behind one of the doors. When I knocked, the door opened and there she was, wearing a pair of strappy red high heels, perfume, and not much else.

It wasn't my first time, but it was the first time with a real woman who knew what she was doing. The experience damn near ruined me for girls my own age.

I clung to the warm glow of that memory, among many others, as Hicks and I rode toward Blackmire. The weather turned on us less than an hour outside of Brownsville, and we found ourselves riding through high winds and driving snow. According to Hicks' little tablet, it was nineteen degrees with eight inches of precipitation expected in the next twelve hours. Not exactly ideal traveling weather.

We huddled in our coats, covered as much skin as we could, wore goggles to keep the snow out of our eyes, and tried to keep our teeth from chattering too loudly. Our one consolation was we didn't have to worry about the infected. The horses could smell them when we got close and steered clear, tails whipping in agitation.

There was a brief stop for lunch, then we plodded on, keeping well away from the highway and using Hicks' GPS to stay on course. Despite the weather, we set a good pace and reached the outskirts of the Chickasaw Refuge by nightfall.

After searching around a while, Hicks spotted a building through the thick stands of pines we had been riding through for the last half hour. As we drew close, I saw a sign for the Walnut Grove Baptist Parsonage, and a squat, sturdy looking little brick house behind it. The distinctive outline of a chimney rose up on the opposite side, and I shivered in anticipation of building a fire. Doing so would be a risk, but as cold as I was, I quite simply did not give a shit. If anyone showed up with bad intentions, I would shoot them down and piss on their grave.

"What do you think," I asked, nodding toward the house.

Hicks nodded. "Works for me."

"We'll stable the horses in the church. I'll brush them down and feed them if you take the first watch."

"Deal."

It was the longest conversation we had all day.

*****

Morning. Planning session.

"First thing is recon," I said.

Hicks took a bite of his flatbread and pointed at a spot on the tablet. "That's where I set up last week. There's a hill there with a big oak tree on top. If you climb up, you'll have a good view of the town."

"Sounds like a plan."

Two hours later, Hicks held my horse's reins while I ascended said oak tree. It had to be at least eighty years old; the trunk was close to four feet in diameter, and the limbs were as thick as my waist. The lowest limb was twenty feet up, requiring me to throw Hicks' rope over it, anchor it to another nearby trunk, and climb up. When I reached the top, I unslung my .338 and focused through the scope.

Ten minutes passed. As I scoured the town from one side to the other, a sad fact became undeniably clear.

Blackmire was being abandoned.

And no sign of the founder or his men.

"Shit."

I climbed down and delivered the bad news. Hicks chewed a piece of jerky, idly scratching his horse behind the ear. The animal dipped its chestnut-colored head and leaned into the soldier's hand like an oversized dog. My own horse, a gelding I named Red because of his rusty coloring, stood aloof, snuffling around in the snow for grass.

"You thinkin' what I'm thinkin'?"

I looked back toward the town and sighed, breath forming a cloud of frosted white. "We need intel."

A nod. "Yep."

*****

The road to Blackmire was fraught with peril, not the least of it Hicks and I. As the townsfolk fled, we picked a good spot on the trail to Watkins road, donned our ghillie suits, and lay in wait.

Most of the passersby were too tough of a target. Raiders in their Army surplus camouflage, marauders in their various crudely-dyed colors riding under embroidered flags, slavers in their dun brown, innocuous, home-spun fabrics. These were hard men and, to a less numerous extent, hard women. Not the kind of people who would back down to a couple of armed Union types demanding information. Undesiring of a firefight, we let the sharks pass and waited for the bait fish to filter through.

It didn't take long.

There was a squat, frail little man in a wagon with an equally squat, frail little woman riding next to him. Drawing their cart was a pair of mules, both looking sickly and underfed. The cargo behind them was hastily stacked, consisting mostly of food, water, a cask of whiskey, a wood-burning stove, a crate with Chinese markings denoting its contents as rifles, and another crate with Cyrillic script advertising two-thousand rounds of ammo. Just a pair of malcontented settlers struggling to start a new life.

And I'm a monkey's fucking uncle.

My hand appeared from nowhere, grasping the harness binding the two mules and holding them in place. I rose to my full height, appearing out of the foliage on the side of the road. The old woman reached back and laid hands on a rifle, only to find a clump of forest swinging into her cart and aiming an M-4 at her head. She stopped cold, hands still.

"Listen," the old man said, hand easing toward a spot under the buckboard. "Just take what you want. We'll get-"

I drew my pistol and pointed it at his face. "We're not here to rob you."

The old man's eyes crossed comically as he gazed down the barrel. "So what do you want?"

"Information. Answer a few questions, and we'll send you on your way."

"All right."

As a show of good faith, I lowered my weapon. Hicks didn't move. "I'm looking for a man named Sebastian Tanner, goes by the alias Blackmire. Big scar on his face, one dead eye. Have you seen him?"

The old man turned his head and spit. "Hell yes I seen him. And if you're out to kill the bastard, you don't need to threaten me for information. I'll give it to you for free."

I glanced at Hicks, then said, "Go on."

"He called a town meeting yesterday, said the Union was sending soldiers and artillery to destroy the place. Told us to get the hell out of dodge while we still could. Then him and his personal guard rode off through the north gate and left the rest of us twisting in the wind. Ain't seen 'em since."

"How did he find out about the Union sending troops this way?"

The old man shrugged. "Radio chatter would be my guess. The Union ain't so careful about operational security sometimes."

I processed that, suppressing a grimace. The next time I spoke with General Jacobs, I would definitely bring that up. "You said they left through the north gate. Which way did they go after that?"

Another shrug. "Hell if I know. If I had to guess, I'd say north, probably toward the 155 bridge over the river. From there he can follow the highways up to Red Blade. That's the nearest Alliance outpost."

"How many men were with him?"

"Eight. His personal guard, all on horseback. Oh, and three pack mules."

"What about his other men?"

The old man spit again. "Deserted. Worthless sons o' bitches."

I glanced at Hicks and gave a little twitch of my head. He stood up and leapt smoothly from the wagon, feet barely making a sound when he landed.

"Go on," I said. "You're free to go."

The old man's eyes narrowed. "You with the Union? Special Forces types?"

I raised my pistol again and drew back the hammer. "Go. Now."

With fumbling hands, he gripped the reins, snapped them, and the wagon tottered forward.

"Come on," I said, looking at Hicks across the trail. "Let's get out of here before someone else shows up."

FORTY-EIGHT

I used to believe I was an expert tracker. Not anymore. Now, I consider myself a marginally competent tracker.

Hicks, on the other hand, is an expert.

"Looks like the old fella was telling the truth," he said, riding a circle around a cluster of barely visible hoof prints. "Nine men on horseback, three mules loaded down heavy. Looks like they went north toward Highway 88."

"So they have a day's lead on us," I replied. "How much you want to bet they already made it across the river?"

"I'd say that's a definite."

We followed the tracks and rode hard, pushing our mounts at a fast pace. If Tanner made it to Red Blade, he was as good as lost. But the airport the community was built around was about a hundred and fifty miles from the 155 bridge, so we had at least four days to catch up with him.

Along the way, there was a buzzing, nagging little voice in my head, like a fly in my ear. I call that voice Instinct, and I had long ago learned not to ignore it. But focusing on it did no good, the harder I tried to work out what the guys in the basement were doing, the darker the lights dimmed. So instead, I cleared my mind, focused on the trail ahead, and let them do their jobs. As afternoon wore on toward evening, less than two miles from the bridge, I swear to God I heard an audible click.

"Stop," I said, tugging back on the reins.

Hicks obeyed, hand straying to his weapon. "What's wrong?"

"Blackmire knew about the Army sending troops this way."

"Okay. So?"

"My name was mentioned a few times in the chatter. I heard it."

Hicks furrowed his brow and dipped his head. "And…"

"We have personal history, Blackmire and me. Also, there's a bounty on my head. A substantial one. If he heard about the attack, and knows I was involved, there's every reason for him to believe I might try to catch him before he reaches Red Blade."

I saw the machinery begin to churn. Hicks said, "So we might be walking into an ambush."

"If you were going to set one up, where would be the best place?"

We both thought about it for a moment, then looked up and spoke at the same time.

"The bridge."

*****

The 155 bridge, according to the tablet, was built on the narrowest point in the river for miles in either direction. But even there it is nearly half a mile wide.

They don't call it the mighty Mississippi for nothing.

Fording was not an option. Horses are good swimmers, but not that good. The cold would sap their strength, and ours, and the lot of us would drown. No go.

We did, however, find a canoe.

Hicks put the horses on a long tether, fed them a double helping of oats, and made a water trough out of an old plastic barrel washed up beside the river. The effort cost us a couple of hours, but that was okay. We didn't plan to leave until well after nightfall anyway.

Neither of us was entirely comfortable abandoning the horses, but there wasn't much choice. The bridge was as long as the river was wide, which meant our only hope of ambushing the ambushers was to get around behind them—if, in fact, they were there. If not, we would simply cross back over, reclaim the horses, and head north. We just had to hope the weather stayed on our side and didn't warm up too much. If the temp got above 26 degrees, and the dead thawed out, the horses would rip up their stakes and take off. Hicks made sure not to bury the tethering stakes too deep just in case.

The water was flat and wide, the current strong but sluggish. I kept the canoe pointed slightly north to combat the river's southward flow, and in less than an hour, we crossed the border into Missouri.

After dragging the canoe ashore, we turned northward and followed the river for two miles, then swung west in a wide arc. The bare floodplain around us eventually turned into a dense patch of forest half a mile from the Missouri side of the bridge. I switched my NVGs to thermal mode, unlimbered my .338—I had loaned Hicks my M-110—activated my FLIR scope, and began a slow, deliberate search.

We stayed on the south side of the highway, spread out at ten meters, maintaining radio silence. There was no need to talk, I could see Hicks clearly with my thermal imager. If he strayed too far, it was a simple matter to warn him with a pre-arranged bird call. He had NVGs of his own, but they did not have FLIR capability, just standard night vision. Same story with his scope.

About three hundred yards from where the bridge terminated on the landward side, Hicks and I belly crawled over a ridge, staying low to avoid skylining ourselves, and paused to search the forest around the highway.

At first, with the scope set at 9x power, I didn't see anything. But then I dialed it up to 20x power and did a grid search.

"Bingo," I whispered, then signaled Hicks to come over.

"How many," he asked when he reached me.

"Four. Not sure where the others are, probably continued on toward Red Blade. Left these guys behind to capture or kill me."

The scarred soldier peered through his night vision scope. "Must be dug in good. I can't make 'em out."

"Center your reticle on the highway where it meets this side of the river. Good. Now pan right to where you see the tallest tree, looks like a pine. Okay, now scan the base of it on the left hand side. You should see a tree cancer."

"Got him."

I gave him instructions to find the other shooter on the south side of the highway and then watched as he moved the scope back and forth between them a few times. "Okay. Ready when you are."

I repeated the same exercise with the gunmen on the north side, then tapped Hicks on the shoulder. "On three. Five...four...three."

Both rifles fired at the same time. The M-110 was loud, but the .338 was deafening. I was glad I had remembered to put in my earplugs.

The glaring white man-outline in my reticle jumped a bit, twitched a few times, and moved no more. The man ahead of him tried to get up from his hide and make a run for it, but I was too quick for him. My second shot leveled him center of mass, driving him to the forest floor. To my right, I heard Hicks fire a second shot, curse, then fire a third.

"Sorry," he muttered. "Was a little low on the second one."

"But you got him, right?"

"Yep."

"That's all that counts."

Warily, we descended the hill, approached the dead bodies, and searched them. Three of them had tattoos identifying them as having served in, respectively, the 82nd Airborne, First Infantry Division, and USMC. The fourth had no such markings, but his gear and weapons were maintained with military-esque attention to detail.

"Pro's," I said.

"Traitors." Hicks shook his head and pointed back the way we came. "Let's cross back and go get the horses, then make camp on this side of the bridge."

"Works for me."

*****

Hicks picked up their trail at first light.

"This is fresh," he said, looking down from the saddle. "They must have stuck around for a while, then left when you didn't show up in a timely manner."

"How long ago, do you think?"

"Not more than a day. We probably missed 'em by a few hours."

I loosed my M-6 from where it was lashed to the saddle and laid it across my lap. "Let's go."

The horses were clearly sore from the previous day's exertions, but we couldn't afford to take it easy on them, not this close to our goal. After following 155 to where it intersected with Interstate 55, we turned northward. The forest gave way to barren fields for a while, then the terrain grew increasingly hilly and eased into another long stretch of woodland. By the time the sun began to dip below the horizon, we had covered over thirty miles. Finally, shortly after nightfall, Hicks spoke up.

"We have to stop, Gabe. We're gonna kill the horses. They need rest."

I checked the sky, looking at the last shreds of midnight blue retreating before the encroaching black. "Let me see the tablet."

"Why?"

"If we're close, they should have made camp somewhere nearby."

"What makes you think we're close to them?"

"Think about it. Would they have set this hard of a pace? Probably not. Tanner expected his men to either kill me, capture me, or at least slow me down. They did nothing of the sort. You said it yourself, the tracks are fresh."

Hicks pondered for a few seconds, then nodded. "You know, you might be-"

There was a whirring sound, a shrill thrum I knew all too well, and then a hammer nailed me in the right side of my ribcage. I had enough breath in my lungs to shout a warning to Hicks, and then he was moving.

The report startled Red, who jumped beneath me and bolted for the cover of the trees. For the first time in my life, I could have kissed a horse and not felt the least bit weird about it.

As we left the road, and the powerful animal wended his way among the trunks, I felt a tug at my back and the distinct *thak* of a bullet impacting wood. The gray matter went on autopilot, calculating the vectors.

I was facing north when the bullet struck me. It hit me in the right side. Then another one grazed my back from the same angle as I rode away, headed northwest. Which meant the shooter was to the northeast, and had been aiming center of mass both times. Judging by the time gap between impact and report, I estimated the range at four-hundred yards. By the sound, it was a 7.62x54, maybe a Dragunov or PSL.

Which meant the shooter was none other than Sebastian Tanner himself.

Red carried me over the crest of a hill, then broke a sharp left to follow Hicks' horse, forcing me to hang on to the saddle horn for dear life. I ducked my head and stayed low, desperately hoping no large branches came along and swept me from the saddle. We soon caught up to Hicks, which seemed to calm Red enough for me to grab the reins and slow him down. Hicks eased his mount to a halt, then turned in his saddle and began digging around in his pack.

"We have to ditch the horses," he said. "They're too loud and too big of a target."

"Agreed." I jumped down, untied my ghillie suit and pack from the saddle, retrieved my weapons, and slapped Red on his haunches. The big animal took the hint and bolted away into the forest. Hicks outfitted himself quickly and then did the same.

"How'd they get the drop on us?" he asked as his horse pounded away.

I stood silently and pondered. If they had spotted us from far away, Tanner would have set up a roadside ambush. Which meant they had spotted us when we were close to their camp. But why the long-range shot? I turned and looked back the way I came.

He knew you were following him. What would you have done in his place?

I would have made camp far away from any buildings. I would have chosen high ground with a view of the highway. I would have set up a hide, then settled in and waited.

So he picks a hilltop, and his men make camp, and he peers through his rifle. He had set a hard pace during the day's ride, and didn't think I would catch up to him. To his surprise, I prove him wrong. So he takes a shot and rallies his men.

"He was waiting for us. Probably spotted us as we topped that last hill. I was wrong, he wasn't stupid enough to assume his men would stop me at the bridge. He's a lunatic. Doesn't care if his own men die. I should have thought of that. Should have stuck to the woodlands and not followed the highway. Stupid of me. That's what happens when I get in a hurry."

"Don't beat yourself up. Shit happens." Hicks stepped closer and peered at my side. "How bad are you hit?"

The pain was minimal, so it hadn't even occurred to me to check. With no small amount of apprehension, I stuck my finger in the hole in my vest and felt around. The puncture stopped at a mushroomed, copper-jacketed wad of lead. The ceramic disc beneath it was shattered, but had done its job and stopped the bullet from penetrating.

Dragon Skin. Best there is.

"I'm fine," I said. "Body armor stopped it."

"Glad to hear it."

The scarred Texan covered me while I donned my ghillie suit, and when finished, I set my goggles to thermal mode and did the same for him. After sorting himself out and activating his NVGs and night vision scope, he pointed to a spot up the hill. "I'm going to set up over there. It'll give me a good view over the hill without creating too much of a target picture."

I looked at the spot and nodded. "Good thinking. I'll set up fifty yards that way. Not much use in radio silence at this point."

"Agreed. How many you reckon we're dealing with?"

"There's probably at least five of them, Tanner and his four men. I probably should have told you this earlier, but Tanner and I went through sniper school at the same time. I know for a fact he graduated top of his class, so don't underestimate him."

"Good to know."

"Also, the fact he was able to shoot me in the dark tells me he has a night vision device. It's probably safe to assume his men do as well."

Hicks raised his rifle and made a scope adjustment. "Duly noted. We should leave the packs here and come back for them later, assuming we're still alive."

After taking a moment to line up my other FLIR device in tandem with my scope, and stuffing a handful of spare .338 rounds in my pocket, I followed him up the hill. On the way, I realized I had dropped my M-6 when Red bolted, and was limited to just my .338 rifle, Beretta pistol, Kel-Tec PMR-30, and backup piece. Not the ideal load out for a firefight, but better than nothing.

When I reached the top of the hill and settled in, cheek against composite plastic stock, it became immediately clear Hicks and I had a major tactical advantage.

FLIR. Forward Looking Infrared.

Night vision is great. If you have it and the other guy doesn't, you're probably going to win. But night vision has many of the same limitations as the naked eye. Take camouflage, for instance. Although night vision gives you a better chance at spotting someone who is heavily camouflaged in the dark, if he is an expert and hides himself properly, he can still get the drop on you. With FLIR, it's a different story. FLIR allows you to see in the infrared spectrum—heat signatures. And no amount of conventional camouflage is going to hide a person's infrared signature, especially when the ambient temperature is less than twenty degrees. In those conditions, a human body stands out like a torch.

Consequently, I spotted Tanner's men with no problem.

FORTY-NINE

They were down the hill about a hundred yards away, closing fast, armed with AKs, equipped with NVGs, spread out at ten yard intervals. I assumed they hadn't spotted us yet, being that there were no bullets ricocheting around my head. I radioed their locations to Hicks, who quickly spotted them as well.

"How you wanna do this?" he asked.

"Pick one and take him out, then back off as fast as you can. We don't want Tanner getting a fix on us."

"Copy. I'm ready."

"Same here. Count us down."

"On one. Three, two, one."

We both fired. I took no chances, aiming center of mass. At a thousand yards, a .338 Lapua magnum round can punch through military-grade body armor like tissue paper. At less than a hundred yards, the match-grade 300 grain projectile I fired was traveling over 2700 feet per second and struck its frail human target with nearly 4900 foot-pounds of energy. In other words, it really didn't matter where the bullet hit. The guy was toast. I watched him fall and caught a glimpse of his back. There was a ragged hole there, roughly the size of a softball. He was dead before he hit the ground.

Then I was moving.

At four-hundred yards, if Tanner had his scope focused anywhere near my position, he had to have seen the muzzle flash. He would also have established a vector on the thundering report, far louder than Hicks' M-110. Which meant if shots started coming, they would probably be aimed at me.

I backed quickly down, worked my way about fifty yards toward the south side of the hill, then climbed back up. As I edged my way slowly over the hilltop, I caught sight of the two remaining gunmen. One flanked right, while the other attacked straight ahead, spraying potshots as he went. There was no sign of Hicks. I followed the guy going straight up the hill until he stopped to take cover behind a tree, then I let out a breath and fired. The bullet caught him in the side, bursting both his lungs and his heart like balloons, and kept on trucking. As the gunman fell, I heard a staccato series of *thak*s as the projectile spent its remaining energy busting through tree trunks.

Scary stuff.

Again, I backed off and started moving northward toward the last of Tanner's men. About forty meters north of Hicks' original position I reloaded my rifle's magazine, then climbed up and peered over the edge. Tanner's man was still moving in the same direction, trying to come at me from the north in a flanking maneuver. Roughly ten yards ahead, unbeknownst to him, crouched the slim, angular form of Caleb Hicks. I followed the gunman with my scope until he passed within a few feet of the stealthy soldier. I almost expected Hicks to stand up and slit his throat, but he proved to be much more practical. When the enemy was past, he simply stood up, placed the barrel of the M-110 against the back of his head, and pulled the trigger. Before the body hit the ground, Hicks was already moving, threading his way among the trees.

Nicely done, kid.

His voice sounded in my ear. "Gabe, what's your twenty?"

I told him. He acknowledged and said he was on his way. When he reached me, he said, "Well that was surprisingly painless."

I tapped my FLIR imager. "Gotta love technology."

"So what now?"

"Tanner is still out there, and he's not going to be nearly as easy to kill as these last four."

"Be that as it may," Hicks said. "We have the advantage now."

I nodded and clapped him on the shoulder. "Okay, I have an idea where that first shot came from. I don't think he's changed position. If he had, he probably would have taken a shot at us by now. We'll separate sixty yards, you on the north side, me on the south, and approach from two directions. You take my FLIR scope and give me your night vision one. I can get by just fine with my goggles."

"You sure?"

"Positive. It'll double our chances of spotting him before he spots us."

"All right then."

I had zeroed the FLIR scope on the M-110 many times, and knew what adjustments to make. Once it was attached to Hicks' rifle, he helped me do the same with his night vision scope on my .338.

"That should be pretty close," he said. "Wish we had time for a few test shots. Don't be surprised if your first shot falls short. You might have to apply a little Kentucky windage."

"Don't worry, I'll figure it out. Or die trying."

Hicks chuckled and shook his head. "Let's get this over with."

"Amen."

It took us the better part of an hour to cover the distance. We took our time, moving carefully, taking great pains not to disturb the foliage around us. Even with the imager at its highest setting, I had trouble making out Hicks' shape among the dense forest. With just the night vision scope, he was a ghost.

There was a bit of sphincter puckering as we crossed the highway, but we made it across without incident. It was a long highway, and even with a scope, I knew Tanner wouldn't be able to monitor all of it at once. The gamble paid off.

The hill Tanner's shot came from loomed ahead, standing at the top of a long, wide hollow bisected by the highway. As I drew closer, the adrenalin began to wear off and I felt a warmth spreading on my side. A quick inspection revealed I had popped a few stitches there.

Forget it. Fix it later.

My hand, which had settled into a dull throb that I could mostly ignore, began to flare into pulsing, burning agony. It also itched like hell. The itching was a recent thing, having started that morning. I hadn't been as diligent about cleaning and re-bandaging it as I should have been, and I worried it was becoming infected.

Another thirty yards of careful walking took me up the slope of the hill where the foliage thinned and the trees stood much wider apart. The voice of Instinct began to chirp again, so I radioed Hicks to stop and wait.

"What's wrong?"

"He picked his hide pretty well," I said. "Is the forest as thin on your side as it is on mine?"

A pause, then, "Yeah. Gonna be hard to sneak up on him through that."

"Exactly. And if this fucker's half as sneaky as I think he is, the approach on the opposite side is probably rigged with traps."

"So what do you want to do?"

"Hang tight. I need a minute to think."

We could try leapfrogging up the hill, but if Tanner got a bead on either one of us, we were toast. The only reason I was still alive was because of my body armor, a thought which rankled more than I wanted it to. Getting up there to him was going to be difficult in the extreme. Unless, of course, we knew where he was. Which meant that, somehow, I had to trick him into giving away his position.

"Okay," I said into the mouthpiece. "I have an idea. Hold position until I call you again."

"Can do."

I backed off slowly, putting about a hundred yards of thick forest between myself and the clearer approaches up the hill.

Then I took off my ghillie suit, lashed a couple of long sticks into a shape like a crucifix, and draped the ghillie suit over it. Then I crept back the way I had come, got as close to the hillside as I dared, and leaned the rig up against a tree.

Not the tricky part.

I unslung my rifle, set its foregrip in the crotch of a low limb, right about the level the stick man would hold it if he were trying to aim, and lashed it in place with paracord. Despite the cold, beads of sweat dripped into my eyes as I worked. That old familiar prickling sensation tingled between my shoulder blades. Once finished, I breathed a shaky sigh of relief and moved a few yards to my right, taking cover behind the trunk of a massive beech tree.

"Okay, Hicks," I radioed. "Keep your eyes on the hilltop. I'm gonna try something here. He might take a shot."

"Roger."

The next part was crucial. The goal was to throw a stick, disturb a tree limb, and fool Tanner into taking a shot at the dummy sniper. If I threw the stick too hard, Tanner would know it was a ruse. But if I did it lightly, just enough to draw the eye, there was a good chance he would take the shot.

Taking up a stick I had chosen for the purpose, I took aim, held it in a light grip, and tossed it. It spun twice through the air, flying in a slow, lazy arc, and, as intended, one end barely kissed a thin branch, gently agitating it. A few seconds passed in silence. Just as I began to think he hadn't seen it, or had seen it and wasn't fooled, a shot rang out. The ghillie suit flew backward, the bullet hitting one of the sticks supporting it.

Hot damn.

"Got him," Hicks said.

Tanner must have realized he'd been fooled, because a volley of bullets began to pepper the woods around me, aimed seemingly at random. He must have figured out that whoever triggered the decoy must not be far from it, and was trying to flush me out.

"Hicks, I'm pinned down. Can you try to draw his fire for a few seconds?"

"On it."

Several shots rang out from the M-110. They must have been uncomfortably close, because Tanner shifted aim and began firing in Hicks' direction. I stood up, drew my knife, and sprinted to where I had left my rifle. A few quick sawing motions later, it was in my hands.

Moving farther up the hill, I caught a flash in my FLIR imager. It was brief, there but for a fraction of a second, but I had it. Raising my weapon, I peered through the night vision scope and waited for him to fire again. There was a slight motion under a pile of leaves between two boulders, and then another flash.

"Gotcha, motherfucker."

The boulders were in the way. I couldn't shoot Tanner, but I could damn well shoot his weapon. As I sighted in, one of Hicks' shots hit the boulder to Tanners left, sending sparks and a spray of granite into the air. The former CIA agent kept firing, undeterred.

Remembering Hicks' warning, I centered the reticle, estimated the range, lifted my point of aim a little higher than I normally would, and fired. The .338's reputation as a competent anti-material rifle held. Tanner's weapon—a Dragunov, by the look of it—slammed against the boulder to his right and fell from his hands, clattering down the hillside. A pair of legs appeared behind the boulders and the tall, lean figure of Sebastian Tanner emerged. He belly crawled backward for a few seconds, then stood up in a crouch and turned to flee down the hillside.

"Like hell," I muttered, then worked the bolt, shifted my aim, and fired again. The reticle was centered on his chest but the bullet went low, hitting him in the right hip. With a shriek of agony, he fell and rolled halfway to the bottom of the hill, coming to a stop not far from where I stood.

Keeping my rifle steady, I approached cautiously. With a cry of effort, Tanner sat up and fumbled for a pistol on his chest rig. I stopped, took careful aim, waited until the pistol cleared its holster, and fired again. Tanner's weapon, and about half of his right hand, spun away into the darkness. He cried out anew and lay on his side, clutching his right wrist.

"The next one will be your head," I warned as I drew near.

Without my ghillie suit, he had no trouble recognizing me. I stepped up the rise and stopped less than ten feet away from him, gun leveled. Blood poured in great streaming gouts from his ruined right hip and mangled hand, sending up shimmering white heat waves in my imager. Unless I missed my guess, he was not long for this world.

"How?" he asked as he lay gasping. "I hit you center of mass. That was a kill shot. You should be dead."

I rapped my knuckles on my vest. "Dragon Skin. Best there is."

He let out a rusty, grating laugh. "Son of a bitch. Why didn't I aim for the head? I should have known you'd have some trick up your sleeve."

I took off my goggles and took a few steps closer, gazing down at him. The moon had emerged from the clouds, shining pale and cold on his ruined face. "Was it worth it?" I asked. "Was it really worth it? All these people dead on both sides, and for what? So you can bleed your last lying in the dirt on a random hillside in middle-of-nowhere Missouri? Why couldn't you just let it go, Tanner?"

He laughed again, his lone functioning eye growing dim. "Why...couldn't you?"

I opened my mouth to reply, then closed it. The eye had gone blank. Empty. No one home to talk to.

I drew my Beretta, waited for the death rattle, and put two in his head. Just to be sure.

For you, Elizabeth.

*****

Hicks radioed his position to me and informed me he was wounded.

"How bad?" I asked, picking up the pace.

"Got me in the right leg, low and outside. Missed the bone and the big artery, but it still hurts like a son of a bitch. Bleeding pretty good, too."

"Hang in there. I'm on my way."

I found him propped up against a tree, rifle across his lap, a wide gauze bandage around his leg. It had already bled through. "Hold still," I told him as I took out my first aid kit. "I'm going to patch this up a little better."

He grimaced and nodded silently.

First, I cut away the old dressing. Then I cut a slit up the outside of his pants leg so I could get a better look at the wound. Hicks was kind enough to detach his tactical light and shine it on his leg. The bullet had gone through and through, leaving a ragged circle of torn flesh in its wake. The bleeding was bad, but not arterial. If I could get it stopped, Hicks had a good chance to recover.

Reaching in my medi-kit, I grabbed a bottle of iodine. "This is going to hurt," I said.

He nodded. "Just do it."

He hissed through clenched teeth as I cleaned the wound, taking my time and doing a thorough job. Once finished, I took out a packet of QuickClot, held the wound open, and poured in the powder, making sure to pack it in both perforations. Hicks ground his teeth and cursed vividly, but remained still.

"All right, the worst is over. Now we just need to wrap you up."

I packed the bullet holes over with gauze, wrapped more gauze around his leg several times, then sealed the whole works with compression tape.

"There," I said. "That should get the bleeding stopped. Think you can stand up?"

"Yeah. Give me a hand."

I picked up his rifle, slung it over my shoulders, and helped him to his feet.

"We need to find the horses," he said. "No way can I make it all the way back to Brownsville on this leg."

"How do you propose we do that?"

"Just get us back to where we turned 'em loose. They'll wander back there eventually."

I frowned at him. "How do you know?"

The young soldier grinned. "'Cause that's where I left the feed bag."

I threw back my head and laughed, then ducked under his arm and supported him as he walked.

"Caleb, my friend, you are a steely-eyed missile man."

FIFTY

The hand was infected.

On the ride back to Brownsville, it grew steadily worse. A red streak started from the base of my diminished left ring finger and began tracing its way across my palm and up my forearm. By the time we rode through Brownsville's main gate, I was feverish, sweaty, and generally felt like I was dying. Which, in fact, I was.

Hicks, on the other hand, was healing nicely. His wound had sealed too much for stitches, so Ethan and the other medics simply cleaned it as best they could, prescribed antibiotics, and put him on limited duty for a couple of weeks. He was examined first, since he was the one on active duty, then they worked their way to me.

"Lucky for you, we have antibiotics now," Ethan said, examining my hand under the olive-drab tent of a hastily erected field hospital. "Just stay in bed for a couple of days. Once the meds kick in, you'll be back on your feet. Make sure you take the full cycle."

"I will most certainly do that," I replied.

Penny showed up an hour later, chewed the medics' asses up one side and down the other for leaving me in a drafty tent for so long, and demanded they move me to a room in her tavern. They took me there on a litter, apologized profusely to the fiery little woman, then fled the building with their tails between their legs. I had a long laugh over that one.

The next morning, I woke up to find Sheriff Tucker sitting on a stool beside my cot, bright sun shining on her face, smiling warmly. "How you doin'?" she asked.

"I've been better."

She nodded. "I gathered that. How bad is it? The medics wouldn't tell me."

"Not very. I'll be on my feet in a day or two."

"I'm glad." She patted my shoulder and was quiet for a long moment, eyes fixed on the wall. The lines of her face were deep with exhaustion, and there were little black circles under her eyes. I tried to imagine what the last week or so had been like for her, then decided I didn't want to know. Finally she looked up and said, "Did you find him? The man responsible for what happened here?"

"I did."

"And?"

I shook my head. "He's not a problem anymore."

She nodded again, eyes troubled. "You know, I should be bothered by that. I've been a cop since long before the Outbreak. Never had much patience for vigilante justice."

"If it makes you feel better, it wasn't justice."

She looked me in the eye, head tilted to the side. "What was it then?"

"Revenge," I said. "Plain and simple."

Her hand came up and traced a scar on my check, fingers gentle and searching. "Is it true what they say? Is it best served cold?"

My eyes closed and I lay back on my pillow, suddenly very, very tired. "No, Sheriff," I said. "It's best not served at all."

There was a rustle of fabric, a brush of soft lips against mine, and then she was gone.

Four days after arriving in Brownsville, Hicks and I arranged transportation for our horses and the loot we took from the Crow Hunters and the Blackmire guards, then gathered our gear, said our goodbyes, and hitched a ride on a transport bound for Hollow Rock.

Along the way, I thought about Sheriff Tucker, and the women of her town, and how hard things would be for them going forward. I thought about Tanner, and his greed and anger, and the destruction such things bring. I thought about my own

498

desire for vengeance, and how things might have turned out differently if I had just let it go. Mostly, though, I thought about Elizabeth, and Eric, and Allison, and the Glover family, and how good it would be to see all of them again.

As the transport trundled along, I thought about how a great many people don't have homes anymore. Those of us who do cling to them and fight hard to protect them because we understand how precious they are. We know the homes we build, the bonds we forge, and the friendships we make are the fire in winter's cold that gives us hope for better times, and better lives. It is why we work, and toil, and plant our crops year after year. It is why people hug their children, and make love, and celebrate milestones, and share food and laughter and all the thousand little touches in between. Because having a home is worth working for, worth fighting for, and if necessary, worth dying for.

And I had been away from mine for far too long.

EPILOGUE

With the approach of May, winter finally lost its grip.

As the daily high temperatures rose, so did the hopes and prospects of Hollow Rock's many farmers. The bulletin board in front of town hall once again became festooned with HELP WANTED and NOW HIRING signs, each one listing a particular farm, its owner, and what terms of payment they were offering. It was plainly obvious the aforementioned farmers had held a meeting and agreed on what wages to offer. They were universal, and much lower than the previous year's.

"That's going to cause trouble," I said to Elizabeth, pointing at the flyers.

She shook her head. "The same thing happened last year before you got here. I held a town hall meeting and forced the farmers to explain themselves, at which point they capitulated and agreed to better terms for the workers. I imagine it'll be the same this year."

"Seems like a lot of unnecessary arguing."

She shrugged. "The farmers want to keep as much profit as they can. It's their land, after all."

"Yes, but without field hands to help them, they aren't growing anything."

"And everyone goes hungry. It's just the way of the world, Gabe."

I frowned and picked up a notice with my diminished left hand. With the infection cured, it had healed quite nicely. The seam of stitched skin over the nub of proximal phalange had settled into a flat, pink thimble of scar tissue. Even the incessant itch had gone away.

"You'd think after everything that's happened, people would learn to be decent to one another. To appreciate what they have and work together for the common good."

Elizabeth's hand was soft and strong as it slipped into mine. "You of all people should know better, Gabe. That's not going to happen."

"Yeah. I know."

We turned away from town hall and walked down the sidewalk, bound for Stall's Tavern. It was just past noon on a Friday, and the town square was busy in preparation for market day. A steady stream of farmers, Runners, and trade caravans poured in through the north gate, prompting Sheriff Elliott to double up the guards and send out extra patrols to beat back the encroaching infected.

In the distance, I heard the steady beat of hammers and the roar of heavy equipment as the newly arrived troops tore down the wooden palisade surrounding Fort McCray and built a larger, sturdier wall. The wooden buildings within the encampment were being torn down also, soon to be replaced by quonset huts and pre-fabricated steel.

Between First Platoon, the new arrivals, and the Ninth TVM, there were now three full companies of troops stationed just outside of town, along with two Blackhawks, an Apache gunship, several APC's, and two Abrams tanks. A hell of a lot of hardware by modern measure.

While the townsfolk appreciated the extra protection, and the extra business, they also understood the reason for such a strong military presence. And they were not comforted in the least.

"You ever hear back from the feds about the insurgents?"

Liz snapped her fingers. "Right, I'm glad you reminded me. Yes, I did. The trial has been canceled. There's a Chinook coming next week to take them all to Kansas."

I sighed in relief. "That's good. Last thing we need around here is to stir up more trouble with the Alliance."

"Amen to that."

501

As we passed by the sheriff's office, I glanced at the front door and wondered what awaited the ten captured insurgents within. Seven of them had tried to attack Hollow Rock, and three of them were associates of the now deceased Sebastian Tanner, a known outlaw and Alliance sympathizer. The first seven were probably looking at lengthy prison sentences at the least, and execution at worst. The other three, because they had testified against Blackmire, would probably be turned back over to the Alliance.

Their trial had been postponed due to the attack on Hollow Rock a few weeks ago, and afterward, Elizabeth sent a message to the recently re-established Justice Department imploring them to take the prisoners off her hands. She had enough problems to deal with as it was, and inciting the anger of the Alliance settlements to the north would do nothing to ameliorate them. The fact that they were honoring her request was welcome news indeed.

As we neared Stall's Tavern, I put my arm around Liz and pulled her close. "So what's the special occasion?"

She smiled coyly. "What do you mean?"

"You never drag me out of the house in the middle of the day. You're too fond of your afternoon nap. What gives?"

"You really don't remember, do you?"

"Remember what?"

She laughed and opened the tavern's door. "And here I thought you had a mind like a steel trap."

As I stepped inside, I was greeted by the sight of several dozen people, some in uniform and some in civilian clothes, all with silly, colorful little pointy hats strapped to their heads. The building's newly installed light fixtures came on overhead, shining upon ribbons, streamers, and balloons. Elizabeth beamed at me as the assembled guests raised their hands over their heads and cried, in unison, "HAPPY BIRTHDAY!!!"

I stopped in my tracks and found myself amid a hail of multi-colored confetti and serenaded by the sounds of kazoos and party horns. Liz clapped her hands together and did a bouncy, excited little dance. I turned my best scowl upon her.

"You did this?"

"No," a familiar voice said from the stage. I looked over to see Eric standing there, smiling broadly, his guitar strapped across his chest. "I did. Happy birthday, you big nine-fingered bastard!"

I was going to throw a chair at him, but then I saw the cake.

Cake fixes everything.

*****

There was food, and drink, and cake, and a lot of laughter. Eric played his guitar and sang for a couple of hours, then came over to my table with a bottle of lukewarm booze. Elizabeth, perceptive lady that she is, excused herself so we could talk.

Eric pushed a full shot glass across the table. "So tell me. What happened?"

Ever since I returned from Brownsville, he had been remarkably non-inquisitive. Probably figured I needed time to sort things out. Evidently, my reprieve was at an end. So I took the shot and told him, start to finish. It took me half an hour, and when I was done, I held out my glass. "The son of a bitch got me twice," I said. "Must be losing my touch."

Eric frowned at me. "If you had been more careful, he wouldn't have. The first time, you let emotion get in the way. You were angry. You didn't act with your usual thoroughness. But you escaped with your life because you had something Tanner didn't."

I caught my glass as Eric slid it across the table. "And what's that?"

"Friends," he said, then downed his shot. "You inspire loyalty and confidence. That's why Ethan and the others were willing to risk their lives to track you down. Yeah, I paid them, but that was just to satisfy their CO. They would have done it for free otherwise. Tanner, on the other hand, ruled by fear. His men followed him out of greed and avarice."

I clanked my glass against the table and shook my head. "But he got me again on the highway. If I hadn't been wearing my armor, I'd be dead."

"Listen," Eric said, "there's good luck, there's bad luck, and then there's making your own luck. You do a good job of the latter. You train hard. You stockpile ammo. You buy the best weapons and equipment you can get your hands on. You make readiness a top priority. Tanner didn't do that. When he took that shot, he aimed center of mass because he didn't have enough confidence to try for a headshot. You wouldn't have made that mistake. But you knew *he* might, so despite the weight, you wore your armor. It wasn't just ceramic plates that saved your life, Gabe. It was thinking ahead."

I studied my drink for a while, then tossed it down the hatch. "Well, when you put it that way…"

Eric grinned, slapped me on the arm, and informed me he was going to go eat cake with his wife.

The party lasted until late in the afternoon, all attendees spirits buoyed by the warm weather and the copious amount of alcohol flowing from the bar. As the sun began to dip to the west, I sat with Liz by a window, feet propped up on a chair, head back, sun on my face, listening to the good sounds of children playing outside. Eric climbed back onstage, much to the revelers' delight, and plucked a few notes.

"Okay folks," he said in his booming stage voice. "One last song, then I'm outta here."

The response was a mixture of cheers and mournful wails that it was the last song of the afternoon. Eric's deft, long-fingered hands began dancing across the strings, pulling music from his finely-crafted instrument until it slowly suffused the room, glowing and warm and dripping with heartache. I felt a small smile pull at the corners of my mouth. *Head Full of Doubt/Road Full of Promise*. The Avett Brothers had long been a favorite of mine, and Eric knew it.

After the opening chords, he began to sing:

There's a darkness upon me that's flooded in light.
In the fine print they tell me what's wrong and what's right.

"What are you thinking about?" Elizabeth asked as I swayed my head in time with the music.

"Nothing," I said. "Nothing at all. It's nice, for a change."

And it comes in black, and it comes in white,
And I'm frightened by those who don't see it.

"I wish I could do that. There's so much on my mind all the time, sometimes it feels like my head is going to burst."

I opened my eyes enough to look at her. "You carry a lot of responsibility. Ever think about delegating some of it?"

She sighed and laid her chin on crossed forearms. "I guess I'm going to have to. Maybe hire an assistant or something. What about you? When will you start going on salvage runs again?"

I shrugged and turned to look out the window. "Maybe in a few weeks. Eric is managing things just fine. I've been enjoying the time off."

"You certainly earned it."

When nothing is owed, or deserved, or expected,
And your life doesn't change by the man that's elected,

Her hand crept across the table, turned over, and made a come hither motion. I reached out and felt her fingers trace over the newly healed stump. "There's something I wanted to ask you about," she said.

A pause. "Okay."

"Don't be mad."

"No promises."

"Allison told me about your conversation with Eric."

If you're loved by someone, you're never rejected,
Decide what to be and go be it.

I sat up and withdrew my hand. "Which one? We talk a lot, the two of us."

"You know which one."

I pinched the bridge of my nose and hissed out a breath. The conversation in question happened a week after I returned from Brownsville. I brought Eric up to speed on the situation with the Republic of California, as well as my bargain with General Jacobs, and asked if he wanted in. He hesitated, eyes straying to Allison working in the garden outside, and said he would think about it. I knew he would talk it over with Allison, but I didn't think it would reach Liz's ears. So much for secrecy.

There was a dream, and one day I could see it.
Like a bird in a cage, I broke in and demanded that somebody free it.

"That's classified information, Liz. How many other people did you tell?"

"No one. You, me, Eric, and Allison are the only ones who know."

"Please make sure it stays that way."

She waved the comment aside. "Why didn't you tell me?"

And there was a kid, with a head full of doubt.

So I'll scream till I die and the last of those bad thoughts are finally out.

I laid my hands flat on the table and stared at them, specifically the one with a reduced allocation of digits. "I was going to. Just didn't know how to say it."

"How about, 'Liz, I made a deal with the head of Army Special Operations Command, and in exchange for the medical supplies that probably saved your life, I offered to become Jacobs' personal assassin.'"

I winced. "It's not like that."

There's a darkness upon you that's flooded in light.

In the fine print they tell you what's wrong and what's right.

She stared at me for a moment, then stood up, came around the table, and plopped down in the seat next to me. Her arms slid around my waist, warm and comfortable, like they were made to go there. "I'm sorry. That was a cheap shot."

"I deserved it."

And it flies by day, and it flies by night,

And I'm frightened by those who don't see it.

The arms tightened, and her lips brushed my ear. "Why do you do it, Gabe? After everything you've been through, after all the years of fighting, why do you feel compelled to risk your life to help others? Why keep putting yourself in danger?"

There was a dream, and one day I could see it.

Like a bird in a cage, I broke in and demanded that somebody free it.

There were a lot of ways I could have answered that, but as I am fond of saying, the best explanation is often the simplest. In this case, it was a parting shot from that broken-hearted woman who slammed a door in my face all those years ago and banished me from her life forever. Maybe someday I would get a chance to apologize to her, but I wasn't getting my hopes up.

And there was a kid, with a head full of doubt.

So I'll scream till I die and the last of those bad thoughts are finally out.

The song went on as I held my new love tighter. She nestled into me, and I laid my cheek on her head, rocking the two of us in time to the closing refrains. Finally, and all too soon, Eric sang the last lyrics.

There's a darkness upon me that's flooded in light,

And I'm frightened by those who don't see it.

When he strummed the final, haunting chord, I opened my eyes.

"I am what I am, Elizabeth. And I always will be."

About the Author:

James N. Cook (who prefers to be called Jim, even though his wife insists on calling him James) is a martial arts enthusiast, a veteran of the U.S. Navy, a former cubicle dweller, and the author of the Surviving the Dead series. He hikes, he goes camping, he travels a lot, and he has trouble staying in one place for very long. He lives in North Carolina (for now) with his wife, son, two vicious attack dogs, and a cat that is scarcely aware of his existence.

46548536R00283

Made in the USA
Lexington, KY
07 November 2015